UPON A WICKED TIDE

Book One in the Wicked Tide duology

Copyright © Kate Craft 2022

First Edition: November 2022

Paperback ISBN: 978-1-7397349-4-7

Hardback ISBN: 978-1-7397349-5-4

For enquires, please visit: www.katecraft.com

UPON A WICKED TIDE

THE WICKED TIDE DUOLOGY
BOOK ONE

KATE CRAFT

Sometimes fate smiles upon us...and sometimes she takes us by the throat and drags us down the beaten path.

— KATE CRAFT.

To my wonderful partner in crime.

Even when the tides are rough, you help me stay the course.
I love you.

CONTENTS

THE FIRST PAGE

Come here and behold a tale like no other,
a perilous yarn of a girl and her lover.
This is the tale of a girl with blue eyes,
whose journey is fraught with peril and lies.
She waits for us now, shall we ponder together?
Who is this girl, to whom is she tethered?

A VOW, A PROPHECY, AND A BOOK

THE GARDEN ISLE

They say dead men tell no tales, but that's not strictly true. I met a dead man once, a man drowned and brought back to life. A dead man walking, so to speak. He didn't walk for long, falling victim like many before him to the sirens' calls. This man told me a story, a tale of the Eighth Sea where the siren king dwells. No one has seen the Eighth, at least none who live to speak of it. But *he* did, the dead man told me before he slipped beneath the waves, never to be seen again.

As the ship rocks gently beneath my feet, I stare at the glistening surface of the Second Sea, the softest sea of them all at full slack, with barely a ripple in sight. Closing my eyes, I grip the ship's rail and listen for what lies beneath.

I hear them. I hear the sirens' call, soft and seductive. The salt on the air tingles my parched lips, a light breeze tussling the waves of my long, red hair. I know that breeze is not enough, yet still I open my eyes and tilt my head back to stare hopefully at where the sails hang limp and derelict.

It's been three days since the winds died, three days of relying on the ship's thrusters to slowly make my way back to the Garden Isle. I often enjoy the solitude of seafaring, finding any excuse to extend my trip knowing the galley is well stocked and the catch kept fresh in the ship's holds. But this time is different, the need for haste has me glancing at the sails with every small gust. I need to get home, back to my guardians – the three sisters.

Marnie, Malka and Malina were born and raised on the Garden Isle alongside my mother and father, so it makes sense I would be left in the sisters' care when my parents perished at sea all those years ago...Nine years and already I had forgotten my mother's face and the sound of my father's voice.

In the years since, my guardians had trained me in the ways of the water and how to hunt at sea. One could argue I became adept at rigging a sail before mastering the art of tying my boot laces. Those lessons have served me well – only twenty years old and already I'm a master captain, a title I wear proudly on the Isle.

To work at sea is a woman's job. While males are typically employed to maintain the docks or build the ships, only women are safe on the open water with the threat of sirens dwelling below. Men are too fickle, their hearts too easily tempted by the hidden promise and naked allure of their song. That's how the creatures like their prey – less resistant, the meat a little tougher. Though, that's not always the case, and for that reason the sisters taught me a song, one to thwart the sirens' lethal lullaby.

I close my eyes now, listening. It's always there, always waiting. I drum a quiet beat on the ship's rail and hum the tune I was taught.

Come here, come now, I dare of thee,
Come see this heart so pure 'n' free.
Come here, come now, oh wards o'er deep,
In exchange for my life, your own death you will reap.

I stop the idle song and shield my eyes, glancing up at the sound of a halyard snapping against the mast and a sail catching on a fresh breeze. The ship pitches forward, as if she were a horse straining at the bit. My stomach flutters, my chest expanding as I grin and race across the deck to crank those clever sails taut once again. Soon, the ship takes off across the water like a prize stallion. With the pulleys secure, I bound up the wooden stairs to the quarterdeck and release the wheel's lock to guide my ship, *The King's Arcana*, home to the Garden Isle.

I SQUINT through the last of the evening sun, to where a lone and familiar woman waves from the shore of Merry-weather. Before long, more figures race along the harbour to welcome me home. With a level of skill rare for my years, I carefully line up the vessel with the dock, slackening the sails and captaining the thrusters well before breaching the rope bollards of the protected siding.

"Curse you, Emery," a small voice calls from below as the ship comes to a rolling standstill. "I've been worried sick! We thought for sure the tides had claimed you."

With a wide grin I vault the rail from the quarterdeck, landing lightly on the dock in front of the harbour master, Pattie.

Scanning me from head to toe, she places two hands defiantly on her hips. "Well, where the hell have you been?"

I jokingly mirror her stance, puffing out my chest and

giving my best scowl. "Well, it's lovely to see you, too. Now why don't you give me a bloody minute to empty these holds," I say, looking appreciatively as the other, younger hands duck past us to secure the ramp and get to work.

"I might be old, but I could still throttle you, Miss Mirabel," Pattie mumbles as she taps her foot.

I laugh and hold my hands up in surrender. "I'm certain you could, though I'm sure Malka and the others would have something to say about that."

At my mention of the sisters, Pattie's whole body seems to tense, her head falling forward to study the wooden decking. I suppose there's only so long we can go without bringing them up. How far along have my guardians progressed through the stages of the plague, I wonder? I almost don't want to know, preferring to remain blissfully ignorant. When I had left four days ago, their skin had already begun to sag with the rapid loss of weight, their aching bodies chilled to the bone.

"I was with them earlier this morning," Pattie says quietly. "It's bad, Emery. You should go. The girls and I will take the catch to the storehouse and lock up."

I squeeze Pattie's shoulder, offering a strained smile as thanks, then turn and stop one of the younger dockhands as she brings up the first load. Opening my satchel, I take four fish from the girl and place them each into one of the wax-sealed compartments, then secure the flap and race for the stables.

Angus – once a wild and beautiful black stallion now far too old for any such fire – whinnies and nods his head in greeting when I reach his stall. I spot the bale of hay tied tightly to the far wall and make a mental note to thank Pattie for taking care of him in my absence. Not bothering with a saddle, I secure the bridle and use the small step ladder to mount Angus, before prompting him forward with a gentle squeeze of my thighs.

Taking the northern road, we race over the low hills until we reach Woodcutter Forest. It's quicker to go through the wood, but the canopy is too dense, and with darkness steadily descending, even a native like myself would almost certainly lose their way. Having travelled this route a thousand times, Angus veers down the left-hand path without my bidding, whinnying his hellos as we pass three goats lazing idly beside the ancient Troll Bridge. I nudge the stallion on, a gentle reminder of our need for haste, and he gallops harder than his age should permit, towards a small light flickering in the distance.

We jump the shallow, iron gate, pulling to a stop outside a long, single-story cottage. Made of stone and wood, it sits entwined with the edge of the forest, twisted vines like stringy moss clinging to the stone walls like long fingers, coaxing the small home back into the woodland's heart. I had promised to prune and cut back those fingers before I left, yet I hadn't, and somehow more of the home has been reclaimed by the creeping forest fauna in my absence.

I push the guilt aside as I dismount. Food was a priority, not gardening. My only mission had been to bring the sisters and villagers something to eat that wasn't poisoned or diseased. The Garden Isle has suffered, our animals tested and culled to half their number to mitigate the plague's awful procession. The only truly safe food now is fish, and I'm the best fisher the island has to offer, so I had to go.

Leading Angus into the open paddock, I close the gate and take the narrow, pebbled path towards the house. A large and crudely painted cross on the front door gives me pause, an instinct of sorts taking charge. Rendered black under the moonlight, I know in the light of day that cross is the colour of crimson, a warning not to enter this house of death. I have nothing to fear from the plague, this cruel curse that destroys some and walks by others. I am immune. Without knocking, I open the door and step inside.

My bag slips to the crook of my arm as a shiver rocks me. It's colder in the cottage than it is outside, where the warmth of summer lingers long after the sun sets. I rub my hands together and head to the kitchen to drop the fish on the side. Taking the lantern from its hook, I light the wick and hold it up as I turn about the room. The place is pristine, with hardly a dish or mug out of place. Pattie must have cleaned. I really do owe that woman a lot.

With the lamplight to guide me, I head to the first of the sisters' rooms intending to check on them one by one. The door creaks as I edge myself inside, and I resist the urge to cover my nose and mouth at the stench of human decay.

"It's about damn time you showed up," a frail voice coughs and wheezes from the far side of the room.

"Sorry, Marnie–" My breath catches as the lamp casts a glow over Marnie's face. Being the oldest of my three guardians, she was once a strong and proud woman, earning the highest respect from the villagers and even the king himself for her healing tonics and maritime skills. That woman is gone now, replaced with a gaunt, fair-haired creature made of bones and loose skin. She lifts her hand weakly, the colour once tanned and palms calloused with hard labour, now diseased and blackened at the fingernails.

"Put that infernal light down," she rasps. I oblige, quicker than I ought to, but the glow of the moon through the open curtains only serves to exaggerate the gauntness of her face.

"Are you hungry? Or maybe I can get you some water?" I ask. What do I do? What *can* I do? I'm not a healer like her, I fish and mend and run the stables.

Marnie shakes her head, at least I think she does. The

movement is so imperceptible, so painful to watch I could cry. I won't. I mustn't. Marnie wouldn't like that.

"Sit over there, Emery. I don't want you coming any closer," she says quietly.

"But why? I'm immune." Marnie and the other healers had devised a test using special equipment to look at a person's blood. Marnie had tested me herself, told me I had *markers* – me and a handful of others on the small isle. "Please. Let me bathe you and change your sheets at the very least."

"Don't fuss, Emery," she snaps, shoulders shaking in a hollow, ragged cough. "Death is close. My sisters and I have held her at bay for as long as we can, but her patience is a brittle thing."

I bow my head, willing back the tears. This is her goodbye, one I'm not ready to hear. I knew this was coming, I'd prepared myself. At least I thought I had. "There must be something I can do," I whisper, my hands shaking by my side.

"There is. I have two instructions, ones you must promise to heed before leaving this house. The first and most important is that when you go to my sisters, you must ignore their requests."

This isn't a particularly odd thing for Marnie to say. She's always been the one in charge and never shies from chastising her younger siblings for their more whimsical ways.

"Okay, and the second?" I ask. Not a promise, but it would do for now.

"The second, is that you must go to the king and call in an old favour. Ask for an estate and enough coin to keep you comfortable for the rest of your days. Live your life *here*, on the isle," Marnie instructs, her voice weak but determined.

"I understand," I say, though I don't understand in the

slightest. The sisters had always been close to the royals, friends I suppose. But what in the world would convince the King of the Garden Isle to give *me*, an ordinary fisher, such a prize? I watch as Marnie sinks deeper into the pillows, and I can't help but take two steps forward. The stench intensifies as I draw near. I need to move her, change her, bathe her...anything.

"Stop, Emery. Leave me be. Death is in the parlour, and plans have been put in place to care for our mortal remains. There is nothing left for you here, so heed my requests, say your goodbyes, and do not return."

The words are cold, but the intent behind them is one of mercy. She's trying to make this as easy as she can, so I gently nod in acknowledgement and turn for the door, lingering on the threshold to look back.

A single tear slips free to roam down Marnie's face, once proud and strong now oddly at peace. My heart breaks.

"Happy Birthday, Emerelda Mirabel. I love you, and I will always be with you. Even Death has no power over that."

"I love you, too," I say, my voice cracking. I leave the room, pulling the door closed behind me, and squeeze my eyes shut at the sound of gentle sobs.

I pause in the hallway, taking a moment to compose myself. Saying goodbye once was bad enough, but three times...

A wheezing cough emerges from the second room, and I push open the door. Malka's condition is worse than Marnie's. Even without sufficient light, I know she's close to passing. The smell of death is potent, intermingled with blood, sweat and faeces. I cough to hide my gasp and blink back the tears.

"Emery? Is that you, sweetie?" a tired but hopeful voice calls out.

I hurry to Malka's side, placing the lantern on a small

nightstand by her bed. She is nothing, barely a speck of what she once was, bright and beautiful. Her once golden hair lays flat and unwashed against the side of her face, drenched in sweat despite her shivers.

"I'm here," I say as I place a hand over hers. "I'll run a bath and get you cleaned up."

Malka chuckles lightly, the croaking rasp more frightening than reassuring. "Pattie wished to do the same, though I imagine she wouldn't have been quite as gentle." Malka's hand shifts beneath mine, each sharp bone cutting a hole in my heart.

"Pattie's a brutish woman, but she cares in her own way," I say, my tone light and easy as I slip my arm around those small, bony shoulders to help her sit up.

She puts a hand on my chest and shakes her head. "There isn't much point in washing a corpse, Emery, and the pain isn't worth it at this point. Besides, who wants to bathe an old lady on the eve of their birthday?"

I stare back, appalled by her flippancy. "You're not dead yet. And my birthday is the *last* thing on my mind."

She smiles up at me, her teeth black and eyes sunken so deep they seem almost hollow. "I have a request for you, one last thing, but one you must obey."

Marnie had warned as much, and instructed I deny their requests. Nevertheless, I nod my head to Malka in a silent vow to at least listen.

"You must never take a lover. It may seem cruel and unjust, but please promise me this much, Emery."

"Why?" I ask. Not a single one of the sisters had ever taken a husband or a wife to warm their beds, but why ask such a thing of me?

"Do you remember the man from the Eighth Sea?"

The dead man that told a tale. "Yes."

"Well, he carried with him an old tale, one that saw you and the end of your story."

"He prophesied my death?"

Malka gently nods her head. "He said that the man you love, a heartless man, will be the one to kill you. So, this is my final request of you, my darling. Do not take a lover. Instead live a long and happy life with *friends* to keep you company."

I've never been in a rush to fall in love, perhaps a matter influenced by the sisters. Don't get me wrong, I've kissed my fair share of frogs over the years, but all the other girls my age are wed and most with babes on the way.

"I understand," I say, once again dancing the line between accepting the vow and simply acknowledging her request.

Malka pinches her lips together and smiles knowingly, but seems to accept this is all I'm willing to give. Prophecies hold no weight on the Garden Isle, where the people are simple and live to fish and breed throughout their easy lives. Prophecies don't exist here.

"Good. I heard you speaking with Marnie. I want you to visit our youngest, and then leave this house forever, Emery." She lifts a hand to my face, brushing away the strands of hair now rough with sea-salt. "I love you so much, and I'm sorry we won't be here to keep you company."

I dip my head, tears rolling down my cheeks. "I love you, too," I say, and stand to step away from her bed. I feel the sickness clinging to me, trying to infect me through the trail of sweat Malka's palm has left on my face. But the plague can't get to me, and a deep and terrible part is thankful for that, thankful I won't meet the same fate as the sisters. I just wish I could save them, too.

I offer one last smile to Malka and close the door behind me as I step into the corridor. The lantern's light paints trembling shadows along the floorboards as my hands begin to shake. One room left. One more sister to bid farewell, and then I'll be alone. I place a palm on the cool stone of the wall. The house is so cold, unnaturally cold, like Death herself truly walks beside me. Marnie had alluded to such a thing, that Death has already arrived and stands by impatiently. I shiver and face the final door.

"Well, come on then, I haven't got all night, Emerelda," Malina chuckles from inside.

I brace myself and push the door open. Inside, the smell isn't quite so pungent, the scent of jasmine barely masking the stench. I raise the lantern, steeling myself for what I know the flickering light will reveal. My heart falters at the sight of the smallest and youngest of my guardians, who never seemed to age and held an unquestionable beauty in both her looks and her heart.

"Come in, come in, I've missed you," she says weakly from the bed. I rush to her side, setting the lantern down and helping her sit up. What once was a pretty button nose is now a darkened mass, yet another cruel symptom of the disease, each finger laying delicately across her stomach as black as coal.

"I brought some fish, would you like some? Or I can get you some water?" I ask desperately.

Malina smiles, her blackened teeth dull against the lamplight. "No thank you, sweetheart. It's past our time and Death is becoming quite the surly madam," she says, her eyes bright and full of a life that belies her words.

I stare silently at the youngest of the sisters, admiring her as I always have. Malina is like a perfect mix of her elder siblings, with Marnie somewhat cold and calculating, Malka warm and entirely too forgiving, and then Malina, exactly in the middle with her tranquil cleverness.

"What can I do? Are you comfortable?" I ask, almost dizzy in my desire to help.

"Comfortable enough, but I would like you to fetch me a box from beneath those floorboards over there." Malina raises her hand and points a long, bony finger to the corner of the room.

A little confused, I do as she asks. Where the boards are worn, I pick out one with scratches along its edge, like a sharp tool had been used to lift it. Unsheathing the dagger from my thigh, I prise at the same spot and the board comes loose, revealing a cloth covered box sitting in the small space between the joists. I reach down and pick it up, not bothering to refit the board as I return to Malina's side.

"Look inside," she says encouragingly when I take the cloth covering and discard it on the floor.

The box itself is beautiful. Made of something akin to brass or copper, the scuffed and time-worn frame is lined with jewels, uncut and brilliant in size. I can only assume they're fake. The box would be worth much more than anything we fishers could afford, and far more suited to the gilded rooms of the Garden Palace.

I open the lid, unsure of what to expect. More jewels? Coins? Instead, I find a silk blanket, and beneath that, a worn leather book. I pull the silk out, holding it close to the lamp to examine the stitched filigree of creatures and soft ocean waves. Mermaids. Sirens. Krakens. All resplendent with golden thread on the bed of deep indigo silk.

"Our mother made that for you," Malina whispers, pulling her hands back to keep from touching the fine material. "The book is yours as well. It's a part of you and something you must use wisely." Her fingers grip the sleeve of my cotton shirt. "I cannot stress that enough. Only read what is allowed."

"I don't understand," I say, returning the silk to the box and taking the book. The spine in bent, and as I hold it up to the light, I notice half of the pages are missing – ripped out.

A golden clasp holds both ends together, and as I go to open it, Malina takes my wrist and knocks the book from my hands, allowing it to fall to the floor.

"Not yet, Emery. This is my final request to you. Please, *please* do as I say."

She releases me and I reach down to retrieve it, placing it carefully under the silk and closing the box's lid. Malina sighs in relief, relaxing against the cushions as she warily eyes the copper case.

"This book is tricky, and offers much temptation, but you must be strong and resist. Tomorrow, on your twenty-first birthday, you may open the book and read *only* the first page."

"Only what is allowed," I say, echoing her previous statement.

She nods her head. "Yes, the book will show you. It will tell you when the next can be read, and not a day sooner. There are consequences to breaking the rules, consequences you cannot afford. I believe it will guide you well."

I stare at the box, now more curious than apprehensive with her words. "Is it a magical book?" I ask.

"Not so much magical as simply something that is. It is the way of our world, of Oceanus. Everyone has a book, though almost none get to read them. This is yours. My sisters and your parents told me to destroy it or send it back to where all the books are kept. But I couldn't do that, not while knowing what you face."

"What do you mean?" I ask. Malina often speaks in riddles or poems, something I once found endearing and wonderful. I don't need riddles now, I need answers. I need a cure to the plague. I need the sisters.

"I read your book, Emery. And while the tides may yet change and the story rewritten, for now I see you need it as much as it needs you. Take the book, listen to its words, and follow your heart. That is all I ask."

I search each line of her face, looking for the answers I need. There are none. Nothing to explain such an odd request. "I'll do my best," I say, again hesitant to offer an empty promise, but giving enough to ease her concern.

"Good. Now, I heard you speaking with my sisters, you have said your farewells and it's time for you to leave."

"Why can't I stay? I want to be here when…" the words catch in my throat, unwilling to voice such a finalising statement.

"In the time it has taken us to speak, my sisters have already passed, and I am close behind. Once you leave this room there will be nothing left for you here. Do not return, do not concern yourself with our remains, Pattie will take care of that. My sisters and I have lived long and full lives, our days made brighter when your parents left you with us."

I stand from the mattress as her bony fingers wave me away. Clutching the box, I walk slowly and stop before the door.

"Don't look back. Remember me as I once was. I love you, Emery."

"I love you, too." I whisper those words softly, and almost hope it's for the last time. Such words should not be used as a goodbye, yet they so often are. I never want to say goodbye again, never want to say…

I don't look back as I leave the room, don't let her see the tears welling in my eyes as I close the door behind me. My body trembles, chest aching with the repressed need to cry. I rush across the hall to my room. Throwing clothes and keepsakes into a large canvas bag, I move to place the copper box amongst the folds, then think better and retrieve a small satchel instead. I don't have much, and it doesn't take long before all of my worldly belongings are pulled together and

I'm ready to go. Looping the bags over my shoulder, I race for the cottage door.

Outside, I take large gulps of air, willing each foot in front of the other. I stop at the paddock and open the gate, using it to mount Angus.

He takes off at a gallop when I snap the reins, the burning lantern from the sister's cottage fading quickly into the gloom. At the ancient Troll Bridge, I pull Angus to a stop and climb down. A warm breeze rustles the trees along the edge of the forest, and the river bubbles as it tumbles down the hill. I'm far enough away now, far enough that even their ghosts won't hear me. I fall to my knees, and weep.

A KING'S GIFT

THE GARDEN ISLE

Angus stirs me from sleep as he grunts and whinnies through the bars of a nearby stall in the dock stables. Ignoring the pounding headache, I stand from the bed of hay, stretching my back and brushing straw from my shirt and breeches as I step from the dark corner into the light flooding through the stable's open doors. Just beyond, the Second Sea laps against the bollards of Merryweather Wharf. Everything about that sight is a lure. The sound, the smell…even the slight taste of salt on my lips.

My heart has always belonged to those waves, something unseen pulling at my chest to explore a world so much bigger than what the Garden Isle has to offer. I had stayed for the sisters, heeded their warnings to ignore that call and stay where it's safe and comfortable. But now they're gone, leaving nothing behind but empty vows, a silk blanket and an old book.

Angus kicks his stall and snorts a protest through his nostrils, as if hearing my thoughts and reminding me this isn't strictly true. I return to his stall, tussling his mane and touching my forehead to his.

"How about we pay a visit to the king and see what this favour to Marnie is about?" I ask him. Angus nickers and bobs his head, seeming pleased by my suggestion.

Taking the blanket and saddle from the racks, I fasten the billet straps and adjust the stirrups before securing my canvas bag and satchel at the saddle's cantle. Once I'm comfortably astride, Angus trots forward without needing the prompt, eager to venture out and get on the road. I guide us from the seaside stables and up the winding path towards the palace.

Months ago, before the plague, the Garden Isle bustled with life. Water deer would wander the open fields, unperturbed by the humans passing by, and people would walk the roads from town to town, selling goods or visiting friends. Now, the roads are empty and the fields left fallow and gone to weed, only those with immunity venturing out to tend to the sick or visit the graves.

As we reach the first town, I cast a grim look to each and every door of the small wooden dwellings we pass. Nothing but the colour red stands out from a town once decorated in beautifully vibrant hues. The red of those crosses, those warnings, brighter than all the rest. Death dwells here.

THE GARDEN PALACE lives up to its name, built to surround the Great Beech Tree, the tallest in existence with branches touching the sky and beyond, and a twisting trunk wide enough to house a city. It's a tree of perpetual life, one that never sheds its leaves or browns in the winter, it stands as it has for centuries, untainted.

As Angus and I pass through the gates to the palace

grounds, I glance to where the guard station remains empty, long since abandoned with the end of the war for the Second Sea. These gates are never closed, the royal gardens never barred to the people of the isle; something I admire about our wise king, whose only policies are to live honestly, work earnestly, and be neighbourly. Since the end of the war, the isle has been a peaceful place, with crime virtually non-existent in a land where the people's king tends to them well... Perhaps I'm mad to want to leave?

My thoughts scatter at the sound of hooves pounding the gravel behind me, and I nudge Angus to the edge of the track. Barely a breath later, a horse gallops past, the rider's long cloak flapping errantly behind him and catching my face like the tail end of a whip. I cry out and try to steady myself, but fail to catch the saddle's pommel and tumble to the ground. Angus nickers and neighs, stepping away to stop from trampling me.

"Are you injured?" a deep voice calls from further down the road. The rider has stopped his horse, his face shadowed beneath the hood of his cloak.

With a palm to my cheek, I stand and glare at the hooded man. "You didn't have to ride so close, what did you expect would happen?" I ask, looking down at my dusty trousers and white shirt now ripped at the elbow.

"Do you require my assistance?" the man asks. He doesn't move from where he sits atop the mare, merely tilts his head and continues to gaze my way.

I sigh, gingerly holding my elbow and wincing at the new tenderness. "No, I don't need any help. Just be careful next time." With my pride a little bruised, I turn from the rider and climb back into the saddle. By the time I'm settled and reorientated towards the palace, the man and his horse are galloping off, kicking up dust and gravel in their wake.

"Bloody urchin," I mutter, giving Angus a pat when he bobs his head in silent agreement.

The path ahead widens as we approach the final set of iron gates. No matter how many times I've come to deliver fish or Marnie's tonics, or at times to visit the princess, the sight never fails to catch my breath. On one side of the stone-built castle, a tall, crystal tower stands shrouded in mystery. Reaching far above the highest spire of the royal residence, I admire the impossible structure, carved to perfection from a single crystal. Beyond the king, nobody is allowed access, and no one knows why or how they came to be – or if they do, they're not prepared to tell a simple seafarer.

I drag my gaze from that tower to the grounds and entrance of the castle. Much like the villages, before the plague this place had once been alive with the graceful flurry of servants and local tradesmen. Now it's a ghost town, straight-faced guards the only hint of a human presence, guards whose only purpose is to stop locals from wandering into the residence without an appointment.

As I pull up before the entrance, one of stable boys recognises me and rushes from the red-brick barn to take charge of my horse's reins. I slide down from the saddle and thank him, leaving both Angus and my duffel in the boy's care, but looping the satchel with the copper box over my shoulder. I take the stone steps to the front door slowly, my palms sweating with the weight of my bold request hanging over me.

At the top of the steps, guards are posted either side of the tall, double doors, each with spears and grim expressions. As I'm about to pass, they both step forward in unison, their spears clanging together, braced crosswise and barring my entry.

"I'm here at the request of the healer named Marnie," I

say, my voice commanding and insistent despite my trepidation.

The guards share a look, that tight line of their lips growing thinner. "Tell her she's too late. There's no longer any need for a healer."

I step back, confused and a little concerned by their response. "The King?" I whisper.

The guard who spoke shakes his head sadly and says, "Our Queen. She passed last night."

Queen Cinder, beloved for her kindness and hospitality. It was she who had cultivated my love of books, often visiting the schooling quarter and ensuring it was governed with as much passion as it deserved.

"You," a familiar voice calls from beyond the palace doors. "Are you here to make a complaint about your accident?"

I lean to the side and peer past the guards to see the man whose cloak had knocked me from my saddle. That cloak is gone now, emerald eyes and a handsome face revealed beneath, one I belatedly recognise as belonging to Ryder, the prince of this isle.

"Your Highness," I mutter, offering a shallow bow. "I am here at my guardian's request and was hoping to speak with your father...but I understand he must be grieving. I'll come back another day."

"Why would you do that? Surely it's more hassle for you to ride back and forth. Come. I'll take you to him now," the prince insists.

The guards grit their teeth but recognise the silent command to let me pass. As I step forward, I hear one mutter a word – *heartless*.

The prince has just lost his mother, and yet with the way he stands and waits for me, not a flicker of emotion stirs beneath those dark lashes. Turning on his heel, Ryder leads me up a winding marble staircase.

With his back turned, I follow closely behind and take the chance to study the prince of the Garden Isle. He's tall – far taller than my scrawny height – with thickly corded thighs and shoulders you could rest the world on. An old but well-kept sword hangs at his side, tapping lightly against the tight riding breeches. The weapon is an odd thing for a prince to carry. He has no need to hunt, or fight, or defend. At least, not anymore. During the war he had defended this isle with a ferocity that spoke to the guard's accusation, the heartlessness; those muscles honed in the throes of battle. But the war is over, and he is royalty, so why carry the sword? I suppose despite the lack of crime here, we are just as subject to invaders and pirates as any other of the richer islands.

"This way," Ryder says at the top of the stairs, leading me down a wide corridor with paintings capturing every inch of the walls.

I admire them as I go, my eyes falling on one in particular. Queen Cinder on *The King's Arcana* with the three sisters. My heart catches at the sight. Cinder and Marnie had been great friends, I suppose it's fitting they each took their last breath on the same summer's night.

"What are you doing?" the prince asks, eyeing me curiously. His raven-coloured hair shifts slightly with the movement, and I'm oddly transfixed.

When he continues to stare, I realise I've stopped walking altogether, one finger delicately tracing the line of Marnie's face on the painting. I pull it back and shove both hands in my pockets. "I'm sorry about your mother."

His curious eyes again fail to flicker with sadness, loss or despair. Instead, his brows crumble slightly in contemplation. "That's nature, is it not? People die."

The callousness of his comment staggers me, and I dip my head to hide the anger rising at Queen Cinder's defence. She was good and kind and loved her children, all children. The guard had been right. He *is* heartless.

Down several further corridors and up a second flight of stairs, Prince Ryder leads me to the highest room in the palace. Unease sits like a stone in my stomach. I've never been to this part of the residence before, nobody outside of the royal family has ever been allowed. It's private, not for visitors, and certainly no place for a young woman calling to settle an old debt on the day following the queen's death.

I nearly tumble in my haste to catch up, to tell Ryder I'll come back another day instead, but I'm too late. He pushes opening a tall, oaken door and steps inside, holding it ajar for me to follow. I do, and immediately regret it.

King Phillip sits with his head in his hands beside a large, ornate bed, where the body of his deceased wife is laid neatly with her hands placed reverently to hide their blackened state. Even from here I see the signs; the dull colour of her once golden hair and the way her dress hangs loosely at her sides, failing to mask the emaciated frame.

"Ryder, you came–" The king stands from his chair, his elation at seeing his son fading to a look of surprise when he spots me standing close behind. "Emery? What are you doing here?" he asks.

"I...I'm so sorry, Phillip," I stutter, offering a low bow.

"She wishes to speak with you. I came to see the body," Ryder says, his tone devoid of any emotion, as if he were here to inspect a new tea set as opposed to his dead mother.

Phillip stiffens, his once tanned but rosy cheeks drained of all colour at his son's callous words. With one hand gripping the bed, Phillip rubs a palm to his chest and sighs deeply. Ryder remains where he is, eyes glazed and body relaxed. I can't help but take a step back, wanting desperately to sink into the shadows and flee this place where I am not supposed to be.

"What is it you wished to see my father about?" Ryder asks flatly.

Despicable. He is completely and utterly despicable. "It doesn't matter," I whisper, shaking my head and taking two steps further back towards the door, towards my escape. The prince doesn't try to stop me, but his father raises his head, his eyes catching my face.

"Wait, Emery," Phillip says, and my feet root themselves to the floor at his command. "Your guardians, they should be here to...to say goodbye. My wife was close to the sisters, they were family to her and she would want them here."

My mouth opens but words fail me, my throat dry and seizing up. The king's face falls and he rakes a hand through his short, silver hair, recognising the grief in my hesitation. He stands and crosses the room in long strides, pulling me into his chest. I want to push away, the stink of death and days at sea clinging to my hair and clothes. But Phillip simply holds me tighter, the familiar scent of his velvet robe redolent of cedar and a temporary reprieve from the aching loneliness.

"You will stay here in one of the palace estates," he says, leaning back to hold me at arm's length. "I owed the sisters a great favour and will repay it with what I promised – a roof and enough funds to keep you comfortable."

I'm staggered by the sudden affirmation, grateful that his memory serves correct, that Marnie was right and that I myself was not required to speak of the debt.

"Thank you," I say softly.

"The sisters saved Ryder's life when he was a young boy. Believe me when I say, this is the very least I can do to return their kindness."

I bow my head, wanting to know more of the story, of *any* story that involves my former guardians. But now is not the time. "I'm so sorry I intruded. I should leave," I say, half turning towards the door.

"You have nothing to be sorry for, Emery." Phillip turns his head to where Ryder has moved to stand beside his mother's body. "That man...I feel with every passing year his heart fades further away."

Heartless.

"Thank you for your kindness, I'll return at a later date," I say, continuing to back away.

Phillip turns his head to where I stand with one foot inching over the threshold. "Don't be absurd. You won't wish to return to the sisters' cottage. Tonight, you will stay in the palace and join us for supper. I will ensure the Moor estate is ready for your arrival tomorrow morning."

I don't care, I just want to get away from this, from death, from the despair so deeply set in the king's olive-green eyes.

"Ryder, take Emery to the guest rooms on the second floor," Phillip says, returning to his wife's side.

Ryder nods his head at the command and turns without a word, heading out the door. With one final bow to Phillip, I offer the same to the deceased queen and again whisper my condolences before hurrying from the room.

THE GUEST CHAMBER IS IMPRESSIVE, the four-poster bed like a throne of silks and soft cotton, with heavy curtain drapes pulled open for the midday sun to bathe the room in warm light. I place my satchel carefully on the vanity desk, ignoring the glint of the copper box and instead moving straight to a high-arched doorway at the far side of the room. I almost sink to the floor at the sight of the bathing pool, made of pretty, textured tiles and set on a raised platform, it fills one half of the room and is large enough for six people.

As I turn the taps to start the water, someone knocks on the door. At my answer, a maid enters hugging the bag I had left on Angus to her chest. Depositing the heavy duffel on a chair beside the bed, she asks if I require further assistance. I shake my head, wanting nothing more than to be alone with my thoughts before dining with the king later this evening, so she leaves without protest.

Water gargles from the bathing room and I hurry in to check its level, quickly turning off the taps and adding salts from a small alcove set into the wall. Stripping from my pungent clothes, I'm about to step into the bath when an odd scratching noise comes from the other room. Curious, I wrap myself in a towel and peek my head around the corner to inspect the bedroom, but nobody is there.

The scratching persists and I follow the sound, listening along the walls and checking beneath the bed. Nothing. I look up to where the copper box sits in my bag and walk over, pulling it out and holding it to my ear.

Scratch. Scratch. Scratch.

I open the lid and push the silk cloth to one side, removing the book. It vibrates softly against my fingers a moment longer, then falls silent. I eye the book warily and remember that today is my birthday. As per Malina's instructions, I'm allowed to read the first page.

Leaving the box and the silk behind, I carry the book to the bathing room and place it carefully on a towel to the side of the pool before stepping into the steaming water. Sinking in, I groan as the salts and warmth work their magic, easing the aches and stripping the smell of death from my skin. I submerge fully, holding my breath and scrubbing my face and hair. The salt won't help the tangled mess, but I'll rinse it properly later. For now, there's no rush.

After three long minutes underwater, I break the surface, filling my lungs and feeding my guilt for finding enjoyment when only yesterday the sisters had passed. Turning onto my front, I rest my arms on the pool's side and dry my hands with a towel before picking up the book.

Against the aged leather, the golden clasp looks new and untouched by time. I flick it loose and flip open the cover. Inside, the binding is frayed where the first half of the book has been removed, but the first page is clear and bright, with a single verse written in red at its centre.

> *The sisters are dead, the mother untold,*
> *and the girl with blue eyes remains lonely but bold.*
> *For she ponders her place and the sisters' requests,*
> *Unsure how to live, not knowing her quest.*

I read the passage over and over, picking apart the sentences. *My* eyes are blue. *My* guardians are dead. *I* ponder the sisters' requests. The similarities are...impossible. Malina had spoken of temptation, of how this book is a part of me as much as I am of it. I expected a fairy tale, perhaps a diary. But this tome seems to speak in riddles of what has already passed. I sit up, holding the book closer, one finger ready to flip the page.

Only what is allowed.

The words echo in my head, and I notice smaller writing at the bottom of the page.

~ *FOUR DAYS* ~

An instruction, the one Malina had warned of. Four days until I'm permitted to read the next page. My finger remains, toying with the weathered edge of the paper. I close the flap, replacing the catch and covering the book with the towel before moving to the far edge of the pool. Temptation indeed. Is it possible for a book to tell your future? For the future to already be written? The thought is frightening...and a little disappointing; the lack of control over what comes next. No. Malina had said the story may be rewritten.

I sigh, more confused than ever as her words tumble incoherently in my mind. Closing my eyes, I once again slip beneath the water, to where there are no riddles, and the world is quiet.

VOYAGE DECIDED

THE GARDEN ISLE

I stare at the skinny, fractured woman in the mirror. My hair is tamed and tied neatly in a side plait, my breeches and shirt clean but crinkled. The clothes are entirely inappropriate to dine with a king, but with little else, I leave the tired looking reflection and head for the stairs to the lower levels.

Unsure where exactly Phillip dines, I stop at the palace entrance where two new guards stand at the open doors in deep discussion with a man. Not wanting to disturb them, I turn my back, searching the empty halls for a maid or butler to guide me instead.

"You there!"

I turn to see the man stumbling back, one guard roughly pushing him away. "Hey, I doubt there's any need for that," I say, storming towards them.

"Oh, thank you. Please, I must meet with the king!" the stranger begs, dropping to his knees before the guards. Dressed in flared harem trousers and a red, open waistcoat stitched with fine threads, I can see he's no beggar. He also isn't from the island, *that* much is certainly clear with the way his hair is fashioned – his head shaved minus a single, long ponytail worn over one shoulder.

While I pity the man, the royal family is grieving, and they have already accepted one uncommon guest today – Me. I step forward and place my hand on the man's shoulder. "You might not have heard, but the queen passed last night and King Phillip is grieving. Would you be able to come back another day?"

The man dips his head, three golden loops in one ear brushing against the dark skin of his cheek. He most definitely is not a beggar.

"But I have nowhere to go," he says, dejectedly.

I wonder at that. Surely with the jewellery he wears he can afford an inn? I suppose it's none of my business. I shake my head with a sigh. "Go to the stables and wait for an hour or so, I'll speak with the king and see if I can house you in my estate until you get yourself settled."

His head snaps up, eyes practically glittering with renewed hope as he thanks me graciously, bowing again and again as he backs away and down the steps.

"Are you sure that's wise, Emery?"

I spin to see Prince Ryder making his way down the stairs, his previous, commoner clothes exchanged for those more fit for royalty – all silk and studded gems, the shirtless waist coat left open to reveal a powerfully muscled stomach beneath.

"What do you mean?" I ask, keeping my eyes stubbornly affixed to his and nothing further south.

Ryder tilts his head to one side. "What if he's a criminal?"

"On the Garden Isle? Not likely," I say with a sharp laugh. Is he worried? *Can* he feel such a thing? "Anyway, even if he *is* a criminal, I'm more than capable of looking after myself."

"Interesting," is all the prince says, eyeing me like a curious specimen. "Come. My father should be waiting for us." He turns and heads down the corridor while I follow behind, admiring the cut of his jib despite the loose fit of his trousers.

The man you love, a heartless man, will be the one to kill you...

I chuckle inwardly at the thought. While the prince does indeed come across as heartless, he's certainly not the type I would fall in love with, at least his personality isn't. If I was to love a man with no heart, such a lacking would need to be a little less obvious. Nevertheless, it doesn't matter. I have no intention of tying myself to any man or woman.

After what feels like an age of wandering down marble floored corridors lined with carefully tended plants and flowers, we pass through two glass doors and step out into a courtyard overlooking the gardens, the Great Tree towering above. Lanterns light the open space, and servants hurry past us with trays bearing an assortment of food.

The King sits at the head of the stone table, his head resting on his hand and nose buried in a book. As Ryder pulls out his chair, Phillip looks up – first to his son, then to me, standing awkwardly by the open doors.

"Ah, you found your way," he says with a kind grin, folding a page in the book and snapping it shut before placing it on the table to one side.

I cringe at that. Malka might have cursed him for such a sacrilege. One must *never* fold the page of a book. "Sorry we interrupted you. What are you reading if you don't mind my asking?"

Phillip glances at the closed book and gently pats the cover. "My wife's favourite, the fable of a young woman who travels to another world to save her family. Though, some believe it is based in truth, the story coming from a traveller to our world."

I laugh, unsure if he's being serious. Otherworldly travel is about as believable as Malka's prophecy regarding my future lover. Still, I don't say that, instead stating I had yet to read such a story, but that I'd like to.

The king hesitates momentarily, then picks it up and hands it to me. "Don't worry, Cinder has at least three copies...*had* three copies," he says, correcting himself. "She would like that one has landed in your care."

I step forward and hesitantly accept the worn book. "Thank you. I'll treasure it." It's true, I love books and everything they have to offer. Whether to learn or to escape to new and exciting worlds, I love the opportunities they provide.

"Good. How are you finding your room? Comfortable enough?" Leading the way for the rest of us, Phillip begins to load food onto his plate, all the while looking at me expectantly.

"It's perfect, better than that, in fact. I don't think I've ever bathed so luxuriously," I say with a chuckle. "Speaking of lodgings, I should mention there was a man at the palace door. He was asking for you, saying he had nowhere to go. I said he could sleep in the estate you offered me until you're ready to receive guests. I hope that's alright?"

Phillip pauses, his eyes narrowing slightly. "I see. And where is this man now?"

I waver a little and wonder if I've taken a step too far by assuming he isn't ready to perform his duties. "I told him to wait for me by the stables," I say quickly.

The king lifts his eyes and dips his head to a guard I had failed to notice hiding in the shadows of the courtyard. With a responding nod, the guard quickly departs, and another enters to take his place.

"You must be more cautious, Emery. Do you know how the plague came to this isle?"

"Yes, the sisters told me it was brought by travellers from the First Sea."

Phillip nods his head, moving the food around his plate distractedly. "That's right. Our shoremen tell me more ships from those lands have been spotted recently on the western coast. None have ventured too close, though. Not in so far as we're aware."

"You believe there might be trouble?" I ask. Being a small waypoint between the First and Third Sea, it isn't unusual for travellers to stop at the island before continuing their journey, though most don't stay for long when they find we have little to offer in trade, other than water and common vegetables.

"Without the sisters' sight, it's hard to be sure if they're merely travellers or the more nefarious sort. That reminds me, how do you intend to inform their mother?" Phillip asks, skipping from one mysterious statement to the next.

"What do you mean by *their sight*? And I thought the sisters' mother was dead?" I ask, pausing mid-cut of my garlic potatoes.

Phillip stares at me, his brows pinching slightly in the middle. "Their witch sight, of course. And yes, I myself only heard news of their mother recently. Apparently, she is alive and well on Aurora Isle."

"Witches?" I scoff.

"Oh dear. It seems I might have over-stepped," Phillip says with a sheepish smile, one hand rubbing the nape of his neck.

I'm not sure it's possible for royalty to overstep anything. "The sisters weren't *real* witches," I insist. "They would have told me." Doubt creeps in the moment I say it, and one look at the king's pitying eyes drives his point home. Their ship is called *The King's Arcana* for goodness' sake. Marnie's potions. Malina's apparent agelessness. Malka's prophecy. The *book*.

"I'm sorry, Emery. I thought you knew," Phillip says softly

I shake my head and load my mouth with soft vegetables in the hopes it might stop me from saying something rude. Did the sisters not trust me? Did they think my mind weak enough to snap at such a confession? Swallowing the mouthful, I lean back in my chair. "Where is Aurora Isle?" I ask.

"The Fifth Sea. I can send a messenger if you wish?" Phillip offers.

I mull it over silently as I pick at the seared fish on my plate. This might be it, my chance to leave, the reason I've been waiting for. "I think I'll go myself." The words flee my lips before I've realised, and I look up to see the king watching me carefully.

"Highness?" a voice calls from the open doors.

We all turn to see the guard from before as he steps through with the stranger I had promised to meet at the stables.

"Is this the man you spoke of, Emery?" Phillip asks.

I nod my head.

"I see." Placing his cutlery down, Phillip turns his full attention to the new arrival. "I don't recognise you. Which sea do you hail from, young man?"

"I travelled from the Third, Majesty," the man says, averting his eyes. It's an odd thing, that fear so evident in his twisting hands and shaking shoulders. Is the Third Sea's monarch so terrible they elicit this kind of response?

"What business do you have here?" Phillip asks, his elbows resting on the table and fingers steepled beneath his chin. The serious king.

"I wish to beg for your protection, Majesty. I ran away from my master and I'm in urgent need of safe passage to the Fifth."

"How oddly fortuitous. It just so happens the captain of

The King's Arcana is considering such a voyage. Why should she bring you along?"

While I assume this means I have the king's blessing to travel, I continue to carefully watch Phillip. This is a side of the man, of the *king* I have never seen before. A side reserved for those outside his kingdom, for those he does not trust.

"As I'm sure you're aware, Your Majesty, the southern isles of this sea are refusing any unsanctioned ships permission to travel through their territory. If your captain requires it, I can guide her through Marooners' Canal instead, the only pass outside their reach. Beyond that, I admit I won't be much use as a guide, but I am prepared to work for my place on the vessel."

Phillip eases back in his chair, one finger tapping on the table as he looks from the newcomer to me. "Well, Captain? What do you think?"

The stranger's eyes snap up to the king, then follow his gaze to me. "*You're* the captain?"

I continue to stare at Phillip. He's testing me, seeing if I heed his earlier warning to be more cautious with my chosen company. "I *am* the captain, and I don't have the papers required to travel in southern waters, so a guide would be helpful..." I finally turn my head from the king to look at the stranger. "You may come, but there are conditions. Those who sail aboard *The Arcana* must be willing to work, and I'll ask that you relinquish any and all weapons before you step aboard."

"You're allowing him to go with you then? Just like that?" King Phillip asks.

I can't turn down a person in need, and the man seems truly desperate. "Yes."

"In that case, I will send three guards and an additional crew-woman with you. And I must ask a personal favour, Emery, while you're in such a willing mood."

Ah, so this is what he's *really* after. "You're my King, your wish is my command," I say with an expectant grin.

"I would like you to take Ryder on your journey to see Mother Witch. I believe she can help him find his heart," Phillip says with a hopeful glance towards his son. The prince continues eating, as if oblivious to the fact he remains in our company.

"Prince Ryder?" I ask, that grin slowly fading as I shift in my seat to regard him. "Do you wish to travel with us?"

Without hesitating he says, "I'll go if that is what my father wants. I'm not sure what the witch can do for me, but I don't object."

That's it. No excitement or dismay, no questions regarding our decided voyage. "Do you feel *anything*?" I ask him.

The prince considers this a moment, those green eyes lifeless as he raises his fork, and with one quick strike pierces the skin on his other hand. Four red dots of blood rise to the surface and Phillip curses, calling one of the maids for something to treat it.

Ryder's eyes remain on mine as he places the fork to one side, allowing the maid to tend to the broken skin. "Does that frighten you, Emery? Being on a ship with a man who feels nothing, no pain, no love, no anger, nor fear?" he asks.

I shake my head, a smile stretching across my face. "On the contrary. The voyage to the Fifth Sea will take several weeks at least. Having someone onboard as intriguing as you might liven things up a little," I say. His answers, however, tell me one thing. Ryder cannot be trusted. Without love, there is no loyalty. And without Fear, there is recklessness. Neither will do, but the king wishes it, and so I must obey.

"Excellent," Phillip says with a weary sigh. "With your permission, Captain, I will assist by having *The Arcana* prepared for your voyage with enough gold for every port and enough food to keep you well."

"You mentioned sending three guards, do you think that's necessary? I'm quite capable with blades and a bow, and I wish to sail without drawing too much attention," I tell the king. A large crew would draw inquisitive eyes, so the less people, the better.

"I cannot in good conscience send you off without protection, the sisters would surely haunt me," Phillip mutters, looking skyward as if the very women in question were watching him now.

"I'll protect her," Ryder says, resuming his meal as soon as the maid scurries away. "I've bested nearly every man and woman you have, so why send any at all?"

Fearless. Reckless.

The king considers this a moment, and as the father and son lock eyes I realise just how much they look alike – both with sharp noses and strong jaws, their eyes cut from the same, perfect emerald.

Phillip shakes his head. "I will send *two* guards then, instead of three. And I won't hear any more on the matter," he states firmly. "As for the crew-woman, Winnie Dawning will be going with you."

I open my mouth to insist that isn't necessary – what with *The Arcana* being cleverly rigged to sail singlehandedly – but the king cuts me off.

"I'm sure you can manage it yourself, Emery. But as you said, the voyage is long, and the offer of a helping hand should not be easily dismissed. Winnie will be useful."

I bow my head to hide my grimace, acquiescing his request. I would prefer *none* of them come. While company is at times appreciated, it's the quietness of the open ocean I love, the silent opportunities. More bodies mean more drama. Perhaps that's why I don't entirely mind the prince joining. He's quiet and reserved.

"How long before your people will be ready to sail?" I ask Phillip.

"Three days should do. My daughter will have returned by then, and she'll wish to see you both before you depart. What shall we do with your estate? Do you plan to return to the isle?"

I hadn't thought of that. Will I return? "I'd like to keep it just in case, if you don't mind?"

"It is your estate to do with as you please," the king says with a smile. He glances up to where the stranger still stands awkwardly fiddling with the end of his ponytail. "What is your name?"

"Ansel, Majesty," the man says.

"Well, Ansel, you may have a room in the palace until your departure, and a guard will remain by your side at all times. Do you understand?" Phillip asks, his tone ten degrees cooler than when he had spoken with me.

"I understand," Ansel says softly then bows his head with gratitude, before being led away by the guard.

As I AMBLE through my bedroom door, I immediately make for the bed and fall on the soft, quilted duvet. I ate far too much, and already I regret it. Ritual states that a week before setting sail, you reduce your diet to the same rations you can expect onboard. I'm not sure how that might be possible when every night in the palace I can expect such lavish and generous portions.

I roll onto my back, letting a hand fall across my face to block the moonlight bleeding through a crack in the heavy curtains.

Four strangers. Two guards, Ansel, and a woman I don't know all living together on the humble deck of my ship. Then there's Ryder, the heartless prince. It's a recipe for disaster. Rules and expectations will need to be set if we have any hope of surviving the coming weeks together.

I bolt upright at the sound of scratching and grip my aching stomach as I move to where I left the leather book in the bathing room. The sound intensifies the closer I get, soft but insistent. I stop beside the bath and stare at the towel as the sound continues, watching the soft cotton vibrate. After a moment the room falls silent, and I uncover the book to pick it up. Nothing. No scratching. No soft vibrations. I flick the clasp and read the first page again.

> *The sisters are dead, the mother untold,*
> *and the girl with blue eyes remains lonely but bold.*
> *For she ponders her place and the sisters' requests,*
> *unsure how to live, not knowing her quest.*

~ THREE DAYS ~

The sisters' mother…a quest. Already the verse is beginning to make more sense, and the similarities to what transpired at dinner only make me wonder more. As I read it again and again, I realise it's changed. Not the verse, but the days to wait before reading the next. Is that what the scratching was? The sound is close enough to that of a quill across parchment, though somewhat enhanced.

But that's impossible.

I think back to what King Phillip had said about the three

sisters, the three *witches*. Had they somehow enchanted the book? Taking it with me into the bed chamber, I'm about to place it back in the copper box when the scratching starts again. I toy with the clasp. Malina had warned of a dire cost. What was the price of knowing your future?

A knock on the door breaks the book's tempting spell, and I hurriedly place it back in the box and into my satchel where it's hidden.

"Emery? May I come in?"

I start at the sound of Ryder's voice behind the door. Of all people, he is not who I would expect as a late-night visitor. I open the door to find him leaning casually against the wide frame.

"Is everything alright, *Sire*?" I ask, the title a bitter taste on my tongue.

"My father says the timetables have changed. My sister arrives tomorrow, and Winnie has agreed to undertake the voyage along with two volunteer guards. With that, we should be ready a day sooner than expected."

So, something *has* changed. My gaze falls to the vanity desk where the satchel lies.

"Will you be prepared to leave a day early?" Ryder asks.

All I need to do to prepare myself is visit the cartographer to obtain the sea charts, and then Pattie to hand over Angus. The King has said he will ensure *The Arcana* is well stocked, so I will leave that to his kindness.

"Yes, that should be fine. Was there anything else you needed?" I ask.

After a moment, the prince leans forward, one hand raising to stroke my cheek. The touch is gentle but confusing, and before I realise, I seize his wrist and hold it away from me.

His eyes widen slightly as he stares at my hand, at my nails lightly denting his skin. "You're a curious creature,

Emerelda. Perhaps I *can* feel something after all?" Pulling his hand from my grasp, he turns and walks away, slipping into a bedroom down the hall.

I close the door and almost turn for the bed when instead I click the lock in place. My heart pounds a rhythm in my chest and I gently touch my forehead to the door. I remember Ryder from when we were children. He was lively and kind and gentle like his mother. This man is different, made of tin, or iron, with nothing at the centre. He *does* frighten me, not that I would ever openly admit that. But at least I recognise it in myself. I'll have to be careful of him.

The man you love, a heartless man, will be the one to kill you...

I shudder at the thought as I undress and climb under the silken sheets of my king-size bed. In three days we will be well on our way and I can read the next page of the book. Hopefully then, I'll have some answers.

CHARTS & CHAINS

THE GARDEN ISLE

The sun has barely risen by the time I'm dressed and making my way down the long marble staircase. The guards smile as I pass through the palace entrance, asking where I'm off to at such an early hour. When I tell them I'm heading into town to take care of some business, they each bob their heads with one stating he will notify the prince, before leaving his post and heading inside the palace.

"Am I supposed to report my whereabouts whilst I stay here?" I ask, a little surprised by the notion.

"I'm afraid Prince Ryder insisted," the remaining guard replies.

What business is it of *his* where I go and what I do? Unsure if the prince intends to shadow me throughout the day, I hurry down the steps towards the stables, hoping to get on the road before he can catch up.

I skid to a stop beside the stable doors, seeing Ryder brushing the mane of the same large and beautiful white mare he'd been riding yesterday.

He turns to me, his expression blank. "You're up early."

"You asked the guards to monitor my whereabouts. Why?" I ask, failing to hide the bite in my tone as I collect my saddle and bridle before walking past the prince towards my horse's stall.

"I assured my father I'd protect you. Surely that means I need to know where you are?" he asks, voice deep and calm.

"I don't need your protection, nor do I want it. Especially here on the isle where it's perfectly safe."

"You're...angry?"

As I tie the last of the straps on the saddle, I sigh and turn to face Ryder. Angry isn't the right word, but of course he would struggle to recognise how I feel when he himself feels nothing. "No, I just prefer to be alone. I have a lot to do today, and I don't need people constantly stopping me to pay their respects to my companion."

I watch as Ryder retrieves a saddle and straps it into place on the mare, then swings up gracefully and pulls the hood of his cloak forward to conceal his face. "Nobody will know I travel with you."

Everyone will know, but fine. Here on the isle, he is the prince, the master, my superior. Out at sea on *The King's Arcana*, that will change. The titles will shift, and I'll be in charge. The thought brightens my mood somewhat, the prospect of once again being free to do and say and *be* who I am. Pulling myself onto Angus, I nudge him gently with my boot, and lead the way from the stables.

AS PREDICTED, for the umpteenth time on our trek I steady Angus at the side of the road to wait as a young woman fawns over the prince. He plays his role well, wishing her health and happiness with a polite nod. The moment we are alone and continue down the road, the real prince returns, his face stoic and blank.

"When is the princess due to arrive?" I ask, eager to fill the silence between us.

"At midday."

The quiet drags on and I'm unsure what to say. While I appreciate this side of the prince and will later welcome it in the small confines of the ship, right *now* I want to gauge him, to understand him a little more. "When did you lose your heart?" I ask.

Ryder tilts his head to one side, his brows crumpling in thought as he takes both reins in one hand to feel his chest. "I don't believe I have lost it."

"Not your *literal* heart, I mean your ability to feel something other than curiosity." I roll my eyes at the fact I even have to clarify such a thing.

"You're the only thing that makes me curious. Something mysterious, something hidden calls out. Can't you hear it, Emery?"

I'm not sure how many times he's said my name now... three, four? Each time is the same, the single word spoken softly, alluringly. "I'm not a *thing*, I'm a person. And there's nothing mysterious about me." Well...apart from the book, I suppose.

Before long we reach the small town of Spriggin, a quaint little place with all but ten stores and a centre square for the artisans to display their work. After a moment perusing the latest leather goods and bladesmith's stalls, we pull our horses to a stop outside a store belonging to the best cartographer on the isle. I snag Angus' reins over a long, iron hitching rail, then head inside without waiting for Ryder.

At the ding of the shop's bell, an old man with long, white hair looks up from his counter, a beaming grin spreading from ear to ear. "Emery! It's been a little while since you last graced my stoop. I heard about the sisters, how are you faring?" Anderson asks, removing his glasses from a crooked nose to clean them.

"Faring as well as can be expected, Anderson, thank you. I'm actually here on business. Do you have charts with each of the eight seas and their sailing routes? I'll need one with all of Oceanus on it as well."

"A world map too, eh? Not planning to leave us, are you? What will we do without our best fisher?" he calls as he ambles down the archives in the back.

"I'm afraid so," is all I say. From the tall stacks I hear the grunts and moans of Anderson pulling his step ladder and moving from shelf to shelf to find what I've asked for. He emerges shortly after with one hand gently touching his lower back, and the other laden with leather tubes each housing a chart.

Looking past me, he gasps and drops his bundle as he stoops to a low bow. "Your Highness! Please forgive me, I hadn't realised you were here," Anderson says quickly. His back creaks and protests with age as he tries and fails to stand straight again, so I hurry to the other side of the counter to help him.

"There's no need for such formalities, but thank you. I'm only here to assist Emery with her business," Ryder says with practiced grace.

I glare up at him as I help Anderson onto a chair and move to pick up the dropped tubes.

"Oh, I see. Will you be sailing together as well?" Anderson asks, patting my hand gratefully as I place the items on the desk beside him.

"Yes, I will be accompanying the voyage as her protector whilst we search for–"

"Adventure!" I say with a tight laugh, cutting off Ryder. "We're off to search for adventure." The Islanders see the prince as a mirror of his beloved mother. Telling Anderson that Ryder is leaving in search of his heart is a can of worms I'm not prepared to open today.

"How exciting, I do miss my adventuring days, but I'll look forward to collecting your stories!" Anderson says smiling up at both of us. "Well, we'd best make sure you have all the charts you need for a safe voyage then."

Ryder says nothing of my lie, but I feel the weight of his gaze as I work with the cartographer to pick out the best charts for our journey. Unsurprisingly, Anderson has nothing for the Eighth Sea, but according to the map of Oceanus, we shouldn't need to venture anywhere near it to get to Aurora Isle.

With the scrolls in hand and Anderson paid handsomely by Ryder, we say our goodbyes and I mentally tick the first job off my list.

"You lied," Ryder says the moment we've mounted our horses and started down the road.

"We would have been stuck there all afternoon trying and failing to explain your heartlessness if I hadn't intervened." As we approach a fork in the road, I pull the reins and direct Angus down the right, towards the coast and the town of Merryweather.

"Where are we going next?"

"To visit the harbour master and check on the ship." I angle myself slightly in the saddle to look back at Ryder. "You can head back to the palace if you like? I wouldn't want you to get bored." More like I don't want him to be there when I visit Pattie. She'll get so excited I'm worried the sight of him might induce a stroke.

"I'm not bored," he assures me.

I groan and take Angus from a trot to a gallop. We remain in silence as we fly down the empty roads, until we're forced to slow as we approach the first houses of the town. To the south, down the worn, gravelled slopes and past the small shop fronts, the sea shimmers invitingly beyond a white sanded beach, and I find myself desperate for the days to pass quickly so I can get back on the water.

Down the narrow side streets, we nod at each passer-by, and I try to keep my eyes from wandering to the doors of each dwelling. This town was hit the hardest when the plague took hold of the isle.

"It's worse than when I last visited," Ryder says from behind me, his voice devoid of sadness as he simply states fact.

I stop outside a small, terraced home the colour of bleached coral, and look up to the see moth-eaten curtains flutter in an open window on the top floor.

"Pattie, I know you're home," I call, not bothering to dismount from Angus. An invitation to enter the home of Pattie Zakeer is as likely as snow in summer.

A moment later, Pattie opens the door with as much enthusiasm as a plank of wood, and rolls her eyes. Recognition dawns, and her complexion quickly shifts to a colour matching the dull walls of her home as she splutters her welcomes to the prince – only pausing to ensure the door at her back is firmly closed so he can't see the messy state of her home.

When formalities are done, she looks to me, both hands raising to sit on her wide hips. "I'll take one guess as to why you're here, Emerelda. You're leaving, aren't you?" she asks, her chin lifting slightly with the accusation.

I dip my head and grin sheepishly. "You can't really expect me to stay cooped up here for the rest of my life?"

"I suppose that doesn't come as much of a surprise," Pattie says, softening slightly. "Malina always knew you were going to sail off one day, though the other sisters were sorely against such a notion."

My smile fades as I remember my guardians' words, their

warnings. "I know. But I have to go. I belong on the sea, Pattie."

With a sigh, she steps down from her porch and reaches up to pat Angus. "I know you do, kiddo. It's done by the way, the sisters are buried and the house is all ash and stone walls now. I'll take care of Angus here."

I raise my head and nod gratefully at her. The sisters had said arrangements had been put in place with Pattie to deal with their remains. Knowing the house is gone, I realise Malina was right. That place had been an anchor, and with it gone the chains binding me to the isle are undone.

KING'S WARNING

THE GARDEN ISLE

The next morning I'm packed and ready to leave well before the maid knocks on my door to inform me the King is waiting downstairs. Dressed in my usual, sea-worthy clothes of a loose white shirt and black breeches with red leather boots, I tie my thick rubicund hair in the signature side plait to keep it tidy, and do one final check in the mirror.

The woman reflected back is different than before, her eyes now clear instead of dull. I'm doing it. I'm leaving, finally venturing further than the Second Sea to new and exciting places. The decision is made, and the notion is liberating.

Scratch. Scratch. Scratch.

I turn to where my satchel lies on the vanity desk. Only one more day and I can read the next page. If it *is* a book that tells my future, I want to know. I want to be prepared for what comes next on our voyage. Or do I? Not knowing is thrilling, it's the very reason I want to leave. If I stay here on the Garden Isle I know exactly what comes next – a life as dull as dishwater.

With a smile, I sling both bags over my shoulder, then leave the room and head down the staircase.

"Emery!" a delicate voice calls from below.

I smile down at Princess Odette who turns from her father to wait patiently at the bottom of the stairs. Looking into those deep blue eyes, with her blonde hair tied neatly in a bun and clad in a delicate dress of blue chiffon, she looks just like her mother did.

"Oddie, it's good to see you! I'm so sorry about your mum," I say, dropping my bags and pulling her into a hug. While I had never felt close to the king or the prince, Odette and I had gone to school at the same time and had quickly become friends. Over the years, as her duties had grown more extensive, our friendship had lost its lustre. Nevertheless, I'm happy she's next in line to rule. The princess not only mirrors her mother's looks, but her temperament is cut from the same cloth too. Being the first born, it will be her duty to rule after her father, and it's one she seems proud to assume.

"I'm so sorry about the sisters, Em. And now you'll have to put up with my brother for the weeks to come. I will pray to the stars for you."

I chuckle, first at her, then at the vacant look Ryder gives her. "He's not so bad," I say with a wink.

Odette scoffs, linking arms with me as we head outside to where our horses are waiting. On the ride to Merryweather, I ask where she's returning from, but Phillip answers in her place.

"The Southern Isles. Despite my wishes, my daughter thinks it wise to form a matrimonial partnership with one of those infernal princes." Phillip shakes his head and looks despairingly to his daughter, who merely chuckles and waves a hand dismissively.

"It's the best deterrent to future war, and long since overdue, Father," Odette insists with a grin. "The oldest prince is a little rough around the edges, but seems gentlemanly enough…I'm sure it will be a good match."

I'm not sure what to say to that. As a princess and future Queen, Odette seems content with her decision to marry and join the two kingdoms. But I wonder how she feels as a young woman, as a person unable to follow her heart and fall in love.

Little more is said for the remainder of the ride, and before we know it, we've reached the port town of Merryweather, where the docks and *The King's Arcana* are both teeming with guards and merchants moving up and down the ramp with boxed goods.

I'm pleased to see Pattie is here, holding a crate of what I suspect is wine or rum. Leaving the king and princess, Ryder and I steer our horses towards the beach to greet her.

"It's a long 'ole way to the Misty Isle, I thought you might like a bit of rum for when the tides are wicked and the fates unkind."

I laugh at that, first chastising her for jinxing our journey, then thanking her as I trade Angus' reins for the crate. "I'll send a bird when I reach the Isle, but you know what those things are like. If you don't hear, just assume I'm well," I tell her.

She nods her head and shifts awkwardly from one foot to the other, then leans forward and pats the top of my head. "You be careful now, Emery. And I'll be counting on *you* to take care of her as well, Sire," Pattie says boldly to the prince.

"That is my duty. Of course I will," he says with a single, cocked eyebrow.

With a final goodbye, Ryder and I head to the dock to where Phillip and Odette continue to check the manifest. Seeming content, the king turns and gestures towards the end of the dock – a signal for the additional crew to step forward from the gathering crowd.

I try to mask my surprise and mild annoyance when two *men* step forward, Phillip's promised guards. Women are usually the preferred protectors at sea. Men are trouble, their hearts and heads unsuited to resisting the sirens' calls.

Perhaps sensing my hesitation, Phillip explains his lack of choice, with the plague diminishing his people and most of the women wishing to stay and care for the sick. This isn't a great start to our journey, but I understand, and so face the two guards.

Both are tall and visibly strong, seasoned soldiers made obvious by the way one hand remains close to a weapon. I hold my hand out to the dark-headed guard on the right, admiring the inky lines and swirls tattooed along the taut skin of his arms. His nostrils flare as he looks away, and I pull my hand back, more confused than offended.

Odette gasps and slaps the back of the man's head. He grunts his annoyance then rolls his eyes when she points at me and unleashes a stream of very unladylike words.

Like a toddler forced to play nice, the tattooed man holds out his hand but still refuses to look me in the eye. I take it and shake once before his hand is pulled back and he wipes the palm down the front of his breeches.

Ignoring the insulting gesture, I turn to the second guard, man just as tall as the first but with shorter, blonde hair. He smiles and holds out his hand, before unabashedly dropping his gaze to travel south, all the way down to my toes with an almost imperceptible nod of approval.

Gods spare me.

"I have strict rules for the men on my ship," I say, voice calm and commanding. "When we're out at sea, I am your captain and Ryder is no longer your immediate commander.

He is a prince, yes, but aboard *The Arcana* he is a passenger and a helping hand. *My* word is law. Do you understand?"

The two guards look to Phillip, who smiles and nods his head. With the king's blessing they turn back and catch me by surprise by offering a low bow.

"There'll be none of that, either," I say, resisting the urge to purse my lips.

A tall woman steps out from the gathering crowd by the end of the dock and races toward us with a canvas bag bobbing up and down on her shoulders. Phillip holds out his arms in welcome and she shyly steps into his embrace.

"Emery, this is Winnie Dawning, our finest engineer, seafarer, and cook," Phillip states proudly. "She's also quite the bowman, should you have need of one."

With such an introduction, I'm keen to judge her skills for myself. Having another woman onboard will certainly be useful, especially now I'm expected to travel with so many males.

Winnie steps forward and eagerly takes my hand to shake it. "I'm so pleased you're allowing me to come. I've never travelled past the Fourth Sea so this will be new!"

I grin heartily back at her, already appreciating the enthusiasm. With beautiful, naturally dark skin the colour of warm oak, and tight auburn curls brushing her shoulders, she's a handsome woman, her only flaw the three long scars pinching the skin along her throat. Only one creature would leave such a mark – sirens, the witches of the waters.

"It's nice to meet you," I say honestly, taking her outstretched hand. "Why don't you and the others stow your bags onboard and get settled?" I ask, pointing to the ship. "Once we set sail, I'll walk you through how the old girl is rigged, it's likely different to what you're used to, but should be easy enough to navigate once you're familiarised."

Winnie and the guards agree, offering their goodbyes to

the royal family before heading up the ship's ramp. Unsurprisingly, Ryder doesn't leave with them. Apparently, he's taking his duty very seriously.

"Where's Ansel, the man who came to the palace?" I ask King Phillip.

"Oh yes, silly me. I must have forgotten to tell him we were leaving," the king says, holding his arms out in an 'oh well' sort of way.

I search the sea of faces by the beach, concerned and eager to leave. At the palace, a shoreman had stopped to give his report of an incoming swell that's due to hit the north side of the isle before late afternoon. I want to be well underway and out of its path before then, unsure when the weather might improve.

The crowd murmurs as someone battles their way to the front, waving his arms to catch our attention.

"Hmm, it seems Ansel made it nonetheless," I say, offering a smirk to the king. "Why don't you wish for him to travel with us?" Phillip isn't the forgetful sort, and it isn't in his nature to be so uncaring.

"Ryder tells me there's magic in him, yet this man pretends otherwise," the king says quietly. "I want you to be careful in his company. The guards have been made aware of my reservations, though I *had* hoped he wouldn't make it."

"It's true," Ryder says, carefully watching Ansel as he races up the dock to meet us. "I can hear it."

"Sorry, so sorry I'm late, Captain," Ansel says breathlessly, dropping his bag to take my hand and shake it. "I still can't believe you hold such a position for someone so young."

"I'll take that as a compliment," I say dryly, noticing the bandages wrapped around his hand for the first time. "You're injured."

He glances down at the crude wrappings as if seeing them

for the first time, then pulls both hands behind his back with a nervous laugh. "Nothing to worry about, I'm just a little clumsy."

Liar. I don't push it, there's no need. "Weapons?"

Ansel shakes his head, but nevertheless Ryder steps around me to do his own search, patting down every inch of the man's clothing and rifling through the small bag. Finding no blades or nefarious items, the prince waves a hand to one side, allowing Ansel to pass.

"Head on up to the deck, I'll be there shortly," I say, and with a polite but wary smile at the royals, Ansel does just that, collecting his bag and rushing up the ramp.

"Be safe, Emery, and please take care of my son," Phillip says, pulling me into his gentle embrace.

I promise him I will as I return the hug and offer the same to Odette, then wave back to Pattie and Angus.

Once Ryder and I are aboard, the dockhands remove the ramp and mooring lines from the bollards, and I move quickly to coil them. Getting straight to work, I ask Ansel and the guards to keep to the side of the ship and show Winnie and Ryder how to crank the sails, but ask that they wait for my go ahead.

Hurrying up the steps to the quarterdeck, I turn the cogs to activate the ship's thrusters, and slowly *The Arcana* crawls back and away from the dock. With both hands on the wheel, my heart all but bursts with excitement as my body moves automatically to bring us about. I call down to Ryder and Winnie and soon the sails snap taut as they catch the wind, the ship surging forward to fly with ease over the water, and away from the Garden Isle.

MAPS & MARBLES

SECOND SEA

With the course laid in for Marooners' Canal and the wind holding up nicely, I lock the wheel to maintain our heading, then descend the stairs to the lower deck where everyone waits patiently.

"Welcome aboard *The King's Arcana*. I assume you've all settled into your cabins below?" Despite its smaller size, *The Arcana* had been built to house eleven passengers, with five cabins and the captain's room beneath the helm and quarter-deck. The size of the crew has worked out well, meaning none will have to share, and affording us each some measure of privacy.

"Winnie, I hear you're quite the cook. The galley is to the stern. I'll leave it to you to acquaint yourself with the mechanics of that later." I look to the two guards and pause awkwardly as I realise I haven't been given their names.

"I'm Caleb and this is Toriq," the slimmer and prettier of the men states as he smiles and rakes his fingers through his short blonde hair. Beside him, the tattooed man I now know as Toriq, eyes me warily as he ties his own, long and darker hair into a messy bun.

"Great, my name is Emery. I'd like you both to start hauling these crates down to the galley and then help Winnie move the perishables into the cooler compartments in the lower holds. The door is in the pantry, you can't miss it."

"Should I help them with that?" Ansel asks, tugging nervously at the golden loop on his ear.

"No, you and I will have a look at those charts and mark where is best in the Third Sea to stop and resupply." One of these days I'll build or buy a water desalinator for this ship, and spare myself the exorbitant prices of traders. But for now, planned water stops are essential.

"There are shallow reefs between here and the south, and by the Barnacle Cliffs, too," Ryder says as he steps up behind me. "I can ensure they are properly located on your chart if that helps?"

"That would be great, thanks," I say with a nod to the prince. As they all turn to do as I've asked, I tell them to wait as I have yet to cover the most important part. "I have some rules to lay down. Men are at risk on the open sea, so you must do as I say when I say it." I walk to where a large crystal hangs from the upper deck of the helm, its colour a pale and dull white. "This is a siren bell. It glows with their song and should give us some warning when they're nearby. There's a smaller one in each bunk as well. If you see it glow and hear it hum, you *must* return to your cabins and allow myself or Winnie to lock you in."

"You wish to fight the creatures on your own? Even women aren't immune to the sirens' call," Toriq states, his tattoos stretching as he crosses his arms.

"Not immune," Winnie says, lifting a finger to trace the scar along her throat. "But we retain enough of our sanity to resist and steer the ship to safety. This is not within a man's gift." She stares at the crystal then turns to me, admiration clear in her wide, honey-coloured eyes. "I've never heard of such a thing, how does the crystal work?"

"It captures their song, resonates with it, and sings back a warning. My guardians designed them but they don't always work, so be on your guard." I wait a little longer and ask if the crew has any questions, but for now, they seem content.

With the chores divvied up, Winnie, Caleb and Toriq begin moving crates to the compartments below and set about the careful management of our supplies, while I lead Ryder and Ansel to my quarters to review the charts and plan our route in more detail.

Inside, I hand Ryder the cylindrical leather cases, then drop my satchel and travel bag onto the large, four-poster bed before moving to open the shutters. Light pours through the windows along the ship's stern and into the cabin so clearly forgotten to time, with dust coating every surface. Neither the sisters nor I had ever really used this room on our trips around the isle, each preferring the cosy cabins below. But now it's as much a statement as it is a necessity for me to sleep here, therefore setting myself apart from a crew of strangers.

With the left wall of the room dominated by rows of books, I beckon Ryder to the long table by the windows and ask him to open the case and roll out the charts. As requested, the cartographer has provided a scroll depicting each sea in beautiful script and meticulously hand drawn lines. We select the two relating to the Second and Third, and I trace my finger to the furthest point south of the Second Sea, to where several islands are drawn of varying sizes, some larger and others smaller than the Garden Isle – The Harrow Lands.

My thoughts return to Princess Odette, set to marry the eldest of seven princes from those lands and rule our small isle at his side in the hopes of reuniting the people of this Region. I don't envy her fate.

"Marooners' Canal should be just north of those lands," Ansel says, following my finger then tracing back along the Barnacle Cliffs to a gorge passing between the two.

"There's a fork in the passage. Which path do we go down? Is one safer than the other?" I ask him. It's unclear from the chart, both looking as long and as thin as the other.

"This is the safest route," Ansel says, pointing to the right. "It's the one my master chose to get us here and we made it through just fine."

"Are you lying?" Ryder enquires, watching Ansel's finger tap the preferred path.

Ansel turns ashen at the accusation, and stutters his quick reply. "Not at all. It's still dangerous, but I can guide us just as my master showed me."

The prince tilts his head to one side, as if listening for something. "What *are* you?" Placing one hand on the hilt of his sword, he turns and takes a single, predatory step forward.

"I...I'm not sure what you mean," Ansel says.

"Enough of that," I grumble, bunching my fist in the sleeve of Ryder's shirt and pulling him back to the table. "We all have secrets, and as long as they put no one at risk, I don't care what they are or whom they concern. Ansel, thank you for pointing the way. How long do you expect it will take us to reach the passage, and how long to get through to the other side?"

"Around seven days to get there, and another day at least to cross through the passage itself," he says automatically.

"The supplies from Phillip should last longer than that, but we should consider topping up somewhere in the Third Sea just in case," I say, pulling up my sleeves and rolling out the second chart. Beside me, Ansel begins to say something, then snaps his fingers, seeming to remember something before rushing from the room.

For a moment, Ryder and I simply stare at the open, empty doorway. I finally turn back to the chart with a resigned sigh. While I would like to respect my crew members' rights to keep their own council, that man and his peculiarities beg all sorts of questions.

I run my finger over the fading blue ink of the Third, trailing it east until I hit the first blotch of what seems to be a long island of desert. I doubt there's much there...and the name of the island unsettles me somewhat. I continue to the next and think back to travellers' tales of the Third Sea and the miscreants, footpads and vagabonds who abound in much of this region. We'll have to choose our watering stops carefully.

Ansel reappears just as my finger finds the next potential waypoint in our journey. "Here, I want you to have these," he says taking my hand and dropping twelve marbles into my open palm.

Eyeing the coloured glass balls dubiously, I place one hand on my hip and fix Ansel with a suspicious stare. "Why?"

"For luck. The Third is a dangerous place, and I want to thank you for having me aboard your ship. Please keep them with you."

More riddlesome things. I tuck the marbles into my pocket with a withering smile to Ansel before pointing to the chart. "Happy now? Can we perhaps get back to business?" I ask. Ansel responds with a solemn nod, his gaze lingering a moment on the bulge of my pocket before raising his head and stepping up to the table.

"You said you're from the Third Sea," Ryder says, crossing his arms and regarding Ansel with a narrowed gaze.

"Not originally, but I've spent a good deal of time on

several of the islands. If we *must* stop to resupply – and I do not suggest it for a second – then I would say...*here* is your best bet." Ansel's finger hesitantly falls on a small island not much bigger than the Garden Isle.

Reading the ornately scribbled banner along the top of the isle, I raise my eyes to Ansel, the question in my tone loud and clear as I say, "Beggars' Cove?"

Ansel bites the corner of his lip but holds my gaze. "I know what you're thinking, but I promise it's the best place to restock, *and* the safest," he assures me.

Again, Ryder and I share a look, his more questioning than concerned. I exhale sharply while rolling up the chart and putting it to one side. I've never been to the Third Sea, so for now, we have no choice but to trust him.

Returning to the chart of the Second, I dismiss Ansel while the prince and I note the various reefs and shoals that exist between our current position and Marooners' Canal. As the crow flies we can make the journey in less than four days, but this sea is littered with obstacles and impediments, forcing us to navigate the deeper waters and avoid such risks.

I'm surprised by how much Ryder knows. He's only a few years older than me, and most men are untrained and thus unable to determine proper sailing routes. I watch as he takes a stick of lead and carefully draws a dotted line around the areas he remembers as being too dangerous to sail. Before long, my attention wanders to admire the way his dark hair catches the light and how his sharp, jade eyes seem to shine in his concentration. He's handsome, I'll give him that.

Ryder drops the pencil and looks about the room. "What's that sound?"

I lift my head to listen, then hear it.

Scratch. Scratch. Scratch.

"Oh...that? Honestly, I have no idea," I say returning my attention to the markings he's made.

"It's coming from your satchel," Ryder says, leaving my side and walking towards the bed.

I hurriedly move from the table to intercept him, but he's quicker than I am and holds the bag in the air out of reach.

"Are you hiding something, Captain?"

My stomach flutters at the sound of his deep, drawling voice saying my title, his eyes inches from mine as I struggle to reach for my bag.

I step back and place both hands on my hips, ignoring the thundering beats of my heart. "Fine. Hand it over and I'll show you," I say, holding my hand out. When he stays as he is with my bag above his head and his eyes piercing mine, I narrow my gaze and remember the change in hierarchy. "Now, Ryder."

He drops his arm and places the satchel on the bed, taking one step back and eyeing me curiously.

With an irritated shake of my head, I remove the copper box from the bag, opening its lid and placing the blanket and book to sit side by side.

"I can hear it," Ryder whispers, touching a palm to the leather facing. "Can you?"

The scratching has long since stopped, so I'm not sure what he means. "You hear it now? That scratching sound?"

"Not a scratch...a hum," he says. Picking up the book, he flicks the clasp and opens the cover to read the first verse.

He's about to flip the page, but I put a hand on his wrist to stop him. "Don't. It gives instructions for when to move on."

"Where?"

I take the book and go to point to the writing at the bottom, but notice it's gone. Does that mean I can read the next? It said *three days* last I read it. But then, it said *four* the first time. Maybe it changed its mind? I scoff internally at such a silly notion. Books don't have minds to change...do they?

I almost drop the tome when the scratching noise comes to life and two words etched in red ink slowly appear at the bottom where the instructions once were. We both wait patiently until the sound stops, my hands shaking as I read the new line:

~ GO AHEAD ~

"I believe it's telling you to read the next passage," Ryder says quietly with a nod, completely unperturbed by what's just happened.

I cough to clear my throat and steady my nerves, then I flip the page and we read the verse together:

> *Our bold young captain heads out to sea,*
> *the witches ignored, she abandons the Tree.*
> *Remember your song, girl with blue eyes,*
> *it serves you well and never lies.*
> *With strangers for crew, she heads for the shallows,*
> *where a ship can succumb to the ocean waves' gallows.*
>
> *To the dawn of her story, she heads with this crew.*
> *To the man with no heart, how do you do?*

~ FOUR DAYS ~

Ryder and I read the passage again and again. If I wasn't sure before, I'm certain now that the book is talking about me.

"Interesting," Ryder says, thumbing the top of the page. "Am I the man with no heart?"

"*That's* your first question?" I ask, snapping the book shut and placing it back in its copper home. I turn and head to a crate by the table where I've stashed Pattie's gifted liquor. Reading the labels, I discover two are bottles of port and the other is my favourite, urchin rum. I pull the cork on the latter and take a large swig.

"I have a number of questions," Ryder continues as he watches me. "Where and how did you come by it?"

I take a seat on the edge of the table and hold the rum out to Ryder. He takes a moment to consider, then retrieves the book and comes to place it beside me before accepting the bottle.

"Malina gave it to me," I say, stroking the worn leather spine. "She said it's a part of me, and that I'm a part of it." A little shaky and unsure, I flip open the cover.

"Where are the other pages?" Ryder asks, his fingers tracing down the weathered spine.

"I don't know, but it's one of the reasons I need to go to Aurora Isle. Yes, I want to explore and to meet the sisters' mother, but I'm hoping she might be able to tell me a little more about the book as well."

Ryder turns to the latest verse and trails his fingers over the rough writing, his skin lightly brushing against mine. "My father told me of books like these. Apparently everyone has one, but they're kept hidden in a great library in the Eighth Sea," he says softly, thoughtfully, as if trying to recall the whole memory.

"Malina said something similar." I turn to the passage and read it again.

"Why does it say you ignored the witches?" Ryder asks, his finger stopping on the second line of the verse.

"Marnie told me to stay on the Garden Isle, and Malka…"

told me I'll fall in love with a heartless man and he'll kill me. "Well, Malka told me to be cautious of men and now I'm travelling on the open sea with four of them."

Ryder continues to read the passage, pausing just before the end. *"To the dawn of her story…*It sounds like wherever we're heading you're on the right path."

I read the line and realise he's right. Perhaps Mother Witch really *does* knows something I don't. What's written above that, however, concerns me more. "We should look over the charts again and make sure we've marked the shallow waters. I think the book is warning us."

Ryder nods in agreement, and we stow the book and rum to get back to work.

ONCE THE CHARTS are marked to the best of our collective knowledge, Ryder and I leave to join the others for the first of Winnie's cooked meals. The moment I step onto the deck, my stomach growls with the smell of seared fish and spiced herbs. With the cooling temperature I had expected the others to want to eat below, so I'm surprised to find the table on the main deck set with pots of steaming vegetables, plates and cutlery.

Winnie smiles shyly at my approach and pulls out a chair at the head of the table, waving to the seat and waiting expectantly. When I sailed with the sisters, there was no fussing or fawning, and the most we typically managed for cooked meals was dried fish with a few potatoes, the food bland but enough to give us strength for the coming days' work.

"This looks fantastic," I say taking the proffered seat whilst admiring the dishes laid neatly before us.

Winnie tucks a stray, dark curl behind her ear and offers a

half grin in return, the scar along her neck rippling as she swallows nervously. She opens her mouth to say something, but snaps it shut when something catches the corner of her eye. Caleb is reaching over the table, his fork ready to claim the first bit of fish. Winnie turns, picking up a long, wooden serving spoon from beside the dishes and thwacks the top of his outstretched hand.

"Ah! What was that for?" Caleb asks, rubbing his knuckles and glaring at our chef.

Winnie harrumphs and raises the spoon a second time but pauses mid-air. "Just you wait your turn. Servings go in order of rank, meaning Emery is first as our captain, then Ryder–"

"Actually, that would make *you* the second, Winnie," I say, picking up my fork to spear a piece of fish with a sly grin to Caleb. "I'm not typically so formal, but if you want to get technical about it, you hold the second highest rank on this ship as the captain's second mate, *then* Ryder."

Winnie beams, and bobs her head as she piles steamed vegetables onto my plate, and then onto hers. Toriq and Caleb glance nervously at Ryder and I cast my eyes his way, expecting the privileged prince to contest his demotion. He doesn't, instead he simply waits patiently as Winnie takes her seat and helps herself to the fish, before then serving himself.

In the initial awkward silence of strangers coming together, I'm grateful the others decided to dine outside. At least out here the quiet is filled with the sound of *The King's Arcana* cutting through the waters. I look up as Winnie stands and heads for where a crate has been left by the companionway, retrieving two bottles, she returns to the table and proceeds to pour a small amount of what appears to be rum in each of our glasses. When she places the bottles at the centre of the table, I note they're each the rare and more expensive flavours – pickled cob and dewberry – likely a gift from the king.

Returning to her seat, Winnie raises her glass and offers a toast, the blues and pinks of sunset reflecting off the crystal glass and lighting the softer features of her face. "To *The King's Arcana*, and to our captain, without whom we would be stuck on land with no call to travel the seas."

I smile sheepishly and rub the nape of my neck. It's tradition to toast the ship on the first eve of travel, but not her captain. I raise my glass with the others and thank them for joining me, before we each clink the tumblers together and down the sweet and fiery dewberry rum.

With such a simple act, or perhaps with the help of a little liquid courage, Winnie's toast seems to loosen the friction between us. Everyone slowly seems to relax, offering stories about our pasts and where we each hail from, about our futures and what we wish for, but mostly of what we expect on our journey together.

In such a short amount of time, the strangers that make my crew become a little less strange as I listen and take note of their tales. With Ansel being the most curious of the bunch – his odd fashion and quiet nature, his gifted marbles and riddlesome requests – I'm eager to know more and so prompt him to enlighten us.

"There isn't much to tell, really," he says, gently laying down his quill and glancing up from a piece of parchment. "I simply wish to meet Mother Witch."

We know that isn't the only reason for his quick dash from the isle. He's running from someone, a master he does not wish to talk about. As Ansel picks up his quill and returns to his writings, I decide it best not to push the issue, at least for now. It's only the first night, and awfully hard to keep secrets on such a small ship. I'm sure I'll find out eventually.

Next, I look to Winnie. With her culinary skills and first-rate knowledge of the seas, I admit she's a valuable addition to our crew. While her character speaks of a natural instinct to mother those around her, she is older than I expected, revealing she turned twenty-eight several months ago.

"Won't you miss your family?" Caleb asks her. "I heard you had long since wed." The glint in his eye doesn't go amiss. He hopes Winnie might correct him, state she is no longer married and looking for the man of her dreams. From that lustful look, I imagine Caleb would be anyone she wants for a quick tumble between the sheets.

Winnie rests her chin on her hand, one finger tapping her flawless dark cheek as she looks to me, as if I had asked the question. "My mother was the last of my family ties, she died of the plague." With a slight angle to her head, she cuts her eyes to Caleb, the look withered, as if proper etiquette was the only thing that compelled her to acknowledge his existence. "And yes, I *was* married. My wife died a long time ago, and I have no intention of taking another."

Caleb's smile drops and he studies a knot in the wooden table with a mumbled apology. With Winnie seeming disinclined to offer any more on the topic, I turn next to the rakish man himself.

I would say Caleb is *pretty*, more than he is handsome. With his shortly cropped hair and lean physique, he doesn't possess the bulking brawn of Toriq or Ryder, perhaps favouring speed and skill over strength. Despite a more childish nature and insatiable flirtatiousness, I would hazard a guess he is a little older than Winnie. He confirms as much when I ask, and I have to say I'm impressed, considering he is also said to be the king's most renowned master at arms, particularly noted for his skills with a blade.

"Why did you decide to join us, Caleb?" I ask, swirling

the rum in my glass and casting a mischievous glance his way. "Not enough women on the isle to satisfy you?"

He grins in return and runs a hand through the short but oddly smooth spikes of his hair. "I was bored. Teaching the royal guards had its perks back in the day, back when those skills were needed in the war for the Second Sea. But these days...I need more excitement!" He raises his glass and tips his head back in a silent prayer to the long-forgotten Gods, hoping our travels won't disappoint.

I was fifteen when the wars ended, when a tense treaty was written and the Second Sea split between the north and southern territories. Ryder took part in those battles, was rumoured to have butchered just as many as he saved despite having barely entered adulthood. I look to the prince now, but he fails to notice my shift in attention, perhaps also conjuring memories of his time on the ocean's battlefield. Or perhaps not. Surely something like that would elicit feelings of sorrow or perhaps regret, yet his face remains – as always – utterly impassive.

As Caleb finishes listing off the desired qualities he hopes to discover in the exotic beauties on our travels, I look to Toriq next. He's a curious one for sure. He has yet to speak, or to offer any sort of insight into his life before joining us. I had spotted his wedding ring during our first meet at Merry-weather Wharf; the small, silver band surprising me for two reasons. Firstly, he doesn't seem the type to marry. At a guess, he's around the same age as Ryder, and while it isn't unusual on the isle to marry young, it simply doesn't suit him. Secondly, he's utterly miserable and sour company at best, clearly unhappy with his choice to join us. So why leave the isle at all? Why leave your family behind? Unless they, too, have fallen to the plague. That might explain his quietness.

"Why did you decide to come, Toriq? A love for the sea?"

I ask, no longer able to stand the stream of unanswered questions tumbling through my head.

"A love for the prince," Toriq says with a cold and quiet glare as he leans back and sips his rum.

My eyes widen at his admission. "Oh, you mean you and he are..."

"Toriq and Ryder grew up together," Caleb explains. "They made a blood-brother pact before our prince became all...empty." He grins at Ryder, who in turn doesn't bother looking up from his plate.

Ansel jumps as Toriq slams his glass onto the table. "Something changed the day Ryder fell into the water and those witches saved him. I'm hoping their witch mother can shed some light on it," Toriq growls. Downing the remainder of his rum, he pours another glass, all the while keeping his narrow eyes trained on me.

My temper frays and I lean forward slowly, resting my elbows on the table as I hold Toriq's stare. "Have I done something to offend you?" I ask. He's been watching me all evening, his hand casually returning to his sheathed blade every time I move or speak.

"Are you a witch, like them?" he asks, that hand flexing on his blade.

"Enough, Toriq," Ryder says coolly. "She's not a witch. Emery is something...different. I can hear it."

"I'm nothing of the sort, I'm just a fisher," I say with a shrug. Breaking the stare with Toriq, I roll my eyes and pull my braid loose, allowing the wavy curls to hang freely over my shoulder. Despite a developing headache, I refill my cup with a drop of rum and no more, knowing there's work to do before retiring to bed.

"Shall I get us another bottle?" Winnie asks when the silence drags on a little longer than she seems comfortable with.

"You're welcome to, but I need to check our bearings and set the course overnight," I say, rising from the table. "Winnie, thank you for the meal, it was wonderful. If you leave the washing up, I'll tend to it in the morning."

"No bother, Captain. I'll get to it just as soon as everyone is finished here," she says with a wide smile. "Goodnight."

I say goodnight to the rest, ignoring the fact that Toriq seems disinclined to return the gesture, then head for the helm. In good practice, I check the stars overhead, noting the long line of the Hunter constellation – the tip of his spear guiding us directly south, and the smaller group of stars in the shape of a Foxling, with a wide, bushy tail.

Taking my sextant, I measure the angle of the Hunter's spear in relation to the horizon, then draw a line on my chart by adjusting for my height above sea level from the quarter-deck, before finally combining this with the data provided by my trusty cartographer. The same is done with the star denoting the tip of the Foxling's tail, and as my second plotted line intersects the first, I now know where I am.

Checking the navigational panel, I note we're heading two clicks southeast, a little off our target, so I correct it, turning the wheel and locking it three clicks to the west and away from the shallows.

Next is speed. Taking a float, I walk the length of the ship to her bow. Then, holding the rope in one hand, I toss the float overboard and count the seconds as its drifts back, clocking the time when it passes the stern. Good. The pace is slow and steady and perfect for sailing through the night.

Returning to my quarters, I take a seat at the desk and complete the captain's log, checking our progress against the sea and star chart. Good wind, good speed, and good company...well, at least Winnie should be. All in all, it's a healthy start to our journey. Closing the log, I glance at the drawer where the book is stowed, but force myself to turn away and instead set about flipping the mattress and making the bed before changing into my night shift. I'm exhausted by the time I climb under the covers, and sure enough, sleep quickly follows as I drift into a world of dreams, featuring a book floating in shallow waters – a ship's gallows.

SONG IN THE WATER

SECOND SEA

Come here, come now, I dare of thee,
come see this heart so pure 'n' free.
Come here, come now, oh wards o'er deep,
in exchange for my life your own death you will reap.

I wake humming the familiar tune, admiring a blue light dancing along the cabin's interior as I wait for the lingering dream to fade. The humming continues, and I turn my head sleepily to the small, siren bell glowing a spectacular cobalt, its light catching the crystal's cuts.

The siren bell is glowing...

I spring from the bed, catching my foot in the covers as I tumble to the floor. Scrambling up, I don't bother to change or grab a shawl, and step out of my cabin to see that same, brilliant blue chasing the shadows from the deck. I hear it now, the siren's call.

"Captain, the bell!" Winnie calls from the companionway.

"Release those nets, then check the men. Make sure they're all in their rooms, and pull the bolts to lock them in," I command. Rushing to port side, I crank the heavy lever and watch as wide nets made of rope and beads of orichalcum slowly stretch out from the rails along the ship's sides like wings. Sirens and orichalcum never mix, the substance supposedly a reminder of their Sea God and his similarly constructed trident. If my song doesn't work, the nets will at least temporarily stop them from clawing their way onto the ship.

I lean over the rail and check the dark and churning waters for movement. The sky had been clear only a few hours before, but now with a blanket of cloud to conceal the moon, it's hard to pick out much of anything. Finding nothing of note, I race to the starboard side, and see it. Less than a hundred yards out, waves break in the high splashes and whitewash of sirens. Dozens of them.

I hurry up the stairs to the quarterdeck and unlock the wheel, placing both hands on the soft wood, ready to steer the ship and blast the thrusters should the need arise.

"Captain!"

I ignore Winnie, instead watching the sirens' approach. Just a little closer…closer. I sing.

> *Come here, come now, I dare of thee,*
> *Come see this heart so pure 'n' free.*
> *Come here, come now, oh wards o'er deep,*
> *In exchange for my life your own death you will reap.*

Winnie approaches the helm, her eyes locked on mine as I continue the familiar verse, letting the lyrics tumble from my lips to the waves below.

The creatures' collective melody morphs into screams and wails the closer they come, my song their poison. I squeeze my eyes shut and release the wheel to protect my ears from their piercing cries. The ship shudders and groans as the sirens launch their bodies against the starboard, the momentum sending me stumbling to one side.

My hips crash painfully into the railing, just as the ship takes a second hit from the sirens' assault, sending me overboard. I had meant to repair the nets along the helm, it was on my list of things to do. How had I forgotten?

I brace myself for the claws and teeth of the monstrous creatures waiting below, their arms outstretched in a terrible, deadly welcoming. Their human faces drawn wide in violent glee, ready for their next meal.

My breath catches as someone above seizes my wrist, the sudden jolt snapping my shoulder taut and slamming my body against the side of the ship. Below, the sirens scream, cursing the interloper, those long nails scraping the air beneath my boots. I look up and Ryder's jade eyes stare back, his jaw tense and his calloused grip tightening as he hauls me back over the rail.

"Keep singing," he roars, keeping one arm wrapped around my waist as he guides me back to the ship's wheel.

I do as he asks, and a chorus of desperate screams and violent splashes continues below, before slowly quietening as the sirens flee from the damning sound of my song.

The King's Arcana creaks and groans her complaints as I finish the last line of the verse. Nobody speaks for several moments after as we watch and listen, waiting for the blue light to fade and to see if the creatures return.

After a long moment, I fall to my knees, clutching my chest and thanking the sisters for their lessons.

"We're likely off-course after that," Ryder says, lighting the nearest lantern to check the charts.

I grip the wheel and slowly check our position against the stars. Confident we're back on course, I lock the wheel and send Winnie to check our speed as I head to my cabin to collect the captain's log before returning to the helm.

"The sisters taught you that song?"

I turn to see Ryder leaning against the rail, his arms crossed and head tilted in wonderment. I open my mouth to answer when it suddenly occurs to me Ryder wasn't affected by the sirens' call. Before I can ask why, Winnie returns to deliver our speed and asks the question for me.

"How are you not halfway to the bottom of the sea, Ryder? And why didn't *you* tell us you know the siren song?" she asks, pointing to me. Looping the float, she returns it to the hook and looks pointedly to both the prince and I.

"It's not an entirely uncommon ability," I explain, failing to realise I probably should have declared it earlier. Winnie raises an eyebrow and crosses her arms, the mother-hen confirming as much. "Sorry, the sisters taught me, but it isn't always effective enough to send them away. I'd rather we don't rely on it."

Winnie softens, understanding. "From what I can tell, we're all savvy enough to know we mustn't rely on any one thing to keep us safe. And it *is* an uncommon ability, actually. I've met barely a handful of people who can hit the exact notes for the song to properly resonate," she says as she slumps down onto the bench seat along the quarterdeck's railing.

I look to Ryder, switching fire to put him in the hot seat. "And you? The sirens' call isn't something men can resist. So how are you here?"

"It's a good thing I *was* here, or you would be dead," he says. When Winnie and I continue to stare questioningly at him, he simply states he has no idea.

I sigh and tip my head to the sky, to where the moon glows from behind the clouds. Barely midnight. I know I'm too frazzled to go back to bed, but the others should get as much sleep as they can.

"You need sleep as well, Captain," Winnie says gently. She

tries to hide the unease behind a smile, but the soft quake of her shoulders betrays that fear as her eyes return to the water.

"I'll keep us safe tonight, Winnie. Sirens rarely attack twice in a single night. You're safe," I lie. I remember a time with Marnie when the creatures attacked in quick succession again and again, three times in one night. Her song had kept them at bay, but *The Arcana* had needed serious repairs in the weeks following.

Winnie shrugs and offers a wide grin, putting on a brave face. "I'll unlock the other cabins before I go back to bed. Night, Captain." Heading for the companionway, Ryder follows closely behind her, casting one last look my way before heading down to the lower decks.

I shiver as the cool night settles in, and head to my cabin to retrieve a blanket, wrapping it around my shoulders before returning to the helm. In the short amount of time it takes, I notice our course is drifting again and mutter a curse as I turn the ship's wheel.

Taking the lead line from a hook adjacent to the float, I cast it over the side, marking the fathoms of depth and sighing with relief the higher they climb. No sign of the shallows. At least not yet. Keeping a steady eye on the water, I leave the line tied to the ship's rail and collect my spyglass, searching for breaks in the waves and rocky formations, anything to suggest trouble.

"See anything?"

I jump at the sound of Ryder's voice, and the spyglass drops to land on my bare foot with a heavy clunk. After listing off several of my more colourful profanities, I snatch up the spyglass and glare at the prince. "Dammit, Ryder. I thought you went to bed?"

"I'm not tired," he says, handing over a mug of warm liquid. I breathe in and melt at the scent of cocoa beans and

vanilla, my glare softening and bringing me as close to gratitude as possible given my throbbing foot.

Moving to the railing, I take a seat on the cushioned
bench that runs along its length and stare out at the ocean.
"Why do you think the sirens don't affect you?" I ask.

"I don't know," he says quietly. For a moment, I think
that's the only explanation I'll get when he continues, saying,
"Maybe they stole my heart when I fell into the sea all those
years ago. Maybe there's nothing left for them to take."

I turn to find him studying me, the soft tresses of his hair
rustling in the breeze. "Do you mean when the sisters saved
you? When you were little?"

"They saved a part of me, I guess. Toriq thinks they're the
ones who took my heart. But I can't think of why they might
have done such a thing."

That would explain why Toriq is so suspicious of me,
perhaps thinking I'm just like them. But Ryder is right, the
sisters were healers and as far as I know, they had no use for
a prince's heart.

Taking another sip of his cocoa, Ryder places his mug
beside the ship's wheel then walks to where I sit, taking the
spyglass to peer through it. He stays like that for a long
moment, and I sip my drink and watch, for once taking the
time to study *him*. The way his raven hair lightly brushes the
tips of his ears. The way the long leather coat fails to hide the
muscles shifting in his back.

"You're trembling," he says, closing the spyglass and
peering down at me. "Did tonight's events frighten you?"

From anyone else, I would take that question as a challenge. "No, I'm just a little cold." I pull the blanket back up
to cover my shoulders and ward off the mild chill. The attack
tonight *had* shaken me, but it wasn't my first time dealing
with creatures of the deep, and it won't be my last.

"Cold?" Ryder stares at the goosebumps on the exposed

parts of my arms then rolls up his sleeves to check his own. Corded muscle under smooth skin is all he finds, with no hint of the night's coolness.

"You don't feel the change in temperature?" I ask.

He shakes his head, then removes his coat and drapes it over the blanket across my shoulders, before returning to the wheel to retrieve his mug. I nearly drop my mug, utterly dumbfounded by the act – such a gentlemanly, caring thing to do. But I suppose while he feels nothing, his parents would have instilled courtly good manners befitting of a prince.

Drawing his coat tighter around me, I breathe in the heady scent of pine and cinnamon, then chuckle at the sheer size of the thing, feeling dwarfed as it nearly swallows me whole.

"Do that again," he says, slowing lowering the rim of the mug from his mouth.

"Do what?"

"That...smile."

I scowl instead. "Women don't like it when men ask us to smile for them," I mutter.

Ryder cocks his head to the side, and I can't help it, a grin breaks across my face and I shake my head in mock dismay at the curious prince.

He shivers, the small act catching us both off guard. "I... feel that." Lifting a hand to his chest, he taps to the beat of what flutters beneath, growing faster and faster. "I feel it, Emery."

I don't know what to say, but watch as something flits across his face, shock and wonderment and...ultimate confusion. Goosebumps rush up his arms to the rolled sleeves and he abandons the tap of his chest to feel along the raised hairs.

Just as quick, the bumps subside and his expression

returns to vacancy, the burning jade of his eyes losing their lustre.

"What *was* that?" I whisper. "I thought you couldn't feel anything." He had stabbed a fork through his hand only a few days ago to prove as much.

"I'm not sure. That hasn't happened for a long…" He trails off and shakes his head. "I can't remember."

"Maybe you should get some sleep," I suggest, a little perturbed by his reaction. "We have a busy day tomorrow."

He nods his head absently, then turns and heads down the stairs and through the door to the companionway without another word, leaving me alone at the helm.

THREE DAYS PASS and a fog bank rolls in, forcing us to blindly navigate the open sea. The day after the attack, I'd discovered the bearing line had come loose, meaning we were well off-course. With no markers to indicate where in the Second Sea we were, the sails were collapsed to half-mast to steady our speed, and the lead line constantly monitored for the shallows.

"There, Captain! I see rocks," Winnie calls from the bow.

I open the spyglass to study the formation and their distance from the Barnacle Cliffs off the port side. Checking the chart, I quickly recognise the markings and realise we're running through a channel in the reef, with shallows either side of us.

"Ryder, give me a reading," I call, keeping the wheel steady and praying his markings on the chart are correct.

"We just hit ten fathoms," he calls back.

The King's Arcana will kiss the seabed at four fathoms, we can sail just fine at ten.

"Seven fathoms," he calls.

Shit.

"Six fathoms."

"Take the reading from the starboard side," I order, holding the ship steady.

"Eight fathoms," he calls back a moment later.

I turn the wheel ever so slightly, guiding her back into the channel, before checking the chart and watching the compass for any deviation.

"We can't stay on this path, we'll hit the rocks ahead," Winnie calls as she rushes across the deck and up the stairs to the helm.

"We'll be fine as long as we time it just right and take this turn here," I say, indicating the chart and our only viable course.

"No way can you make that," Winnie squeaks unhelpfully.

"Yes, I can. Now take the other lead line and monitor the port side," I order calmly.

I glance down to where Caleb and Toriq stand by each mast, waiting to adjust the sails at my command. I call down to Ansel, telling him to come to the helm and stand by the thruster cogs. Winnie is right, this is going to be tight. Turn too late and we'll collide with the rocks ahead, too early and the ship's hull will drag along the shallow reefs either side of us.

"Caleb, Toriq, when I say, draw the sails to full mast. Not yet though," I call down. They both nod, Toriq stepping closer to the main mast. I smile in anticipation, enjoying the challenge despite the danger.

"Six fathoms," Ryder calls from the port side. I pull the wheel slightly to the right and wait.

And wait.

And wait.

"Now!" I call, spinning the wheel and watching as Toriq

and Caleb loosen the furling lines. The sails snap taut and *The King's Arcana* surges forward, masts groaning as the port side dips towards the waterline in a tight turn.

"Ansel, twist that cog to ninety degrees." He does and we each hold on as the ship tips steadily further over.

The Arcana jolts, her keel scraping along the coral reef as we pass the last of the tall rocks jutting from the surface. "Now the other one!" I call to Ansel.

He does as I've taught him, twisting the first cog back to its original position, then moving to the next and hurriedly turning it as I spin the wheel back to starboard. The port side slowly pulls away from the water's surface, righting the ship to sit straight in the water as we pull away from the shallows and back out to the deep.

The crew cheers and whoops as we put distance between us and the rocks, Ryder and Winnie's readings reflecting greater depth. We made it. I stroke the wheel of *The Arcana*, silently thanking her and the sisters.

"Bloody kraken, you did it!" Winnie says, returning the lead line and clapping me on the back. "No wonder you're the best on the isle."

"Not quite, we still took a beating on that reef. I'll have to drop the anchor and do a dive to check the damage," I say, sobering my excitement.

"Ah, come on! That was impressive. I thought for sure we were crab meat back there," Winnie says with a laugh. I chuckle along with her, not ready to admit that I was close to the same assumption.

"Well done, Captain," Caleb says as he and Toriq make their way up the stairs to the quarterdeck.

"Good job yourselves, you both got those sails going quicker than I thought you would. I suppose having a few men onboard isn't all bad," I say with a wink to Winnie.

"And to think, you often sail by yourself," Caleb says with

a look skirting the line between admiration and lust. "I think I'm in love."

"I wouldn't have been able to guide her through that bend by myself. I'm good, but not *that* good."

"You can guide me to bed, if you wish? I think you've earned it," Caleb croons seductively, earning a swat across the back of the head and a sour look from Winnie.

Between chuckling at the two bickering crewmates, I calculate our position and set the bearing to avoid a number of dangerous shoals close to our heading, before making a note in the captain's log. I shake my head in wonderment as I work. Only four days into our journey and twice we've faced Lady Death and sailed away. I'm not sure whether our voyage is blessed, or cursed.

"We should stop sooner rather than later, the ship is taking on water below," Ryder calls up from the companionway.

"Definitely cursed," I mutter to myself. "Toriq, Caleb, can you two furl and lash the sails. Ryder, help Winnie lower the anchor, we should still be shallow enough."

"What are you doing?" Ansel asks nervously behind me.

"Looks like I'm going swimming."

MERMAID'S PROMISE

SECOND SEA

Stepping off the last rung of the ship's ladder, I clench my teeth and shiver as my body slips into the water and a soft wave laps against my cheek. Above, the others stand watch as I take a deep breath and dive below. I follow the arch of the ship's hull, leather gauntlets protecting my hands as I carefully feel her barnacled belly for the damage we know is there. While we had mended the small holes from the inside, the pressure of the sea against the ship's bandage means it won't hold for long. I make a note of the length and depth of the damage, then rise to the surface with the calculations in mind. Climbing the ladder from the water to the upper deck, I take Winnie's hand and climb over the side.

Everyone waits patiently as I relay my assessment, relaxing slightly when I assure them all I'm well-equipped to temporarily patch the damage.

When Winnie feels sure there's nothing for her to help with, she excuses herself and heads to the galley with Caleb and Ansel to start preparing supper. I'm confident two guards will be enough, with Toriq and Ryder to watch the water and keep a wary eye on the siren bell for any unexpected guests.

"Are you sure you have everything you need?" Toriq asks. He had been evidently surprised by my sailing skills when it came to avoiding the rocks. That surprise is gone now, his usual, cold doubt slipping back into place.

"More than sure. It'll take a few days, but I can fix her up well enough to last a few more weeks on the water. Looks like we'll have to stop at Ansel's suggested port for proper repairs when we get to the Third Sea though."

I head to the storage cubby below the quarterdeck and open the hatch to where three barrels are tucked neatly side by side. Prying open the lid of the first, I hold my breath and grimace at the repugnant smell that wafts from the open container filled nearly to the brim with greenish gloop. I dip my hands in and pull free an oozing canvas bag, before closing the lid.

Toriq's face pinches in horror as I drop the small sack beside the ladder, the saturated material leaking onto the deck by his feet. "What in divine hell is that?" he asks, taking several paces back and holding his nose.

"Suckerweed," I say with a strained grin. "Smells foul, but it's the best fix for a broken ship." Opening the bag, I pull out a slimy length of the seaweed. Almost instantly it comes to life, wrapping itself around my arm, the minuscule suckers latching onto my skin painlessly. "Oh no you don't," I mutter, pulling it free. "They should be enough to stop the leak, but they won't stick around much longer than ten days at best. Ryder, can you throw these down to me one at a time when I ask for them?"

He nods his head at my request, watching as I climb over the rail to descend the ladder. He grips my hand, stopping my descent and I look up questioningly.

"Be careful," he says quietly, his eyes moving from mine to watch the water below.

"That goes without saying," I mumble, slipping my hand free and continuing the descent. It's difficult to tell if his concern for my safety is born from something deeper, or if he's simply being pragmatic, knowing he needs me as a captain despite his own skills at sea. My thoughts return to the task at hand as my body slips into the frigid water once again and I duck below the waves.

Lining myself up with the first of the ship's smaller wounds, I hold the weed to the hull with one hand and stroke along its spine, willing it to connect with the splintered wood. Soon enough, the plant stretches its length along the hull until it finally goes rigid, refusing to move after a few experimental tugs. The whole process for one weed takes no less than three minutes, and my lungs are burning when I finally surface and signal for the next. Ryder drops it down, and the steady routine begins again.

Before I know it, hours have passed and the sun is slipping below the horizon with the repairs only half complete. When the last weed of the day lands in the water beside me, I'm about to dive when bubbles rise up from beneath.

Ryder calls out a warning but the sound is lost as a tug on my ankle sucks me underwater before I can take a proper breath.

A rasping laugh rumbles through the wash and I fumble for the knife on my thigh, pulling it free and slashing at the scaled hand gripping my boot. That laugh turns to a gasp as my foot springs free and kicks the creature in the face. I swim for the surface and break through, dragging air into my lungs.

Ryder is halfway over the railing, his eyes practically glowing as Toriq strains to hold him back. I reach for the ladder, but not quick enough. With a strangled cry, I'm pulled below once again.

"That wasn't very nice, Emerelda Mirabel," a voice calls from below. I watch, both awed and terrified as beautiful red hair rises to fill my blurry vision, the silky body of a mermaid swaying in the current before me.

The vision of the woman suddenly blurs with whitewash as bubbles surround us both and strong, calloused hands wrap around my arm. The mermaid hisses and swims back as Ryder swipes at her with his blade, the movement slowed in the water as he drags me to the surface.

"A man, Emery? you fool!" the mermaid hisses.

Ryder and I break the surface to find Toriq halfway down the ladder. With one hand on the ladder and the other cupped under my backside, Ryder launches me out of the water, and I grab Toriq's hand.

Hearing Ryder grunt below, I look down to find the mermaid grappling with him, all the while trying to avoid the sharp tip of his blade. Being quicker in the water, she slips behind and knocks the dagger from his grasp, wrapping an arm around his throat to drag him under.

"Stop!" I call, holding one hand out towards the sea creature. Surprisingly, she does as I ask and releases Ryder. "Your kind is always after something, always dealing in trade. What do you want?" I ask her.

"I only wish to talk," she says, her jagged teeth flashing in a smile. While sirens appear half like us – a hauntingly beautiful imitation of humans crossed with the tail of great fish – mermaids belong entirely to the sea, all scales and teeth and bargains.

"Let Ryder come aboard first, then we can talk," I offer carefully, with no room for open interpretation.

The mermaid considers this a moment, then relents – unsurprisingly – with a trade. "He may go up, but you will come down." The gills along her neck flutter, and she dips lower in the water so that only the top of her head and ruby red eyes remain visible, waiting for me to object.

"She's coming up with me," Ryder demands sternly, looking from the mermaid to me.

"Do you *promise* not to harm me?" I ask her. The sisters had taught me that, unlike sirens, mermaids aren't the type to kill humans – but are more prone to stealing from them instead. Their promise, however, is binding, and far more valuable than the empty words of humans and sirens alike.

She bobs her head in the water and I smile wryly at the tricky beast, "Nice try, but I need you to *say* it."

The mermaid claps her hands in applause for catching her out, then rises from the water to say the words, "I promise not to harm you, Emerelda."

As Ryder and I pass each other on the ladder, he stops halfway and silently questions my decision. He doesn't know the sea and its creatures like I do. With the mermaid's promise the risk is nullified, unless her sisters lurk below. With that in mind, I keep a dagger firmly in my grasp and enter the water.

The mermaid rushes towards me, and wraps her two, scaled arms around my neck. I freeze where I am and allow the cold embrace, suppressing a shiver as her gills brush against my skin.

"How delightful to meet you in person," she says as she pulls away.

"How do you know my name?"

"Everyone knows the name of Emerelda Mirabel. Every creature of the deep wants a little piece."

Her words only serve to confuse me more and she cackles, seeming to enjoy this. "Will you explain?" I ask, despite knowing the risk of asking her favour.

She taps a clawed finger to her chin. "Hmmm, what will you give me?"

I must be careful not to promise that which I do not have. I call up to Toriq, asking for one spoon, a knife and a fork. "Will that do?" I ask the mermaid.

Her eyes glitter with delight and she claps her hands again. We wait as Toriq retrieves the cutlery then returns to cast them over the side. With astounding speed and grace, she leaps up from the water to catch the offered items and cradles them gratefully as she splashes back down beside me.

"Now, why do the creatures of the deep know my name?"

"Such a forgetful girl, Emery. Of course we know you! Your name is written in songs across the eight seas…some of love, though some sing of hate. The sea queen wishes to meet with you. This is how we know your name."

"The *queen*? Why?" I ask, suddenly more wary of what might lurk beneath.

The mermaid tuts with disapproval at my second question, wagging a long finger in my face. "Only one."

"I can offer you more." *No more than I can give*, I remind myself.

"Meet me on the western docks of Aurora Isle, only then will I tell you what you wish. I live there you see, but you must *promise* to come and swim by my side when I call for an election."

"Election?" What an odd word for a mermaid to say.

She tilts her head and chuckles, the sound closer to the dying cry of an injured bird. "Of course. I wish to minister the mermaids, silly girl. With you by my side I'm sure to win…or possibly perish for consorting with you at all. We will see, I suppose. Do you *promise*?"

"Emery," Ryder warns from above.

I'm heading to Aurora Isle anyway, and she hasn't put a time limit on our deal. Mermaids don't lie, and I have little to lose in our bargain. So many questions, and this creature might know the answers. I thought the seas' ruler was a king, not a queen, and why does she want to meet? What songs do the creatures sing in my name? Why *me*?

"Assuming our journey goes as planned, I *promise* to meet you there on a date that suits me, but that is it. I will swim with you, but I will not *speak* for you during these...elections," I say, being sure to cover my bases and not give too much.

"That will do," she says, her wide grin revealing multiple rows of teeth. "My mere acquaintance with you will set me high above the others." Drifting closer, she removes her necklace and hands it to me. I study the small, silver pendent of a conch shell, turning it over in my palm to admire the speckling of gold leaf faded over time. "My name is Alina. When you reach Aurora Isle and you are ready, call my name into the shell, and I will surface to meet you."

I nod my head, mystified by her instructions, then watch as she smiles and sinks beneath the waves, clutching her cutlery, and her promise.

Slipping the silver necklace over my head, I climb the ladder, my arms protesting with the weight of my sodden clothes and a day of working on repairs.

"Are you okay?" Toriq asks as he and Ryder offer a hand to help me over the ship's railing.

"Fine. Just tired...and confused," I say, surprised but appreciative of his concern. I glance to Ryder, his breathing slightly heavy as he rakes a hand through his hair.

Toriq drops his gaze to the side, his voice a mumble as he says, "Thank you, Emery."

"For what?" I ask

"For putting Ryder's life before your own when you took his place in the water with that creature."

The fact that Toriq believed the mermaid might have hurt me speaks to his inexperience at sea. Nonetheless, I smile back and hope he might now give me a fair chance and abandon his assumption concerning the sisters stealing his friend's heart.

We all turn at the sound of footsteps crossing the deck to find Winnie setting the table for supper. Still drenched and slightly chilly, I tell her I'll only be a moment as I hurry to my quarters to change.

A small movement at the helm catches my eye, and I look up to see Ansel leaning over the banister, his dark skin shining with sweat as he continues to stare at where I'd climbed up the ladder.

I wave to catch his attention and his head snaps down to look at me. With a nervous smile, he waves back, then turns and scurries down the stairs to join Winnie and assist with bringing up the food. I stare after him, and ponder the look he'd worn before he left, before he'd slipped back into what I'm quickly beginning to think is a facade. A look of both wonderment…and knowing.

As we all sit down to eat, I inform Winnie and Caleb of the events they missed, answering questions and educating them on a mermaid's quirks. Predictably, Winnie is already well versed in the tricky ways of the creatures, but Caleb and the others find it fascinating.

"I thought you knew about the political underbelly of the sea," Winnie says to me as she slurps a spoonful of steaming fish stew. "Though, I suppose you're a bit young for that. I was only little when the last of their elections took place."

"The sisters mentioned the ruler of the seas in old stories, but I never thought she was real," I say. Taking a spoonful of stew, I close my eyes and enjoy the sweetened broth, the saltiness cleverly masked with herbs and a dash of honey.

"Truthfully, I thought it was a *king* that ruled the Eighth, so that surprised me," Winnie notes somewhat distantly.

"Me too," I say, and Ryder nods in silent agreement.

Winnie sighs and scratches her head. "I know mermaids live in their own sort of hierarchy under the king, or queen I suppose. It sounds like Alina is looking to rule her kind."

"Was she pretty? I've heard they're seductive beauties," Caleb asks, leaning forward on the table to waggle his eyebrows at me.

"You're thinking of sirens," I say soft and seductively, my breasts squeezing together as I lean on the table towards him with a smile...and then flick the tip of his nose.

He yelps and Winnie all but howls with laughter as he rubs the abused appendage.

"Sirens don't need to look at a man to seduce him," I say, chuckling lightly as I lean back. "One song and you'll happily give them your very soul. Mermaids on the other hand don't intentionally hurt humans unless provoked. Though sometimes their playfulness can get a little out of hand," I finish with a look of warning to Caleb in particular. He strikes me as a man who would chase a skirt to the bottom of the sea if she showed any sort of interest. I'll have to keep my eye on him.

The rest of the meal is spent swapping tales of travel, with Winnie being the most experienced having delivered messages as far as the Fourth Sea's northern isles. I envy her, truly humbled as I listen to her tales of pirates, barren wilderness, and far flung places.

My experience lies only in the Second Sea, where my calling as a fisher had kept me too busy to venture further afield. That's about to change, and the more she speaks the more excited I become.

Once everyone is finished, I once again offer to help with the dishes, but Winnie won't hear of it, insisting I'd done the work of three women carrying out my repairs today. She isn't wrong, and I thank her, gratefully slipping away to return to my quarters.

As I undress, I rub the hairs along my arms, each coated in sea salt. What I wouldn't give for a moment in that bath in the king's Palace back on the isle. I shake my head at the thought, disappointed in myself for barely lasting a week at sea before wishing for the comforts offered on land. It seems I've grown spoilt in the few days spent in the palace.

Putting on my night-shift, I crawl under the bedcovers and listen to the faint scratching coming from the desk at the centre of the room. What is it writing now? Has my promise with the mermaid shifted fate? Tomorrow is the fourth day, the instructed amount of time before being allowed to turn the page. The scratching stops, leaving only the sound of waves lapping against the side of the ship. Sleep first, my questions can wait.

A BOOK OF LIFE

SECOND SEA

O nce awake and dressed for another day of tending the ship's wounds, I wander outside to find Winnie is already in the water, with Ryder ready on the deck with more suckerweeds. I walk over to where he waits for her to resurface and place my hands on the rails, peering over and waiting with him.

"Winnie wanted to help. Apparently, you seemed quite tired last evening," Ryder says idly beside me.

I nod my head and smile. Yesterday had been long and my muscles aren't in the best of moods this morning with the aching aftermath. Still, I'll want to check her work, unsure if she's familiar with the suckerweeds' picky disposition. They have to be held just right, with just enough pressure to encourage them to bond with something as hard and unfor-giving as wood.

Winnie surfaces and grips the lower rung of the ladder before looking up to call for the next weed. Spotting me, she waves and offers a happy good morning. I wave back, telling her to stay where she is, then climb onto the ship's railing and dive overboard. The water is cool and calm and a welcome relief to the dry heat above.

"I was hoping to spare you the water today, Cap," Winnie says with a grin as I swim to her side. "What's the matter, don't trust my skills?"

I smirk and give her a small splash. "I would be a fool to trust what I have yet to see."

"Good answer," Winnie says splashing me back then calling up to Ryder for the next. Without my weight-belt, I follow after Winnie as she dives underwater, checking the repairs I had done yesterday. She must have been at this for a while. At least six more weeds have been fastened to the hull, secured exactly as I had done. She lines up the plant and strokes along its spine, waiting patiently for it to stick before kicking to the surface.

She grips the ladder and takes her time to recover, the strain in her eyes making it clear she hasn't held her breath like this in quite some time. Most who are trained in ship repairs can hold their breath for three times the length of any normal human. I'm proud to say I frequently beat that, often testing and pushing myself in training when I head out on the water.

"Have you eaten today?" I ask before she calls for the next suckerweed.

"Not yet. I wanted to get at least five more done before taking a break."

"That's a bold goal," I say with a laugh. She coughs as a wave laps against the boat to splash her face, and I realise how shallow her breathing has become. "Come on, I'm starving and haven't got a clue what's what in the galley. Why don't you start breakfast and I'll secure the next weeds before joining you?"

Winnie shakes her head fervently, then stares back at me, wanting desperately to finish the task she's set herself.

I sigh then call to Ryder for another two weeds. "We'll be quicker if we work together."

"But you did all the work yesterday," she mumbles back.

"I'm the captain, and *The Arcana* is my responsibility. Yours is to make sure me and the rest of the crew have the energy to do what needs to be done." I put a hand on her shoulder. "And it's a job you do brilliantly."

She beams at me, and I can't help but smile at such a youthful response. She's seven years my senior, and yet her reaction speaks to the high regard within which she holds me. I'll have to keep that in mind. Winnie is kind and caring and always on hand to help wherever she can. But she needs the affirmation, to *know* when she's being helpful or doing a good job; the words of others perhaps holding more sway over her than they should.

With the weeds in hand, we dive down to secure them, then carry out the same manoeuvres with the next two before taking the ladder up to the deck.

I make a point to hold my stomach and groan dramatically. Winnie grins, promising to get breakfast underway just as soon as she's changed. I smile back and watch as she hurries down the companionway, passing Ryder as he walks towards me with two steaming mugs.

"I understand you are probably warm enough on a day like this, but I'm told the cocoa will give you energy," he says, handing me one of the mugs. When I gratefully accept and turn to sit at the table, he looks at me with his usual level of speculation. "Aren't you going to change?"

"There isn't much point. Like you said, it's warm enough that I'll dry off soon, and there's still more repairs to do. I'll get back to work once breakfast is settled."

"Have you read the next page yet?"

I stare into the steamy liquid of the cup, avoiding his eyes. Truthfully, I'd spent a good portion of time this morning holding the book in my hands. But with a day of repairs ahead in the dark waters of the Second Sea, I was frightened of what it might say. "I'll read it later, once the ship is patched," I say carefully, hiding that fear.

"Why? The book offers advanced warning to threats. It seems unwise to ignore that."

I flick my eyes from the cup to his face, to those curious green eyes. He's questioning my judgement, and he's right. I should want to know everything I can whenever I can. When I mumble as much and stand to head for my quarters, he cuts me off, telling me to sit and drink while he retrieves it for me. A little non-plussed by his insistence, I tell him where it is, and sit back to enjoy the quiet of the breezeless morning.

Today is a good time for the wind to die. We won't be setting sail until the repairs are complete and monitored to ensure they hold. I wonder what the others will do with their time; if Caleb's hobbies extend from weaponry to more creative talents; whether Toriq reads or perhaps draws – his persona suiting the tortured artist stereotype.

On our days at sea to date, when the chores are done, Toriq and Ryder usually take to sparring under the watchful gaze of their tutor, Caleb. Winnie on the other hand prefers to find a quiet corner with a book from my quarters when she isn't cooking a culinary masterpiece. Then there's Ansel, who continues scribbling away at whatever it is he writes, his hands freshly bandaged with each new day.

I have yet to see Caleb and Toriq this morning, but Ansel sits in his usual spot on the bench beside the helm over-looking the ship...and me. I pretend I don't see him and watch from my peripheral as he readjusts his position, trying to better hide himself from view.

As Ryder walks from my cabin with the book, Ansel's head peeks over the railing, watching as the book is placed on the table in front of me. I look up at the odd man, seeing that same, knowing look. "Why don't you join us, Ansel?"

He ducks behind the railing with a muttered oath, then reappears a moment later sliding a hand down the back of his shaved head and along his ponytail with an awkward grin. "I wasn't spying!"

"I never said you were. Come on, I have a sneaking suspicion you might know a little more than you're telling us." The command in my tone leaves no room to object, and Ansel ambles down the stairs and over the open deck to where Ryder and I sit at the table.

"What is that?" he asks, taking a seat beside me.

"You tell me," I say in challenge, sliding the book to sit in front of him.

He reaches forward and takes it in both hands, idly stroking the spine as if comforting an old friend. "Have you read any yet?"

I lean back in my chair, assessing and failing to understand the way his eyes and mouth pull down softly in sadness. "Only a little, only what's allowed," I say, and when Ansel bobs his head in return, it's all the confirmation I require to know that he is indeed familiar with such books. More so than Ryder and me.

"It's a book of life," he finally whispers. "One volume in a library of millions. How did you get it?" he asks, flicking the golden clasp to release the two facing covers.

"It was passed down to me by my guardians before they died. I don't know where they found it."

Ansel's sadness deepens, a small sound passing his lips when he opens the book and notices how many of the pages have been ripped out. "Why would anyone do this?" He fingers the loose binding, then sighs and snaps the book closed. "You must be careful, Emery. The few I've seen who get their hands on their own books almost always succumb to temptation. They change, become greedy for information and power."

"Who writes the books?" Ryder asks as he leans further forward on the table.

Ansel seems to hold his breath as he shrugs and slides the book to sit in front of me. I'm certain he's lying, yet I can't for the life of me understand why he would. His concern is palpable though as he averts his eyes from Ryder's questioning gaze.

I open the book and flip to the second page to check the instructions have disappeared, allowing me to move on. They have, so I turn to the latest verse.

> *A mermaid's meet is at best a curse,*
> *for their trickery and games tend to lack in worth.*
> *But our girl with eyes as blue as can be,*
> *must honour her promise or succumb to the sea.*
> *Don't be hasty, do as you're warned,*
> *and perhaps you'll avoid the sirens' scorn.*

~ FIVE DAYS ~

Sirens again. What warning does it mean? One I'm yet to receive? I glance up at Ansel who quickly looks away. More bloody riddles.

I'm about to question Ansel further when Winnie hurries across the deck with two hot plates and places them down on the table, waving her hands and blowing on them.

"Kraken's breath, they were hotter than I thought." Her smile fades as she registers the tense atmosphere, then notices the book and reaches across to pick it up. She doesn't get the chance as Ansel snatches it from the table and holds it close to his chest.

"No! This is *only* to be opened by the captain, and *only* to be read when she allows," he says forcefully with a cold look of warning to Winnie.

Winnie holds up her hands and puffs out her cheeks in a dramatic retreat. "Sorry, I thought it was just any old book. I was curious to see if I'd already read it."

Ansel's reaction only further confirms that he's hiding something. "You and I are going to have a long and private chat in my quarters at some point soon, Ansel," I say, watching him closely and holding my hands out.

He places the book in my open palms, then stands from the table. "Your wish is my command, Captain," he says solemnly, then heads for the companionway without staying to eat.

"What the barnacles was that all about?" Winnie asks, lifting the lids from the trays to present to us a platter of bacon and scrambled eggs. As if summoned by the smell, Caleb and Toriq appear in unison from below deck, each eyeing the food hungrily.

"Have any of you heard of a book of life?" I ask as the two men take their seats.

They glance to one and other questioningly and shake their heads, while Winnie casts her eyes to the leather bounded pages on the table beside me and says, "*Should* we know?"

"Perhaps not," Ryder mutters quietly, shifting his gaze from the book to me with hidden meaning.

I'm not sure I see the harm. If anything, being a part of the crew I believe they're entitled to know when the book might warn of future dangers. Deciding to go with my gut, I tell them all about my curious inheritance and what it seems to speak of; both a past and a future yet to be properly written.

Caleb openly scoffs and devours his second slice of bacon, while Toriq raises one brow disdainfully. I open the book, and slide it over, instructing them to read only the first three pages. It takes a moment, but slowly the words sink in, and Caleb drops his spoon, taking the book in both hands to study it closer.

"You're the girl with blue eyes, the one the book speaks of?" Toriq asks.

I nod and take a bite of buttery scrambled eggs. "It would seem so. Naturally I'm not the *only* girl in the eight seas with blue eyes, but everything else seems to fit."

"It warns about the sirens...and the shallows we faced yesterday," Caleb says, reading the second page over and over. He turns to the third and his tanned skin seems to pale. "What's the warning? The one that avoids the sirens' scorn?"

"I'm not sure," I say truthfully. Over the past ten days I'd heard and received many warnings. Stay on the isle. Don't read too much. Be careful of Ansel. Keep away from men. Don't make deals with tricky mermaids. So many warnings with no clue as to which I should really take heed of. Naturally I should look to obey them all, but a little clarification would be nice.

Caleb is about to flick to the fourth page when Ryder leans over and snatches the book from him. "You will not read further than the captain permits. The book seems to be spelled, and to go against its instructions may incur a debt. Is that clear?" he says, making sure not only Caleb, but Toriq and Winnie nod their heads and acknowledge his command.

"Prince Ryder is right to be cautious, Emery," Toriq says. "If this book gives warnings of the future, some might find that an attractive advantage." When Winnie and I share a confused look, he explains. "Picture a betting man. He might be tempted to kidnap you and the book, forcing you to stay by his side and commit to actions that in turn predict not only your future, but his own."

"I hadn't thought of that," I admit, kicking myself for the lack of foresight.

"You have nothing to fear from us, Emery," Winnie says softly, placing her hand over mine. "I'm glad we have your trust."

While I won't admit such a thing aloud, it isn't that she has my trust, or that any of them have it, I simply hadn't applied logic to my thinking. I smile back, knowing she deserves nothing less and take the book from Ryder, closing it and securing the clasp before putting it to one side.

Once everyone is finished with breakfast, Winnie and Caleb leave to tend to the dishes while I return the book to my quarters. Ryder follows behind me, closing the door as we enter and leaning against it.

"Ansel knows more than he's letting on," he says. "I don't want you alone with him at any time. I know you asked to speak privately with him, but I want to be there."

I laugh sardonically as I close the lid on the copper box and tuck the book in the desk drawer, not to be touched for five more days as the instructions read. Turning to face him, I cross my arms. "The only person who gives an order on this ship is me, Ryder. *The Arcana* isn't exactly big, I'm certain to be alone with Ansel at some point."

"I promised my father I would protect you, Emery. So that's what I'll do. He warned us about Ansel, perhaps *that's* the warning the book speaks of."

I shake my head, there's no way to know that. Ryder isn't wrong, Ansel is holding something back. But while I sense fear, trepidation and something quietly different about the man, I've never felt a sense of malice.

"I *am* being cautious, Ryder. And I'm quite sure I could put Ansel down if the need arose."

Ryder's expression remains impassive, but I swear a flicker of annoyance flashes as he narrows his eyes. "You're so quick to dismiss the help of others. Why is that?" he asks.

"I accept help when I need it." The sisters were very pro-independence and had taught me as much, making sure I had all the tools to care for and defend myself should I ever have the need.

I walk towards him, hoping he might get the sense that this discussion is over. He remains where he is, his back leaning against the door, his arms crossed. This close, I know what I've seen isn't imagined. He's irritated, a muscle ticking in his jaw, his eyes hard and unblinking.

"Please move, I have work to do before heading back into the water." Either at the sound of my voice or the cut of my words, the look of frustration passes, replaced with his customary inscrutability as that flicker of emotion is buried once again. He steps to the side and opens the door, letting me pass through.

I head to the quarterdeck, my frustration growing with the traitorous rhythm of my heart. Something about the prince's eyes, about the way he hovers and stares at me unabashed...I'm affected by it.

The man you love, a heartless man, will be the one to kill you...

I'm not so sure it's Ansel I need to worry about. With each passing day, every time I'm alone with the prince and his heartlessness slips, my own heart seems to falter a little more; seems to beat a little faster. I place a hand to my chest and take several breaths to calm the storm, replaying Malka's warning over and over in my head.

Taking the captain's log from beside the wheel, I settle on

the bench to update it with the extent of the damage, repairs and amount of suckerweed used. After some consideration, I write the number *five* at the bottom of the log, reminding myself of the days that must pass before opening the book in the hopes of reducing temptation. Flipping to the back, I'm pleased to note our dedicated chef has updated the stock lists, subtracting the food we've consumed thus far, and indicating we are a long way from running out of the essentials.

I glance up at the sound of voices coming from the bow, and see Ryder heading towards Ansel – who has settled himself, as he usually does, with his papers and quill.

Seeing Ryder approach, Ansel quickly folds the pages to conceal his work, and nods his head at whatever is passed quietly between them. As Ryder walks away, Ansel looks to where I'm sitting, and smiles, then opens his notes and continues writing. Whatever the exchange was, it doesn't seem to have perturbed Ansel, if anything, he appears more at ease.

Placing the logbook back by the wheel, it's almost precisely noon, so I set about establishing our position. We would have hit the channel today if not for the sirens, the shallows, and *The Arcana's* poor calibration. According to where we are now, if the repairs hold and we weigh anchor early tomorrow, we'll arrive at the passage in three days. Not too bad, all things considered. I think back to the Book of Life. It would be nice to know what to expect.

"We should read the next page," Caleb calls up as he paces back and forth on the lower deck. He stops and looks out beyond the bow, to where Marooners' Canal sits as a natural break in a coastline aptly named the Barnacle Cliffs.

I turn the wheel and regard the chart again, using the thrusters and carefully lining up *The King's Arcana* to fit perfectly through the narrow entrance to the canal.

For three days Caleb had continued to make the same request, or had suggested we head further south and take the longer route. If not for the damage to the hull, I might be inclined to take the risk and attempt to slip through the southern territory instead. I had done the calculations carefully with both Ansel and Winnie and determined the closest, safest port to be through the passage in the Third Sea, at Beggars' Cove. The Harrow Lands south of us are at least fourteen days away, too long for the repairs to hold.

"Will we fit?" Winnie asks, concerned as she joins me at the helm.

"We will," I assure her. "And we're not reading the next page, Caleb."

Caleb turns and looks at me sharply, his fists bunching. "You're relying on *his* word that this is safe," he says, storming up the stairway to point at Ansel. "He's not even a seafarer!"

"I agree with Caleb," Toriq says to the surprise of everyone. Making his way up to the quarterdeck, he pushes past Caleb to join Winnie and Ansel on the bench by the port railing. "I think, just this once, it might be worth the risk. Marooners' Canal is renowned for its two routes, one more dangerous than the other. Ansel claims the right, but I'm certain it's the left."

"No, the left is the route of riches," Ansel says with a shake of his head. "It's a lure."

"I heard the richest path is the safest," Winnie says, suddenly unsure.

I groan and look to Ryder leaning against the stern. He merely stares back and shakes his head, unsure which is the correct path.

"Just a quick peek, Cap," Caleb says. "What's the worst that can happen?"

"That's the problem, I don't *know* the cost of failing to follow the book's instructions. And considering where we're heading, I'm not sure *Marooners'* Canal is the place to find out. The hint is in the name," I mutter.

Caleb throws up his hands dramatically and sits on the bench, leaning his back over the ship's rail. "We're all going to die."

"That's not helpful," I growl. "Ansel, how long before we reach the fork in the passage?"

"We should reach it by this evening…why?"

Then I have until this evening to decide. Read the book?

Don't read the book? "Winnie, how comfortable are you with steering the ship through this?" I ask.

We all go quiet as shadows loom over *The King's Arcana* and we pass between the cliffs. Living up to the name, long-dead barnacles cling to great heights, their forms petrified to rock. It comes as no surprise that the moment we pass into the canal, a chill sets in, the passage cast in perpetual shade and drawing a shiver from the crew.

Keeping my hands firmly on the wheel, I keep *The Arcana* steady as we crawl along, using only the ship's thrusters to propel us forward at an acceptable speed. A large overhang looms above, and I hold my breath as the main mast barely scrapes underneath.

"Honestly, Captain?" Winnie says, cringing at the sound of wood grating against rock. "I'm not sure I would be comfortable taking the helm in a passage this narrow," she admits, belatedly answering my question as she hangs over the rail to run her hand along the cliff wall.

I don't blame her. The passage is far narrower than I'd expected. Ansel continues to assure me that before long the canal opens out. Until then, I won't be moving from my position at the helm, I can't. One accidental jerk of the wheel would see *The Arcana* kissing the cliff walls.

A large rock falls from above and cracks against the lower deck. We all look up to see small creatures with black eyes and shaggy white fur scurrying along the cliffs, darting in and out of the small caves higher up.

"Chimera," Winnie whispers. Hurrying from the helm, she races down the steps towards the door to below deck. It shuts behind her with a loud bang, and we stare after her.

"Did she just...run away?" Caleb asks nobody in particular. "How bold to leave her captain to face the chimera alone."

"She isn't alone," Ryder says, unsheathing his sword as he

moves to stand behind me. "As long as we keep quiet, they shouldn't be a problem."

The companionway door bangs open and we all flinch, watching as two of the chimera snap their heads to peer down at the intruders, *The King's Arcana* passing below.

With a bow and two quivers stocked full of iron-head arrows, Winnie remains on the lower deck and readies her weapon. King Phillip had mentioned Winnie's skills as an archer. I hope she doesn't get the chance to prove him right.

"We thought you'd run away to hide," Caleb says softly down to her.

She turns and cocks an eyebrow in a questioning glare. "Good to know you have such a low opinion of me."

"Silence." The command from Ryder is quiet but deep, and nobody speaks as we slowly drift through the canal, each watching the walls for any sign of an impending attack.

THE SUN HAS LONG since set by the time the channel opens out. It won't be long before we reach the fork. I play each warning over and over in my head; Ansel's warnings, the book's warnings not to read ahead. Marooners' Canal is home to many a sea creature, the worst being sirens. But which route is right? Do we read the book for another clue?

"Not long now, Captain," Ansel warns as we approach a formation of rocks shaped like an anchor. Just beyond that is a graveyard, the bones of ships jutting from the water in an ominous warning of how these cliffs can respond to careless pilotage. Ansel guides me well, and we weave *The Arcana* through the deepest parts, avoiding a similar fate to the wreckage around us.

"Ryder, get the book," I say quietly, spotting a fork in the passage ahead. Time has run out. I will use the book this once to help guide me.

"No, Emery. You mustn't," Ansel hisses quietly, glancing up worriedly at the chimera scurrying above. "Patience isn't just a virtue, Captain. It's a necessity. You *must* not read ahead."

Ryder pauses by the stairs, making sure I've made up my mind. I nod my confirmation, and he turns and heads to the cabin to where he knows I keep the book.

"Thank the Gods. You're making the right choice, Cap," Caleb whispers, patting me on the shoulder and returning to his seat on the bench.

His words are empty, offering me no comfort whatsoever. There's no way of knowing the consequences of peeking too soon at a future not yet properly written.

I slow the thrusters to barely a quarter of their capacity, making it slightly more difficult to steer, but giving Ryder the time to return with the book before we make the ultimate decision. Left, or right? The path of riches or the poor man's passage?

"Something is happening," Ryder says as he takes the stairs two at a time. "It's scratching."

"This is a bad idea, Emery. *Please* reconsider," Ansel cries clutching my arm.

"Why are you so against us reading it?" Toriq asks Ansel. "You don't know the consequences any more than we do, so why protest so much?"

I shake off Ansel and take the book from Ryder, sucking in a quiet breath as I lift the catch and open the book to the third page. Everyone gathers around as we read the instruction:

~ TWO DAYS ~

Whatever the consequences, we face them together, as a crew. I look to each member and everyone but Ansel nods their head, ready to accept whatever will come to pass. I slip my finger under the weathered page and flip to the fourth, and immediately regret it.

> *Patience, patience, you must not peek,*
> *now a curse is set, the penance bleak.*
> *I will say this, a warning to note,*
> *beware of the one with the golden cloak.*
> *The girl with blue eyes will be tempted thrice,*
> *take none, but one, or pay the price.*

Bugger. Is it too much to ask for a little clarity? I close the book and sigh as I hand it back to Ryder.

"I told you. I *told* you it was a bad idea," Ansel hisses, but it doesn't go amiss that he seems...relieved by something.

"It said to beware of a golden cloak," Winnie whispers, looking to me.

"Ansel, you said the left passage is the route of riches, correct?" I ask. He nods his head in response. "Then we take the right. A golden cloak sounds like something you'd find where there's treasure."

I turn the wheel to starboard taking us down the chosen route. Too late to change our minds now, even with the thrusters, we'd be lucky to reverse our way back to the Second Sea and avoid the rocks. Again, I'm good, but not *that* good.

"You made the right choice, Captain," Ansel whispers quietly in my ear. My gut seems to scream differently, begging me to try the thrusters, to get away. I bite down on the fear, keeping a wary eye on the chimera watching above, some breaking into a chatter, as if laughing at the foolish travellers below.

～

I REST my arms on the felloe of the ship's wheel and shift my weight to one leg. I need a break from the helm, need to sit or lie down, just for a moment. It's been hours since the sun set, hours of coasting through the perilously narrow gorge, with no room for error. I lean back and grip the handles of the wheel, the callouses burning along my palms.

"Coming close to the side, Captain," Caleb whispers from port side. I turn the wheel a fraction to the right at his warning, away from the jagged rocks of the cliff wall, then look to Toriq on the starboard side. He gives no sign that I've pulled us too far and continues to sweep his lantern from left to right over the rails.

Winnie's lantern bobs unsteadily at the front of the ship, its glow – enhanced by interior crystal mirrors – casting a beam into the darkness ahead and lighting our way. The light bobs again and I search the open deck for Ansel. He's sitting by the main mast with his inks and papers, seeming to stare into space.

"Ryder, tell Ansel to switch with Winnie, she needs a break," I say.

He stands from the bench along the rail and walks over to stand beside me. "She's not the only one, Emery."

I shiver as he rubs a hand over my shaky arm, the warmth of his palm seeping into my skin. "I'm fine, but I need that beam steady and the watcher alert for rocks ahead. Go."

Pulling his hand back, he turns and makes his way to Ansel. I watch as he stops under the deck light next to our resident scribbler. He seems to say something, yet Ansel doesn't respond, just continues to stare into nothing. Ryder puts a hand on his shoulder and Ansel jumps up, knocking his papers to the deck. Words are exchanged and Ansel nods his head as he scrambles to pick up the pages, hastily writing a few notes, then folding them over and turning to relieve Winnie.

"What was that all about?" I whisper as Ryder steps up to the helm.

"Magic," Ryder says, scratching his jaw and returning to his seat on the bench. "I can hear it when he writes, like the magic you use when you sing to the sirens." Turning his head, he looks over the rails to where Ansel has taken the bow's light, keeping it straight and steady ahead. "He seemed to be lost in a trance...or he was sleeping with his eyes open. It was hard to tell with such little light."

As I've said before, I don't mind people having secrets on my ship, we each have our own burdens to bear. But magic is different, it comes with risk and temptation. The moment we make it out of this Gods-forsaken passage, Ansel and I will be having that private chat I'd asked for. It can't be long now, once the sun is up and Winnie has had a break, she can take over the helm and allow me a short reprieve.

"Captain," Toriq warns from starboard. I pull the wheel a fraction to port.

"Whoa, Captain," Caleb calls from Port. I grit my teeth and shift a fraction back to right, then wait.

A loud screech penetrates the quiet, resonating along the cliff walls in a harrowing echo as *The King's Arcana* scrapes her portside along the barnacle covered rocks.

"Shit! Winnie, ready your–" Winnie has her bow unslung and an arrow knocked before I can finish the order. "Ryder, take that lantern and search the higher walls of the cliff for chimera."

He does as I ask, unhooking the lamp and twisting a cog in its base to open the interior mirrors. A sharp beam of light shoots out and he sweeps it along the surrounding walls.

"They're not moving," he says.

I look up, catching the odd glow of the furry, white creatures' eyes as the light passes, but none descend. I had never come across the beings myself, but I know enough about them from second-hand accounts. Known to attack larger ships, they are said to be blind, hunting their prey through the clever use of echolocation. We had alerted the vile creatures to our presence, so why are they not attacking?

"I thought these things were supposed to be bloodthirsty, ready to attack anything loud enough to get their attention?" I whisper to Ryder.

"They are. Something, or someone is keeping them at bay."

We both look across the deck to where Ansel stands at the bow, his back turned to us, his light steady across the passage ahead. Even Caleb and Toriq are quite clearly perturbed by the chimera above, checking the walls higher up every now and again before continuing to watch the water.

A second screech pierces the air, *The King's Arcana* shuddering as her hull catches on the canal bed. I look to Toriq and Caleb who stare back shaking their heads. We haven't hit the sides. I look to Ansel, but he stares dead ahead, one arm looped over the rail as he holds the lantern high.

I squeeze my eyes shut as *The Arcana* screams her complaints, her belly taking a beating. We can't slow the thrusters. If we stop here, we'd be lucky to get her moving again.

"Ryder, increase speed by one quarter," I command. He turns to the panel behind to twist both dials as I've asked, and *The Arcana* rocks forward, her complaints growing. We hold on as she judders and jerks over the rocks.

"Bend ahead, Captain," Ansel calls from the bow. I curse and glance up, but the chimera remain as they are, blindly lurking.

The Arcana slows and I tell Ryder to increase the thrusters a quarter more. Two bumps and a crack, and the floor falls from beneath us as the ship clears the reef and moves into deeper water, her speed now too great for the approaching bend.

"Reverse both thrusters at half speed," I call quickly to Ryder. He turns the dials and the ship begins a steady slow. "Full!" I snap. We're still too fast. He twists it again and the tight bend approaches. I watch as Ansel's light casts a shadow up the looming cliff wall, the turn so tight it appears to be a dead end.

"Cut the left thruster and full forward with the right." I turn the wheel and *The King's Arcana* soars around the bend, her bow cracking against the wall, her port side screaming along the rocks. A final jolt as the stern strikes the cliff face, and we emerge coasting into an open lagoon, cocooned on all sides by the Barnacle Cliffs.

"Ryder, reverse both thrusters and bring us to a stop." He does as I ask, and *The Arcana* glides along the still waters for a moment longer then slowly comes to a sailing stop. Leaving the helm, we join the others on the lower deck and drop the anchor.

"Well done, Captain," Winnie says with a shallow breath. She keeps her bow down but armed, still unsure of what dangers lurk in the large lagoon.

"We're not out yet," I remind her. "Where's Ansel?" We all look to the bow where he had been standing only a moment before, only to realise he was gone. "Check the water," I say, taking the lamp from the main mast and moving to the starboard rail.

"Over here, Cap. He's in the water!" Caleb calls from behind me.

I race over the deck to stand beside him and cast the light over the side. "Where? Where is he?" I'm frantic now. Only the Gods and ghosts know what lies in the murky depths of these waters.

"Over there." I follow the beam of Caleb's light to movement in the water. Ansel, swimming away from the ship towards the shore of a large cave.

"What the hell is he doing?" Toriq growls.

"Here's something you might find more concerning, Emery," Ryder calls from the bow of the ship. Pushing away from the port rail, I head to where he stands and watch as he proceeds to guide his lamp along the canyon's walls. "I believe we've hit a dead end."

TEMPTED THRICE

MAROONERS' CANAL

I pace along the deck, watching Toriq, Caleb and Ryder cast their light along the walls of the lagoon. It's clear the passage once continued through the eastern wall at one time or another, but now the rubble of a rockslide blocks our exit, trapping us like fish in a barrel. There's no choice, and I wanted to avoid it, but we'll have to use explosives to blast our way through. *The Arcana* was lucky to make it past the sharp bend and the shallows in the earlier parts of Marooners' Canal, and I'm not prepared to tempt fate twice.

"Who here has experience setting an explosive charge?" I ask, turning to the crew. To everyone's surprise, Winnie puts her hand up with a lopsided grin.

"I've set my fair share in the past. You want to blow through that passage?" she asks dubiously, following Caleb's light to the eastern wall. "How much do you have? We don't know how far back that rubble goes, not to mention..." She glances up and around the cliffs surrounding *The Arcana*, "we might end up bringing more rocks down."

"I'm open to suggestions," I say, crossing my arms and

eyeing each of the crew hopefully. Only grimaces answer as everyone shakes their heads.

"What have I got to work with?" Winnie asks, handing her bow to Toriq.

"Go to my quarters and look under the bed, there are several boxes of high explosive putty, fuses and some detonating cord under there–"

"You sleep with explosives under your *bed*?" Caleb asks me with a chuckle. "A woman after my own heart."

Ignoring him, I continue my instructions to Winnie. "Take what you need, form a plan and make use of these three," I say, pointing to the men. "But I want someone on watch at all times. The chimera seem to be keeping their distance, but I don't want to take any chances."

"What are you going to do?" she asks warily.

"I'm going to collect our deceptive little comrade from that cave," I grumble.

"You think Ansel led us here knowing we would be trapped?" Toriq asks as he slings the bow over his shoulders.

"He was too calm. When have you *ever* seen that man calm?" I ask in return. "Anyway, I'll have to swim, the ship's boat is damaged...yet another repair to have done at Beggars' Cove," I mutter with a sigh.

"You're not going alone, Emery. I'll come with you," Ryder says with a cool calm. I'm tempted to object, more concerned about protecting the ship, but he's already moving to drop the ladder over the port side.

"There's something...different about Ryder," Toriq mumbles quietly. He turns to look pointedly at me with a warning. "He's the brother of your future queen. Protect him with your life."

I roll my eyes and put a hand to my chest with the promise to do my best, then turn and head towards Ryder.

"You have any blades on you?" I ask him, giving a curtesy pat of my own weapons strapped to the belts on each thigh.

He shakes off the long, leather coat and places it to one side, revealing a leather bandoleer fastened over his shoulders and around his chest, with three small daggers strapped to each side. I whistle my appreciation, mostly for the beautiful blades but partly for the tight fit of his shirt.

Stepping closer, I slip one of his knives free and take his hand, placing it in his palm and closing the fingers over. "Always have a weapon ready when you enter the water. If something lurks below, it will go for *you* first, and I'm too tired to save you," I say with a wink.

He doesn't smile in return, just stares and lifts his free hand to tuck a loose strand of hair behind my ear, then reaches down to brush my thigh with his fingers.

My heart pounds so heavily against my chest, I can't help but worry its call may alert every siren in the eight seas to our location. I glance down as Ryder's fingers leave my thigh and something hard and metallic bumps against my hand.

"It seems sensible for you to carry a weapon as well then," he says quietly, then turns and climbs over the rail to descend the ladder.

I follow after him, muttering a curse to the seductive power of men, and shiver as I slip into the water. Slow and steady, careful not to splash the surface, we make our way to the cave.

Above, the pink and amber rays of dawn begin to creep up into the sky, but it doesn't diminish the glow emanating from deep inside the cavern. As soon as our feet touch sand, we each release another blade, making sure both hands are up and ready to fend off an attack. I remain hopeful that perhaps Ansel only swam to shore to get out of the water as soon as he could. But my gut says otherwise.

We sneak into the open mouth of the cave and follow the

glow to where the light pours through a crack in the rock. I should fit just fine, but I'm not sure about Ryder, what with him being easily twice my girth. I motion with my hand for him to stay put and slip inside the crevice. Voices drone from further in and I carefully wriggle my way through, stopping just before the opening on the other side, then slowly peer around the inner chamber.

Flames burn from sconces along the walls, their light glinting off endless mounds of gold bars, silver coins and uncut jewels littering the floor. One could buy the Fifth Sea with so much wealth, those lands home to the richest of kings and queens.

"I must have it! I'll bring it to her, I promise!" Ansel's voice pleads from the far corner of the cave. Clutching the rock, I lean further in, trying to see who he's talking to.

There, on a dais by the chamber wall, Ansel kneels at the feet of a figure. A man, judging by his size...a man with a golden cloak.

I slip back into the shadows and mutter an oath. He's led us straight to the very thing the book warned us about. A laugh echoes along the cave walls, the sound almost ethereal in its lightness.

"Perhaps she may claim it for herself," the voice says. "Step into the light, Emerelda."

I grit my teeth and step from the crevice into the golden chamber. "You know who I am?" I ask, taking one step closer to Ansel and the cloaked man.

Ansel spins at the sound of my voice, jaw dropping and face twisted in horror. He turns back to the man and crawls closer. "She must not choose, please!"

"What's going on, Ansel?" My voice echoes back, enhancing the clear threat in my tone. I take another step forward and flip one of the blades in my hand, sorely tempted to launch it at him. Ryder's hand grips my shoulder, stopping me from getting any closer as he angles his body slightly in front of mine.

"Ah, the heartless prince," the cloaked figure says, his voice a seductive song.

"He's magic, Emery. Not another step," Ryder warns.

The figure lifts his hands, sliding them along the hood until it drops to his shoulders. "Heartless, yes...but the prince is no fool it seems."

I step back, instinctive fear taking over. Ryder's hand falls to my wrist, perhaps the only thing keeping me from running. I stare in horror at the leather-faced creature, not a *man* at all, but a harpy. A messenger of the only remaining God of this world. The God of the Seas. Poseidon.

"You need not fear me, Emery. I've been waiting for you, the one girl with blue eyes, the one with the choice," the harpy croons. Across his back the cloak rustles; his hidden, feathered wings shifting it slightly upwards to reveal thin legs and clawed feet. Half man, half bird, these beings are long since thought to be mythical; grim story-book characters invented to frighten children, warning them that should they lead a life of wickedness, the harpies will come and gobble them up.

"What mark? What choice?" I ask, my voice wobbling and causing the creature to smile.

"I have *three* items for the blue-eyed girl. You may take as many as you wish. But be warned, too many or too little and the giants of the sky will turn their eyes to you. This was offered to a boy once, a boy in another world who took what he wanted and succumbed to the giants' wrath. I leave it to you."

Ansel turns to me, a pleading look in his eyes. "Remember the warning, Emery. Remember what the book said."

The girl with blue eyes will be tempted thrice,
take none, but one, or pay the price.

Three items. Three temptations. "What are my options?" I ask, stepping closer to the harpy. Ryder moves as if he were an extension of my shadow itself, his hand leaving my wrist to stretch protectively across my body.

"I have three items of note, or the clothes off my back. The first is a powerful sword, one so sharp it can cut through any substance. The second is a cap, granting its wearer a wealth of knowledge. The third is a pair of boots, bestowing the gift of great speed. The choice is yours, Emerelda Mirabel."

"Take none...but one," I whisper to myself. The harpy has offered three enticing items...*or* the clothes off his back. Take none of the items, but one piece of clothing? I mull over the words of warning and consider my options. Take too little and the sky giants will set their sights on me, so I can't take *nothing*.

"Emery, choose the–"

"SILENCE!" the harpy booms, cutting off Ansel and kicking him to the gilded floor. Gold and silver coins scatter and roll away, clinking and crunching under the harpy as it steps off the dais to place one taloned foot on Ansel's chest. "The girl must choose."

The golden cloak flaps to the side, revealing the feathered torso of the creature. The words of an old fairy tale spring to mind and I think back to what the sisters once told me, about the harpies and their cloaks, gifted from the Gods to hide their presence from the humans.

"Your cloak," I whisper.

"Say again," the harpy sings, extending one hand towards me.

"I choose your cloak. I accept *none* of the items, but *one* piece of your clothing."

"Interesting," Ryder mumbles beside me. He tenses and shifts slightly forward as the harpy falls silent and walks towards us.

"And you, heartless prince? What can I tempt you with this day? Perhaps I can remove that curse of yours."

"He wishes for nothing," I say, steeling myself and looking straight into the harpy's eyes.

"Curse?" Ryder whispers. I nudge him with my elbow, and he looks down at me beside him. "Yes, Emery is right, I wish for nothing but–"

"Just *nothing*," I say again, cutting off his inadvertent wish.

The harpy smiles and tugs at the tie to his cloak, pulling it from his shoulders and wrapping it around me. "Well done, Emery. You chose well, and so the next gift, I give for free."

I remain still, showing no sign of accepting what could quite easily be another temptation.

The harpy unfurls his large wings and flaps them once as if stretching out long limbs, then leans forward and touches a finger to my lips. "A kiss is the most powerful force there is," he says. "The right kiss, at the right time, by the right person, can break even the most cruel of curses. Remember that." He looks from me to Ryder, then steps back and returns to the small platform, the feathers of his tail displacing the wealth of coins as he walks. Turning back to face us, he winks, folds his wings around his body then fades away.

I sink to the floor and release a heavy breath, taking the folds of the golden cloak in my hands to admire the glimmering celestial material. Slowly, the colour fades and darkens, the material turning from gilded silk to a common, crimson velvet. All around us, the room shimmers as brilliant jewels fade to nothing, and every coin and golden brick turns to sand.

"Emery–" Ansel squeaks, his words cut off as Ryder stalks forward and lifts him by the front of his shirt.

"I think you have some explaining to do," the prince says quietly, calmly.

"Put him down, Ryder." I sigh, exhausted from Marooners' Canal and the sheer terror of facing the harpy. "He's right, though. Perhaps now is a good time to have that chat, Ansel."

Ryder drops Ansel to his feet. "Start by telling us what you are, because I know you aren't human."

I expect Ansel to object or look mildly affronted by the accusation, but instead he kneads his knuckles on each of his temples with an expression closer to panic.

"I'm a genie, okay? There, I said it," he says crossing his arms. "I didn't want to keep it from you, Emery, but my kind is coveted for our gifts…and you already have so much temptation on your plate with the book."

I stare, open-mouthed at Ansel. A genie. I'd met such a being only once before, a travelling man who had stopped on the Garden Isle for a few days before resuming his journey. "Genies don't have masters…what are you really running from? And why did you bring us here?"

Ansel sighs and kicks the sand at his feet. "We *do* have masters, of a sort. But we rarely meet them. Do you know the purpose of a genie?"

"I believe I do," Ryder says. "It's why you're always distracted and scribbling your notes. It's the reason your hands are always bandaged." Ryder turns from Ansel to me. "They're the scribes. The ones who write the books of life. Written in their own, enchanted blood."

My jaw might have touched the floor with that revelation.

"I thought genies offered wishes to those who befriended them?"

"No. We offer favours, advice and at times foretell the outcome of someone *doing* as they wish. We do not *grant* their desires."

"Then this master…"

"Each genie is assigned to one person and his or her book. My master is the one I write for, but what I'm willing to give is never enough for her, so I had to escape." Ansel finally lifts his gaze from his feet to stare at me, his expression so pitiful, it almost overrides the part of me that wants to throttle him.

"Why bring us here?" Ryder asks.

"I need the harpy's cloak." Ansel crosses the space between us and drops to his knees at my feet. "Please allow me to borrow it until we reach Aurora Isle. In return I will grant you a favour, three favours in fact, any of your choosing. And I'll promise to abide by them."

I can't help but think that's oddly specific. "Why do you need it?"

"The woman I run from has ties to a witch capable of tracking me. The cloak will do as it's designed and shield me from her magic."

I sigh and drop my head into my hands. This is all a bit much, and after such a terrifically bad day, I'm hardly surprised when the quiet throb of a headache starts tapping a beat behind my right eye. Untying the cloak's strings, I pull it from my shoulders and hand it over to Ansel.

He hurriedly rises to his feet and takes the material, securing it in place and looking at me gratefully. "Thank you–"

"Don't thank me yet. You should have been honest with me from the beginning, Ansel," I say in quiet anger. He looks down at his feet and nods his head sadly. "But, from what you tell me, I don't blame you for being cautious. For my first favour, I want open honesty from now on. Do you accept?"

"You're wasting one?" Ryder asks, one eyebrow cocked questioningly.

"It's not a waste. I feel a genie's honesty might come in handy in the days to come, especially when it comes to interpreting that bloody book."

Ryder seems about to object, but his words are cut off by a muffled boom. Another quickly follows and the ground trembles at our feet.

Realisation dawns as Ryder pulls me to one side, his body arching overing mine to protect me from the falling debris.

"Those idiots have already started," I shout over the rending rock. Turning on my heel, I race for the chamber's entrance and slip through the tight crevice, hurrying towards the beach with the others close behind.

Across the water, in the middle of the lagoon, *The King's Arcana* rocks with the waves of the explosion. Smoke rises from the eastern wall, and as it clears, the light of dawn streams through the newly exposed gap, one just big enough for *The Arcana* to fit through.

"I think Winnie's trying to get your attention," Ryder says as he points to the ship. Sure enough, Winnie is waving one arm in a wide arc, the other hand holding a dazzling blue light.

The siren bell.

"Get to the ship!" I command, racing into the water. We're barely halfway across the lagoon when I hear it, the song of the seas' most vicious of creatures. Ansel is falling behind, the weight of the cloak holding him back. I mutter a stream of obscenities as Ryder and I swim back for him, pulling the cloak to lessen his load.

We make it to the ship just in time to see the splash of sirens crashing around the sharp bend behind *The Arcana*.

What's more disturbing, is that the water around us seems alive with movement, like the waves are made from soft, wet fur...

"Weapons out, the chimera are in the water!" I yell, alerting the others as I reach down and pull Ansel the rest of the way onboard. "Caleb, Toriq, Ansel, back to your cabins, now!" I race for the mechanism to crank the nets, then turn to face the water, a blade clutched in one hand, the other gripping *The Arcana's* port rail. I sing.

> *Come here, come now, I dare of thee,*
> *Come see this heart so pure 'n' free.*
> *Come here, come now, oh wards o'er deep,*
> *In exchange for my life your own death you will reap.*

I finish the verse but the sirens' melody remains unchanged, with no pained cries of protest from the creatures. The song isn't working. Is it the curse the book spoke of – the bleak penance for reading its pages too soon?

"Ryder, thrusters full ahead!" I call, racing for the helm.

"Captain!" I turn at the stairs to the quarterdeck to see Winnie grappling with Caleb, and Toriq on his knees beside them, clutching both hands to his ears. "It's the men! They're ensnared!" she cries.

The ship jerks forward and I turn to check where Ryder has twisted the thrusters, sending us coasting towards the new, eastern passage. Thankfully his face remains calm, the sirens' call failing to capture his mind. But those eyes speak of something different, wild and burning green, like something small and deep within him *wants* to enjoy this, *wants* to fear it...but can't.

"Ryder, take the wheel and get us out of here!" I shout. He glances down and briefly hesitates but nods, then points behind me.

I spin at the sound of a guttural scream to see Ansel racing across the deck from the companionway towards me, a scimitar raised above his head and murder in the contortion of his face. I hold my ground, waiting for the right moment, then duck. The *shing* of his blade rings in my ears as the scimitar slices the air above my back. I drive forward catching him around the waist and slamming him down onto the wooden deck. He attempts to raise the sword as I straddle his waist, his body writhing beneath me. I catch his sword wielding hand and slam it down, then catch his other wrist and do the same.

"They want *you*, Emerelda," Ansel hisses, his voice foreign and unfamiliar. He tries to lean up, snapping his teeth at my face like a rabid animal as I struggle against his strength. With no hands free, I lean my head all the way back, then slam it down on the bridge of his nose. The back of his head cracks against the solid wood and his eyes close, body slumping to lie still. I breathe a sigh of relief, clutching my throbbing forehead and wiping the blood trickling down my face.

Winnie yells, gripping her arm as she stumbles back, her shirt covered in blood. I call her name then kick Ansel's fallen scimitar towards her as I unclip my blade and reach for the other, patting only the empty leather holster. I must have lost it in the fray. I search the surrounding deck when the sound of scurrying feet forces me to look up, straight into the razor-sharp teeth of a chimera.

Instinct forces me to raise my blade in defence and it plunges deep into the creature's belly as it leaps into the air to attack. I'm forced to my knees and scream as a second lands on my back and sinks its fangs around my shoulder. It jolts and shudders, releasing my shoulder and falling to the deck with an anguished wail, one of Ryder's blades buried to the hilt in its fur.

"Emery, take over the helm," Ryder shouts, that fire in him growing stronger. I stagger to the stairwell and make my way up, taking his outstretched hand.

"Help Winnie first," I order him, then take the wheel as he leaps over the balustrade to land on the lower deck. Just ahead we're almost upon the newly blasted exit. We have to fit, we *have* to.

I momentarily abandon the wheel to check the stern, looking over the rail for the maelstrom of churning water or the graceful, deadly limbs of the sirens. An arm reaches from below, skin sizzling from the beading of orichalcum along the recently repaired netting. I jump back and shriek as the siren's long nails rake across my chest, shredding my shirt but failing to catch the skin beneath.

"Captain!"

I turn back at the sound of Winnie's call to see we're heading straight for the passage, but just off course. I grip the wheel and turn slightly to port, righting us as we slip between the fractured rock walls.

The King's Arcana groans and wails as her sides scrape along the walls. I see the tantalising pale blue just ahead, the glistening water of the open sea – we're close – *so* close.

"Ready the sails!" I holler to Winnie and Ryder below. Only grunts and clanking blades reply as Ryder blocks the heavy swing of Caleb's sword and Winnie battles the chimera one after the other as they launch at her in a frenzied attack.

"They want *you*, Emerelda, the blood of their kin," a cold voice snarls.

I snap my gaze to Toriq slowly approaching from the stairs, his eyes wild with a manic desire to answer the sirens' call.

"Fight it, Toriq!" I scream.

Ryder kicks Caleb in the chest and turns at the sound of

my voice. Gritting his teeth, he raises one of his daggers to throw it at Toriq.

"Don't you bloody dare!" I scream, pointing down at the prince. Ryder pauses and mutters something under his breath, then turns as Caleb jumps to his feet and continues his attack.

Toriq chuckles as he climbs the last step, a sneer curling the corners of his mouth. "They want you. They will love me if I give them what they crave."

I'm trapped, unable to release the wheel to defend myself or risk condemning the ship to the sharp rocks either side. I take a breath and sing the first line of the song, but it's cut short by Toriq's harsh laugh.

He drops the blade from his hand and races forward, ducking the swing of my fist and reappearing behind me to wrap his forearm around my neck in an effective choke-hold.

"Emery, hang on!" Ryder calls to me from below, all the while blocking the crushing blows from Caleb's sword. Landing a carefully timed punch, Ryder takes the chance to try and get to me, but isn't quick enough. He roars as he's again forced to deflect Caleb's relentless attacks. "Toriq, hurt her, and I *will* kill you," he growls.

My throat compresses beneath Toriq's tightening grip, my lungs burning with the desire to breath as I struggle to maintain my grip on the ship's wheel.

Toriq rests his chin on my shoulder, whispered threats dripping past his lips and into my ear.

It's exactly the moment I've been waiting for.

With one hand still on the wheel, I drive the heel of my palm into his nose and wait for the sickening crunch of cartilage snapping before thrusting my hips back. As Toriq steps back, movement from the lower deck catches my attention – Ryder racing for the helm.

"No, ready yourself to raise the sails!" I wheeze down to

him, gasping as Toriq's arm returns to my throat. I jab my heel onto his foot and again he steps back, howling with pain. Without wasting a breath, I turn and finish with a roundhouse kick, sending Toriq spinning to the deck at my feet.

The Arcana squeals and shudders in protest as her starboard side grazes the rock wall, I take the wheel and pull her back into the centre of the channel.

Nearly there.

Golden sunlight bathes the blood-spattered ship as we pull from the shadows of Marooners' Canal, the open Third Sea yawning before us and filling the horizon.

"Now, Ryder!" I call down. The sails fly loose at my command and *The King's Arcana* jolts, her wings hungrily embracing the breeze and propelling us forward.

PAIN & DESIRE

THIRD SEA

With the wind on our side, I'm confident the sirens have no hope of keeping up with *The Arcana*, so I maintain her speed with full sail and maximum thrusters. Below, the remaining chimera are screaming, the sunlight burning their already delicate eyes. Winnie and Ryder go to each, stabbing a blade through their hearts, both for our safety and to put the vile creatures out of their misery.

Toriq stirs on the floor beside me and I eye him warily as I re-establish our position and rig the wheel to our new bearing. "You back with us, Toriq?" I say, crouching down and holding a dagger to his throat.

He peers up through the curtain of dark hair fallen loose from our brawl, his eyes settling on the blood still blooming from the chimera's bite on my shoulder. "Did I do that?" he asks, sounding surprisingly regretful. It's no secret the man doesn't like me.

"No, you tried to choke me instead. I believe you wished to offer me to the sirens in return for their undying – or in their case *dying* – love.

Toriq shakes his head to chase the last of the sirens' spell from his mind, then gingerly touches a hand to his swollen nose and jaw. "I'm sorry. I could see you, and I knew what I was doing, but I couldn't stop myself."

Slipping my blade back in its sheath, I use my good arm to help him stand then smile and point to his bloody and almost certainly broken nose. "Don't worry, I got a few good hits in myself."

Toriq and I turn to see Ryder breathlessly mounting the last step to the helm, a scimitar in one hand slick with the black, tar-like blood of the chimera, and the crimson hue of human blood.

"Oh Gods, did you stab Caleb?" I ask, hurrying to the rail and leaning over to search the bodies below.

"No. This is Winnie's blood from where Caleb sliced her arm. I believe she might need medicinal aid," Ryder says, his eyes never leaving Toriq.

I catch Winnie's gaze and she waves up wearily, her injured arm hanging loosely at her side. Turning to Ryder I tell him to head below deck to the empty cabin where our medical supplies are stashed. We will treat everyone up here on the open deck, where we can be ready for any kind of secondary attack.

With one final look to Toriq, Ryder turns and heads down the stairwell to do as I've asked. Taking Toriq's arm, I lead him down to the lower deck, mindful of his somewhat staggering walk and concerned he might trip and fall. It goes to show just how much the sirens' call affects the men – if I were to try and help Toriq down a set of stairs any other time, I'm certain he would throttle me.

Settling Toriq on an empty seat by our dining table, I turn next to where Winnie is trying to rouse Ansel.

"Captain, your shoulder!" she cries, pulling her hand from

under Ansel's head and letting it bump against the deck as she stands to examine me. The knock seems to do the trick and Ansel stirs, attempting to roll onto his side and waving an arm threateningly to those who wish to pull him from sleep.

Winnie and I chuckle as we reach down and lift him into a seated position. His eyes flicker open as he grumbles his annoyance, then squeals in horror as he scrambles back from the black and bloody mess of chimera bodies littered around him.

"By the Gods! Captain, I remember, I tried to *kill* you!" he says, clapping a hand to his mouth as if speaking such a claim somehow makes it worse.

"And your nose suffered for it," I say with a smirk. "You aren't to be blamed for falling prey to those beasts. Come on," I tell him, linking my arm under Ansel's and heaving him up.

"Ummm, what the *fuck?*" a familiar voice calls, and we all turn our heads to where Caleb is sitting on the deck, eyeing the headless body of a chimera sitting bloody in his lap.

"Nice of you to join us," Winnie says wryly. "You owe me a new shirt." She fingers the sliced material and winces at the deep cut beneath.

"Winnie..." he whispers, remembering what he'd done at the behest of the sirens. She shakes her head and offers him a pitying smile, then walks over to help him to his feet.

"My father didn't provide as much medicine as I had hoped," Ryder calls as he emerges from the companionway and crosses the deck carrying three boxes.

"That looks like more than enough to me," I say, stepping forward to help him.

He pauses and holds the boxes away to one side as he eyes the blood on my shoulder, then skirts around me to place the boxes on the table. "One is liquor. I figured some might need it if the needles and string are required. They say it calms the nerves."

"That's thoughtful, thank you," I say.

He looks sideways at me, unsure of my meaning. "It's practical, of course I thought if it."

I shake my head, hardly believing that this man can be capable of showing such hidden depths of emotion one minute, then an utter lack of understanding the next. I turn to head for the helm when he catches my wrist, drawing a hiss from me at the pain in my shoulder.

"Where are you going? That needs to be treated," he says, pointing to the wound and pulling me back to sit on one of the empty chairs. "Take your shirt off."

"I beg your pardon?" I stutter, flicking my eyes from him to the crew around us.

"I can't treat you with that in the way, you need to strip," he replies blankly.

Beside him, Winnie stifles a giggle, while Caleb looks up hopefully and nods his head in agreement with Ryder.

I smile dryly at both men, then get to my feet. Reaching into one of the boxes, I take some cloth, a roll of bandages and a bottle of iodine. "I'm going to check our heading and then I'll treat my own bloody wound in the privacy of my cabin."

Caleb looks vaguely devastated by this news while a muscle ticks in Ryder's jaw and he watches me leave for the quarterdeck. Away from the prying eyes, I place the items beside the wheel and take a breath, squeezing my eyes shut and pulling the bloody, brittle shirt from the edges of the wound. Dark spots threaten to cloud my vision, so I stop and silently vow never to venture through Marooners' Canal again.

Turning my attention to the pieces of parchment on the

table to the side, I roll up the chart of the Second Sea and instead concentrate on the one outlining the Third. Drawing my finger from where we exited the passage, I drag it to one of the first isles we should come across. Beggars' Cove.

A feeling of unease gnaws at my gut. We had trusted Ansel before and almost been killed. For a *cloak*, of all things. He had promised openness and honesty as one of his favours. With that in mind, I step past the wheel and stand by the rail overlooking the lower deck, gripping it for stability.

"Ansel," I call down. He looks up expectantly. "With my favour for honestly in mind, do you still suggest we dock at Beggars' Cove?"

He dips his head and ponders this for a moment longer than I feel comfortable with, then looks up. "Yes, Captain. Not the safest, but the carpenters there are second to none."

I suppose that's encouraging. *The Arcana* could do with a good carpenter to fix her wounds. Beggars' Cove is the second closest isle on our heading, the first being Hangman's Knot – and I'm not too keen to see how it earns that name.

Turning back to the charts, I note the isle's location and our relative heading, and ease the ship slightly northeast before rigging the wheel to keep her steady and on-course.

"He's hiding something."

I nearly jump out of my skin at the rough sound of Ryder's voice behind me, then turn and scowl at him for his sneakiness. "You mean Ansel?" I glance down to where the man in question attends to Toriq's nose, then allows the same to be done for him. "He's always hiding something," I say with a wave of my hand.

"Then why trust him? Why not dock at another island?" Ryder asks.

"Because Beggars' Cove is one of the closest, and *The Arcana* is in serious need of repairs," I explain with a sigh, turning and leaning back against the rail. I could sleep where

I stand, even the throb of the wound wouldn't keep me awake for long. But the day is new and there's much to be done if we have any hope of reaching the isle before *The Arcana* sinks. Gods only know what the damage is like to her hull after the beating from the passage.

I feel myself slipping to the side and grip the rail, sighing when Ryder's warm hand travels to my waist, wrapping tightly around and holding me up while the other cups my chin and tilts it up to face him.

A scowl flickers beneath his dark lashes, his ever-present impassivity temporarily misplaced for...concern? Anger?

"A chimera's bite is riddled with poison. Come, you need treatment." He tugs my hand and pulls me gently away from the helm.

The better part of me, the stronger, independent captain of *The Arcana* wants to object, to tell him I'm quite capable. But I'm too tired. I trail numbly behind as he guides me down the stairs and towards the stern, barely registering the others as we pass and enter my quarters.

He closes the door behind us and directs me to take a seat on the edge of the bed. I groan as he lifts my arms above my head to remove the shirt, and a giggle bubbles up my throat at a tickling sensation trailing from my shoulder down to my armpit. I look down to see the fresh beads of blood and black, tar-like liquid oozing from where the shirt has reopened the smaller markings of the bite.

"Well, that doesn't look too healthy," I mumble.

"You should have treated this immediately," he says, leaving the room temporarily to retrieve the medicinal items I'd stashed by the helm. He returns barely moments later, or perhaps it was longer than that. My mind seems to dip and sway with the gentle rhythm of the cruising ship, and I try to lie back on the bed. He catches my wrist and hauls me back into a seated position.

In the next breath, the prince of the Garden Isle kneels at my feet, one large hand gripping my thigh, the other capturing my waist and lower back as he leans forward and puts his mouth to the wound. I gasp at the suddenness of it, my fists weakly bunching in his shirt, torn between pushing him away and pulling him closer. Pressure builds along my collarbone as Ryder draws the poison from where one of the chimera's fangs punctured, spitting a mixture of blood and ichor into a small pot by my side. He moves to the second puncture and once again goes about sucking the wound clean.

I'm grateful for the privacy of the cabin. The sensation of Ryder's lips on my skin is a heady mixture of pain and pleasure. I groan and let my head fall back as the stubble of his chin scrapes along my chest. He leans away, spitting the last of the black substance into the pot before wiping his mouth. Reaching for the iodine, he pulls the cork and douses a cloth.

"I'm told this will hurt," he warns.

I nod my head, prepared to welcome the pain, anything to calm the unsettling, *unnatural* throbbing between my thighs. He places the cloth to my skin and fire erupts beneath it. His grip on my waist tightens, forcing me still as he roughly cleans the site. Reaching for the bottle, he tips the contents over my shoulder, and I clench my teeth, forbidding a scream from escaping. Finally, he places a clean cloth over the wound, then proceeds to bandage my shoulder and upper arm.

"Here, drink this now, and then again later this evening. It should fight off whatever remains in your system," he says, lifting a small vial to my lips. I take the tangy liquid down my throat and grimace at the foul taste of jewelweed and gentian root.

"Thank you," I say, already feeling my senses return with the effects of the quick acting tonic. "I don't know what I was thinking leaving that as long as I did." Granted, I had been more concerned with putting enough distance between *The Arcana* and the sirens, and then making sure we were on the right bearing to make land before we sunk. But still, he was right to worry, assuming Ryder is capable of feeling such a thing. I look up into his questioning gaze, and smile.

He steps back and sucks in a breath. Concerned by the hurt on his face, I stand to go to him but stumble instead as *The Arcana* bumps along the waves. He reaches out and catches me, pulling me to his chest where the thump, thump, thump of his heart beats rapidly within.

I lean back, holding my breath as he dips his head down, his gaze travelling to my lips. With that iron grip once again circling my waist, he lifts his hand and touches me there just as the harpy had done. His head slowly dips lower, and his breath fans my face.

The man you love, a heartless man, will be the one to kill you...

I turn my head to the side, looking away, anywhere but those burning jades with the power to light a fire in my soul. His hold on me loosens and I slip from Ryder's embrace, moving back to the bed to grip the post.

"The harpy said I was cursed," Ryder says quietly.

I close my eyes, remembering all too well what the harpy had said, of his implications regarding my kiss and the ability to break the most dire of curses. Still, Malka's warning echoes in my mind. I have feelings for Ryder, inexplicable feelings for a heartless prince. One kiss could be all it takes for him to claw his way deeper into my heart, where I'm not ready to let anyone in, never mind the very man who might one day take my life.

"We'll figure out a way to break it, Ryder. I promise." The words are hollow and meaningless. We have a pretty good idea what might break his curse. Is it wrong of me to be so hesitant? Marnie's sour expression enters my mind with a scowl. *Always look out for yourself, first and foremost,* she would say. And in this regard, I think she would be right. I need to know more before I make any rash decisions, after all, what if his curse turns back on me? I turn to Ryder, a look of apology on my face.

"You're...frightened?" he asks, stepping forward and stroking a finger along the crease of my brow.

I take his hand softly in mine. "I'm cautious," I offer in explanation, though the words only seem to confuse him more. "I can't help you, Ryder. Not yet. Not until I know more."

He drops his hand from my face and tilts his head to one side. "I don't understand, but I respect whatever it is you seem to be considering. Just know this, Emery. I would never hurt you. I've sworn to do the opposite and would forfeit my life in seeing it through."

"That's right, you swore to your Father–"

"No," he says softly, cutting me off. "This vow is for me, I protect you because something inside me wills it...wants it."

Again I'm lost for words, but a swell of warmth radiates through me.

Turning on his heel, Ryder leaves the cabin and I sink to sit on the corner of the bed.

I believe him. How could I not? His actions have only ever suggested his wish to protect me. The prince fulfilling his duty. For now, I'll stick to my instincts and wait. If Mother Witch is anything like the three sisters, surely she can help. She will know what to do. I just need to keep my lips to myself until we reach the Aurora Isle. I reach up and touch a finger to the soft skin where the last of Ryder's touch remains.

With a frustrated sigh, I drop my hand and stand from the

bed, moving to retrieve the open bottle of rum from the case below my desk. Popping the cork I take a swig, rinsing the lingering taste of the tonic from my tongue. Turning to stare at the door where Ryder had left, I release a long sigh. Damned men.

SIREN'S KISS

THIRD SEA

After taking a moment to compose myself and to let the rum do its magic, I return to the open deck, pleased to find the clean-up has already begun.

Between them, Caleb and Toriq are dragging the bodies of the chimera from the deck and loading them into barrels. I was initially concerned they had simply chucked what remained of the creatures overboard, but they had seen the value in keeping the carcasses, the chimera often sought for the medicinal properties in their poison.

I search the deck for Winnie, growing mildly concerned when I fail to find her. I sigh with relief when she appears from the companionway a moment later, wearing fresh clothes and a sour look on her face. Seeing me, she heads over.

"How are you feeling, Captain?" she asks, her frown deepening at the sight of the bandages visible beneath the collar of my shirt.

"Fine, thanks. Ryder treated me. How's your arm?"

She rolls her eyes and casts a look to Caleb who's staring our way with an expression caught between shame and outright fury. "It's barely a scratch, yet the man seems compelled to fuss as if I've lost the whole limb."

"He feels guilty," I say, chuckling at Winnie's ruffled disposition.

"Well, he shouldn't. And it's no excuse to offer a tumble between the sheets. If I ever take a man to my bed, which isn't likely, he won't be *that* lecherous oaf."

"He offered to bed you?" My eyebrows shoot up, and I turn my gaze back to Caleb, who has the good sense to look mildly embarrassed. "That's bold. Doesn't he realise he's not your type?"

Winnie had told us all about the death of her wife on our first night aboard the ship, and her vow never to take another. With that knowledge in mind, I'm surprised Caleb even bothered to try.

"Overconfident doesn't begin to describe Caleb. Men like him think everything can be solved with a quick poke," she says shaking her head despairingly.

I laugh aloud at her adept description of his skirt-chasing antics, then lace my good arm over her shoulder. "Well, I suppose you can't blame him for trying. You're quite an impressive woman."

She wriggles from beneath my arm and turns to look at me, her eyes searching for any hint of teasing. There's nothing but honesty in the gentle smile I return.

"Winnie, from the moment you set foot on my ship, you've been invaluable," I say.

Her cheeks flush and she grins back. "Easy, Captain, or I might just fall in love with *you*."

I wink playfully. "Careful what you wish for. I have too much fire in my soul to settle down. But I'll take your friendship if it's on the table?"

Winnie feigns grief at my words, placing both hands over her heart and pretending to sway backwards, then straightens with a sigh. "Well then, as your friend and your crewmate I should tell you, I checked below deck and we're taking on water again – not much, but we need to properly tend to the worst of *The Arcana's* wounds. I estimate she won't last much longer than three days at sea as she is."

My grin fades with her words and the captain in me instantly returns to take charge. "At this speed we should make it to Beggars' Cove by tomorrow evening." I glance at the dull, inactive crystal of the siren bell and take a moment to think, weighing each option carefully. I trust Winnie's judgement, but I should really check for myself.

Then there's the sirens to consider. While they clearly aren't close, they could be tracking our bearing and waiting for us to slow or stop. It's risky, especially without my song. I lift a hand idly to my throat, hoping my voice isn't lost forever.

"Captain?" Winnie asks, interrupting my thoughts.

"I need to get in the water to assess the damage properly," I say, moving to the main mast and cranking down the sails.

"You shouldn't, not with that wound on your shoulder," she insists, following close behind.

"We haven't much choice, Winnie. It'll be quicker with both of us doing it, and I won't have the men underwater drawing all manner of sea creatures to our location."

Winnie chuckles as she cranks the rigging on the second mast. "You have to feel sorry for the poor bastards, not being able to swim freely in the ocean. I never really understood it myself."

"Something to do...ugh, with their pheromones," I say through my teeth as I secure the sail tightly to the mast. I roll my shoulder experimentally and groan at the aching pain along it, then turn and head up the stairs as Winnie goes to the store to collect our weight belts.

"Why are we stopping?" Ryder asks as he follows to stand beside me at the wheel.

"I need to check the hull for major damage. It's another day and a half before we reach our port, and I'd rather not sink before we get there." Using the spyglass, I scan the horizon for any sign of land or rocks. Ansel had monitored our speed at agreed intervals and noted it down as I'd asked. With that in mind along with our bearing, we should soon be in sight of Taro's Teeth in the north.

"You aren't going in the water with your wound," he states firmly.

I resist the urge to remind Ryder he has absolutely no say in what I will and will not be doing, instead focusing on the task at hand.

There, north of *The Arcana*, a series of rocks jut from the water. Taro's Teeth. Marked on every chart with a warning skull, the place a known death trap for any vessels passing too close, with an undercurrent strong enough to drag even the most powerful of ships to its core. I take a cursory check of our location against the chart and note our depth, then turn the thrusters to full reverse and wait until *The King's Arcana* goes dead in the water.

"Did you hear me?"

"Yes, Ryder, I heard you just fine," I say with a bite and a look of warning as I turn the thrusters off. "Please go and lower the anchor and prepare to stand guard." I don't wait for his response, or his argument. I hurry down the stairs and call the others to the main mast where I relay my orders.

"Okay, we want this to be fast so we can get moving again. Ansel, stand guard at the stern, Toriq at the bow, Caleb and Ryder centre port and starboard. As soon as Winnie and I are out of the water, Toriq raises the anchor while Ryder and Caleb go to full sail. Ansel, you will set the thrusters to full ahead."

"You think the sirens are trying to catch up?" Toriq asks, his eyes leaving mine to search the waters around us.

"I'm not willing to take the chance either way. Winnie, take starboard, I'll take port." I turn on my heel and head for the rail to drop the ladder. Gripping the side, I wince at the pressure in my shoulder then glance up sharply as Ryder takes my hand and gently helps me over.

"Once you're done, I'll pull you out of the water with the ladder. Don't try and climb," he says.

I raise an eyebrow, a little dubious of his request. These ladders are heavy enough on their own, never mind with a person dangling from them. Nevertheless, the hard look in his eyes informs me it's a note not worth mentioning, and I begin the decent.

Taking a breath, I dive below, following along the bites and cuts on the hull from Marooners' Canal. It's bad. Worse than I'd thought. After trailing a path from one end to the other, I find one spot with a hole too deep to ignore and decide it must be plugged before we can continue onwards. I quickly resurface and swim on my back, using my legs to take me to the ladder.

"Throw me down two suckerweeds," I call to Ryder.

He disappears momentarily, then returns and drops both plants overboard to land in my arms. I dive once again, biting back the temptation to whimper underwater. Reaching the spot, I allow one of the plants to attach to my arm as the first is secured to the hull. My lungs are burning by the time I've secured the second. I begin my ascent when something catches the corner of my eye, something gold, catching in the light. Slowly, as if unsure, a siren rises from the depths below.

I slip the blade from my thigh and hold it up to the creature, briefly realising it's the rarer of the species, a male. The scales from his muscular stomach all the way down to a bright red fin glitter like gems, each catching the broken light from the surface as he rises to a stop in front of me.

"Do not fear, Emery," the siren croons, the timbre of his voice a song on its own despite the bubbles purging from the gills at his neck.

I fumble with the clasp of my weight belt and release it, my body slowly rising to the surface with the innate need to breath. My eyes remain fixed on him as I go, watching with absurd curiosity as he ducks below to retrieve my belt then returns and holds it out to me in an offering.

I eye the belt warily, my mind screaming with the question as to why I'm still alive. He bobs in the soft current, patiently watching, rising with me. Like the females, he's beautiful. With hair seemingly made from long, gilded threads, it fans out around him in a mesmerising dance to the rhythm of the soft current.

The top of my head breaches the surface and I risk breaking eye contact with the siren long enough to pull in a breath, long enough to hear the shouts of panic onboard *The Arcana*, long enough to see Ryder mount the rail.

"Stay!" I shout to him and point to the ladder. I dive back down, setting my sights on the threat at hand as I slowly, carefully make my way back to where I can safely meet Ryder.

"Do you want this...*thing*, or not?" the siren's voice rumbles through the water, his two, pointed ears twitching as he holds up the belt.

Where are the other creatures, his brothers and sisters? Or has he abandoned them for a chance to play with his food alone? I carefully take the proffered item in one hand, holding the blade up with the other. The ladder bumps against my back and I tuck the belt between my legs and reach for it.

"Wait, I have come to help you, Emery."

My hand freezes inches from the ladder as my obscured

vision remains locked on the shimmering orbs of his deep, blue eyes. Sirens don't help, they maim and kill.

"Please," he hums.

Bubbles break from my mouth in shock at the simple, pleading word from a siren's lips. I jab my knife forward in warning, then bob my head in acceptance. I will hear him.

Brilliant teeth flash in a smile, then he soars through the water and pulls me into his embrace, our lips colliding. I thrust my dagger to his gut, but he catches my wrist, the strength of a siren far outweighing that of a wounded human. I grip the ladder with my other hand and bang it against the hull, a call to those above. My shoulder screams as I'm hauled from the water, my mouth still captured by the creature, the half man clinging desperately to my body.

He pulls away, breaking the kiss with a smile and drops to the water. Hands grip my arms and clothes as Ryder and Caleb haul me over the railing, and I cough and splutter, trying to expel the water and taste of the salty, stolen kiss. Scrambling to my feet with one hand holding my throbbing shoulder, I peer overboard to where the siren still remains.

"Wait for my departure, then sing, my love," he says, his eyes glittering with delight. "I'll always be near." With a somewhat cheeky smirk, he winks, then dips beneath the surface without another word.

"Captain!" Winnie squeals, pulling me into her embrace then checking me head to toe for any further injuries. She stops at my shoulder, fresh blood oozing and spreading along my shirt. "She needs treatment–"

"No, do as I've ordered. Anchor up and sails to full mast, we're getting out of here, *now*," I command. Everyone hurries to their duties as I head for the helm, ready to hit the thrusters to full as soon as the anchor is secured.

Before long, *The King's Arcana* is back to full speed and we're gliding across the water on our bearing to Beggars'

Cove. As I hold the wheel to steady our course, I consider the siren's words.

Sing.

Taking a breath, I sing the sirens' poison.

> ***Come here, come now, I dare of thee,***
> ***Come see this heart so pure 'n' free.***
> ***Come here, come now, oh wards o'er deep,***
> ***In exchange for my life your own death you will reap.***

Far in the distance, the lonely wail of a siren cries out. My song is returned, the curse broken...with a kiss. I put a finger to my lips and smile knowing I can once again defend *The Arcana* with my voice. Why though? Why was it returned from a *siren* of all creatures, the one my song hurts the most?

"Captain, I know it's early, but everyone is damn near starving. Could you eat?" Winnie calls from below.

My stomach rumbles on cue to her question. "I'm *so* hungry I'm quite sure I could devour the reserves of a small village," I say. Winnie giggles and takes that as a yes, then heads down to the galley to begin her preparations.

Checking the ship's course one final time, I lock the wheel and turn for the stairs.

"I was about to come and get you," Ryder says as I reach the bottom step. He points to my shoulder and holds up a bottle of iodine, cloths and bandages in explanation. I wave him to follow behind to my quarters, knowing full well I'm not up to the task by myself.

Once inside, he closes the door and points to the bed, going about the same routine as before.

With the last of the adrenaline coursing through me, I'm suddenly much more aware of everything Ryder does. How he helps to lift my shirt, his eyes lingering ever so briefly on my bare body. More often than not, sailing by myself or with the sisters I would go without a cover band for my breasts, finding the material uncomfortable. But with three men aboard my ship, I had made sure to dress as I felt was appropriate, and was now thankful for the forethought.

"It's not as bad as it looked. You still need to take the second dose for the poison tonight though," he says, dabbing the wound methodically but much more gently than he had before.

"Thank you. You seem well versed with treating the wounded." More than that. I had been impressed when he'd concocted the anti-venom for my snakebite back on the Garden Isle, but from what I can tell, he seems knowledgeable of medicine in general.

"I've treated myself on several occasions. I learn as I go." Placing the cloths to one side, he wraps the bandage over and around my arm, tying a tight knot at my bicep when he's confident the entirety of the bite is covered.

Leaving me on the bed, he packs up the iodine and dirty cloths and heads for the door, stopping with his hand grasping the handle.

"What's wrong?" I ask hesitantly.

He turns, leaning his back against the timber frame. "That siren, why did he..."

Why did he kiss you? That's what Ryder wants to ask. Why would I kiss a creature of the deep, but not him? "I don't know," I say truthfully. "I didn't have much say in the matter, he just launched himself at me."

The thin glass of the iodine bottle cracks in his hand and Ryder holds it up curiously, idly registering his own, white-knuckled grip and the trickle of blood pooling in his palm. "I don't...understand."

Rising from the bed, I hurry over to him, taking the leaking bottle from his hand and placing it on the desk before pushing him down to sit on the wooden stool. "Bloody idiot, you don't even know your own strength," I mutter, holding his palm to the light to check for any glass in the cut. I find none and pick up the bottle, oddly annoyed to find it's empty.

"Stay here a moment, I'll get another one," I say, opening the door and heading to where we left the medical crates by the main mast. Taking a bottle and several more bits of cloth for Ryder's hand, I hurry back to my quarters to find him up and staring past the bank of windows along the stern.

"I don't understand this…thing that's happening, Emery. My thoughts are wrong, impractical."

I place a hand on his cheek, my heart breaking at the confusion shaped in the crease along his forehead. I take his hand and lead him back to the stool where I can treat his wound against the light.

"What thoughts, Ryder? Maybe I can help you make sense of them," I say, dousing a cloth with iodine then dabbing it to his skin. I expect a jolt or a hiss, only to remember he feels no pain.

"I want to jump in the ocean, I want to hunt that siren. It's an impossible thought, and yet every fibre of my being calls for me to take action."

I pause as I reach for the bandage. Could it be…no, certainly not. Not from the prince. "Sirens are a threat. When people face something that might cause them harm, they react in two ways. They fight, or they flee. It sounds like your body still wishes to fight, even though the threat has long since passed." That's probably all it is, no deep-seated emotion that speaks to other, more fanciful feelings.

"I see. Interesting," he says quietly, turning his gaze from the water to watch as I tie the knot and secure his bandage. "What about now? Right now, the sense is similar, my body wanting…" He reaches up and touches a hand to my cheek.

I shift back, my own version of fight or flight coming thick and fast and leaning towards the latter. "I don't know, Ryder,"

I lie, busying my hands with gathering the cloths and bits of broken bottle. "Winnie will be bringing the food up soon. We should head outside and wait for them." Yes, we need to go somewhere public, where people are around and a bed isn't in our immediate vicinity.

"Have I offended you?" he asks softly.

Hardly. Everything about him is a lure. The way the dark layers of his hair brush against a strong, rugged and perfectly symmetrical face. The way his eyes shine and seem to bore into my very soul. Even his body and tanned skin are enticing, forged with hard training and in battles fought to defend the isle, every muscle taut and hard and warm.

"No, Ryder. You haven't offended me. Though, if you keep me from a hot meal much longer, I might start taking offence," I say with a weary smile.

The corner of his lips twitch ever so slightly, and for a breath of a second I think he might smile back. I've never seen him smile. I wonder what such a thing might look like on him.

He stands, brushing past me to hold open the door and I sigh as one look at his face tells me the heartless man is back.

WORDS OF WARNING

THIRD SEA

The remainder of the day is spent tending to wounds and cleaning the upper deck of *The Arcana*, the chimera blood and ichor a foul-smelling stain on the once pristine oaken skin of my ship. Even now, when the sun has long since set and a shared exhaustion settles in, nobody leaves when their bellies are full of Winnie's expertly cooked evening meal. Instead, bottles of rum are passed around the table and we each settle under the stars to discuss the bizarre series of recent events.

"I thought harpies were a myth," Winnie whispers with a shiver, as if the words themselves might conjure the beings. "How did you know to choose the cloak?"

"I suppose we can thank Caleb's incessant nagging for that," I say with a sly look his way. "If we hadn't read the book early, I wouldn't have known what to do."

Caleb scratches the back of his head and looks from Winnie to me. "That may be so, but you lost your voice because of that, and the both were seriously hurt. Sorry, Captain," he says ruefully, handing me the bottle of dewberry rum. I take it and shrug my shoulders automatically, regretting the action as a sharp pain ripples through me.

"I'm sorry I lied to you all. It's *my* fault you were hurt," Ansel says softly from the end of the table.

"As fun as it is to watch you lot throw a pity party for yourselves, we *all* contributed to what transpired," I remind them. "At least Ansel is protected from his master's witch now, and my song has been returned, albeit in the most bizarre way."

"That's right!" Winnie shouts, pouting her lips and smacking them together suggestively. "What was it like, kissing a siren?"

"Not as vile or as deadly as I might have imagined," I say truthfully. Beside me, Ryder frowns, lifting his glass and tipping the contents back into his mouth.

"When the sirens attacked, when they took control of my body, I wasn't compelled to kill you," Toriq mentions thoughtfully.

"I know, apparently you wanted to deliver me to them instead." Ansel had said something similar, that the sirens *wanted* me. I look down the table to him now, hoping he might have seen or heard something to explain why the sirens seem intent on my capture.

He fidgets, pulling his hands into his lap and looking away. "I promised you honesty, Captain, and I can honestly say I don't know why they want you."

"But you know *something*." It's not a question because it isn't difficult to detect – despite the relatively cool evening, he's sweating like a priest in a bordello.

"Your origins are...different, Emery," he says reluctantly, as if forcing the words out as he idly plays with the end of his ponytail. "I don't know much, but I know your ancestors come from the Eighth Sea, the sirens' birthplace. Perhaps that has something to do with it?"

Shocked glances are exchanged with Ansel's confession, and I try to steady my breath. "How do you know that?" I ask calmly, tapping a finger on the table.

Ansel sighs and refills his glass before taking a long sip and returning his gaze to mine. "Because my brother is the one who writes your book. I was told to find you, told the exact time, on the exact day and the exact place I was meant to be when we first met." he says softly.

"Seems you know a little more than you thought, Ansel," I bite out, my calm slipping ever so slightly.

"I don't, honest!" he says, reaching over to take my hands. "My brother and I haven't seen each other for over twenty years. The last I heard was his charge had been born, and was forced into hiding because of who he wrote for, because he writes for you. I don't know why and I don't know who wishes him harm. All I know is that when King Phillip told me your name and that of your ship, I knew it was you I was meant to find."

I release a heavy sigh and sip at my drink. More riddles. More questions. Perhaps I should have listened to Marnie and stayed on the Garden Isle, where life was simple, albeit dull.

"I didn't know humans dwelled in the Eighth Sea," Toriq says to break the silence.

"Oh, they do, a whole kingdom of them," Ansel replies wistfully. "It's truly a beautiful place, at least it was, before the sea queen took the throne."

I stand from the table, wobbling slightly from the liquor. I'm too exhausted to absorb this, to analyse it and figure out how it pertains to me and my beginnings. Were my parents born in this kingdom in the Eighth? Are my grandparents still there, alive and well?

"Emery?" Ryder asks softly when I fail to move or speak.

"We should all get some rest. Considering Ansel's

predilection for half-truths, I can only assume there's some form of trouble to find at Beggars' Cove." My words come with a harsh snap and Ansel drops his head dejectedly. Ignoring the guilt, I bid them all goodnight and head for my quarters, closing and locking the door behind me.

A knock comes shortly after and I don't respond, just wait for whoever it is to tell me their business.

"Make sure you take your second dose," Ryder's voice drifts through the wood, followed by his footsteps walking away.

For once I feel somewhat in tune with Ryder, confused by the turmoil of raging emotions. I'm furious with Ansel for keeping this from me, yet I understand why he did. I want more from the genie, more than he has to give, more than he feels he's able. After undressing, I take the antidote from the desk and swallow it in one, grimacing at the taste but appreciating its sobering effect as I crawl into bed.

Even the vexing questions are unable to compete with my exhaustion, and soon enough I quickly fall into a deep sleep, dreaming of red riding cloaks, and a kingdom made from frozen starlight, hidden beyond the cliffs in the Eighth Sea.

I WAKE to find the sun has long since risen above the windows of my cabin and nobody has come to get me. Peeling back the covers from my sweat drenched body, I groan at the throbbing ache in my shoulder and pray to whoever might listen that we find a healer once we make port. Dressed in one of my last clean shirts and breeches, I tug my favourite red leather boots onto each foot, and try to tame my hair into a respectable plait over my good shoulder. Deciding my appearance is as good as it's likely to get after weeks at sea with fitful rest and nowhere to properly bathe, I leave my quarters to check on the others.

Winnie is the first I see, and after saying good afternoon, she hurries to the galley to fetch me some breakfast and cocoa. Caleb and even Toriq break from their training and wave their hellos from across the deck. I wave back and head for the helm to find Ryder sitting on the bench with the captain's log open on his lap.

"Why didn't anyone come and wake me?" I ask him, checking our position before collecting the spyglass from the table.

"We all agreed you needed the rest more than we did," he says, looking up from the log. "Have you read the next page of the book?"

I flounder slightly, surprised I had completely forgotten about it. "No, not yet. I'll get it once Winnie brings up breakfast." Opening the spyglass, I look towards the bow. A sliver of land shimmers in the distance, peeking over the heatwave on the water.

"It's Beggars' Cove. We passed Hangman's Knot early this morning," Ryder says, anticipating my question.

"We've made good time. I didn't expect to hit the island until this evening." At this speed we'll dock by mid-afternoon. This is good news, meaning we can find an inn and settle before the light fades.

"Breakfast, Captain," Winnie calls from below.

I tell her I'll be there in a moment and turn back to where Ryder is watching me. "Are you coming down to read the next page?" I ask.

"You're sharing it with everyone?"

"As long as you all sail on my ship, I feel you each have a right to any information it might offer."

He nods his head in agreement and returns the log to sit

beside the wheel, then follows me down and goes to gather the others while I retrieve the book.

Once we're all settled, I sip at my cocoa and lay the tome flat on the table so everyone can see, then flip the catch and turn to the fourth page, curious if the warning remains. It does, though an additional sentence is written at the bottom, reading:

~ *Well Done* ~

Ansel smiles and mumbles something under his breath as he reads the line, then looks up, eager for me to turn to the next. Not wanting to wait another moment, I flip to the fifth page, and everyone hushes as we read the verse together.

> *After days and days of battles and rhymes,*
> *the girl with blue eyes is forced to resign.*
> *With the ghost of a kiss, she can finally sing,*
> *but it does her no good with the Beggar King.*
> *The ship is distressed, her wounds left agape,*
> *our girl has no choice but to barter and shake.*
> *Remember your marbles, let them fall to the ground,*
> *so that when you are lost, you soon will be found.*
>
> *Hello brother, I've missed you these years.*
> *Guide our queen well, she will conquer your fears.*

~ *FOUR DAYS* ~

A soft sob breaks past Ansel's lips, and he holds a hand to his mouth as he reads the last lines of the verse. I want to embrace him, and at the same time relentlessly interrogate the man. Ansel had given me marbles on the first day of our voyage, telling me to keep them close.

"Ansel, why did you give me marbles?" I ask, keeping my voice as even as possible. The others look up, each well aware of his deception in the past.

"Here we go again," Toriq mumbles, turning in his chair to face Ansel.

"*He* told me to, it was the last thing my brother said to me," Ansel says pointing to the book and leaning away from Toriq's increasingly suspicious glare.

"And did he happen to tell you *why* he wanted me to have the marbles?" I ask. Trying to get any information from the man is like asking a stone to play chess. Pointless and disappointing. I had hoped we were past this now, that he would be willing to share whatever little morsels he felt might be useful.

"I've told you everything I can, Emery," Ansel whispers.

I sigh and pick up my mug, taking a long sip of the hot cocoa before looking again to Ansel. "You must understand our reservations. I'm convinced you know more than you're telling us."

Ansel smiles sadly and says, "I do know more, but I give you what I can. You must know I would never wish to see harm come to you." He leans across the table and takes the book in his hand, his fingers trailing over the puzzling rhymes. "My brother risks a lot by giving you as much as he does. It's why he writes his warnings in riddles."

"Where is the risk? Who do the genies answer to?" Winnie asks quietly with a cautious look to the sky.

Ansel shakes his head and places the book back down. This is all he will give, though it's easy to see how desperately he wants to tell us the rest, to tell us who writes the laws of the genies, and who they all answer to for breaking those laws.

"Thank you, Ansel, that will do," I say, smiling softly. His shoulders slump and the tension seeps away. This is the very reason he ran from his master, for knowing too much and giving only what he was able. I won't be the cause of his distress, not when I consider that what we glean from Ansel and the book is already so much more than any average sailor.

"What about the rest of the verse?" Winnie asks as she spins the book to face her. "From the sounds of it, we're going to meet a king of beggars and be forced to barter with him."

"It's *this* line that concerns me," Caleb says quietly as he trails his finger over the verse. "It sounds like you're going to lose your way at some point, Captain, hence the marbles."

"You're not to wander off by yourself when we reach the isle, Emery," Ryder says, the command in his tone unmistakable.

I drag a hand down my face, calming my rising irritation. "I'm not some errant child, *Ryder*, I'm your captain."

"And I'm your protector, so you *will* do this, you *will* keep at least one of us by your side at all times."

It doesn't go amiss that the others seem to hold their breath as they glance back and forth between us, unsure who to back in the battle between their captain and their prince. I glare openly at Ryder, who proceeds to stare calmly back.

"We're just a little concerned for you," Winnie says gently. "First the sirens, now this beggar king and a warning that you might lose your way...I'd like to stay with you, if you'll allow it?" Winnie places a hand gently over mine and I immediately soften.

"I have no intention of wandering off on my own, and I have *every* intention of taking the necessary precautions." I look at Winnie and catch her victory grin. "*Winnie's* company I can tolerate, *yours* not so much," I say pointedly to Ryder.

My half-hearted insult rolls off his shoulders with the shrug he gives in return. "Winnie is an adept fighter. She will do well enough to guard you when I cannot."

"Don't I know it," Caleb says, the admiration clear in the soft way he looks at her now. "From the bits I can remember during the siren attack, she's a firecracker with a blade."

We each laugh at Winnie's humble embarrassment as her cheeks flame and she takes my roll of hard bread and chucks it at him.

Taking the book, I close it and secure the clasp. There were several warnings in this verse, so much to unpack and prepare ourselves for. So much temptation. Without a second's thought, I hand the book to Ansel.

"Captain?" he asks, slowly taking it.

"Against my better judgement, I'm already tempted to peek, to see what Beggars' Cove has in store for us. I won't risk losing my song again, not when we have so many more days at sea ahead of us."

Ansel's brows rise and cheeks dimple as he smiles with an almost fatherly pride. At least with this I know I can trust the genie. The love he has for his brother will serve me well with my scribe's instructions for Ansel to guide me. I believe when it comes to the book, he will do just that.

CITY IN THE SAND

BEGGARS' COVE

With the sails lowered, *The King's Arcana* glides seamlessly towards the worn and crowded docks of Beggars' Cove. From the name alone I had certain expectations, ones of a barren land devoid of life and hope. From the helm I see quite the opposite as I peer out across the flotilla of ships, some moored to the long line of docks, others anchored just offshore in the inlet.

The port itself is rampant with activity, people bustling from the ships with crates of goods, while others clean and polish the decks and balustrades. But beyond that, past the long seawall and towering entrance to the harbour, a city made of clay and sandstone sits idly in an open desert.

There is life here, life in the music that carries on the wind from a festive city in the sand, and in the faces of those at the dock already awaiting the newest ship's arrival. I reach behind and turn the thrusters to slow our approach, timing it perfectly as we come to a stop at our mooring.

"One gold to moor for a day, five for seven days, Captain," a young boy calls from below.

I lean over the side and request a lease for seven days,

unsure how long it might take to tend to *The Arcana's* broken hull.

The boy nods and hurries back the way he came to relay the order to the harbour master, while I head to my quarters to collect my purse for payment. By the time I make it back to the main deck, the dockhands are diligently securing a ramp to the ship and the boy has returned with a much older man who ambles up the ramp and holds out his hand expectantly as he peers over his comically large spectacles.

"Do you have repairs below the water-line?" The old man asks, counting each of the coins and going so far as to bite one experimentally.

"Yes, do you have a dry dock?" I ask.

The old man bobs his head as he scribbles on his parchment and hands me a promissory of lease for the ship's mooring. "We do indeed. Should be free in an hour or so." With one wrinkled, bony finger, he shifts his glasses down his nose and glances around the ship, shaking his head at the various stains of blood and black tar. "I assume you'll be wanting her serviced too, that'll be ten gold altogether."

"Ten!?" I stutter. *Beggars' Cove* my ass, more like Pirate's Snare.

"That's fine," Ryder says, stepping forward and removing ten gold coins from a very full purse. He hands them over to the harbour master who smiles a toothy grin in return. When I look up questioningly, Ryder leans over and whispers the king's name in my ear, reminding me of his father's wish to pay for whatever we might need on our journey.

"The boy here will take you to Wayland Square where you'll find the carpenters and blacksmiths. They're a devilish lot, but they'll tend to your ship well enough," the old man says with a wave as he hobbles over the ramp.

"What about the chimera, Captain?" Winnie asks quietly as she points to the barrels.

"I'm sure there will be someone in the city who wants them. Leave them where they are for now. Is everyone packed and cabins locked?" Each nod their heads and indicate to the bags gathered by the main mast. "Ansel, have you taken care of your charge?"

"Yes, Captain," he says, knowing I speak of the book and cautious of saying more around the boy.

Picking up my travel pack, I ask the dockhand to lead the way, telling him we'll need safe lodgings for the next seven days as well. He excitably suggests a tavern run by his uncle, situated in the city's central quarter.

Having never travelled to the isle and unsure where might be best for us to stay, I motion for Ansel to follow along beside me as we step from *The Arcana* onto the dock. As he and the boy fall into easy conversation, I'm afforded the chance to take in my surroundings.

Back home on the Garden Isle, the docks would be quiet and sleepy. Other than the king's fleet, kept tucked away on the western side of the island, we only had three boats to boast of and small towns filled with locals who are born, raised and die having never ventured farther than the Barnacle Cliffs. Here is different, it's a traveller's island, a place where people come from far and wide to settle or trade or perhaps just in passing. As we approach the sea wall and towering harbour entrance, the sounds, sights and smells speak of an eclectic mix of cultures from across the eight seas.

I look up as we pass beneath the sandstone arch, then into a bustling city with buildings seeming to rise from the sands themselves, each pale and golden, but not dull. Long cotton verandas spanning over alleyways and shopfronts dazzle the eye in a rainbow of colours.

I jump to the side as a horse and cart barrels past and onwards up the high street with barely a thought for those in the driver's way. Another follows soon after, a steady stream of the isle's incoming and outgoing goods to and from the port. Ansel had been right, this is probably our best bet to repair *The Arcana* and to obtain whatever it is we need.

"This way, Cap," the young boy says, beckoning for me to join the others. It's difficult to pay attention to any singular thing as we're led from one alley to the next. I watch, mesmerised, as we're guided into a square with belly dancers performing to a quartet of musicians, then into another, smaller square with drunken gamblers trying to pick a fight.

"Stay close, Emery," Ryder whispers as he steps around, putting himself between me and the brawlers.

I would roll my eyes and tell the prince to lighten up, but the further we walk from the city centre, the more his protectiveness becomes warranted. Beggars' Cove indeed. The further west the boy leads us towards the city limits, the smaller the houses become, more dilapidated and decayed with an obvious lack of wealth. As we exit yet another alley, I almost tumble over the legs of an older man lying in the street with barely a rag to his body. I stop beside him and reach for my purse, wondering how the others could so easily walk by without a care.

"Stop," Ryder says, taking my leather wallet and tucking it into the pocket of his trousers. He takes my arm and pulls me along, past more and more unfortunate, homeless families forced to find shelter from the sun under ripped verandas and crumbling homes.

"Why wouldn't you let me give him something?" I ask, more confused than annoyed.

"Look around you," he says, keeping his gaze trained ahead.

That's exactly what I'm doing, and the more I look, the more I wish I had to give. "What's your point?"

"Can you offer them *all* what you offer to one? Because

that's what they will expect. I've seen poverty like this, Emery. It's dangerous." He stops and points to a young girl standing at the end of an alley, her hands held out for coins. "Stay here, and watch."

Not wanting to lose the others, I whistle to get Winnie's attention and she turns, stopping the others in the street. Staying where I am as instructed, I watch Ryder cross an open market and head for the alley. Taking my purse from his pocket, he stops by the girl and leans against the wall, exchanging words with her, then hands over the purse. She bows her head gratefully and slips it under her thin tunic, then turns to Ryder and exchanges more words. He pats his pocket and holds his hands in a visual gesture that he has no more to give. Then, the most unexpected thing happens next.

I call out a warning as a boy approaches Ryder from behind, a dagger clutched in his two small hands. Ryder turns at the last second and grips the child by the throat, knocking the blade from his hand and then throwing him into the young girl. Both land in a heap on the floor, then scramble to their feet, each baring an angry snarl before linking hands and racing down the alley and out of sight.

Barely fazed by the somewhat horrifying interaction, Ryder saunters back to stand beside me with a look of warning. "Where one beggar stands, another is close behind," is all he says, taking my hand and leading me away.

Still a little flabbergasted by the children's actions, I barely think to respond when Winnie asks what we were doing.

"I was demonstrating the risk of handing out coins to beggars," Ryder explains.

Winnie nods her head, her mouth stretched in a thin line. "It's true, you have to be careful in places like this. I'm all for helping those in need, but a little caution is advised."

I hate that. Perhaps growing up in a place where crime

and true poverty is non-existent has made me a little naive in this regard. I *will* heed their warning, but I don't have to like it very much.

I follow along in silence, partly concerned I might slip up and highlight my inept understanding of the wider world's issues, partly because seeing these people in such a state of disrepair is twisting my gut.

"Here we are!" the boy calls jovially from the front. He's clearly used to this side of the city, though not born from it, if his tailored shirt and trousers are anything to go by.

"Why don't you hang around a bit and show us the way back to your uncle's tavern when we're done?" I ask, my confidence clearly shaken as I look to the others for any sign of having suggested wrongly.

Winnie nods encouragingly my way and the boy grins at my offer, settling himself on a short stone wall outside what I expect is a blacksmith's forge.

"I'll be right here," he says and then points across the road. "You'll find Monty over there by the stables, he's the best carpenter on the island."

I thank him and head across the smoky square to where horses and donkeys are confined to surprisingly spacious stalls. Beside that, a forge blazes heartily and a bladesmith hammers away at the beginnings of a broad sword. Beside that we stop at the first door in a long line of murky, glass-fronted shops, where a sign reads: *Master Monty ~ Carpenter*.

A bell dings above as I open the door into an open room, the uneven floorboards cluttered with lopsided tables. After a moment of waiting, curiosity drives me forward to where layers of parchment lie on one of tabletops, each featuring drawings of clever inventions or a ship's blueprint.

"What language?" a deep voice calls out.

I turn to where a young man has appeared by the back door, his frame oddly wiry with an obvious muted strength in the taut muscles of his bare forearms. Taking a rag from a line of hooks, he wipes the stains of blue dye from each hand and stares back at me expectantly.

"Second Sea," I say quickly, thankfully the main and most common language used across the eight. "But I know a little of the Fourth's tongue too if you prefer?"

"Not at all, Second Sea I can speak, my Fourth and Fifth are rusty at best. How can I help?"

"My ship is in need of extensive repairs to the hull. Are you Monty, the carpenter?"

"I am. What's the damage? Canon fire?"

"Shallows. The entire hull will need tending to," I say woefully.

Monty shakes his head, the hair from his messy bun falling loose to sit across his shoulders as he walks across the room to a long, oak desk. Pulling open one of the drawers, he proceeds to take out a book and flips through the pages.

"Sounds like a big job, I won't be able to fit you in for at least fourteen days from today." He closes the log and takes a seat on the chair before resting his arms on the desk. "Unless, that is, you can make it worth my while to bump you up the queue?"

I smile, already expecting such a deal to be brought up. "I leased a dry dock for seven days and I want the ship sea-ready before then. How much do you want?"

"Hard to know without seeing the lady and assessing the damage. I have a bit of time now if you want to take me to her?"

I'm eager for the others to get to the tavern and settle in, it's been a long couple of weeks at sea and they could do with the rest. "Ryder and I will take you." I turn to address the others. "Ask the boy to take you three to the tavern, then tell him to come and collect us from the docks," I tell Winnie.

She seems unsure, likely thinking back to my earlier

promise to stick by her side. She exchanges a look with Ryder, a motherly request to take care. He seems to understand and nods his acceptance, then the four turn to leave.

"Something troubling you, Captain? Most crews that dock here can't wait to go their separate ways," Monty says as he strokes his chin.

I pace about the room, stopping by another table with pages of engineering plans. After a moment of inspecting them, I turn back to Monty, who remains relaxed in his chair. "Shall we go? I'd like to conclude our business for the day."

Monty smiles and holds his arms wide as if to say, what's the hurry? He's young, certainly no older than I am, but his confidence speaks of years living amongst cut-throats and con artists. This is probably why my look of irritation only serves to amuse him further.

With a grin, he stands and tucks several notes under his arm before brushing past me and through the front door of the shop. Ryder and I follow closely as he leads us back to the docks down different alleys, ones cleaner and less derelict than the others.

"I suppose you haven't been here before then?" Monty asks, turning to walk backwards. "I'm sure I'd remember if you had."

I raise a brow at the younger man's wink. "In a city this big, I doubt that. Some of us have been here though," I mumble, offering no more.

"I see," is all he says, then turns to face forward as we enter the harbour.

After several long words with the harbour master, Monty confirms that the dry dock is free and accompanies us on *The King's Arcana* as we navigate her to the far end of the harbour. From there, I gently pilot the ship into a special siding before the gates are closed behind us and the water pumped out, leaving *The Arcana* naked on long trestles with all her wounds on show. It's the first I've seen this ship out of water, and I can't help but grimace as we descend the ladder to the dock, where I can truly assess the damage to her hull.

"What the blazes have you done to her?" Monty whispers. Walking the length of the pontoon, he drags his hand along *The Arcana's* belly, then ducks and gasps at the state of the keel. "This is a lot of work to do in such a short amount of time."

I cringe inwardly, though manage to keep my face neutral. "I imagine you're capable enough, and I need it finished as soon as possible. If I had the tools, I would do the repairs myself and be done with it in two days."

Monty looks doubtful but regards the ship once again. "I can have it done in three if I bump you ahead of the others. Let's call it an even hundred gold."

I nearly choke on my tongue. I expected it to be expensive, but that's double my original estimate.

I'm about to negotiate, but Ryder steps forward and offers his hand to shake and seal the deal. "Fifty now, fifty when the job is done," he says.

Monty's eyes widen in surprise. He, too, had probably expected at least a little resistance to his robbery. He steps back and again scratches the short stubble on his chin as he continues his assessment of the ship. "As you seem to be a couple with...respectfully deep pockets, I could line the hull with a protective layer as well," he says, inspecting one of the deeper gashes in the ship's belly. "For an additional fee, of course."

"Of course," I mutter.

"What sort of protection?" Ryder asks.

"I can apply a layer of metallic sheeting. It might take an additional day, but she'll stand against any shallows, and even canon fire, to an extent."

"Is it heavy?" I've never heard of such a thing, but I think back to the carpenter's drawings in his shop, of the blue-prints and cleverness of his designs.

"Not at all, it's light weight but extremely durable," Monty assures me.

"How much?" Ryder asks.

"Another hundred."

"Do it."

I look between Ryder and Monty as they shake, a little annoyed that I wasn't consulted first. Though I must admit, I'm curious to see what the young man can do, plus Ryder is paying, so I don't complain.

With the fee settled at two-hundred now, Ryder rummages around his travel bag and pulls out two full purses. After counting off the agreed amount, he takes one half and hands over the rest.

"Half now, half when the job is done," I tell Monty. "You have four days."

Monty offers a low bow and tucks the heavy wallet into the deep lining of his trousers, then shoos us away so he can get to work.

A DANGEROUS RUMOUR

BEGGARS' COVE

Thieves' Lair…that's the name of our inn. I stare up at the wooden sign cast in lamplight as Ryder hands our young guide a coin for his efforts. Why can't we stay someplace with a nicer name? Somewhere like, Rum Central, or Safe Haven?…Thieves' Lair is just asking for trouble.

With a sigh, I follow Ryder through the tavern's open door, and the gnawing concern in my gut quietens a little.

A thin veil of smoke hangs lazily on the air, a sweet smell emanating from the right side of the room. I focus in on a lonely group there, each splayed out lazily on two long, leather daybeds in front of a stone-built fireplace. Despite the rows of seating along that side of the room, they're the only ones to reside, everyone else seeming to keep their distance.

A woman with short, dark hair sits in the company of three men, her slender legs crossed one over the other as she idly admires the dancing flames and crackling logs. Raising a long, golden smoking pipe to her lips, a silver bangle reflects the soft light.

"Pirates," I whisper, recognising the silver band welded

forever in place on their wrists. Somewhere on that silver cuff will be the crest or banner of their captain, a totem denoting their loyalty.

The woman glances my way and I turn to study the left side of the tavern, where an open arch leads to the watering hole, a place away from the snug where customers can sit to eat and drink.

A familiar voice echoes from within, around the corner and out of sight. Curious, I leave Ryder to sort our rooms, while I investigate the noise.

"Captain!" Winnie cries, rising from a table at the far end of the crowded bar. Toriq looks up and offers a solitary nod, while Caleb, already inebriated, holds up a tankard and waves it around, gesturing for me to join them.

"Later," I call over the din, waving back and smiling as Winnie purses her lips in a petulant pout.

I return to Ryder waiting by the foot of the stairs, and together we follow behind the attendant asked to show us to our rooms. At the top of the first floor, the old man points to a door at the far end of the corridor, hands me a key, and then leaves. Just one key.

"Where's your room?" I ask Ryder.

"We're sharing."

"No we bloody are not," I stutter, holding the key defensively to my chest. "Go get your own room."

"This is the last they have. We can go somewhere else tomorrow when it's light." Plucking the key from my hand, he brushes past me and opens the door. Inside we're greeted by garish green wallpaper slightly peeling from the corners, but the room is surprisingly spacious, with simple furnishings and a deep, standalone copper bathtub. But only one bed.

"And where exactly do *you* plan to sleep?" I ask, raising one eyebrow questioningly.

He points to the double-bed. "You're small, so we should both fit comfortably enough."

"I'm not *small*," I mutter, mildly affronted. But that's hardly the issue here. I don't want to share a bed with Ryder...at least the sensible part of me doesn't.

"You should bathe," he says as he drops his pack on the worn, wooden floor then heads for the tub. The taps squeal with protest as he starts the water and I expect him to leave to allow me to undress. He straightens and turns, his eyebrows pinching together when he finds I've made no effort to remove my clothes.

"First of all, it's rude to imply a lady smells," I say, lifting a hand to rub my temple. "And secondly, how about a little privacy?"

He considers this for a moment as he looks to the door. Below, the sound of laughter filters through the floorboards, followed by grunts and smashing glass.

"I'm not leaving, but I'll turn around if that makes you more comfortable?"

I stare back, a little staggered by his boldness. I open my mouth, then close it, deciding it's hardly worth the argument. Twirling my finger and coughing suggestively, the prince takes my hint and turns to sit on the bed as I hurriedly strip my clothes and step into the near scalding tub. Careful not to wet my bandages, I sink as low as possible, groaning as my muscles begin to relax and the salt and filth washes away.

"That's...pleasurable?" Ryder asks softly, curiously.

I lean my head back, closing my eyes and lapping the water over my chest. *Orgasmic* is a better word for what I'm feeling, but being alone with a man in my room, a man I'm sore to admit conjures more than a little desire, that particular word feels somewhat dangerous. "It's...nice," I say instead.

Ryder shifts on the bed, rolling onto his back. I'm about to tell him off, but his eyes are sealed shut, honouring his promise not to peek.

"Is it the heat that pleasures you?" he asks.

The deep lilt of his voice is so close, and more words spring to mind, more thoughts and imaginings, things I really shouldn't be thinking. I grit my teeth. "Shush, you're ruining my bath."

I glance up when he remains quiet, and my breath falters. Ryder's eyes are open, and he makes no move to pretend he isn't staring, instead interlinking both hands behind his head. His gaze leaves mine, and my body ignites as his eyes slowly travel down, over my shoulders, my breasts...

He frowns when he's forced to stop there, my position in the bath preventing him from seeing more. I grip the side of the tub and wince, the muscles in my injured shoulder tensing. Ryder rolls from the bed and crosses the room before I can voice my objection. I try to sink deeper in the water, moving my hands to cover the private areas of my body.

"Don't," he says softly, catching my wrist. "I want to see."

Good sense tells me to protest, begs me to send him away. But I don't. He releases my hand to hang loosely over the side, then moves slowly to stand behind me. Leaning over my shoulder, he captures my other wrist and pulls it from the water to grip the side instead, baring me completely.

"This is beauty," he whispers in my ear. "It...stirs something in me." He kneels behind my head, his breath fanning along my neck and drawing goosebumps as his hands trail across my skin, careful to avoid the wounds as they wander down.

"Ryder..." The word is barely a breath, and I close my eyes, a whispered moan escaping my lips as his fingers graze my nipples.

The door to our room bursts open and I shriek, trying to cover my chest as something close to a growl rips from Ryder's throat. Caleb freezes, immediately registering my position in the bath, and Ryder who stands and moves to block me from view.

"Sorry, Cap. I didn't realise you were bathing, *or* that you had...company," Caleb stutters. Behind the looming mass of Ryder, I can't see our intruder's expression, but he sounds more amused than remorseful.

"That's why people knock," I say through gritted teeth. "Out! Both of you!" Ryder turns to face me, and I jab a finger towards the door. "Now!"

He hesitates a moment longer, a rare look of anger slowing fading from his eyes. Finally, he turns and leaves, pushing Caleb out ahead of him before pulling the door closed behind him.

The warmth seems to flee in Ryder's absence, and I sink lower in the tub, taking my time to rub the goosebumps puckering the skin on each arm. I've never been one to run from my problems and bury my head in the sand, but I'm strongly considering bunking with Winnie tonight...

"Coward," I mutter. Standing from the tub, I pull the plug and walk to where my bag is resting on the bed. Pulling out the last of my clean shirts and breeches, I put them to one side and wander around the room naked, letting the cool air filter in through the open window and calm the remnants of Ryder's touch. I need to get a grip. Malka's warning squawks alongside the harpy in my head like a maniacal bird.

Heartless man.

Death.

A kiss can break the curse.

I want to kiss him. I want to do *more* than that. But at what cost? One little kiss doesn't mean I'm destined to fall in love with the man...but it won't end with just a kiss. I know that. Nakedness will follow.

With a shake of my head, I quickly dry myself and start to dress. I'm hungry, that's all it is. Some mead and a bit of food and my senses will almost certainly return.

Liar.

Once suitably dressed, I open the door to find Ryder sitting on the floor with his back against the opposite wall of the corridor. He looks up, the glow from a lantern above his head casting a shadow over his face. Is he brooding? Perhaps it's just the light...I don't stop to dwell on it, instead locking the door and making my way to the stairs.

As Ryder and I enter the bar, several men burst into song, only stopping to down their tankards and call for another. Towards the back appears just as crowded, though slightly quieter with patrons chatting amongst themselves. One table in particular steals my attention, where a woman sits bathed in a cloud of smoke billowing from a golden pipe tucked between her two, ruby red lips.

I glance to the left, where Winnie, Toriq and Caleb reside in the same spot I'd seen them earlier...at a table uncomfortably close to the pirates.

Winnie looks up as I push my way past drunken patrons. "You both missed the last call for supper, so we had to order for you," she says, pulling out a chair for me to sit in, then pushing one bowl to me and then another to Ryder as he takes an empty seat beside me.

Caleb tries to catch my eye as I glance around the room, all the while smiling mischievously. "Where's Ansel?" I ask when I fail to find the genie amongst the throng of customers at the bar.

Toriq drains the last of his soup and answers the question before Caleb has a chance. "He retired early and said he'll meet us down here for breakfast."

That makes sense I suppose. The genie is a bundle of nerves, so I doubt dining in a crowd of likely ruffians would sit well with him. Smiling, I take the spoon and hungrily work my way through the cold stew, not caring that it's tasteless and overcooked. Before long I've drained the contents and move straight to the mead, taking several hearty glugs before noticing the others are staring.

"Bloody hell, you were hungry," Winnie says with a giggle. "Does that have anything to do with what Caleb walked in on?"

My cheeks flame and I shift a glare to the fair-haired gossiper.

Caleb laughs and stands unsteadily from the table as he holds up his empty tankard. "Next round is on me!"

"Nothing happened," I mutter when Winnie continues to stare my way with a wicked grin.

Ryder, thankfully, has the good sense to say nothing of what *almost* happened, and with that thought I'm grateful Caleb had interrupted when he did. I catch the frown on Toriq's face and find I'm in no mood for his judgement.

"What?" I ask him.

"I don't understand. How does he..." Toriq looks to Ryder and leans over the table, lowering his voice. "What about your curse? I thought you couldn't feel?"

Ryder eases back in the chair and lifts his glass. "I'm still cursed, and I *can't* feel." He seems prepared to leave it at that, then turns his stare to me. "Except for Emery. Something about her...scratches."

How lovely, I make the prince itchy. "That's curiosity, Ryder. You should take note, and avoid it," I say glumly.

Caleb returns to the table with three tankards in each hand, all frothing and spilling over the top. He hands two to me, insisting I have some catching up to do, and for once I'm inclined to agree. Draining the last of my first tankard, I take up the second and raise it, asking to what we should toast.

"To friendship?" Winnie suggests sweetly.

Caleb stands and holds out his drink. "To our captain, for sailing us through Marooners' Canal in one piece."

I chuckle, embarrassed but pleased with his choice, and we each raise our drinks in good spirit to finish the toast.

"Did I hear that right? You came through Marooners' Canal?" The woman, the pirate I'd seen with the smoking pipe, turns and leans back in her chair to regard us.

"Damn right, there's no finer captain than ours," Caleb boasts, smacking a hand against my back. Suddenly registering who it is that's spoken, his eyes fall shamelessly on the exposed tops of the woman's breasts.

The pirate smiles, revealing a silver tooth that shines against skin so white, she could be sculpted from snow. We all watch curiously as she stands from her chair, curling a loose strand of short, coal black hair behind her ear, then turns and proceeds to straddle the seat, giving me her full attention.

"I'm impressed," she says, looking back to the men at her table. "Not many ships survive that passage, what with it being a siren lair."

"Not many at all. How did you do it?" a voice asks from behind her.

I glance behind the woman to who had spoken and find several, male dwarves, most of them heavily muscled and sporting beards or a well-kempt goatee. While my own crew has proven themselves time and again, I'm a little envious of the woman and her companions. Coming from an isle of frozen tundras and palaces carved from ice, these men are renowned for both their seafaring skills and their mines – laden with jewels supposedly guarded by large, winged beasts. I've never believed that last part myself, but I've seen their maritime skills first hand.

"It's her voice, it scares them off," Caleb says in answer to the dwarf's question. "Go on, Cap. Sing!" He yelps as Winnie wraps a fist in his shirt and tugs him back down onto the seat beside her, before she looks worriedly from me to the woman.

"My ship has a double mast and thrusters fitted to the stern. She's fast," I say, hoping my explanation will placate the woman and she'll leave it at that.

She narrows her eyes, leaning further forward in her chair. "Your companion wishes you to sing, and I'm curious myself. Won't you oblige a fellow captain?"

Not just a pirate, but a pirate *captain*. Damn. "My crewmate is drunk. Trust me, my voice is nothing special." I take a long drink of the mead, my gaze steadily remaining on hers.

The woman twists a strand of the dark hair and pouts prettily; her lips dyed a bloody crimson. "So, you *don't* know the siren song then? The one supposedly used by witches to repel the loathsome creatures?"

I cut a warning look to Caleb as he opens his mouth to say something, but Winnie clamps a hand over his lips and prevents the words from forming. Nevertheless, the damage is done as he nods his heads and looks at me adoringly, clearly too drunk to understand.

"Oh, *that* song?" I say, trying to make light of it. "Sure, I know it. Not very effective though." The last thing I want to do is offend a pirate captain on our first night, especially with *The King's Arcana* in the state that she is and no means of escaping the island. My crew is capable in a fight, but for all I know, the woman's crew could outnumber mine.

"I find that difficult to believe, especially as you made it so easily through Marooners' Canal," she says with a predatory grin.

"Like I said, it wasn't effective. We got through that passage using explosives and speed." It wasn't a lie; my voice had been cursed at the time.

"Sing for me," she coos.

I stare back at the green-eyed captain and her crew of dwarves waiting eagerly for me to acquiesce. Here, in a tavern full of people, a feeling of dread settles in the pit of my stomach. The siren song is no secret, there's a small number of captains like myself with the gift to repel the creatures, or so I had been told by the sisters.

Still, the way this woman is staring at me – like I'm a prize pig ready for slaughter – something doesn't sit right. "Maybe another day when I haven't had so much to drink. Captain to captain, I'm sure you wouldn't want me to embarrass myself in front of my crew." I raise the tankard to my lips and down the last dregs. It's a challenge, and her narrowing eyes have determined as much.

She stands from her chair and plants one leather-booted foot on the seat as she raises her glass. "Tomorrow then, we shall all dance to the siren song!" she calls.

Everyone in the room turns and lifts whatever drink they have in a drunken, celebratory salute. With a wink to me, she returns her chair to sit amongst her crew without a backward glance.

"You bloody idiot!" Winnie hisses softly as she tugs at Caleb's ear. "Now look what you've done."

Caleb chuckles and holds his ear, looking from Winnie to me with a look of bemusement. "What? Am I not allowed to boast about my captain?" he asks.

I groan and push the empty tankard to the side. "I'd rather you don't talk about me at all, Caleb. Especially not around pirates."

"Pirates? They're not pirates," he says with a scoff.

I tap my wrist then point to the other table. He follows

my finger, looking to the woman's wrist as she holds a hand of cards in the air and slams them on the table in victory. His face drains of colour when he registers the silver band.

"Idiot," Winnie mumbles again as Caleb turns back and begins a steady stream of apologies.

I lean forward and lower my voice against the din. "Keep your wits about you. I'm not bothered if you get rip-roaring drunk when you're not expected to sail, but our business will stay exactly that – *our* business. Understand?"

Caleb, Toriq, Winnie and Ryder each nod their heads solemnly, and with my mood soured, I decide to head to my room. Ryder stands to follow me up, and I place a hand on his chest. "You can stay with Toriq tonight."

He looks at me and shakes his head. "No. As I said before, you are not to be alone while we remain on this island."

It takes everything in me to suppress a growl. For a heartless man, he sure knows how to induce irritation. Winnie chuckles and offers to stay with me in Ryder's place, but I feel I'll be setting a dangerous precedent if I bend to the prince's whims tonight.

"Thank you, Winnie, but no. I will be staying in my own room, by myself, under lock and key with a dagger under my pillow. I have no need for company, and certainly no need for a protector tonight." I turn to Ryder and tell him he may come to my room and collect his bag, then turn and leave. The funny thing about a look of confusion, is that it looks achingly similar to hurt or anger. From the way Ryder's gaze had drifted to the floor, he'd appeared hurt by my rejection.

He follows close behind, up the stairs and down the corridor, then waits as I fumble with the key to my door. I'm a little tipsy, the main reason for wanting to stay on my own tonight – the more you drink the worse your decisions become, hence I rarely allow myself more than I can deal with.

As we enter, Ryder closes the door and moves to the bed where he left his bag. "Why won't you allow me to stay with you?" he asks, hefting the sack over his shoulder. "The book warns of danger."

"Well, it doesn't say I'll be attacked in my bed, and I've yet to see any sign of a beggar king in our midst," I say waving my arms to indicate the empty room. Feeling a little dizzy I take a seat on the bed and hold my head in my hands.

"Emery..." Ryder kneels before me and places a hand on my thigh, then tucks his finger under my chin, tilting it up so I'm forced to look at him. "Let me stay with you tonight."

I shake my head. "No, Ryder. The warnings from the book aren't the only ones I need to consider, and I don't trust myself with you."

"What warnings?" he asks, something perilously close to concern and anger flashing behind those green eyes. "If you're in danger you need to tell me. Let me stay with you."

There it is again, that hurt, etched in the creases around his eyes. I could tell him about Malka's prophecy, about my heartless future lover, my killer. If I tell him, then I'm admitting to the fact that I have feelings for Ryder. I'm not ready to confess such a thing...not yet.

I stare down at him, at the way he kneels before me, a prince bending before a simple seafarer. I stare at his lips, full and entirely too enticing. "I'm confident your curse can be broken with a kiss, Ryder. But at what cost?"

"You think there's a cost to this?" he asks placing a finger to my lower lip.

I close my eyes and breathe in the scent of him. Despite days at sea, he has somehow managed to smell tolerably good, just his usual pine scent mixed with sea salt. "There's always a cost to that," I say, taking his hand in mine. "I can't be your curse breaker, Ryder. Not yet, not until I figure some things out. For now, there's too much risk to me."

"You keep saying that, but I fail to see what you mean." He stands before me and steps closer, dropping his bag and running his fingers through my hair. "I want you, Emery. I've never wanted for anything, but this...this is different." He lifts one knee and places it between my legs to rest on the mattress, one hand gently pushing my shoulders down until my back rests against the soft bedding.

"Wait," I say, the single word half-hearted and barely a whisper.

"You're touched by magic, Emery. Your entire body hums with it, and calls to me specifically...perhaps designed to intoxicate me." As if looking for the source, he slips his fingers under my shirt, his calloused palms abrading the skin along my stomach. "I want to explore you, I want to understand you," he murmurs, lifting the shirt up and over my breasts.

As he leans further forward, his thigh brushes the apex between my legs, eliciting a moan from somewhere within me. He stops, seeming surprised by the noise, then pushes his knee deeper and watches as I squirm beneath him. One hand pulls the tubular band down from my breasts, and his breathing turns shallow. He lowers his mouth and I all but buck under his weight as he takes my nipple in his mouth.

"Ryder..." I whisper, not sure myself what I'm about to say next. Stop? Keep going? Touch me here, there, and everywhere?

He pulls away and scrambles back from the bed, as if snapped from a spell at the sound of my voice. "What was that? Is *that* magic?" he asks breathlessly. He runs his fingers through the loose layers of his hair and takes a further step back.

I lean up on my elbows, not bothering to replace my shirt

as he's not only seen, but felt, touched and tasted what I now have bare. "That's desire, Ryder. I suppose you've never felt it?"

He shakes his head and appears almost boyish for a moment, despite that dark look in his eyes. Against the lamplight, his face is half cast in shadow, dark desire intermingled with a look of calm wonderment.

"Have you ever lain with a woman?" I ask, my own curiosity bubbling to the surface.

"Once. My body reacted to the stimulus, but everything else...nothing. I felt nothing." His eyes narrow, dark lashes concealing the lingering passion still burning at his core. "I need you."

I bite my lip and a rumble emanates from his chest as he steps towards me. "No, Ryder," I say softly, holding up a hand to his hard chest. "You should go." I tilt my head towards the door, but my prince is torn, half of him in shadowy doubt though with no understanding as to why, and the other half wanting to explore more of what just happened, the feelings he'd been robbed of so long ago.

Turning, he picks up his bag and heads for the door, then hesitates. "I'll be across the hall. Call if you...need me."

The door clicks shut behind him, and I scramble from the bed to flick the bolt. Turning around, I slide down to sit on the cool floor and put my head between my knees. That was close. A little *too* close.

A DEAL TO DIE FOR

BEGGARS' COVE

The next morning, Winnie, Ryder and I go in search of a healer while the others go about trying to secure a buyer for our chimera carcasses. It's not a pleasant job, so I'm surprised when Caleb offers to take it on over breakfast. I smile as I think back to Winnie's motherly harrumph, insisting it was the least the man could do after causing such a fuss last night.

My thoughts are derailed as we pass through the central district, where musicians play openly on the street for customers enjoying their breakfast on the tea-rooms' open verandas. Despite the odd and eclectic combination of instruments, the sounds they produce in harmony is intoxicating, tempting those who pass to sway with the persuasive rhythm.

I chuckle as Winnie takes my hand and spins me around in a series of twirls, then releases me to offer her own little parting jig to the musicians' songs. As we continue east towards the healers' quarter, the music recedes into the general hubbub of the city, and we each peer into shop fronts offering tailoring services with impossible price tags. I think back to the western side of town, where people are forced to scrape and scavenge for money or food. The poor living on the doorstep of the wealthy.

Who governs this island, I wonder? Who would allow poverty to sit beside such wealth? I understand there will always be those with more than others, but the dereliction of the western quarter was...unacceptable. Or at least it *should* be considered so by any ruler.

Through several more alleys, past cobblers mending boots and down boulevards belonging to distillers, we follow the signs to a small row of shops, each offering services that deal in alchemical potions, healants and fortunes.

"What did he say this place was called?" I ask, scanning the various hanging signs and plaques. During breakfast, the owner of Thieves' Lair had stopped by our table to offer welcome at his nephew's behest. When we spoke of needing a healer, he'd told us of his friend, an old lady named Orwen, and kindly provided directions.

"This should be it," Winnie says, coming to a stop beside a dusty sign with the very thing we were told to look for – an odd symbol of two, golden triangles joined by a circle, the emblem worn and weathered from years of surviving the city's sandstorms.

Beyond, the windows are so grimy it's difficult to tell if anyone might be inside. Winnie steps up to the small dwelling and raps her knuckles on the door. After a moment of no response, we're about to step away and look for another when the door creaks open and a voice calls for us to enter.

As I step over the threshold, I almost gasp, enamoured by the shop. Gold and copper talismans hang from the low lateral beams, with multi-coloured silks tied to the rafters and bubbling pots of alchemical creations strewn across several oak tables. It's another world in this little store, a witch's haven.

"Be with you in just a moment," someone calls from the far end of the room.

I turn to see a small woman with long and slightly dishevelled auburn hair. Unlike the innkeeper's description, she isn't old at all, very young in fact, her small frame straining as she grinds some herbs with a mortar and pestle. She swiftly moves to check a large alembic, used for distilling medicine or even alcohol.

Watching her work reminds me of Marnie and how she would spend hours in the back room of the sisters' stone cottage brewing potions of all sorts for the villagers on the isle.

"Right, stand back!" the woman calls.

We all take one step back as the woman hurries to the opposite side of the room and ducks behind an overturned table. Beside the alembic, a glass beaker containing an effervescent mixture turns from a pretty pink to an alarming shade of black as it bubbles to the surface.

"This is it," the woman says excitedly, donning a pair of goggles and rubbing her hands together.

We each take a few steps further back and watch as the liquid begins to glow. Despite being in a closed shop, an odd breeze picks up, the very air in the room seemingly drawn to the liquid itself.

All of a sudden, the glow fizzles out and the liquid burps...then explodes. We each look away, Ryder doing his best to cover Winnie and me from the stray shards of glass propelled outwards.

"Damn. Damn it all to hell. Why didn't that work!?" the woman cries, distraught at her potion's reaction. She stands from her hiding spot and storms to the table, inspecting a book lying on a stand beneath a protective glass box.

"What *was* that?" Winnie asks warily, brushing shards from her shoulder.

The woman jumps and turns, as if only truly seeing us for the first time. Lowering her goggles to hang loosely around her neck, she sighs and ties her long hair into a messy ponytail as she answers Winnie. "*That* was supposed to be a portal. I'm so close, I'm just missing something." With her hair out of the way, she busies herself cleaning up the broken glass. "Sorry, did you come to see me?"

"That depends, are you Orwen, the healer?" I ask, keeping my distance as she wipes the table and discards the cloth in a large kiln – the effect summoning sparks and blue flames.

"She isn't here anymore. She went...travelling, to find her sisters." Wiping her hands on her apron, the woman steps forward and holds out her palm in greeting. "I'm Evelyn, Orwen's former protege. What can I do for you?"

I introduce myself and Ryder steps forward to do the same. Winnie, however, keeps a wary distance, still staring at the blue flames in the kiln as she says, "Sorry, did you say a portal?"

Evelyn blinks twice, then bites her lip. "Ah, I shouldn't have told you that...I'll treat you for free if you keep it to yourselves?"

Considering how fast we're burning through coin, I jump at the opportunity for free service and accept the alchemist's offer. She points to a small table and asks us to take a seat as she gathers several cups and loads them with an ominous red liquid from one of the alembics.

"Don't worry, it's just tea," she says with a giggle when we each hesitate to take the proffered cups. "So, what's ailing you?"

"I suffered a chimera bite to my shoulder, and Winnie has a wound on her arm," I explain. "We also have one who suffered a broken nose, but it seems to be healing nicely, and other cuts and scrapes to tend to as well."

Evelyn nods and heads for the front door to flick the lock before asking us to remove our shirts so she might better inspect the wounds. "Ah yes, both are simple enough to treat, and I see you removed the poison. You'll need a salve and Winnie will need some additional ointments to prevent infection, but other than that you should be healed up by tomorrow morning."

I thank Evelyn as she hurries about the room, mixing liquids and referring to a second, smaller book on one of the far tables. Out of curiosity, I decide to ask, "Where does the portal take you?" The notion of inter-dimensional travel is right up there with the winged beasts rumoured to guard the dwarves' mines – laughable.

"Well…I suppose there's no harm telling you the rest now I have your word not to go running your mouths to the locals," Evelyn says as she grinds away at a mixture of who knows what. "Orwen had been working on the concoction for years, telling me about a world with flying machines that can carry you across the world in a single day, and great buildings that touch the sky."

"Is that so," Winnie says with a sideways glance my way.

Evelyn smiles and shakes her head. "That woman had visions. She spent most of her life looking for the right potion to create a portal to this other world. And a few nights ago, she finally did it. I watched her slip through, but the damn thing closed before I could follow or ask how she did it. I only need one more ingredient, and I'm getting close to narrowing it down."

"That all sounds…interesting," I say, with a quick wink Winnie's way. She doesn't believe Evelyn for a second, but I'm suddenly unsure, thinking back to the book King Phillip had given me, about another woman who had crossed through realms to save her family.

"I know, I know, you think me a loon. But you asked, and I answered," Evelyn says as she scrapes herbs into one of many clever apparatuses before striking a match and lighting the wick of a small oil burner used to heat the liquid. "This will take a little while to simmer, why don't you all come back later. I should have it ready by this evening."

Thanking the alchemist, we take our leave and wander back through the city. There's only one other item on my agenda for the day – to find a new inn. Preferably one that doesn't have any pirate captains hanging around, and with enough rooms that we won't have to share.

We stop at the first one we find on our wanderings through the tailors' high street, and already I'm put at ease by the sign that reads: *Dreamscape*. Unfortunately, the interior leaves much to be desired. It's barely mid-morning, yet patrons lounge around the lower levels, each with a scantily dressed man or women in their laps. Quickly realising we've wandered into a bordello, we turn and head back out onto the street to keep searching.

The entire afternoon follows in a woefully similar manner, with most inns doubling as whorehouses, drug dens or gambling holes. The few more respectable establishments we do find have few rooms available, and in a city such as this, I'm eager for the crew to stay together under one roof.

"It's getting close to evening, Captain. Should we head back to see the healer?" Winnie asks. I'm reluctant to admit our defeat, but sigh and nod my head. "What do you think about that portal nonsense?" she continues, leading the way back through the narrow alleyways.

"I heard there's a portal somewhere in the Eighth Sea," Ryder says, barely interested but contributing, nonetheless.

It's the first he's spoken today, and I wonder if he's feeling alright, or if he's thinking about our interaction last night.

"I heard that as well," I say. "But I've yet to see any proof of such a thing." The thought is interesting though, the notion of other worlds, other realms so close to our own.

Just outside Evelyn's front door, we stop at the sound of an excited squeal coming from inside, followed by a rumble and smashing glass. Whatever the alchemist is up to, it doesn't sound good.

"What's this?" Winnie asks. Hanging on the door are two small vials and a leather-bound package with a note attached to it. "The note is for you, Emery."

I take it from her and open it for all of us to read.

> Miss Emery,
> The pink vial is for Winnie, the blue one is for you along with a few additional salves as a gift.
>
> I won't be seeing you again, I found the last ingredient and I'm off to find Orwen.
> Pleasure to meet you!

Winnie and I share a look as we finish reading the note. Inside, the shop has gone mysteriously quiet. Compelled by our curiosity, we open the door. The same chimes and trinkets that once hung delicately from the ceiling are now littered across the floor with broken glass and overturned tables. That same floor, once a darkly stained oak is now covered with sand, as if a storm had blown through and somehow been confined to the shop's interior.

We scan the singular, square room for any sign of Evelyn, sure we might find someone or something after the noise we had heard before, but she isn't here. There are no other exits, no trap doors, no open windows…yet nobody is here.

~

"IT MUST HAVE BEEN a bird or something," Winnie murmurs quietly, swirling the spoon around her soup. With little else to do, we had left the healers' quarter and returned to Thieves' Lair to meet with the others for dinner. Winnie had been quiet the entire walk back, and even now as she picks at her food, she mumbles half-formed attempts to explain the mysterious events at the alchemist's shop.

"I think Evelyn actually did it, I think she travelled or portalled or whatever they call it," I say, smiling when Winnie slowly raises her head with a pointed look of disapproval.

"No you don't. You're just saying that because you know it's bugging me," she says, finally taking a spoonful of soup.

"That's not true, how else do you explain the sand?" I ask, shamelessly enjoying her befuddlement. "Not to mention all that crashing and banging. There were no other exits…unless there *was* a portal."

"Don't be ridiculous, *Captain*. There's no such thing," Winnie insists matter-of-factly. Looking up, she nods to Toriq as he enters and weaves his way between the tables to meet us. "We ordered food for you. Where's Ansel and Caleb?" she asks.

Toriq releases an annoyed breath and summons an attendant to take his drink order before answering. "Ansel will be along in a minute, but I haven't seen Caleb since this morning. He said he would meet me here at midday, but he still hasn't shown up."

"Did he say what he had planned for today?" I ask, a little worried by the admission. Despite last night's display, Caleb doesn't seem the type to stand up his friends.

"Just that he was heading to the weapon district to purchase a new blade. I went there looking for him though, and they said he'd been and left a while ago." Toriq looks up as the attendant returns with soup and a tankard of mead, then tucks in, clearly ravenous despite his concern.

"Do you think we should go out and look for him?" Winnie asks.

Ryder shakes his head and looks to the windows where the last of the sun casts a shadow over the room. "No, we would be wise to stay off the streets at this time of day. Caleb is big and skilled enough to fend for himself.

"I suppose that's true," I say, relaxing slightly. "Besides, knowing Caleb he's likely on the hunt for a little tail at one of the bordellos." I chuckle and offer Winnie a reassuring smile, one she fails to return, instead looking mildly annoyed by the notion. I glance next at Ryder, the prince's lack of concern yet another reminder of his curse. Most would be at least a little worried when one of their comrades disappears.

"Captain!"

I turn in my chair to see Ansel hurrying through the throng of diners to our table. He's out of breath and clutching a bag to his chest. Looking from left to right he leans down and whispers in my ear.

"What's wrong?" Winnie asks, looking from me to the very distressed genie.

"Well, we know where Caleb is," I mutter, standing from my chair. "That pirate from last night is holding him hostage. Apparently she's in the next room and wants a chat."

Winnie, Toriq and Ryder stand with me, and I'm grateful for the backup. Leaving our half-eaten meals, we follow Ansel to the other room where the woman in question sits with three of her crewmates by the fire, each smoking from their long pipes and relaxed on a daybed.

Seeing our approach, she places the pipe on a silver tray and regards us with a grin. "Lovely to see you again, Captain Emery. I suppose I should properly introduce myself if we're to do business. My name is Captain Snow."

The fact she knows *my* name tells me either Caleb or Ansel has talked. I glance to the genie beside me and he shakes his head, already knowing my question. Caleb then. What else has our friend told the pirate and her crew, and how exactly had they extracted the information?

"Where's Caleb?" I ask, keeping my tone steady enough to hide my concern. "Have you harmed him?"

Snow holds a hand to her chest and looks to her retinue of Dwarves on the adjacent daybed, all feigning injury at my question. "I would never do such a thing, dearest Emery. Unfortunately, your unwillingness to share your voice with us last night has driven me to act far outside my accepted boundaries of behaviour. We're desperate, you see."

"Desperate for what?" The book's warning rings in my head...*Our girl has no choice but to barter and shake.*

"For your song, of course," Snow says with a roll of her eyes.

"You want me to sing for you?"

Reaching to the side, Snow plucks a bright red apple from a bowl of fruit beside her pipe and rubs it idly against her chest before taking a bite. "Eventually. First, I want you to visit the Beggar King on the east side of the island and retrieve a small trinket. It's a music box, a shell, much like the one you wear around your neck," she says, pointing to the silver conch gifted to me by the mermaid.

"Why do I get the sense there's a catch to this? Why not go and get the box yourself?" I ask.

"I'm not finished yet," Snow snaps coldly. "The Beggar King is not to be taken lightly, and this device isn't any old thing. With it, I can record your song and protect my crew on our travels."

Ah, now I see. Though, I struggle to understand how this device works in such a way as to capture my voice as she says. "And why haven't you gone to collect it yourself?" I ask.

"As I said–"

"I know what you *said*, but you're going to have to give me a little more than that if you expect me to traipse off into the desert."

Snow crosses her legs and taps a long, ruby-red nail on her thigh. "I can respect that. The Beggar King is a cannibal, and his preferred prey is young children. While my crew are clearly fully grown men, the king's sight is waning, and he is just as likely to mistake their height for that of a youngling," she says with an apologetic look to her three comrades. They each smile and roll their eyes, unbothered by her claim. "He also has a henchman, of sorts. He's the one who lures the children from their beds."

Beside me, Ryder makes a contemplative noise in the back of his throat, likely wondering the same thing I am.

"If that's true, aren't you concerned something might happen to us? Not only will you fail to get the box, but my song goes along with me," I note. Her mention of the Beggar King's taste for human flesh rattles me more than I'd like to admit, and I cross my arms to prevent any obvious fidgeting.

Looking from me to the others standing behind, Snow grins and places the apple to one side, then picks up her pipe and takes a long draw before answering. "That is a concern, I'll admit. I've asked others to retrieve it for me, and offered a great deal of coin in return. But there isn't a damned soul on the island willing to go anywhere near the man. Therefore, I'm choosing you and your crew for two reasons. The first, is that you all seem closer than most. Everyone in this city – both visitors and residents – are all out for themselves. We could kidnap a member of another crew and they would just as soon leave him or her behind. You're different."

"And the second reason?" She isn't wrong, the innkeepers nephew had remarked similarly, pointing out how most crews go their separate ways as soon as they've docked.

"I have it on good authority that your cloak is made of quite a special material." Snow points a long finger to Ansel, who shifts slightly to hide behind Ryder.

"How much did that little weasel tell you?" Winnie hisses at the woman.

Captain Snow chuckles, nearly coughing on the inhale of smoke. "Your friend didn't tell us, the dwarves are familiar with such items, though it's been a long time since any of us have seen one."

When Ansel moves to interject, one of the dwarves, a little stockier than his friend with a very impressive beard, holds up his hand. "Don't bother. We know that's a harpy's cloak. We used to craft them for the messengers before they all died out. I'd love to know where you found it." He eyes Ansel and the red cloak with a glare, as if suspecting we stole it as opposed to coming by the item legitimately.

"I'd like to see that Caleb is unharmed before I agree to anything," I say. Beside me, Ryder noticeably stiffens but says nothing.

Snow smiles and crosses her legs, the very picture of patience. "Of course. My man will take one of you to see him," she says, waving a hand to the quieter of the dwarves. He stands on cue and walks to the door.

"I'll go," Toriq says, and follows him out of the inn.

Little is said while we wait for Toriq and Snow's man to

return. Winnie does a turn about the room, pacing back and forth in a flurry of concern and frustration. I take a leaf out of Ryder's book and do my best to appear as bored as possible, while Ansel hides behind the very disinterested looking prince.

"I don't want to do this, you know," Snow says quietly. "But I must. I've met three others with the gift of the siren song. Each time they've slipped through my fingers, and more men are lost to those infernal creatures."

"I thought Dwarves were immune to the sirens' call," I say. It's one of the reasons they're known as some of the better seafarers.

"Immune to their call, yes. But not to their claws and their strength. With the song we can fight back, or avoid fighting at all," she says softly.

We all turn as a bell dings and Toriq steps through the front door. He nods his head, telling us Caleb is well and being moved to another location. I figured the captain would move Caleb the moment they revealed his whereabouts, it's what I would do were I in the business of kidnapping.

"You have my word no harm will come to your friend," Snow says solemnly. "Bring me the box so I can record your song, then I will return him to you."

The captain holds out her hand to seal the deal and Ryder takes a single step forward, as if prepared to shake on my behalf. Instead, he takes my hand in his and implores me to carefully consider. I already have. The book warned this would happen, that I would be forced to strike a bargain. I never thought it would be to save Caleb's life.

Turning to Captain Snow, I shake her hand. "I'll do it."

THE BEGGAR KING

BEGGARS' COVE

As we all enter my room, I'm pleased to see a pile of recently washed clothes on my bed – one of the inn's better services and a relief to know I won't be spending the next few days in the desert wearing stinking clothes. When Winnie turns to leave, informing us she needs to pack, I ask her to wait and address them once the door is closed.

"Winnie and Toriq, I'd like you both to remain here." When Winnie opens her mouth to object, I hold up a hand and explain my reasoning. "You're the only one I trust to keep an eye on the ship's repairs, Winnie. And I want Toriq to remain as your protection."

Her mouth falls open and she crosses her arms looking aghast that I would think she needs such a thing.

"I mean as your *back-up*, should you need it," I amend with a chuckle.

"I want to go with you and Ryder," Toriq says, also crossing his arms defiantly.

"This isn't about what you *want*, Toriq. I'll hazard a guess and say Ryder isn't prepared to stay here while I seek out this

Beggar King?" I look to Ryder who nods his confirmation. "See? And I need Ansel with me so I can use the cloak and give it back to him as soon as we have what we need. You're the only one left to stay and assist Winnie."

Toriq hesitates, then mutters an oath as he leans back against the wall. "I understand, it's just...I promised his father I would watch out for him."

I laugh sardonically as I remove the bag from under the bed and begin to pack. "Yes, I know, and you don't trust me to keep him safe. You've made that perfectly clear."

Sensing an argument, Winnie and Ansel slip out of the room, Ansel saying he'll meet us downstairs when he's packed. Ryder takes a seat on the floor and leans his back against the tub, stating he's ready to leave when I am.

"You've earned my trust, Emery," Toriq says as he lingers by the door. "You earned it the day you took Ryder's place in the water with the mermaid. I just...he's my friend," Toriq says.

"I believe it's rude to talk about someone as if they aren't in the room," Ryder says from the floor. I smile down at him, noting he isn't annoyed by this, but again merely stating fact, as if wanting to educate us on the right etiquette.

"I'll take care of him," I say softly to Toriq.

"You had better," he mumbles, then walks over to the bed and drops a piece of folded parchment beside my bag. "The dwarf that showed me to Caleb gave me that. It's a map with the route to the Beggar King's cottage."

I open it up and turn to sit on the edge of the bed. "If this is to scale we could make it there in half a day if we hire a few horses." Folding the map and tucking it into my pocket, I'm reminded of the marbles Ansel had given me and collect them from my bag, tucking them in alongside the parchment. "Snow doesn't know about the book yet...the sooner we get Caleb back, the better."

Toriq nods his head reluctantly. "I figured the same. I'll see what the innkeeper can arrange," he says.

I look up as the door clicks shut with Toriq's departure, then stand and return to packing my things. "You've been very quiet today," I say without looking at Ryder. "Something on your mind?"

He waits a moment before answering. "You."

One word…Apparently that's all it takes for my fickle heart to begin tapping a beat, or perhaps it's the way he says it – all dark and serious. "Oh, I see." I want to kick myself for asking in the first place, but my next question is just asking for trouble. "Is it about last night?"

"You know it is. I think I want to finish what we started. I also believe your deal with Snow is a mistake."

"You *think* you want to finish?" That doesn't inspire much confidence. I realise I should be happy about this. But I'm not. Not at all.

"I don't know, Emery. I never know," he says softly, running a hand through his hair and sighing. "I meant what I said about your deal though. The Beggar King sounds like bad news."

"You don't say?" I ask sarcastically. "Which part exactly? The part about his dietary preferences? Or the evil henchman who charms the children away?" If I thought we had any other choice, I would avoid the east side of the island like I would the plague. "What other option do we have, Ryder?"

Without hesitating, he says, "We could leave him, leave Caleb and this place."

I turn on the prince, my face twisted in disbelief. "I won't have that sort of talk amongst my crew. As Caleb's captain, he's my responsibility until he decides to leave my ship. Loyalty is everything, and nobody gets left behind. Do you understand?"

"I do," Ryder says evenly, holding my stare. "I understand

your codes, and I won't say another word of it...unless the risk to your life becomes too great. Then I will be forced to intervene."

The words are a cold threat, not to me, but to Caleb. "I thought he was your friend?" Back on the ship, when Toriq had put me in danger, Ryder was prepared to throw that dagger and kill him. "Don't you care about them? Even a little?" I whisper.

Ryder's eyes narrow and he rises from the floor, taking three long strides to stand in front of me. "What part of my affliction do you fail to understand, Emery? I feel *nothing*, I care for *nobody*."

I step back and try to look away, but his hand captures my chin, the other snaking around my waist to pull me against his chest. "I won't lose you. Not for Caleb, Toriq, or any of them. I'll kill them myself before I allow that to happen."

His warmth permeates the skin beneath my shirt, and I raise a hand to brush the dark hair that's fallen across his face. "Ryder, you claim not to care, but what possesses you to act like this, to protect me?"

His eyes widen and he relinquishes my chin, taking a wary step back. "I...I don't know."

I sigh and shake my head, anger dissolving into exhaustion. "Go get your bags and meet me downstairs," I say, turning my back to him.

He lingers a moment before the door opens and closes with a soft click. Packing the last item, I secure the clasp on my bag and loop it over my shoulder. "This is why it's always better to sail alone," I mutter to myself. "Nobody to rescue, and no infuriating princes to deal with."

〜

As promised, Toriq, Ansel and Ryder are waiting outside with three horses saddled and ready to go. I'm not sure how Toriq has managed to do it at such a late hour, but I suppose from the loud and lively music drifting from the centre of the city, most don't go to sleep until much later.

"I hear you're off to the east side of the island," the innkeeper says as he comes through the front door with four heavy skins of water. After draping a pair across each of the horses' backs, he strokes the hind of mine. "You shouldn't go. It's against our laws to seek out the Beggar King," he says, finally turning to regard me.

"Against the law?" I ask. Under the lantern hanging above the entrance, he looks younger than I suspect he is, the copper tones of his hair changing colour with every flicker. He's somewhat handsome; strong and fit with a kindness found in the soft features of face.

"Make sure you don't tie your horses too tight to any mooring," he says, ignoring my question. "That way, if you die, they can break themselves free and find their own way home."

My face drops. "That's encouraging...albeit ominous," I mutter.

His eyes linger on mine a moment longer. "Be careful." Taking my hand, he lifts it to his lips in a kiss so gentle it makes me blush. Then he turns and wishes us luck as he heads back inside, all the while mumbling something about fools for a crown.

Before we depart, I issue my orders to Winnie and Toriq, telling them to check in with the carpenter in the morning, and to let him know I will be out of reach for at least the next couple of days. They both promise to do as much, and to keep an eye on *The Arcana*.

Ansel begrudgingly hands the book over to Winnie, with his own strict instructions not to peek or she may be tempted to inform me of anything wicked coming our way. She vows to keep it safe and clutches it to her chest.

As I go to mount my horse, Toriq approaches and helps secure my boot to the stirrup, keeping a hand on my lower back as I climb up. "Remember the book's warnings, Emery," he says as he adjusts my stirrup straps.

I grin down at him. "Don't worry, I'll protect our prince."

He shakes his head and turns to walk back to the inn, his words barely audible as he says, "It's not *him* I'm worried about." He disappears before I register his meaning, and we each wave goodbye to Winnie as we motion the horses onward.

With the city's night-time revelries in full swing, we have no hope of guiding our mounts through the throng of dancers and drunks on the main street, and so we're forced to stick to the city limits, tracking along the high wall to where we're told is an eastern entrance. It seems the west isn't the only derelict side of town. The further we venture from the wealthy city centre, the worse the state of living seems to become.

I stop my horse before he tramples a poor, shivering man lying in our path. With such poor light, it isn't until we skirt around that I see the flies and rats tugging on the loose flesh. Not shivering at all, but dead.

I call a warning back to Ansel behind me, then turn my head to the side as I nudge the horse on, but the sight isn't much better. Each alley we pass houses starving children huddled under blankets, or women hidden in the dark shadows, opening their legs for a desperate bit of coin.

"I think my father's heart would break at such a sight," Ryder says from the front.

"And you? How does it make *you* feel?" I ask.

Ryder waits a moment before answering, perhaps searching himself for an answer. "I feel...nothing." He shakes his head, knowing that isn't the right response, but it's an honest one.

I remain quiet as we continue down the alleyways, resisting the urge to stop and help everyone we pass. I have never wished for a position of power, no more than I already have. Looking upon these unfortunate people, with the quiet rumble of laughter so close by, I want to conquer this city. I want to enforce a system that helps those in need. It's a whimsical fancy as I have neither the power nor the know-how to achieve such a thing, but I want it, nonetheless.

Just ahead, Ryder veers right, through a tall archway and out of the city. The tension in my chest steadily eases as I follow him through and leave the city walls behind, much as it does when I leave the dock and sail out to sea. Only this isn't an open ocean of water, it's an expanse of desert dunes beneath a sea of stars overhead. The sight summons a wave of awe and light trepidation; the empty desert concealing unseen threats. Nevertheless, I'm already in love with it. I urge the horse onward and take off to the top of the first dune, stopping at its peak to better appreciate the view.

"It's good we're travelling at night," Ryder says, pulling his horse up beside me. "This desert is loaded with iron, so the compass won't work." He points to one of the constellations, each star dull against the moon's light. "We can follow the Wooden Boy all the way to the eastern side of the island."

The story of the Wooden Boy and how he came to be a star is one of my favourites, a tale about a carpenter and his magical creation. It always came with the warning, that should you tell too many lies, the gods would spirit you away and force you to watch over the world, watch those you love from afar for the rest of eternity.

"Does that mean we won't be able to come back until tomorrow evening?" Ansel asks worriedly as he shifts in his saddle. "What if we need to make a quick getaway?"

"Let's hope it doesn't come to that, but either way it's just as possible to navigate during the day without a compass. We'll be fine," I promise, tapping the horse forward and on through the desert.

As WE RIDE across the barren sands, we stop every now and again to water the horses and offer them cubes of sugar. These creatures are used to the harsher environs – unlike Angus. My old horse would have puffed and grunted his unhappiness with the sands and slower pace, wanting instead to race across rolling hills as we so often did together. I miss the horse, but I know Pattie will treat him well.

As the moon slowly carves an arc across the sky, I find time passes more quickly than expected, the hours spent swapping fables regarding the constellations, all slightly different as they're passed through generations. We each fall into silence once again as dawn slowly spreads across the horizon, casting a glow on the ocean as it grows in the distance. To the left of our heading, a small cluster of houses begins to emerge, and we head that way.

"According to that little map, this is the only village for several miles, so we should be in the right place," Ryder informs us. Taking the reins in one hand, he unfolds the parchment and aligns the town with the markings on the page.

"It looks abandoned," I say, noting the absence of smoke from the chimneys, and that some of the houses are entirely reduced to rubble.

"Considering what we've heard about this man, I wouldn't be surprised if he's the only one living there," Ansel mumbles quietly.

"How will your cloak hide me from him," I ask, suddenly

curious about its magical abilities. "I thought it only hides you from the witch."

Ansel pulls the material tightly around his body with one hand, caressing the red velvet like an old friend. "A harpy's cloak will shield you from anything or anyone you wish. Whether it's a single person or an entire race. The messengers would use it to hide themselves from humans in general, whereas I only wish to be hidden from my master's magic."

"I see. That might come in handy if I lose my song again. We can all hide under your cloak until the sirens just go away," I say with a laugh.

Ansel smiles back and shakes his head. "It's a wonder how you can joke when you're about to meet with such a despicable man."

"Emery isn't going to meet the Beggar King, I am," Ryder says absently, still examining the map.

"That is factually incorrect, actually," I say, leaning over to take the paper from him. "According to the book, I'm the one to meet this king. You two can wait nearby in case I call for help." Suprisingly, I hear no word of complaint from Ryder, and lift my eyes from the map to study him.

He's staring at me, the muscle in his jaw working overtime, probably in his best attempt not to say anything. He knows I'm right, and with the marbles in my pocket and the cloak, I'm confident this will go well...mostly.

Pulling up to the first house, we dismount and lead our horses into an adjacent stable, making sure to fill the stone troughs with enough water to keep the animals happy.

As it turns out, my earlier assumption had been correct. The houses here have long since been abandoned, with no obvious signs of life on the streets, broken windows, front doors left open and tiled roofs collapsing through lack of care.

"Do you smell that?" Ansel asks.

I nod my head and we each look up as the first smoke of the day rises from one of the dwellings. We follow it along the open road, not so much a road as a break between houses, any sign of paving long since lost to the desert sands.

I stop at a bend and peer around the side of a house, seeing a lonely, detached cottage at the end of the small street and close to the shore, with smoke spiralling from the chimney stack.

"That has to be it," I whisper. "Ansel, give me your cloak." He unfastens the string and pulls it from his shoulders, briefly hesitating before handing it over. "I'll give it back just as soon as I'm out of there," I promise.

"How are you going to sneak in?" Ryder asks, leaning close to peer over my shoulder at the small home of the so-called King of Beggars.

I grin as I fasten the cloak around my shoulders. "That's where you two lovely gentlemen come in. I'll need you to create a bit of a distraction so that when he opens the door, I can slip right in with him none the wiser."

"What sort of distraction?" Ansel asks warily.

"Anything loud enough to get his attention," I reply. Pulling the hood up, I turn to face the cottage and think of the Beggar King, willing the red riding cloak to hide me from his sight.

Keeping as low to the ground as possible, I race across the open street and duck to sit below one of the front windows. I hold a hand up to others, asking them to wait a moment. Then, as slowly and as quietly as possible, I lean up and peer inside.

Two, cloudy red eyes stare back from a sunken face, and I scramble away from the window. Something moves across the street – Ryder making his way to me with a dagger in each hand. Rising to my feet, I motion for him to stop just as the door to the cottage opens.

"Who has come to visit? Don't be shy, it's been a long while since I've seen a friendly face," the Beggar King croons. Stepping out from the doorway, the light finally reveals the man in full, and the blood drains from my face with what I see.

With a back hunched from age, the beggar's spindly fingers clutch delicately to a walking cane as he takes another tentative step forward and searches the street.

His eyes, as red as the blood of those he consumes, squint in the early morning light as he brushes long strands of greasy grey hair from his face. But it's not his age that turns my stomach to lead...it's his clothes. Garbed in a dress made of stitched leather, I can see as clear as day it isn't made from the hide of animals, but that of *humans*.

My eyes fall to a patch near the bottom of the dress – a face, skinned and stretched and stitched into place, forever capturing the scream that was cut short. Empty eye sockets, empty mouths, tufts of hair lining the bottom of the dress stare back and I'm forced to turn away.

I have to move. I have to get inside before my courage flees completely.

Slow and careful not to drag my feet, I take one step after the other towards the very man I'm compelled to run away from. He continues to search and taps his cane against the bottom stone step in irritation. I'm close now, so close I can smell the human decay, the metallic scent of dried blood, something only odious when presented in great amounts. This man, this *thing*, reeks of it.

I'm halfway through the door when his head snaps towards me. I'm sure one of the many bones in his neck must have dislodged, as his body doesn't move, only his head. My hand rises to my mouth, and I hold my breath as he sniffs the air...and smiles. He knows I'm here, but he doesn't know where.

I'm ready to bolt from the door and abandon our mission when a loud crash comes from further down the street and Ryder steps back into view. Walking forward, he drags his blade along the stone wall of an abandoned house, and the old man whips his head back to its natural position.

"I thought I could smell another. Though, not as close as I thought," the Beggar King cackles softly. "What business have you? I'm an old man with nothing to offer," he says with a light and withered cough.

"I'm lost and need directions," Ryder says, the lie falling smoothly from his lips.

The beggar mumbles and mutters his annoyance at being disturbed for such a thing, and I take this chance to slip through the doorway and into the small cottage.

Outside, the voices drone, and I wonder if it's enough to drown out the gasp I'm unable to hold back. Captain Snow had not been lying. Even if I had failed to see the beggar's choice of fashion, the skins stretched and hanging over the fire would be enough to banish the last of my doubts.

Morbidly, I can't seem to take my eyes off them, or perhaps it's preferable, because the next thing my gaze happens to fall on is a shelf lined with jars filled with a murky green liquid...and human organs. A heart. Intestines. Several kidneys. Closing my eyes, I hold my nose and cover my mouth to keep from retching.

Beyond the skins and idle body parts, the room is a hoarders dream, with boxes and keepsakes strewn on every surface. I move to the first and quietly shuffle through piles of clothes in search of the music box. Snow had said it was similar in shape to my necklace, though much bigger. It shouldn't be too hard to spot.

I move from one box to the next, trying not to think of the children these items once belonged to. Growing frustrated, I quickly move to the next, then freeze as the door to the beggar's home clicks shut behind me.

I turn slowly to see the old man by the door, only just noticing the large emblem burned into the wood behind him. I'm sure it's a witch's seal, but I'm not sure what its purpose is until the door handle starts to shake, and a banging erupts from outside.

"I wasn't finished," Ryder calls from the street as he pounds on the door. Despite the fragile nature of the wood, it fails to budge, the emblem barring any unwanted guests.

I tiptoe back to stand betwixt the wall of jars and the first of the human hides, while the beggar moves to a table and writes a note. After a moment he whispers a few words, then casts the page into the fire. As he turns from the fireplace, his foot catches on a tower of boxes I had been searching, and they topple to the floor. I must have moved them in my haste because he seems surprised, then looks down suspiciously before casting his clouded, rheumy eyes around the room.

I stop breathing as his gaze lingers over the jars and he slowly makes his way to where I'm standing. Stopping inches from my chest, his breath fans across my cheek, the smell putrid and rotten. I pull the cloak tighter around me as he reaches up and retrieves a jar. With the container held at such an angle, I'm horrified to see the contents staring back at me as the beggar dips two bony fingers into the murky liquid, plucks out an eyeball, and pops it into his mouth.

It's almost too much. I sink to the floor and focus on anything but the horrid man standing beside me. Then I see it. The music box. Hidden amongst timepieces, jewellery and other miscellany scattered across the floor from the fallen box. Despite my temptation to grab the thing and race from the house, I wait. Outside has gone oddly quiet, and I suspect Ryder would not have stopped trying to get the beggar's attention unless he had a good reason for it.

When the beggar finally moves away, I cross quietly to the window and peer outside. Ryder is there, and so is Ansel. Both are sitting on the sand, placidly, absently staring at the house. My confusion fades and a crippling horror settles in when the putrid stink of the beggar's breath tickles my cheek.

"I thought I smelled something sweet."

I turn and scream as the old man latches those bony fingers onto each of my arms, holding me in place, preventing me from running.

"What is this magic? Why can't I see you?" he crows, his voice no longer sweet and innocent, but now an abrasive sound that grates against my very soul. A shiver races up my spine as he leans in and smells my hair.

Outside, Ryder and Ansel barely flinch, yet they must have heard me scream. The old beggar cackles in my face as I struggle against his grip. Gritting my teeth, I pull my head back then smash it against the king's face. His nose cracks and he releases me to stumble back, howling in pain and outrage.

I race to the fire and snatch up the music box, then push past the beggar to pull the handle on the door. It doesn't move. I search for a lock and flick the bolt, but still the door refuses to open.

"Going somewhere? I don't think so," the beggar says, turning towards the door. "You're a little old for my tastes, but you'll do nicely in a stew with my latest catch."

A small sound emanates from somewhere in the room, somewhere above. I glance up, my eyes hunting the rafters for what I fear made that noise. A soft gasp escapes my lips when I find what I hoped I would not.

A young boy hangs hogtied to the ceiling, no older than ten, his mouth agape and blood dripping down to a small pile of straw in the corner. Not just any boy, though. I recognise that face, that soft, red hair and tailored clothing. The innkeeper's nephew, the same young boy who had shown us around the city and guided us to the carpenter. He whimpers when our eyes finally meet, and his mouth moves, the absence of a tongue making it difficult to speak.

I had nearly left this boy. Left him to a gruesome, bloody death at the hands of the Beggar King. I want to cry and throw up and kill all at once. Something glints from the corner of my eye, the beggar picking up a large butcher's knife, already bloody and slightly rusted with age. He takes one careful step my way, sniffing the air and listening for whatever sound I might make.

This man will die today. It isn't a decision I take lightly; murder never should be. But it's the easiest decision I've ever made. Placing the music shell on a table to one side, I unsheathe my own dagger and hold it up. Behind the beggar, the boxes and items still lay strewn on the floor; a large, open fire just beyond. Keeping low, I hold my breath and race forward. Catching the hand with the butcher's knife, I drive my weight forward as my shoulder plows into the Beggar King's belly. He trips and I drop to the floor, looking up just in time to watch as the wretched man tumbles into the fire.

He screams and clutches his head, his greasy hair catching alight almost instantaneously. The leather dress barely flickers, merely curls with the heat as the skin beneath bubbles and blisters. Somehow, he stumbles from the fireplace in a blazing, maniacal rage towards me. Jumping to my feet, I raise my dagger and plunge it deep into the beggar's gut, twisting the hilt for good measure.

The beggar wails, clutching the wound with wide, unseeing eyes. I lift one foot and drive it hard against his chest, sending the king of nightmares back to hell, as he tumbles and crashes onto the logs to thrash amongst the flames, before falling forever silent.

I turn and hurry for the rope that will allow me to lower the innkeeper's nephew from the ceiling, then stop as the door to the cottage creaks open, a tune slowly drifting in.

Above, the boy groans and tries to shake his head. I tell him I'm coming, that I'm going to help him...but my legs refuse to move. Instead, I'm falling to my knees and they crack painfully against the stone floor. I stay there for a moment, unable to move, only able to blink as the strange, lilting melody seems to bind my body.

"I should thank you for killing my master," a voice whispers from the entrance to the cottage. "But you cannot have the Beggar King's throne. That is for me, I've earned it."

Whoever is speaking steps through the door, a small flute clasped in both hands. Captain Snow had warned of a henchman. This man with long black hair is as thin as a rake and half starved, not just from a lack of food, but of affection judging by the hungry look in his eyes.

He steps forward, one cold and bony hand lowering to brush the stray stands of hair from my face. I shiver as he leans down and whispers in my ear. "Don't fret though, you will be my queen."

MARBLES IN THE SAND

BEGGARS' COVE

RYDER'S POV

...

I can't move. All I can do is watch as this skinny, dark-haired man drags Emery from the cottage. Her eyes find mine and something erupts deep inside me at what I see there. Fear, I'm almost sure of it.

I open my mouth to talk, to reassure her, but the words fail. I take in a ragged breath and listen as the man mumbles to himself and to Emery. Dropping her by the side of the sandy road, he heads back into the house, emerging shortly after with the charred remains of what I suspect was once the Beggar King's head. Strolling past Emery, he turns and walks away.

For a moment I wonder if that's it, if all the henchman wanted was a trophy of his former master. The discordant sound of rickety wheels being pulled along the sand tells me otherwise, and sure enough the man returns with a horse and cart.

He grunts as he hefts Emery onto the cart, then climbs onto the horse and kicks him on.

With every bit of strength I have, I move my head to follow as she passes, and tap two fingers against my pocket in the hope she will understand the only message I can offer.

Her eyes widen and she tries to move her hand, whimpering as she hooks one finger on her pocket. They pull away and out of sight before I can see whether she manages to reach for the marbles.

How many hours has it been? I sit on my knees, unable to move as the sun crawls over the sky to sit directly above. While my arms are covered by the thin, cotton shirt, I'm conscious that my neck and face have been exposed to the heat for longer than advised. This is probably the only benefit to my curse. No pain. As the flute's effects wear off, I turn my head to see Ansel flopped on his belly in the shade by one of the houses. At least his skin won't have suffered.

Slowly, I rise from my haunches and straighten my thighs, before carefully lifting one leg to try and stand. I manage it, just about, and stumble make my way over to Ansel.

"Can you stand?" I ask him. I'm not sure If I have the strength to help him yet, but I place one hand on the wall and lean down to grip his arm.

After several attempts, Ansel finally manages to stand, albeit unsteadily, and holds the wall to keep himself up. "We have to follow the marbles," he says, his eyes already searching the ground where Emery had been strapped onto the cart.

"I'm not sure she was able to get to them," I say, taking a few tentative steps towards the next house. I pause at a small sound coming from the Beggar King's cottage, almost imperceptible against the soft breeze.

"She did. It was long ago written that those marbles would help her rescuers find her," Ansel assures me. He glances up and meets my suspicious look, then sighs. "No, I didn't know this would happen, just that she would need them."

I have no reason to distrust Ansel, not because I deem him trustworthy, more that I doubt he would have handed the cloak to Emery had he known they would be separated for this long.

When I fail to hear anything more from the cottage, I wave for Ansel to follow along. "Come on, we need to get to the horses and follow the tracks before the wind picks up."

We half expect the horses to be gone when we round the corner to where we left them. Thankfully, the small, broken-down stable remains cast in shadow, and their water barely half consumed. It would not have aided us to find our rides burned and aching of thirst.

Opening the gate, I take the reins and use the small stool to assist in climbing onto the saddle. Ansel waits as I lead both mine and Emery's horse from the stable, before attempting the same.

"We'll have to ride slowly until our strength returns," I say as we head back down the street to follow the tracks. "Don't fall off, or you'll struggle to get back on and I'll have to leave you behind."

Ansel makes a noise of complaint behind me, but says nothing, instead gripping the saddle with one hand and heeding my warning.

We find the tracks easily enough and follow them through the streets and out into the open desert where they veer towards the west...back towards the city. For some reason, it's the last place I expect him to go. Then again, I wouldn't have expected him to kidnap Emery, either. What does he want with her?

That feeling deep inside me tenses again, and I hold a hand to my chest. My heart is beating much faster than it ought to. Perhaps a secondary effect of the flute's magic? No...It's her. Thinking about Emery with that man...my heart continues to thrum beneath my fingers and my fists clench.

"Are you okay?" Ansel asks beside me.

It's only when I turn to look at him that I realise my teeth are bared, and I'm curious to know why that is. "I'm fine. Why do you ask?"

"No reason," Ansel says with a false smile as he looks away. I think I've made him uncomfortable.

Despite all that's happened, luck is on our side as the light breeze remains steady and the tracks easy enough to follow. Even when night descends and the light fades, the glow of the moon is enough to guide us.

"What's that?" Ansel asks from beside me.

I follow his gaze and easily recognise the structure dead ahead.. "I believe it's the well we passed last evening. He likely stopped to refill his water skins. We have enough, so we'll move on."

"Barely! What if we run out? We should stop, Ryder, it'll only take a moment."

Despite Ansel's logic, my gut is telling me no, that we should continue and make up the distance between us and Emery. I stroke along the side of the horse's neck and sure enough the fur is damp beneath my palm despite the night's cooler temperate. He's right.

We pull up next to the well, only to find no bucket, and no rope to haul the water up. Both items had been present the last time we had passed this way. I lean over and peer into the deep well, though nothing but darkness winks back.

I'm about to turn away when something laps against the water below.

"Ryder, look!" Ansel slides from his horse and kneels on the sand, taking a fistful and letting it drain though his fingers until only a small, glass marble remains in his palm.

I jump down from the horse and almost hurl myself down the well in my haste. "Emery!" Some invisible force grips my chest and makes it hard to breath as I wait for a response. Nothing. Only the soft sound of water lapping below. Perhaps a small animal has fallen in? If it were Emery, she would surely respond.

"At least we know she's alive," Ansel says softly, placing a hand on my shoulder. I believe he's trying to comfort me. Do I need comforting? With his words, the vice on my chest seems to ease a little, so I suppose I do.

"Let's go," I mutter, climbing back into the saddle and once again taking the reins of Emery's horse. With a tap to the animal's side, we break into a canter and continue along the tracks left behind by Emery's captor.

By TWILIGHT we make it back to the southern city with six marbles collected along the way. I must admit, I'm impressed by Ansel's keen sight, as I have yet to find a single glass ball. At the same time, I find it strange the marbles were visible at all.

My mood takes a dark turn and I mutter a curse as we step from the sands onto the cobbled paves of the city's outer rim. With no sand, the tracks disappear, making it impossible to determine which way they went. Bouts and cheers roar from the city centre, and we follow the noise in the hopes that someone might have seen them pass.

As we exit the alley and guide our horses onto the long,

central street of the city, a bonfire rages in the main square. People race past us, some shouting gleeful praise while others jeer – *he's dead, he's dead*.

I lean down from the horse and snatch the collar of a young man. "Who's dead?" I ask.

The young man looks up and sways on his feet from drink. "The Beggar King! Our children are safe, and a new king is decided – the champion who stole the beggar's head!" He pulls himself free from my grip and skips towards the fire, holding up a bottle of rum and joining the cheers of all the rest.

"That lying swine. *That's* why the henchman wanted the king's head," Ansel murmurs, pulling the horse up beside me.

I motion the horse forward, searching the crowd for the gaunt face and coal-black hair of the man I know to be here. *He* incited this celebration. He has claimed his victory, now he will surely bask in the moment.

There.

Emery's captor stands at the centre of the celebration, holding a spear with the scalded remains of the Beggar King's head mounted on top. Sliding down from the horse, I push my way through the throng of people with Ansel close on my heels.

At the grunts and protests from those I pass, the scraggy man looks up and sees me. Against the fire's glow, his face twists and he stumbles back, reaching for the musical pipe secured to his belt.

For a reason unbeknownst to me, I smile at that look, the same look Emery had worn when he'd dragged her from the cottage. Fear. My smile widens. Good, he *should* fear me.

Launching through the last of the crowd, I snag the front of his baggy, smelly shirt and lift him off the ground. "Where is she?" I growl, my tone as much a shock to myself as it is to him.

The cheering dies down and someone steps forward to intercept. With one hand holding Emery's captor, I take a dagger from the holster on my chest and swing it in a wide arc to deter those who might approach. Turning back to the man, I tighten my grip. "Where is she!?"

"He's your new king, release him!" someone shouts from the crowd.

"He saved us!" calls another.

Ansel turns and holds his hands up defensively to the looming, angering mass. "No, you're wrong. This man *lied* to you. It was our friend who killed the Beggar King. This man—" Ansel grunts as a stone cracks against the side of his face.

People bend to gather more projectiles and I hold the dagger to the skinny man's throat.

"Enough of this silliness," a woman calls delicately above the crowd.

I look for the owner of that familiar voice, and find her sitting comfortably on a crate, a golden smoking pipe in one hand, a shiny apple in the other. Captain Snow.

"You will not harm another hair on their heads, or you will answer to me and my men," she says with a wicked grin. On cue, seven of the finest and strongest looking dwarves I've ever seen, step from the shadowed alley to stand behind their captain, each wielding a sharp weapon of some sort to emphasise her point.

"Thank the Gods," Ansel says softly. "Please, Captain Snow, this man took Emery. He's hidden her somewhere."

I snap my head to where the skinny man is cackling softly and tighten my grip on his throat.

"Did you follow the marbles?" he rasps, his fingers clawing at my hand. "I lay them out so prettily for you."

I raise him higher off the ground and watch for a moment while he squirms. "I'm not going to ask you again. What did you do to her?"

"She did leave *one* marble for you to find, did you not see it?" he gasps.

It clicks. The marble by the well. That hadn't been a small animal at the bottom, but Emery herself. Something pools in my stomach, a weight of sorts.

I release the man and barge through the crowd to my horse, ignoring those who rush past me to attend to the man. The piper will die, either by my hand or by those he has wronged when they find out who he truly is.

Captain Snow chuckles from where she sits. "I find it strange that you all seem to care for the very man who would steal your kin in the darkness of night." She takes a bite from her apple then casts it to the ground and watches as it rolls to the skinny man's feet. "Don't you know? This is the Pied Piper, the very man who lured your children from their beds."

LOST AND FOUND

BEGGARS' COVE

I grip the wall of the well, and for the umpteenth time fail to climb more than a few feet. My fingers slip, palms scoring along the sharp rocks as I splash into the water below. It's a miracle I hadn't drowned when that horrible little bastard threw me down here, but at least my head has stopped bleeding. I touch the cut along my hairline and hold my fingers up to the fading moonlight. Feeling lightheaded, I sit in the water, submerged up to my chest, and lean back against the wall.

It was a terrible feeling, hearing Ansel and Ryder so close with no way to call out. Without the marbles, they'll never find me. Did Ryder and Ansel at least manage to help the young boy in the Beggar King's cottage? I can only hope they did.

My head throbs and I know better than to close my eyes after suffering an injury to the head. But I can't help it, I'm so tired. Just for a moment, just to rest my eyes, then I'll try the climb again.

EMERY... EMERY... "EMERY!"

I jolt awake and throw out a fist to beat back the Beggar King. Only it's not the red eyes I expect, or the bony, spindly fingers of the horrid man gripping my shoulders. Green eyes stare back from a beautiful face, barely visible in the moonlight.

"Ryder?" Despite being half submerged in water, my voice is cracked and broken, and I cough at the dryness clinging to the back of my throat.

"Here," he says, scooping water into his palm and holding it to my lips.

I take a sip, refusing to look away. I've heard the desert can conjure images, things that trick the mind into believing something that isn't really there. Mirages, I believe they're called.

"Is she okay?" a small voice calls from above.

I crane my head back and peer up to the top of the well, where the distinctly bald head and long pony-tailed genie leans over the rim.

A sob breaks through me, and I slump forward into Ryder's arms. They *are* here. They came for me.

"She's alive," Ryder calls up as he strokes my hair. His arms wrap tightly around my back, holding me to him — almost as if he, too, fears this might not be real.

"How did you find me?" I ask, leaning away to look up at him. A storm of emotions passes between us in the time it takes to answer my question, emotions I thought him incapable of feeling.

"We found the piper. He hinted you had been left where the first marble was dropped, so we doubled back." Ryder raises a hand to stroke the side of my face. "I'm sorry we didn't find you sooner."

"I'm just glad you found me at all," I say lightly, wiping the tears from my cheek. "I thought I was a goner for a little while there." I chuckle, but it only seems to make his frown that much deeper.

"Why are you doing that? Why smile when it's so clearly false?"

I smile again, this time genuinely. "Because I'm a captain, Ryder. I have to be strong or how will I hope to lead us through our troubles?"

He shakes his head and stands to tower over me. "There's a time to be strong and reliable, and a time to lean on others. Now is the time to rely on me. I won't let you go again, Emery. That much I promise."

I quietly nod my head, staggered by how much I believe him, by how much I truly feel I *can* rely on him after so little time together. "I don't suppose I can rely on you to get me out of this damned well then? I'm not sure I have the strength to climb up that rope."

"You can rely on me for anything, Emery." Without another word, he bends down and hoists me over his shoulder, then takes the rope in both hands and begins the climb.

"Oh Gods! Are you okay, Captain?" Ansel calls, pulling Ryder over the lip of the well and standing back as we topple onto the sand. I can't help but chuckle as Ansel falls to his knees beside me and begins to sniffle.

"I'm all right," I assure him. "A little scraped and bruised and in desperate need of some good rum, but other than that, I'll be fine." I look past him to the horses, noting only two of them. "What about the boy?"

Ryder and Ansel stare back at me quizzically. "What boy?" Ryder asks.

Oh Gods. "The boy in the beggar's cottage, you didn't find him?" Of course they didn't, *I* barely saw him, and I was in there a lot longer than they might have been. "We have to go back and get him."

"*You* need to go back to the inn and, as promised, *I'm* not letting you out of my sight. Ansel can go and collect the boy and the music box," Ryder commands

"By...by myself?" Ansel asks in a small voice.

"No," I say with a grunt as I stand on wobbly feet and make my way to the horses. "I don't want Ansel going anywhere on this island by himself. Plus, the boy will be terrified, he'll need a soft touch to calm him after such an ordeal." I curse and swear as the waterlogged cloak seems to weigh me down, then suddenly remember. Turning back to Ansel I hurriedly unfasten the strings and pull the cloak from my body.

"You should wear it, Emery, you're cold," Ansel says with a soft smile.

"That's kind, Ansel, but after the day I've had, I'm not willing to risk your mysterious master finding us next." I hold out the cloak and wait for him to take it, then wrap my arms around my body and stand by the horse waiting for Ryder.

With an obvious reluctance, Ryder walks forward and removes his coat, draping it over my shoulders before bending to lift me onto the saddle. I shiver as he climbs up to settle behind me, his warm arms snaking across my sides as he takes the reins.

"We don't have long until sunrise, so we'll be riding faster than you might feel comfortable," he warns. I barely have time to agree when he snaps the reins and the horse breaks into a gallop, following the constellation of the little Wooden Boy, to find the little *broken* boy, hopefully in time to save his life.

THE SUN BEATS down as the sea finally comes into view, turning my aching shivers into uncomfortable sweats even after having removed the long coat. When we finally pull to a stop in the abandoned town, I dismount and stumble towards the Beggar King's cottage.

Inside, still hanging from the ceiling, the boy's eyes are closed and it's impossible to tell if he's still breathing.

"Ansel, get the end of that rope and lower him down as gently as you can, Ryder be ready to catch him just in case." They each do as I instruct, and I chew my nails to splinters at the painfully slow descent.

When the boy is finally cradled in Ryder's arms, we lay him on the ground on his stomach and I go about sawing the ropes from across his body keeping him hogtied. As each of the binds snap free, an angry, bloody mark is left across his clothes and skin. When the last is cut, I roll the boy onto his side, careful to go no further should he choke on the blood from his missing tongue, then I check to make sure he's breathing. Seeing the soft rise and fall of his chest, I almost cry in my relief.

"Emery...his tongue," Ansel whispers, kneeling beside me.

"I know, we need to get him out of here. He needs help as soon as possible. Ryder can you–" I stop as Ryder lifts the boy gently into his arms and carries him out of the cottage. I'm about to follow when I remember the very thing that got us into this mess in the first place.

Turning around, I walk to where the music box lays on a small table. As I reach down and pick it up, I stare into the fireplace, where embers still glow and the headless form of the Beggar King remains, burned to a crisp.

That's the first life I've ever taken. Faced with my own warring morality, I turn from the fire and walk out of the cottage with no regrets. In that single, violent act, I've made the world a better place.

"Ansel, get on your horse and I'll pass the boy up to you," Ryder says, then waits patiently for the genie to comply.

Turning to his own horse, he helps me into the saddle before climbing up behind me. With the absence of stars, we can't afford the risk of losing our way in the desert, so Ryder leads us along the coastline, and back to the sandy city.

It's well after mid-day by the time we make it to the docks, and the boy has yet to wake. As we guide our horses through the towering entrance and into the city streets, I'm surprised to see Thieves' Lair is buzzing with customers, some scrambling over others to try and peer through the windows.

"That's them!" someone shouts from the small crowd. People turn and gasp as they point to Ryder, and then to me.

"Are you Emery? Are you the one who killed the Beggar King?" a young girl asks as she approaches our horse.

"What's going on?" I ask Ryder, turning in my saddle to look at him.

He doesn't answer and instead dismounts and leads the horse to the front door of the inn, pushing aside those trying to crowd us.

Once we're as close to the door as possible, he reaches up and pulls me down gently to herd me inside the inn, with instructions to stay put whilst he helps Ansel. Unslinging the satchel with the music box, I set it on the floor beside the leather daybed and wait, still confused by all the activity.

"Emery!" Winnie calls from the stairs. Racing down, she closes the distance between us and pulls me into her arms. "I thought we'd lost you for sure! Captain Snow said you had been left somewhere in the desert and we...well, I was worried for you," she says softly, stepping back to assess the damage.

"What's going on, Winnie?" I ask, pointing to the mayhem beyond the windows.

Before she can answer, Ryder appears through the front door with the boy in his arms and Ansel close behind him.

With everyone inside, the innkeeper hurries forward and sends the onlookers away, closing the door and securing the bolts. "Well, you haven't half caused a fuss," he says with a chuckle, wiping beads of sweat from his brow. "How are you faring?"

"I'm well, but..." I point to the innkeeper's nephew as Ryder turns to face him. Recognition dawns in an instant, and the innkeeper races forward, bundling his arms under the boy to take him from Ryder.

"Hansel!? Oh Gods, what happened to him? Where was he?" he shouts, hurrying to lay his nephew on the daybed.

"We found him with the Beggar King. His...his tongue was removed, he needs a healer," I say as I move to stand beside him.

"I'll go, bolt the door behind me" Winnie says, squeezing my shoulder before heading for the door and racing outside. She knows where the healer district is, and I trust her to appreciate the need for haste. I close and bolt the door before turning back to the boy and his uncle.

"Come on, Hansel. Wake up, lad," the innkeeper whispers as he strokes the boy's hair. "Why isn't he responding?"

"He's likely in shock and he lost quite a lot of blood," Ryder says kneeling beside them. "Though, I'm confident he'll live once his wounds have been tended to. Do you have any smelling salts?"

The innkeeper nods his head and points to the bar. "I have a jar in there beside the whiskey for waking drunkards."

Calm and unhurried, Ryder leaves us and heads for the bar in the adjacent room, reappearing soon after with a jug of water and a jar of pink, crystalline salts.

Beside me, Ansel rubs his hands together nervously and in an effort to distract the genie, I ask him to go and find Toriq. Despite his exhaustion from the past few days, Ansel shows no sign of complaint and heads up the stairs to check Toriq's room.

Ryder steps up to the innkeeper and asks him to move aside, then pops the lid on the salts and leans down to hold the boy up. Concerned for his nephew, the innkeeper tries to intervene, but I hold him back. The prince has a nose for this sort of thing, he's surprisingly well-versed in medicine, and I trust him.

As the jar is held under his nose, Hansel turns his head, finally stirring from sleep with a coughs and gargling scream as the pain settles in. After a moment, he leans back heavily on Ryder's arm and looks with tearful eyes to his uncle.

"Hansel! Oh, thank the stars," the innkeeper cries, falling to his knees beside him, he takes Ryder's place in supporting the boy's head, then at Ryder's instruction, tries to get the boy to drink some water now he's roused.

I turn at the sound of Ansel's voice, seeing a very unhappy looking Toriq descending the stairs behind him. As Ansel goes to take a seat by the fire, Toriq moves to the window, peering through the glass at the curious faces loitering outside the inn and trying to see inside.

"What's going on, Toriq?" I ask, coming to stand beside him. Outside, people gasp and point, waving for others to come and see.

Toriq mutters a curse and moves to block me from their view, then gently guides me away from the windows. "Apparently you're their new queen."

I blink, certain I've misheard, and he fills in the blanks of what I had missed during my confinement in the well. Everything about the Pied Piper, and the citizens claiming him as their champion and king. I open my mouth to say something, but what *do* I say? Wobbling, I lift a hand to my pounding head, feeling dizzy as hundreds of question enter my mind all at once.

I barely register Toriq as he gently manoeuvres me towards the fire and onto one of the leather seats. I had earned a crown by way of murdering the old king. None of it makes sense. If the old man was, in fact, a *real* king, why was he living in the middle of nowhere? Why hadn't someone killed him long ago?

One thought in particular stands above the rest. Only days ago, I had wished for the power to effect change in such a broken city. Now I'm a queen. I sigh and lean forward to hang my head between my knees. I guess that's why the saying goes, *be careful what you wish for*.

DECISIONS DECISIONS

BEGGARS' COVE

S inking into the bath, I finally relax as the filth and grime of the past few days slips away. Not long after our arrival, Captain Snow arrived at the inn with nought but a smile, and upon seeing the music box, promised to return with Caleb this evening and join us for dinner.

I can't help but muse that pirates are a funny bunch. Only a *pirate* would be confident enough to believe that dining with the friends of her captive is a normal state of affairs. Still, she promised me no harm had come to Caleb, and considering Snow's natural beauty, I'm sure he probably enjoyed a good portion of his captivity.

After allowing myself time to soak and wash my hair, I reluctantly pull myself from the bath and dress for our evening meal. Checking my appearance in the mirror, I'm no longer the frightening sight I had been earlier in the day, and I hope the boy is faring a little better too. Thinking of him, I strap the dagger to my thigh, more for comfort than necessity, and decide to check on young Hansel before meeting the others downstairs for dinner.

I open the door to my room and almost trip on the body lying outside my door. Thankfully, it isn't dead, as it grunts and rolls over.

"Ryder? What the devil are you doing outside my door?"

"You wouldn't let me *inside* your door, so I made do out here," he says nonchalantly as he stands and brushes the dust from his trousers.

I stare incredulously back at him, but am pleased to note he's at least taken the time to bathe and change his clothes. He even shaved, though only a trim, leaving a small dusting of stubble.

"Have you seen Hansel yet?" I ask, turning and locking my door. He shakes his head but notes the innkeeper believes his nephew is doing well, and has a healer stationed by his bed through the night, just in case.

"You need food," he says taking my hand and leading me towards the stairs.

"I need more than food," I mumble. I need rum...and therapy.

With the city fussing over news of the Beggar King's death and their new champion, the innkeeper had graciously decided to close the inn to any and all patrons for the night, allowing us the privacy to collect our thoughts and make a plan.

Down in the bar, the absence of the usual crowd is appreciated, but more than that, I'm thrilled to discover a feast waiting when we arrive. My mouth waters as I stare at the tables pushed together, and maids continually emerging from the kitchen with platters laden with all sorts of exotic looking foods.

As we approach, Toriq surprises me by standing and pulling out a chair for me while the innkeeper hurries over with two jugs of what he promises is his finest gin.

"You didn't have to do this," I say, feeling thankful but a

little awkward as he gushes his appreciation for saving his nephew. "We did what anyone would do. I'm just glad we found him before..." The room turns quiet and Toriq surprises me again by squeezing my thigh reassuringly.

"Hansel is doing well. Without his...well, I'm not sure he'll ever speak again, but at least he has his life to be thankful for. And we *are* thankful, Miss Emery, more so than a solid meal and a bit of drink can make up for."

The boy may yet speak. One of the villagers on the isle lost her tongue after developing a strange lump. It took many years of practice, but eventually she was able to communicate quite well. I say as much to the innkeeper, and he looks hopeful despite the doubt clearly written in the creases along his brow. As he leaves us to our meal, we're about to tuck in when a familiar, silky voice calls out behind us.

"Starting the celebrations without me? I hear we have a new queen in our midst."

I cringe at that word, *queen*, and turn to see Caleb walking towards us with Captain Snow and three of her dwarves just behind him. I move to stand, but he places a hand gently on my shoulder and tells me to sit.

"Captain...Emery," Caleb stutters, unsure what to say. His eyes harden and he stands tall, then steps back and offers a low bow.

"Oh Gods," I mutter, rolling my eyes. "Stop that and sit down so we can eat, I'm bloody starving and the food is getting cold." All of this thanking and fussing and attention is starting to make my head hurt, and my stomach is in knots I'm so desperate for food.

As Caleb takes a seat between Winnie and Ansel, I go to grab what looks like a chicken leg drizzled in something utterly mesmerising. Captain Snow steps up to the table and I almost burst into tears, but politely drop the chicken and turn to her.

"Glad to see you survived. Where's the box?" she asks, casting her eyes around the room for her prize.

Ryder reaches into the satchel behind his chair and holds it up for her to see. When Snow lifts a hand to take it, he moves the device out of reach and points to the empty chairs. "Food first, then business. Emery needs to eat."

Snow rolls her eyes and orders her men to sit, and I take that as my cue to dig in. Taking the chicken leg from the platter, I groan at the honey drizzled glaze and quickly devour that, then three more, before moving on to something different.

Across the table, Winnie watches me with something close to dismay, her lips pinching when I load my plate with vegetables and an assortment of carved meats. Already suspecting the cause of her frustration. I lower my plate and lean forward so the innkeeper's maids can't hear.

"Don't worry, your food is still the best I've ever tasted," I say with a wink. My suspicions were correct, and Winnie smiles before finally tucking into the food, her jealousy abated. "This gin, however, is unbeatable," I say, lifting the bottle to inspect the name and brewer.

One word spans the label: Canty, with the distillery being Thieves' Lair itself. I'm impressed to say the least, and decide we'll have to purchase a case to take with us when we finally leave this place.

When we're all comfortably full, the drinks are topped up and Snow begins the discussions. "So, you're a queen now. How does that feel?" she asks as she leans back in her chair and loads the pipe with fine tobacco.

"Honestly? I don't understand any of it. If all you had to do to inherit the throne was kill the beggar, then why has nobody killed him before now?" I ask, taking the first sip of the oddly sweet and tangy gin and relaxing in my chair.

"Oh, people have tried. My men and I dock at this island

at least once a month, and every time there's a story of a new challenger. You're the first woman though, perhaps that's why the Piper didn't intervene."

I shudder at Snow's mention of the man. "He said he wanted to make me his queen."

The glass in Ryder's hand cracks under his grip, and he stares down at it in surprise, before setting the pieces aside and calling the maid for another.

"You also had the hood on your side," Snow says, eyeing Ansel and the red riding cloak longingly.

"From what I hear, that creature didn't seem like the sort who would be accepted as king," Winnie says, and I have to agree. It's yet another thing I fail to understand about this island.

Snow leans over and takes the jug, pouring herself another healthy dose of gin before settling lower into her seat to share what she knows. "The story goes, that when the king of the cove presided over the city, he was respected and loved. One night, his unusual tastes were discovered by a servant who happened on the king consuming the uncooked flesh of a young girl. The servant fled the castle and told everyone who would listen, but nobody believed him. Worse, they beat him half to death for what they thought were lies. Not long after the event, children began to disappear in ones and twos, and rumours spread of a pied piper enchanting away their young, only to be consumed by the cannibal king."

"Who *was* the Piper?" I ask.

"Do you know what 'pied' means?" Snow asks with a wide smile, seeming to enjoy her story's alluring effect on everyone at the table.

"The Piper was the servant, the one that tried to warn the people," Ryder says. "The word 'pied' refers to the colour of his clothes, and is thought to be a shortening of the word 'magpie'. Royal servants traditionally wear black and white attire to denote their status. I assume this man was no different?"

Snow claps her hands together. "That's right. After being beaten to a bloody pulp by the city folk, the servant wished for revenge, and so returned to the king and offered to work for him. When the citizens discovered this treachery, they banded together and went to the palace to kill the king. Instead, they found the scattered remains of the missing children, and a note stating that for every attempt on his life, five of their young would be taken. The king kept to his word, and for every attempt, the attackers failed to return, and the children went missing. It became an unwritten law that nobody was to go near the Beggar King, and that children weren't to leave their homes after dark."

Nobody speaks as we try to process Snow's story. The innkeeper had warned me that seeking out the Beggar King was breaking this city's law. I hadn't understood then. These people have suffered terribly, their children paying for the mistreatment of one man in the name of a king that didn't deserve their loyalty. And now they're looking for their new queen.

What am I supposed to do with that? I have my own quest to attend to. I realise, then, how empty my prior words had been, when I'd wished to help these poor people. I touch my neck, as if feeling for the invisible chains snaking up to trap me in a role I'm not prepared to fulfil.

"Captain?" Winnie asks.

I look up to the faces around the table, all looking to me expectantly. "What do we do?" I ask, the words more strangled than I'd like.

Snow sighs and takes a long draw from her pipe, before releasing it slowly. "You're in a pickle, that's for sure. This city lives and breathes by its traditions. Only those who are born to the current power, or who take it by blood, can rule.

They won't accept anything else. Those who have tried to take up the mantle in the years since the Beggar King's exile have all been killed."

"Brilliant. Then in order to get out of this, my only two choices are to give birth, or to let someone run me through with a sword?" I ask.

Toriq and Ryder snap their heads to me simultaneously; Toriq with an angry scowl, and Ryder with a hard look of determination. Apparently, those options are *not* on the table.

"We could run?" Winnie suggests, biting her fingernails. "Surely they won't chase Emery down and drag her back." Beside Winnie, Ansel vigorously nods his agreement.

"I wouldn't be too sure," Snow mutters. "Worse than that, the city will descend into chaos. Sorry, Emery, but you're the first cause for hope these people have had in a long time," she says with an apologetic look.

"But I don't know *how* to be a ruler," I groan quietly.

Toriq leans forward and pours another drink, then offers it to me and says, "Well, you captain a ship well enough, why not an island?"

I give him a sideways look. "Why are you being so nice to me all of a sudden? You're freaking me out."

Everyone laughs and he smiles as I take the glass and throw back the contents, letting the drink sit in my mouth before swallowing it.

"You nearly died, Emery. It changes a man's perspective," is all he says in return.

While I appreciate this new and far more pleasant version of the man, I'm not sure I like the look in his eye, the softness there.

For the next few hours, ideas are bounced around the table regarding how I might be able to avoid taking on my new, queenly role. The best we have so far is faking my death, with the second being to accept the crown and immediately step down from my duties. Somehow, I feel it won't be quite so easy.

Additionally, Captain Snow seems inclined to remind me again and again, that with my new position comes the threat of others who might wish to challenge my place on the throne. Challenge as in trial by combat...to the death. This seems to distress more than just me, as Winnie and Ansel visibly begin to sweat, while Caleb, Toriq and Ryder look positively bloodthirsty at the notion.

"I have a suggestion," the innkeeper says from the doorway.

I hadn't seen him standing there and wonder just how much of our conversation he's heard. His quiet voice nevertheless breaks up the squabble between Winnie and the men as she condemns their apparent outright enthusiasm for a fight, and we all turn to hear him out.

"You seem reluctant to take what is quite rightfully yours," the innkeeper continues, "and I can understand that. I think I know of a replacement. If you're interested?"

"Who did you have in mind?" Snow asks, leaning forward curiously.

"Me," he says, straightening his spine. He steps further into the room, looking taller and stronger than the few times I had seen him. "Now, I know what you're all thinking – what would a tavern owner know about ruling? And you'd be right. But I grew up around here, I know the people, and I owe you a great debt. The throne would be yours the moment you want it, but I would be glad to do my bit in the meantime."

I take a moment to consider this, looking to the others and to Snow in particular. She raises her eyebrows at the humble innkeeper's suggestion, but makes no move to mock or outright dismiss him.

"Aren't you concerned about the people who might want to challenge you for the position?" I ask.

The innkeeper smiles broadly and crosses his arms. "You needn't worry about that. I make the best gin on the island, there's not a man nor woman who would wish me harm. And those who do will soon think twice, I have enough loyal customers to keep me safe."

Everyone at the table can't help but laugh at the man's reasoning, but we're in no position to deny his claim. The gin we've been drinking all night is some of the finest I've ever had.

"Sounds like the best plan so far, Captain," Winnie says. I nod my agreement and she shifts her gaze back to the innkeeper. "How do we go about doing that?"

"Well, with your permission, Miss Emery, I'll send word to the rumour-mill tonight, telling them to spread the news that their queen will address the people tomorrow afternoon. By morning, the whole city will know."

I appreciate he's trying to get things moving as quickly as possible so we can leave, but it all feels a little *too* quick, a little too rushed for something so important.

I groan and place my head in my hands to try and focus my thoughts. Nobody speaks, giving me time to weigh and consider my options. There are none. Like Winnie said, this is the best, if not the *only* choice we have.

"Do it," I grumble. "Send word." I sit up and look pointedly at the man prepared to take on such a momentous task. "I don't even know your name."

The innkeeper smiles and walks forward before offering a bow. "My name is Tomas. Pleased to officially meet you, Your Highness."

I smile up at him and hold out my hand. "Don't accept if you're at all unsure about your decision. I may not be able to return to this island, or worse I could very well die on our travels." The eight seas are home to many deadly places, and I want him to know exactly what he's in for. "Are you prepared to accept this role indefinitely?"

He steps forward and takes my outstretched hand as he kneels before me. "We have much to discuss, but if you're willing to put your faith in me, I won't let you down."

With that, I shake and accept his offer to take my place on the throne. With *that*, a commoner by the name of Tomas, the distiller of a gin known as Canty, and owner of the Thieves' Lair...becomes prince regent.

A RELUCTANT QUEEN

BEGGARS' COVE

Despite an entire evening discussing plans with Tomas, I'm hesitant to step from the inn when the time comes to address the city today. Yesterday I was a captain, today I'm a queen. *Today*…I'm a married woman.

The marriage is a lie of course, only wed by word of mouth and not by contract, all to help the citizens of Beggars' Cove swallow the bitter pill of accepting a new ruler. Still, it doesn't sit well with me, and from the way Ryder is pacing beside the fireplace, and Toriq is scratching a hole in the leather, I'm not the only one.

"Are you ready, Captain?" Winnie asks, coming to stand beside me and fussing for the tenth time today over the state of my hair. "Ansel and I will head straight for the ship and ready her to make sail as soon as you're finished. *The Arcana* looks fantastic by the way, I can't wait for you to see her," she adds, hoping to lift my spirits.

Her words pull at my heart and just about do the trick as my anxiety quietens a little. I've missed *The King's Arcana* and the open sea, and I can't wait to get this over with and leave Beggars' Cove behind, at least for now.

"Ah, my beautiful wife," Tomas calls as he walks down the stairs in his best harem trousers and finest silk coat. He falters on the last step as everyone turns and regards him with a stony glare. "Just kidding, thought I might try and lighten the mood," he says, chuckling.

"Let's get this over with," I say, sighing and holding my hand out for him to take.

With Ryder guarding our front and Toriq and Caleb watching our backs, we step outside onto the street and the entire city seems to erupt in a mighty cheer. I smile and wave as we make our way to the main square, passing shops and tea-rooms and taverns, all with signs stating they're closed for business to attend the royal speech. Every alley is filled with eager faces trying to peer over the crowd, every corner of the street packed with hopeful men, women and children. I swallow, my throat parched and nerves frayed.

With a glance towards Tomas, I relax slightly as he squeezes my hand and leans in to whisper in my ear. "You can do this. These are good people and they will respect this decision. I'm sure of it." He straightens and smiles as a young girl races forward from the crowd. He knows her well, the child's mother a maid in his establishment. Releasing my hand, he bends down to pick her up, carrying her through the street to the city square.

The crowd quietens as we climb the steps of the fountain that marks the centre of the city, and like a ripple in the water, every single inhabitant present in the streets and alleys, all take a seat on the cobbled paves. You could hear a pin drop a mile away, nobody daring to speak for fear of missing what we say.

Steeling myself, I step forward to address them. "Thank you all for coming today. As I'm sure you all know by now, I killed the man you once called your king. I have no regrets. I only wish his life had been taken that much sooner."

The crowd erupts in a cheer, and I wait for them to quieten before continuing. "What some of you won't know, is that I am a visitor to this island. I am not a citizen, I am not your friend, nor am I member of your family. But I hope, one day, I can serve to be your queen. Until that day comes, until I have learned and lived and earned the right to take on such a role, I entrust this city, this island, and all who live here to someone who *is* a citizen, a friend, and your family. Your Regent. My husband." Purposefully, and with meaning, I step to one side and hold out my hand for Tomas to take my place.

Releasing the young girl, he steps up and regards the shocked faces of the people. "Things are about to change around here, but I will serve you well," he says with a confident smile.

Before Tomas can continue, someone stands from the crowd, causing Ryder, Toriq and Caleb to unsheathe their weapons in warning.

The same person, a man, holds his hands up defensively and looks to Tomas. "So, not only did you bag yourself a beauty, but a kingdom as well? You always were a lucky blighter, Tomas...I mean, Your Majesty." With a genuine smile, the man bows.

Most in the crowd laugh and joke with only the few giving looks of suspicion or disquiet. Everyone though, every person no matter their age or their feelings on the matter, stands and bows before their new king and queen.

With that, Tomas continues. "Now, Your Queen will be taking a leave of absence. As she said, she wishes to travel the world and learn ways in which she can help our kingdom to the best of her abilities. Do you all accede to her wishes?"

I snap my gaze to Tomas. This wasn't a part of our plan, what if they say no? My shoulders sag with relief when the crowd hollers their appreciation for my efforts some even crying their wish to support my mission.

Tomas turns to me and smiles. Before I know what he's doing, he wraps an arm around my waist and locks his lips with mine.

He's lucky. If we weren't in the company of an entire city, I'd rattle his teeth with my knuckles.

I suck in a breath as he breaks the kiss and stares cheekily down at me. "Thank you, Emery. Thank you for saving our city and for entrusting me with these people. I'll make you proud and look forward to your return."

I blush and mumble an oath, but eventually smile back, unable to help myself when the atmosphere cries out for celebration. "Perhaps I'll see you soon," I say, unable to offer him more.

He takes my hand and kisses the top softly, prompting another round of applause from the crowd. "I'll be waiting, My Queen."

AFTER A STEALTHY ESCAPE from the city square, Ryder, Caleb, Toriq and I head for the docks. Despite Winnie's assurances to have the ship ready to sail by our arrival, *The King's Arcana* is still partially out of water, the dry dock still in the process of being filled before the gates are opened. But I'm grateful for that, as from here I can see the tremendous work carried out by our carpenter-shipwright, the same man who is waiting beside the ship now in a heated discussion with Winnie, and Ansel stood off to one side looking as awkward as usual.

"Captain Emery," Monty practically sings his relief, all the while glaring at Winnie. "I thought you might like to appreciate your new and improved ship before she properly takes to the water."

"I do appreciate it, and I see you fixed the tender as well," I say, admiring the small and newly mended boat hanging from ropes to one side of The Arcana's smooth, metallic hull. "Won't we sink with all this sheeting though?"

Monty laughs sardonically then chastises me for underestimating him. "Of course she won't sink. It will, however, be a hell of a lot harder for sirens to get their claws in, and for reefs to do any major damage."

Ryder steps forward to where Ansel is waiting with our bags, and takes out a purse before handing over the remaining balance in gold for the repairs. In the meantime, I scan the long row of docks for Captain Snow or her ship, and see it moored at the far end.

It's a beautiful vessel and speaks to her prowess on the open seas, boasting three masts and enough room to house a small army. As the breeze picks up, I watch as her flag flutters in the breeze, the chosen emblem an apple with one bite missing, and an axe.

"Looking for someone?" Snow calls from somewhere above.

I glance up and see her lying idly on The Arcana's railing, her head turned to watch the going ons below. "I didn't want to leave without honouring our bargain," I call up.

"I felt quite the same, hence I'm not leaving this ship until that song of yours is mine." Snow raises the music box as if to prove her point.

After instructing the others to head on up the ladder, I turn to Monty and Ryder, regarding the carpenter as he gleefully counts his coins. Once content that the amount has been paid in full, he calls on the dockhands with instructions to open the dry dock gates once it's sufficiently flooded.

"It's been a pleasure, Captain Emery, or should I call you,

Your Highness?" he asks with a chuckle. When I wave off the title, insisting 'Captain' is just fine, he tucks the purse into his pocket before offering what I hope will be the last bow I ever have to endure.

Naturally, with Ryder's proclivity for over-paying, the carpenter all but begs us to return soon, before bidding us farewell and hurrying along the docks to spend his newly earned wealth.

I'm about to climb the ladder after Ryder when I spot someone limping past Monty, trying to wave us down as they slowly make their way towards us.

Small, with curly red hair, I recognise the boy instantly and hurry along the dock to meet him halfway.

"Mi–" Hansel stops and puts a hand to his swollen mouth, the natural instinct to speak and say my name catching him off-guard.

I put my hand on his shoulder and crouch so that our faces are at the same height. "I'm glad to see you're doing better, Hansel. I have a friend who lost her tongue. It took a long time for her to speak, but she does so beautifully now, so don't worry."

Hansel smiles back, and winces at the consequent pain. With small tears in his eyes, he puts a hand to his chest and pats the space above his heart.

"Are you trying to say you love me?" I ask, feigning a gasp and a swoon then chuckling along with his silent laugh and shy shake of the head.

He pats his chest again, then places his hand over my heart, his eyes already conveying what he so desperately wants to tell me.

"You're welcome, Hansel. But I'll need some repayment," I say, standing to my feet and placing both hands on my hips. "First, I need you to look out for your uncle. But more importantly, I never want you to give up hope. Don't let that old

Beggar King steal more than he already has. You're young and strong and have so much yet to do. Can you promise me that much?"

Without waiting a beat to consider, Hansel nods his head with a determination that makes my heart swell with pride. He's so young to have been through something like that, but he's alive, and that's what counts. With a wave I turn and leave, calling back my hopes to see him again soon.

By the time I reach *The Arcana*, the dockhands have opened the gates and I reach into my pocket and offer them each a coin for their work, then jump the small gap and climb the ladder.

"How's the boy?" Snow asks, taking my hand to help me over the rail.

"He's well, all things considered," I say as I glance over the side to the empty docks. Turning, I face Snow and her men and hold out my hand. "Let's do this. I'm eager to get as far from here as possible before the people change their minds and drag me back."

Snow chuckles and holds up the shell. With two fingers, she pinches a small dial on its side and twists it anticlockwise until we hear a sharp click. With that, she smiles, looks to me and says, "Okay, Emery. Sing."

> *Come here, come now, I dare of thee,*
> *Come see this heart so pure 'n' free.*
> *Come here, come now, oh wards o'er deep,*
> *In exchange for my life your own death you will reap.*

I sing the familiar verse three times before she holds up her hand, motioning for me and everyone else to be quiet. Pushing the small dial in and twisting it clockwise, she holds it high for all to hear my song, my voice, as if I myself were singing the tune. My hand goes to my throat. I know it isn't me, but the sound is so clear I can't help but check.

When the verse is complete for the third time, Snow passes the shell to one of her men and holds out her hand. "It's been...interesting, Captain Emery."

"Likewise, Captain Snow," I say, taking her hand in a firm shake. "Next time you feel compelled to kidnap one of my men to get me to do your bidding, think twice," I warn with a faux smile.

She grins back and heads to the ship's railing, then turns her head to regard me for the last time. "It all worked out well in the end. I secured your song, and you inherited a kingdom." She pauses and looks out across the docks to where an unfamiliar crew is readying their ship to make sail. "Odd day to be heading onto the water, is it not?" With that, she mounts the rail and salutes, before dropping over the side to land on the dock below. Her men jump after her, each whistling and singing an odd tune about heading home after a long day of work.

Home.

I turn to Winnie at the helm and smile. "Take her out to sea, Winnie."

PUZZLING RESCUE

THIRD SEA

With our bearing set to the southeast, I pick up the captain's log and head down the stairs to the lower deck. Ansel is already there, scribbling what we now know is someone else's story. I wonder who they are, and if their tale is as convoluted and as a perilous as this one. It seems unlikely, and I hope the genie has nothing but warnings of trip hazards or unexpected rain on sunny days.

Placing the logbook on the table and leaving Ansel to concentrate, I walk to the starboard side of the ship and look out over the water. The Third Sea is almost as quiet as the Second, but much easier to navigate with little to no warnings of shallow reefs seen on the chart. It should make for an easy sail over the next three days to the pass. This should have been the easier stretch of our journey, with Beggars' Cove being a quick stop before moving on.

"It only gets more difficult from here," Winnie says as she walks up behind me. "Not many make it past the guardians from Fourth to Fifth, hence I've never travelled any further."

The Guardian Pass, two stone giants that bar the crossing

between the two seas. Both as alive as any human, they remain the last of the sky giants on Oceanus. If Marooners' Canal is considered tough, the guardians are nigh on impossible, their price too steep for most to pay.

"I think I have a plan for that," I say, keeping my gaze on the soft waves of the Third sea. "The giants are rumoured to ask the highest toll a sailor can pay, and I can only think of one thing."

Winnie sighs and leans forward to rest her arms on the railing. "I trust you with my life, Emery. So, I hope you're right."

I finally turn to look at her. We haven't been sailing together for long, and yet I feel the same way. I trust her. All of them, in fact. I shake my head and smile at that, at such an absurd thing.

"I best go get some dinner on before Caleb complains," she says, straightening to tie her curly, black hair into a tight bun.

I watch as she goes, laughing when Caleb catches her by the companionway and enquires about our evening meal. Seeing Ansel put down his quill and fold his pages, I head back to the table and sit beside him to open the captain's log.

Where to begin? Repairs to the ship I suppose. Working from memory, I note each of the carpenter's fine restorations and the additional shielding along the hull. I close my eyes and feel as *The King's Arcana* cruises effortlessly through the water, and note in the log that despite her metallic skin, she seems swifter than normal, more streamlined.

My quill hovers over the next entry, wondering if I should mention the Beggar King and my reluctant inheritance of his crown. I decide against it, just in case the log is somehow lost, and my identity revealed to those who might seek to ransom me.

Finally, I note our current heading and projected timeline

before reaching the Fourth Sea, then close the book and lean back in my chair to close my eyes. With the previous evening spent with the newly appointed Prince Regent Tomas to discuss his plans for the city, I'm ready to drift off and catch up on all the sleep I've missed these last few days.

"Captain?"

I groan and crack one eye open to glare at Ansel.

He chuckles and taps the pages lying on the table. "It's way past time, don't you want to read the next verse?"

I moan again and squeeze my eyes shut. "No, not really. I'm barely over the last ordeal, I'm not sure I could take another warning right now," I mutter, putting a finger to my lips in a muted request for silence.

"What's that you said, Ansel? It's already that time?" Toriq asks, coming to join us.

I open my eyes and tip my head heavenward with a long sigh, praying to whoever is up there to grant me some peace and quiet. "I'll read it when Winnie comes up with the food. If you're free, maybe you should check if she wants any help?" I suggest to Toriq.

"I already offered but she insisted one man in her galley was more than enough." Taking a seat beside me, Toriq glances around the deck. "Have you seen Ryder?"

That's a good point, I haven't seen our prince since we left Beggars' Cove. "He's probably in his cabin catching up on sleep...something I'm sorely tempted to do myself," I mutter, giving him a pointed look.

"Actually, I believe he was by the stern not too long ago. He might still be there," Ansel says pointing towards the back of the ship as if to make his point clear. "He looked concerned, maybe you should check on him?"

When it comes to the prince, Toriq is a gullible as they come. It's an incredibly rare day when the prince looks anything other than vacant, so I chuckle when Toriq rushes off, and turn and smile gratefully to Ansel for his clever distraction. Leaning my head back, I settle in under the warm sunshine as I slowly drift off to sleep.

"We have a problem," Toriq says, snapping any hope of a little shuteye under the late afternoon sun.

I slam my hand on the table. "Curse you all, can't a captain have a nap on her own deck?" I ask, sitting up straight and pointing an accusing finger at Toriq. Seeing the concern in his frown and Ryder striding up behind him, I lower my hand and sigh. "Fine, what's the issue?"

"We're being followed," Ryder says, taking a seat at the table. "I believe it's the same people we saw readying their ship at Beggars' Cove. They aren't flying a flag, but the vessel is about the same size and has been following in our wake since we left."

Unsurprisingly, Ryder looks completely unperturbed by this, which means very little when I consider the fact that it's him. Though, I'm not too concerned myself. *The Arcana* is built for speed, so I'm sure we can outrun them. Not to mention, if it is the same people from Beggars' Cove, I only saw a crew of about three. And with our crew consisting of several good fighters – not including Ansel – I'm confident we can handle a fight if it comes down to it.

"Ansel, can you head up to the helm and set both thrusters to full?" I ask. He nods and packs away his pages before doing as I ask. "Ryder, have they been gaining on us over this time."

"Yes, but not by much. I'm confident we can outrun them."

"Excellent. Well then, gentlemen, if you don't mind, I'd like to get back to what I was doing before you interrupted. Unless you have any more pressing matters that require my attention?" I'm getting a little grumpy now, but if I go to my cabin and sleep I likely won't rise until the next day, and despite my earlier reservations, I *am* interested in reading the next page of the book.

Thankfully the two have nothing left for me, so I prop my feet on the table and sink into the chair, enjoying the wonderful hum of *The Arcana's* thrusters as she picks up speed.

~

IF THE CREW thought I was grumpy before, then I'm positively incensed when I'm woken from my nap by Ryder tackling me to the deck. I try to push him off, and when that fails, I raise my fist to thump him. A loud boom pierces the air and we both cover our ears.

Cannon fire.

"Get off me!" I yell to Ryder. He rolls to one side but keeps a hand on the centre of my back, trying to keep me low. I swat it away and stand tall to search the horizon, waiting for the next boom as my indicator to duck. It doesn't come, and I spot our stalkers from Beggars' Cove.

It seems in the short time I've slept, their ship has caught up, though not entirely. They're still a ways behind us, making it odd that they would bother firing.

A boom rings out and Ryder tugs me down as *The Arcana's* stern takes a hammering. Damn, their canon is mounted on the bow.

Keeping low, I make my way to the stairs leading to the quarterdeck. Up there I'll be at most risk, but I have to check the thrusters.

"Where are *you* going?" Toriq asks, pulling me to one side and pinning me against the stairs as another canon rips through the stern's balustrade.

"Thrusters," I say, wriggling from his grip. "Go to my cabin and get the explosives."

He grinds his teeth, looking concerned as he blocks me from another round of canon fire. "Go now!" he says, releasing me.

I bound up the stairs knowing the next round will be fired in less than a minute. Behind the helm, both thruster dials remain on full, so I struggle to imagine how they've managed to catch up. Racing towards the broken rail at the back of the ship, I peer down to where the thrusters sputter and burp in the water, the metallic blades coated with slimy green seaweed.

I yelp as I turn and crash into Ryder's chest, and we both race from the stern and tumble down the stairs as the next canon ball hits.

I roll to one side, checking myself and Ryder for any sign of serious injury. "Well, at least they're not trying to sink us," I say. "That's a win."

"What the hell are you talking about? They're blowing *holes* in your bloody ship!" Ansel squeaks from behind the overturned table.

"Their trajectory is high. They're trying to get us to surrender," I call, the adrenaline conjuring a giggle at Ansel's laughable idea of a hiding spot. I turn as Toriq approaches with the box of explosives and begin setting the charge.

"Oh, you have *got* to be kidding," Caleb says as he and Winnie appear from the companionway.

I look up, following his gaze to where the siren bell begins to glow...and smile as I place the explosives back in the box. "Winnie, I need you to lock Ansel, Toriq and Caleb in their cabins." I turn to Ryder. "Help me raise the orichalcum nets."

"Or you could sing?" Toriq asks, bewildered that I hadn't thought the same thing.

"Now why would I do that, when for *once* the creatures can be of some use to us?" I reply with a grin. "Go to your cabin before you lose your head," I say, ducking as the next boom rings across the ocean between us and our attackers. The hit doesn't come, and I risk taking a peek at the stern.

Sure enough, the crew consists of three men and a woman I had failed to see at the docks. She is most likely their captain. The canon is no longer stationed at the bow, they've moved it to starboard side.

As the others return to their cabins, I hurry to *The Arcana's* righthand rail and search for the churning ripples of approaching sirens. I see it, then I hear their song.

From the rail, the orichalcum nets extend across the water, and moments later Ryder comes to stand by my side. Together we watch, and wait, and hope that the sirens will, at the very least, split up to attack both ships. But something strange happens. The bubbling mass beneath the waves is changing its path.

We walk towards the stern, watching as the sirens descend on our attackers with frightening force. Onboard, the men are screaming, holding their hands to their ears and begging for the song to stop. One rises from his knees and walks in a mesmerised daze to the side of the ship. Their captain, the only woman, screams and races forward. But she's too late, and he topples over the side, the water exploding in a frenzy where he falls and turning pink as he's ripped apart beneath the waves.

Neither Ryder nor I speak, unable to look away from the diabolical carnage before us. These people don't deserve our pity, but they have it, nonetheless. To fall victim to a siren is not something I would wish on many.

Winnie steps up quietly behind us as the first of the creatures manages to board the other ship. They were fools to take to sea without protective nets or ample training with a weapon. The other two men are to fall prey as the sirens sink their claws into flesh and drag them over the side.

The woman is left to last, swinging her sword frantically from left to right. As if remembering at the last minute, she takes out her pistol and cocks the hammer. The sirens sneer and cackle in chorus, not a single one concerned by the weapon pointed toward them. It's likely a single shot pistol. She's a dead woman either way.

Turning the barrel to her temple, she cries and mutters quiet words to a god that turns away. The sirens scream and lunge, outraged that the human would seek a quick and peaceful escape. The woman looks up and we lock eyes. She pulls the trigger.

I turn my head before her body crumples to the deck, and my gaze falls on something else. The golden-haired siren from before, the one who kissed me and broke the curse is staring back.

Unlike the storm of sirens scrambling around their victims' ship, he swims patiently through the water, keeping pace with *The Arcana*, and watching only me.

A fire erupts on the other ship, and the main mast begins to fall. Quickly, the distance between us begins to grow, and the male siren smiles. In a foreign tongue, he calls to his kind and the creatures respond, abandoning the ship and returning to the water. He looks up and waves something green in the air, then ducks below the waves.

As *The Arcana* picks up her usual speed, I realise the object the siren beheld was seaweed. He must have removed it from the thrusters, allowing us a quick getaway.

"I don't understand," Winnie whispers. "Why didn't they attack *us*, as well?"

I continue to watch where the mysterious siren disappeared and shake my head. Turning to check the bell, its blue glow begins to fade, signalling their departure. "I have no idea."

~

Everyone remains around the table after dinner for a number of reasons. We all wish to discuss the puzzling event with the sirens, and we still have the next page of the book to read. But mostly we linger and take our time because the closer we get to the notoriously cold Fourth sea, the less we'll be able to dine under the stars on a balmy night.

"It was the same creature from before, the one who kissed you," Ryder says, his tone mildly accusatory. "It seems to be tracking us."

"I'm not sure how, and I'm not sure why, but it seemed to me like the sirens were coming to our aid," I say, just as puzzled as the rest of them.

"But sirens don't *help* anyone," Winnie murmurs. "Though, that blonde one seems to feel something for you, Emery."

Again, I'm not sure why. Yet another question to add to those already stewing in the recesses of my mind. Keen to change the topic, I turn to Ansel and ask him for the book. He reaches into the satchel by his side and places it on the table before sliding it my way. Everyone shuffles their seats closer to my side of the table, each with their own nervous habits. Winnie smacks Caleb's knee as it thrums a beat beneath the table while she continues to bite her nails.

I flick the catch and open the book to the first page, carefully navigating to page four, where suddenly the last sentence of the older verse makes a little more sense.

> *Guide our queen well, she will conquer your fears.*

Queen. It's the vaguest warning we've had yet. Not simply a pet name or a turn of phrase, but an actual title. A warning that I was to inherit a crown. I shake my head and tuck my finger under the page, quickly checking that the instructions have disappeared and I'm allowed to read on. The space below the verse remains blank, so I flip the page, and read:

> *The beggar is dead, and the city freed,*
> *their king will do well, he will plant the first seed.*
> *Rest and recover, girl with blue eyes,*
> *the killer, the royal, and the one who must die.*
> *The journey for now is soft and quite fine,*
> *but the Fourth Sea is cold, so beware of the climes.*
> *There's an island to note, where the lost ones are left,*
> *perhaps stop, take a breath, and ease the bereft.*

~ SIX DAYS ~

I could panic about the fourth line of the verse, but I had already expected as much with the Guardian Pass looming in our near future. Leaning back from the book, I push it farther forward for the others to get a better look, and sip at my cocoa.

"Why are you so calm?" Toriq asks, pointing to the very line I'm trying not to concern myself with. "This says you're going to die." He taps the page more forcefully and slides the book back towards me.

"I know what it says," I assure him, snapping it shut and securing the clasp. "And it's nothing to worry about, at least for now."

"Nothing to...have you gone mad? When *should* we worry about it? When you're already *dead*?" Toriq growls, getting more heated than I've seen him.

"What's going on with you?" I ask, eyeing him suspiciously. "You've been acting strange since Beggars' Cove. Where's the man who sits in the corner and broods and says little to nothing?" I look down and notice he's removed his wedding band, only a thin white line remaining against his tanned skin. "Did something happen?"

He looks down to the finger in question and tucks his hand under the table. "Nothing of note. I'm moving on, that's all," he says, pouring himself a drink. "Forgive me for being concerned for my captain's wellbeing."

This is more than that, it's more than mere concern. "Something else is bothering you," I say, hoping to coax a real answer from him.

"I care about you, alright!" he shouts, throwing his hands in the air. "I thought you were just some witchy girl who steals people's hearts and who hurt my friend. I was wrong, you're loyal and fierce and brilliant, and I...I've come to care for you."

Winnie giggles, breaking the shocked silence and drawing a scowl from Toriq. I thought he hated me. I suppose he *did* at one point.

"Why are you so angry then?" I ask, still a little confused by his reaction. Winnie sighs woefully as Toriq lifts his head slowly to look at me, the disdain clear in the thin line of his mouth.

"Never mind, Captain. Can you *please* explain why you fail to feel concerned by the book's warning," he asks, lifting his glass to take a very long sip of his drink.

Winnie and I smile at one and other, our earlier discussion springing to mind. "I can't risk saying it out loud, so you'll just have to trust me. You'll know closer to the time," I promise them all.

Ryder narrows his eyes and taps two fingers on the table, but relents and nods his head, confident I know what I'm doing. The others seem less sure as they continue to stare my way, each waiting for an explanation.

Not prepared to submit myself to further interrogations, I stand from the table and insist I help Winnie with the dishes while the others retire to their cabins.

As we collect the plates and head down to the galley, I try to figure out how I'm going to word my own line of questions. I hadn't offered my help for the sheer joy of it. When Winnie had been reading the verse, she seemed to recognise something, something she tried to keep hidden. And I want to know what that *something* is.

Placing the dishes in the wide sink, I fill the bowl as she heads up top to collect the glasses before re-joining me. "Tell me," I say when the last of the men have passed and bade their goodnights.

She sighs, unsurprised by my command, and takes a cloth from the galley side as I pass her the first plate. "I know the island the book is talking about. It's where I came from," she says softly.

"I thought you were born on the Garden Isle."

Winnie shakes her head as she takes the next plate to dry. "I was ten when I finally decided to sail there," she says, her voice catching at the end."

"Ten? You sailed Marooners' Canal at the age of *ten*?" Even by my standards, that's more than a little impressive.

Winnie chuckles, almost dropping the plate. "No, Gods. I sailed *around* the passage. Anyway, I made it and haven't looked back since...well, not until I read the book's suggestion to go there." She rubs the plate until its bone dry, actively avoiding my gaze.

"We don't have to stop there. We have enough to make it through to the Fifth Sea now," I say. Like she said, it was only a suggestion, not a requirement set out by the book of life.

"No," Winnie mumbles, drying her hands and turning to

lean against the side. "I understand why it says we should, why it says to 'take a breath' specifically." She looks up at me, her brown eyes shining with a fear I don't understand. "There's a lagoon on the island, and at the bottom is something that might help you if all else fails with the guardians. It's a witchlight, Emery...it brings people back from the dead."

THE LOST BOYS

FOURTH SEA ~ THE ISLAND

The next three days pass as calmly as the book promises, with no mermaids, sirens, pirates, or cannibals to note. Only one person remains ill at ease. Winnie has barely spoken to anyone since our discussion in the galley. I've tried a number of times to approach her, but she always turns to busy herself and refuses to join us for meals.

I shiver as the breeze picks up and pull my quilted coat tighter around my shoulders as I look from the bow to port side. Just in the distance, a crystal tower looms on the horizon, one identical to those found on the Garden Isle. One day I would like to find out exactly what those towers are for, but today I simply admire it. With that in sight and the gradual drop in temperature, I know we've crossed into the Fourth Sea. Only one more to go and I'll finally have the answers I desire from Mother Witch.

I turn in my seat and look out across the deck. Ansel is scribbling, as per usual, while Toriq and Ryder attend to their daily routine of sparring throughout the afternoon, taking notes and lessons from Caleb.

I would often join them, enjoying the chance not only to learn from a master swordsman such as Caleb, but to relieve the boredom.

Sitting alone at the helm, Winnie stares out across the sea, a lost look in her eyes. I wish she would lean on me more, tell me about her past and why it pains her so much. At the very least, I'd like to know more about this witchlight she feels sure is the real reason behind the book's suggestion. I've never heard of such a thing, a tool that can summon someone back from the dead. I shiver, more at the thought than from the cold.

"Captain," Caleb calls from mid-deck. "You're not joining us today?"

The cold rushes through me and I start to head over. Perhaps a quick spar will help ease my stress over Winnie, or at the very least warm the chill in my bones. Removing my coat, I resist the urge to rub my arms and bounce on the spot, instead accepting Ryder's sword and taking a stance to battle Toriq.

After re-fashioning his hair in a messy bun, Toriq remains where he stands – muscles bunching as he lowers his centre of gravity and loosens the hold on his weapon. Primed and ready.

I launch into a full-frontal attack, raising the sword and swinging it down in a move that, against a less skilful opponent, could cleave a skull in two. He easily parries, then swings his sword down and to the side before nudging me back with his elbow. I stumble a few paces and he assumes the stance again, waiting, always waiting for his challenger to make the first move. With a wide grin, he lifts his hand and curls two fingers, beckoning me forward, baiting me.

"Cheeky devil," I murmur, but don't rise to his taunts, not yet. I take a step to the right, then another, careful of my footing as I slowly circle. The moment his foot leaves the ground, I strike. He brings the sword up but only just in time, and he has yet to find his feet. I swing again, and again, each fall of the sword that much closer to a fatal hit. Knocking his weapon high, I lunge, driving my shoulder into his chest, before plunging the blade into his gut.

Toriq coughs and clutches his abdomen. "That hurt!"

I laugh and bow, signalling the end of the match, then throw the wooden training sword back to Ryder. "You can't go easy on me just because I'm a woman, Toriq. That won't do anyone any good."

He mutters something under his breath then straightens to look at me. "Okay then, let's go again."

I waggle my finger at him and tut. "Now, now. We all know training should be done with a clear head and not with silly notions of revenge." Picking up my coat, I swing it over my shoulder, feeling quite pleased and much warmer than before, then sashay my hips as I walk away throwing back a victorious grin at the grumbling Toriq and laughing Caleb.

Winnie spots me heading up to the helm, the remnants of a smile on her lips from watching our match quickly fading as she tries to move past me on the stairs.

"Not so fast. We need to talk," I say, blocking the stairs.

"I should really go and prepare–"

"Dinner can wait," I insist, taking her elbow and gently but firmly leading her to the bench by the port rail. "You can't keep shutting us out, Winnie. I know I'm your captain, but I *had* hoped you might consider us friends enough to be able to confide in me."

Her eyes glance shyly to mine, and she smiles sadly. "I do consider you a friend, Emery. I just...don't want you to think less of me."

I sink back against the rail and sigh dramatically. "How could you think so little of me?" I ask, giving her a wink. "Come on, out with it."

She shuffles and fidgets on the bench for a moment before settling. "I was their leader, the one who looked after the lost boys on that island all those years ago. I eventually decided to leave, part of me scared, the bigger part tired of the same bedtime stories, the same fights, the same berries and shrubs for dinner. So, I built a raft. I didn't have the skills or materials to build it for more than one person, and planned to leave by myself."

I whistle softly and lift both arms to relax them across the rail. "I couldn't have built a raft at that age. So far I'm nothing but impressed."

"Well, aside from the fact that I tried to abandon the boys, I was caught on the eve of my departure by my second in command." A soft smile curls at the corner of her lips, and she ducks her head. "Peter was out foraging with three others when they found me loading what little supplies I had onto the raft. He told me I had to stay, that I couldn't abandon them. He went to fetch more people, asking the other three boys to watch over me until he returned."

"But you managed to convince them to join you instead?" I ask, starting to put the pieces together.

She bobs her head, a stray tear falling to her lap. "Two of them, yes. The third tried to stop us, a boy call Chubs. I hit him over the head with a rock, he might be dead for all I know," Winnie cries, the longstanding emotional dam finally breaking as she bursts into a flood of tears.

I draw her in and hold her close, rocking us both back and forth. "Hey, do you know how hard it is to kill someone with a rock?" I ask, holding her back and smiling softly. "It's hard for an *adult* to do, never mind a bloody ten-year-old!"

She chuckles but the sobs continue, and I pull her back into my chest. "Winnie, you were a child. You were doing what you needed to survive. Where were the adults? Your parents?"

Winnie sniffles and leans back, wiping her face on the sleeve of her coat. "We don't know. The boys just appear at random, wandering through the forest. What frightened me the most, is that when they get to a certain age, eighteen perhaps, they...vanish, and we never see them again.

"What do you mean?" I ask softly.

"I don't know, Emery. One told me of a voice that calls them to the mountain, but they always go, every single one of them, disappearing forever. I arrived when I was four, I think. My memory is fuzzy, but I'm the only one to ever arrive by boat. That's all I remember, a small boat and two people leaving me on the sand. They were sad, I think." She shakes her head, as if hoping it might knock something loose, then sighs.

"You don't have to come with us, Winnie. You can stay on *The Arcana* and wait for us to return."

"No. This has been a long time coming, and everyone I once knew will have disappeared by now." She stands and smiles down at me, her eyes tired and swollen from the tears. "I think I'll head to bed. It won't be long before we reach the island."

I watch as she leaves, my heart breaking for this kind and compassionate woman, wishing I could shoulder some of her burden.

I WAKE at first light when a sharp knock raps on the door of my cabin. Having predicted to arrive at the island no earlier than midnight, I had posted an overnight watch to ensure the ship was anchored within tender distance of the shore.

After quickly dressing, I head for the main deck, noting the sails are furled and *The Arcana* at anchor as I cross the deck to the starboard side. Squinting against the predawn fog, a small island peeks though the mist, wild jungle capturing the amber light. According to my chart, this land is barely half the size of the Garden Isle, with only a single mountain at its centre and several sandy inlets visible.

As expected, there's no dock in sight, meaning we'll have to use the tender to make our way to shore. With the skiff only designed to carry four people, it had been decided the night before that Ansel and Caleb would remain with the ship and therefore take up the night watch, knowing they could alternately catch up on sleep throughout the day with one always guarding the ship.

I turn and make my way up the stairs to the quarterdeck where Ansel and Caleb are in deep discussion. Caleb had made it plaintively clear he wasn't pleased about being left behind, but he and Toriq had drawn straws, with Toriq winning...or losing depending on how our trip goes.

"One of you can go and get some sleep now if you like?" I ask.

Ansel and Caleb share a look before the genie finally admits what's been troubling them. "I'm not sure stopping here is a good idea, Captain."

I take a seat on the bench and hold out my arms, regarding them both with open curiosity. "How so?" I can hardly fault their concern. After Beggars' Cove and Marooners' Canal, I'm hesitant to stop anywhere but our final destination at this point.

"Two reasons," Ansel continues. "First is the place itself." He turns his head and gazes past the fog to the island's low mountain and jungles, then leans in to whisper. "It's unnatural, Emery. Do you see the way the fog fails to shift despite the wind?"

I *had* noticed that, and I was trying not to dwell on it. "I agree, it's...bizarre. What's your next concern."

Ansel swallows, his lips puckering in annoyance. "Oh,

well, the second is the witchlight Winnie told us about. They're dangerous things and most were destroyed by the coven leaders. I could hardly believe it when she told us there's one on this island."

Again, their concern is well grounded. The witchlight is rumoured to bring people back from the dead, but bringing back a soul is another thing entirely. Winnie had seen fit to warn me that while the body will always reanimate, it's often too late for the soul as Death herself comes to collect. And Death isn't known to give back what she has already claimed.

"Truth be told, I'm not sure I want the thing either. But Winnie is insisting the book is giving us a clue, like it always does."

"You assume my brother is infallible...but this is proof against that, Emery," Ansel warns. "You must not claim the witchlight."

Caleb speaks differently on the matter, more concerned by the book's warning regarding my certain death. He feels by having the light, we at least have a backup plan should things go wrong. I'm inclined to agree.

We all turn as Ryder approaches the stairs to the helm, a somewhat sour look on his face. "If this light can save Emery, then we're getting it, and I won't hear any more on the matter," he says, looking pointedly at Ansel.

It's rare we see the authoritative *prince* in Ryder, when more often he is the warrior, the protector...the unfeeling one. Ansel withholds what amounts to a squeak, and bobs his head in quiet acquiescence.

"Are Winnie and Toriq awake?" I ask Ryder, eager to diffuse the tension.

He looks down at me, as if only just noticing my presence. "Yes. Winnie is gathering supplies and Toriq is waiting by the ladder."

A little taken aback by the sharpness in his tone, I watch

as Ryder turns and heads down the stairs. Caleb, equally as surprised, meets my questioning stare and shrugs softly.

I meet Winnie as she emerges from the companionway with a leather bag filled with sandwiches and water skins, and we both head over to the ladder to find Toriq already lowering the tender.

Heading down last, I take a seat at the back and use one hand to pump the handle and activate the propeller, while using the other hand to guide the rudder, taking us to shore.

"Be on the lookout," Winnie warns softly as the tender beaches on the white-sanded shore. "They'll already know we're here."

Stepping onto the beach, we each take a corner and haul the boat further up the sand so as not to lose it to the changing tides.

A wall of varying trees wrapped in thick vines and ivy loom in front of us, the call of birds and exotic creatures sounding from within the forest beyond.

"This place reeks of Death," Ryder says, stepping close to my side and clasping the hilt of his sword.

Winnie nods her head and hesitates, but eventually takes the first step, leading us on as she beats a path through the dense foliage.

At her command, we remain silent as we follow along, each listening for the rustle of leaves or snapping twigs. Not a single noise feels out of place. If the children, if these lost boys are hiding, they're very good at it.

Ansel had been right regarding the unnatural elements of this place. Back on the ship, the air had been close to freezing, but since passing through the fog and leaving the beach, my shirt slowly dampens with sweat beneath the heavy quilt of my coat. Perhaps the jungle operates on a micro-clime, enhanced by the dense vegetation?

As the ground inclines the closer we come to the mountain, we stop for a break, forced to remove our coats when the rising heat becomes too much.

While Ryder, Toriq and I each take a seat on a fallen log, Winnie stands and looks around, squinting through the trees and inspecting our surroundings. With a cough to clear her throat, she takes a knee, her hands shaking as she reaches into her bag and pulls out two sandwiches. Despite only being midmorning, I'm already famished and reach forward to take one.

"Stop," Winnie whispers, pulling the food away before quickly assessing the trees again. "Sorry, Emery. But these aren't for you." She stands and turns in a tight circle, holding her arms out wide. "Well, are you going to come out and say hello, or not?"

Whoops and hollers answer her call as ten young boys emerge from the jungle to surround us.

On either side of me, Ryder and Toriq stand and unsheathe their weapons, prompting me to mutter an oath and pull them each back down to sit on the log.

Covered with leaves to decorate and camouflage their bodies, and mud to hide the shine of their skin, the wild boys bounce around in a wide circle, howling and yipping like animals as they prod the air with their sharpened sticks.

"Now you stop that right this instant," Winnie calls, putting a hand on her hip and pointing to each boy in turn.

The boys titter and snort their amusement, one going so far as to say, '*you are not mother*'.

Winnie harrumphs, then holds her hands up in defeat. "I guess we'll have to eat these sandwiches ourselves then." Bending down, she picks up one of the wrapped parcels and throws it to me with a wink.

I understand her game and unwrap the paper, taking the bread and sniffing it with a look of pure delight. "Wow, this smells fabulous." I cast my gaze around the circle of boys, watching as they slowly come to a standstill. All at once the spears are dropped and they race towards her bag, each snatching at least one parcel with the quicker and bigger boys getting two.

I'm torn between chuckling and crying as the boys gobble down the small feast. They're so skinny, the rags they wear clinging to thin arms and legs. Being an orphan myself, I'm suddenly overwhelmed with gratitude for having been raised by the sisters. These boys had been abandoned on the island, left to starve and fend for themselves.

Two of the younger ones begin to scrap, one protecting his second sandwich from the other. Winnie moves to try and pull them apart but takes an elbow to the nose for her efforts. Again, Ryder and Toriq try to intervene, but I hold them back as two of the taller boys step forward and break up the spat, plucking the sandwich and holding it in the air.

"This is for Father," the tallest boy states, glaring at the others. "We will take Mother to see him too." He looks up to Winnie, who rubs her nose and smiles.

"I would very much like to meet your father," she says, then turns to me. "If that's okay with you?"

I nod, just as curious as the others to meet this mysterious parental figure when we all now know the boys only remain on the island to a certain age. With that decided, the little rascals jump to attention and offer a funny salute to the oldest, then turn to us and proceed to pull at our clothes.

Their excitement is infectious, some whispering about the sandwiches and how they wish they had a hundred more. Others wonder at our size and ask if we're giants, to which we aren't really sure how to respond. To tell them we are adults might incite a panic or confusion, with the boys wondering why they never become adults themselves. And they would be right to ponder such a thing.

By the time we reach the lost boys' encampment, the sun

is high and beating through the exposed gaps in the canopy. Back on the ship the halyards had begun to freeze in the cool clime, but here it's hotter than the deserts of Beggars' Cove.

I wipe the sweat trickling down my neck and glance up into the trees at the sound of running feet. Several faces stare back from rickety walkways stretching high up from tree to tree, each leading to small huts and further bridges made from vines and tightly bound logs.

"This is different," Winnie whispers, awed by the sight above. "It wasn't anywhere near this big when I lived here."

The boys release our hands and race ahead to where several large huts sit side by side on the forest floor, their roofs thatched and held together with reeds likely sourced from a nearby river. At the centre of the commune sits a large fire pit, with a number of the younger children lying idly about or making crafts with twigs and bark.

They each jump up with our arrival, looking warily from us to the boys who had led us here. We wait by the edge of the clearing while words are exchanged and the sandwich is presented as if it were a reverent offering. The children clap their hands excitedly and wave for us to approach.

"We'll take you to Father now. Come on, in here," the sandwich bearer says, taking Winnie's hand. We follow along as we're led into the central and tallest of the ground huts, built to surround the base of a great tree. Being a singular, round room, with one quick glance it's easy to tell there's nothing inside.

"Winnie?" a voice rasps from the centre of the room.

I step to one side, peering around Winnie and the boys to see where the voice had come from. My heart leaps into my throat at what I see there.

A boy...though, not entirely. What speaks is something impossible – a teenager, his body gnarled and rooted into the bark of the tree at the centre of the hut, as if that tree and the boy were becoming one.

"Winnie?" the wooden boy calls again with a laboured breath, his eyes a clouded grey and neck stiff with the growing bark. The wood groans as he smiles. "I knew you would come back. I've been waiting."

WITCHLIGHT

FOURTH SEA ~ THE ISLAND

"Peter?" Winnie whispers, stepping up to the tree and falling to her knees. "What...*how* are you still here?" she asks, her voice cracking under the weight of what she sees.

The boy's face cracks painfully as his smile only widens. "I didn't go to the mountain like the others. I wanted to wait...for you," he whispers.

Winnie cries and throws her arms around the tree, around Peter. I step forward instinctively, protectively, frightened the tree might try and absorb her too. I find my breath when she steps back and taps the side of Peter's trunk, prompting a wince from the mutating boy.

"You bloody fool," she says with a sob. "I never said I was coming back!"

Peter grins again, some of the bark encroaching on his face breaking away and falling to the ground. "Did...too," he barely manages to say. "The woman calls to me, Winnie."

A woman? I think back to Winnie's tale about the older boys who spoke of hearing such a voice, before wandering up the mountain and disappearing forever.

"Won't you tell me a story, Winnie? Just one more?" Peter asks, his hope the last shining light in his failing vision.

Tears roll down my cheeks at the tree's innocent request, and beside me, Toriq sniffs and tries his best to wipe the drops before they fall. I look to Ryder, wondering, hoping that perhaps this will be the thing to break down those walls. Nothing but curiosity stares back as he turns from Peter to stare at me.

"Of course I'll tell you a story, Peter, just like I did before," Winnie says, holding a hand to his cheek. Turning to the younger boys, she instructs them to fetch the others, stating she will tell them all a great tale of the lands beyond this one.

They race from the hut without having to be told twice, and shouts of excitement fill the jungle as the word is spread.

With only a small amount of space offered inside the hut, Toriq, Ryder and I step outside to allow more room, and young faces rush past to find a spot on the floor. Winnie waits for the last of the boys to gather before beginning her long tale of sirens, mermaids and pirate captains, and I quietly beckon for the others to follow me to the fire pit.

"What the hell is this place?" I whisper when we're comfortably out of earshot.

"Death," Ryder says, staring back at the hut where the children laugh and gasp at Winnie's story. "This whole place is…wrong. We shouldn't be here."

Toriq and I are inclined to agree, but what about the boys? There are too many to help, too many to ferry aboard our ship. I look back to the hut and don't even bother to count. There are at least a hundred small faces, all boys, with not a single girl amongst them.

Seeming to understand my concern, Toriq leans over and puts a hand on my shoulder. "We could go to one of the islands in the north and bring back more ships. That's assuming the children *want* to go. They seem...content with their lives here," he says. It's true, and his observation eases me somewhat.

THE LIGHT HAS ALREADY BEGUN to fade by the time Winnie finishes her story. The children leave the hut, all yawning and rubbing their eyes sleepily as they climb the ladders and return to their shanties in the canopy.

We wait by the fire for Winnie to appear, but she doesn't, and we don't go to her, instead giving her and Peter the space they need to be reacquainted.

Is this why the book had brought us here? *Ease the bereft*, it had said. None of the children seemed so afflicted, but perhaps it was for Winnie's sake? I bite down on an apple we had found on a nearby tree, wishing I had brought my bow and arrows to hunt.

"Perhaps we should abandon the witchlight?" I mumble, more to myself than the others. "Maybe we really have achieved what we came here to do, to help Winnie."

Ryder shakes his head, but before he can say more, Winnie steps up behind him and takes a seat beside us.

"I still think we're here to get the light, Emery," she says, taking a stick and poking at the embers. The fire burps and pops satisfactorily, coming back to life as she adds more kindling. "Peter is gone."

"Gone. You mean..." I take a long breath and look to the forest floor. "I'm so sorry, Winnie."

"I never thought I would see him again, but he was waiting all this time...At least I got to say goodbye."

"Do you know what happens when they go to the mountain?" Toriq asks softly, conscious of her pain, but desperate to know more.

"As I told Emery, all I remember is that when the boys

reached a certain age, they would hear a woman calling for them. Each would go willingly to the mountain to meet her, and none would return." Her voice breaks and she holds her head in her hands. "All this time Peter could hear her but refused to go. He told me that one day he sat by the tree and stubbornly, *openly* refused the woman, then fell asleep. The next morning he was unable to move, and over the years his body slowly started the process of becoming one with the tree."

"It's not magic," Ryder says matter-of-factly, his tone and expression unfeeling. "I only feel magic from one place, and it's coming from the far side of the island.

Winnie sits up and wipes her tears while nodding her head. "That's probably the witchlight. We'll leave at first light to get it," she promises. Turning to me, she takes my hands in hers and kisses each of them softly. "Thank you for being patient and giving me today, Emery. Thank you for giving me the chance to say goodbye."

AFTER AN UNCOMFORTABLE NIGHT under the stars, we're all tired and achingly hungry when we leave the children's canopy city this morning.

Following Winnie's lead, we head for a nearby river and follow its course upstream, stopping only to refill our water skins and to catch and cook what she insists is a very tasty treat.

I stare at the water slug dubiously, but tuck into the meal nonetheless, only to find it's oddly similar to fish. Absolutely ravenous, I devour my portion and resist the urge to suggest we find another.

If not for the strangeness of the place, I could see myself returning here to explore the jungle and enjoy the sights.

High in the trees where they know they are safe, jungle creatures watch as we pass, some squawking, others howling, perhaps in greeting or to warn their kin.

Winnie and I chat as we walk, talking of plans to help the children escape the island, and openly wondering if they would wish to leave at all. Slowly throughout the morning, the stream widens to become a river, and the roar of water comes from somewhere ahead.

We step from the jungle into a wide, open clearing, a great waterfall spilling from the mountain's belly high above. I lift my hand to shield the sun's glare as I follow the long curtain of water. Above the spray, multicoloured birds with long, feathered tails soar in and out of the rising mist, as if cleaning themselves in a fun and inventive way.

"This place is beautiful," I whisper. "Is this the lagoon you were talking about?"

Winnie nods and stares wistfully at the turquoise waters below. "The witchlight is beyond the waterfall. It's a difficult swim, but I came close once. I can hold my breath almost twice as long as the last time I tried, so I'm confident we can make it now."

"Maybe I should go instead?" I say, looking worriedly from her to the water. "I can hold my breath for longer than average."

"No, there's an underwater cavern with a few twists and turns involved," Winnie says as she begins undressing. "You can come with me, but you certainly can't go on your own."

"Wait," Ryder says, taking my arm as I begin to remove my shirt. "I'm unable to hold my breath for long, so I won't be able to follow."

"We're not asking you to follow," I say, tugging my arm from his grip and pulling the shirt over my head as I silently thank the gods Winnie and I had decided to wear underwear today.

"I agree with Ryder. What if there are sirens down there?" Toriq asks, crossing his arms. "Considering you were warned of an impending death, I'd also rather you stayed here."

"Well, I would rather you two take a step back and stay here while Winnie and I go and get the witchlight," I say stubbornly.

The book's prediction doesn't speak of here and now. But I can't tell them that. Not yet. Before Toriq and Ryder can object further, I discard my clothes to one side and walk towards the water's edge. With a sly grin I look back, wave at them, then dive in.

When I surface it's to a symphony of expletives from Toriq, and something close to a growl from Ryder.

With a netted sack tucked under one arm, Winnie giggles as she wades into the water. "You drive them mad, do you know that?" she asks as we swim towards the waterfall.

"The feeling is mutual," I mumble in return. "Don't get me wrong, I appreciate their concern – to a degree. But they have to trust me as well. Trust that I know what I'm doing."

Winnie rolls onto her back to swim the rest of the way, telling me about her deceased wife and the similarities between us. Apparently Winnie seems inclined to take the men's side, saying her wife was just as hard-headed and as stubborn as me.

I follow her lead and roll onto my back, enjoying the coolness of the water under the midday sun. "Also, I don't want you in here alone in case a siren *does* show up," I say.

"Oh, they don't come here. The same goes for mermaids. They never seem to come past the fog, almost like they're scared or something," she says. "Don't get me wrong, this island is…strange. But it still kind of feels like home."

I want to ask more, but we reach the waterfall and she ducks underwater. I follow, taking a breath and diving to swim beneath the churning falls above. Just ahead, the wide mouth of a cave opens up and I follow Winnie through until she heads for the surface. Breaking through, I'm lost for words as I look up, the walls of the cave a veritable treasure trove for both the eyes and the pocket. Lining the cave and reflecting the light from the water are rocks of natural crystal, some pink, others blue, but most white and all at least the size of my fist.

"Come on," Winnie says, tucking her finger under my chin to close the gaping hole of my mouth. Again, I take a breath and dive below, following closely behind as she weaves her way through the underwater tunnels. She was right, I never would have found this place on my own.

My lungs burn by the time she surfaces again, and I begin to worry this might be too much for her. Winnie coughs, holding a fissure in the rock as she heaves in several heavy breaths. With a promise that we're nearly there, she dives, and again I follow.

Through the blurry darkness of the water, something glows in the distance. So far we've been relying on sunspots, cracks in the rock above to light our way. But this tunnel is darker than the rest and growing narrower, too narrow to swim side by side. My panic subsides when the space finally opens up, and Winnie ascends...slowly...too slowly. I take her arm and kick for the surface, breaking through, but too fast. My head cracks on the ceiling and I yell bloody murder, then check on Winnie. She's okay, but only just. Getting out of here is going to be another matter altogether.

"Where is the witchlight?" I ask, taking the netted sack from around her shoulder and guiding her to a natural handhold in the rock. Even with our heads brushing the ceiling, the water reaches our chin.

"Right below us," she says, her breathing haggard. "It isn't too deep. I just need a quick stop."

"Stay here, I'll go down and get it," I say. She starts to

object but I'm already plunging below. I had assumed the glow from before was the result of a crack in the cave's ceiling, and for the most part I was right. But the deeper I get, the more that light is concentrated in one area, until my fingers touch an oddly shaped rock on the bed of the cave. The light from the rock grows brighter, as if resonating with my skin...no, not my skin. The light *throbs*, the beat in rhythm with the one pounding in my head, my heart. I head for the surface, clutching the small object in my hand.

"I got it!" I cry, breaking through the water more carefully this time to avoid the low ceiling. I glance around, eager to show Winnie, but she isn't here. Tucking the object into my netted bag, I duck below to search the water.

There, floating down, down...

I swim desperately and clutch at her shirt. There isn't enough room in this cavern to try and revive her, I'll have to swim to the next. I power through the water to the small opening of the tunnel, the skin on my hands and back and shoulders scraping painfully along the wall as I hug Winnie to my chest and shimmy us through the gap.

My lungs are burning already, and we're barely halfway to the air pocket. The muscle in my left leg begins to spasm and I beg the ocean herself to stop it from seizing. One cramp and we're both dead if I don't make it to the next cavern.

Light glows ahead and I almost cry with relief. Calling on a new, untapped reservoir of sheer will, I pour everything I have into my legs and kick for the surface. We break through and I scream with the effort to keep Winnie afloat.

Filling my lungs, I'm forced to tread water as I check her breathing and heart rate. Her heart is slow, and only getting slower. She's not breathing. Pinching her nose, I furiously kick my legs to keep us afloat and breath into her mouth as best I can. One...two...three – I try to pump her heart with sharp, rhythmic hugs, but I don't know if I'm doing it right. I try again and again, repeating the same movements and willing her to live.

I gasp as the water around us sways and bubbles, and a beautiful, elegant face emerges slowly from beneath. Pulling Winnie to my chest protectively, I hold the rock above my head, ready to fight whatever has come to prey on us.

"You," I say when I recognise the male siren, the one who had saved my song, and saved us from capture. "How did you find us?"

He swims forward until he's close enough for me to see the vivid turquoise in his eyes, like the lagoon itself had seeped into their depths. He raises one hand and strokes my cheek, catching the tears I didn't realise were falling. "I followed these," he says, his voice soft and sad as he touches a finger to his lips. Looking down at Winnie, he frowns, the skin shimmering lightly along the creases. "You should not be here, Emery. This island is not a place for your kind."

"Please," I whisper. "Please help me get her out of here."

He frowns again and all but snarls his disapproval, but takes Winnie from my arms. "Stay here. I'll come back for you," he says.

My head feels heavy, but I nod and tell him I'll stay, I'll wait for the siren to return. It's not a sentence I ever thought I'd say, at least not in this lifetime. He smiles and strokes my hair, whispering words in his foreign tongue, then slips beneath the water with Winnie.

I pat my cheeks with one hand, surprised by how quickly I'm beginning to fade. When that doesn't work, I give each cheek a hard slap and curse witchlights, and magic books, and underwater caverns for landing me in such a sticky spot.

"What are you doing?" the siren asks, swimming towards me.

Spooked by the sudden sound of his voice, I let go of my handhold and sink into the water. A strong, lightly shimmering arm wraps around my waist and pulls me back to the surface.

"Emery," he calls, the single word laced with concern.

"Humans don't like it when they're snuck up on," I mutter, coughing up the lagoon's salty water.

He chuckles, the sound throaty and warm, not cold and cruel like it should be. The concern remains, and he frowns again as he touches his fingers to the back of my head. "I thought I tasted you," he says, his fingers coming back pinkish with blood. Once again, he puts them to his lips, and for a brief second, his irises flash like rubies. "I need to get you out of here. Hold your breath, Emery. Don't fall asleep."

He pulls me into his embrace so our bodies are flush, every muscle taut and hard as if carved from steel cables. Taking a breath, I wrap my arms as far around his chest as they will go and try to cling on as he dives below and races through the cavern tunnels. My arms slip, but it doesn't matter, his hold on me is unrelenting. In a fraction of the time it would have taken me to swim the distance, the siren breaks through the spray of the waterfall and carries me to the shore.

Ryder is in the water waiting for us to surface and wades in deeper to pull me from the siren's embrace. As I'm passed from creature to man, I catch the barest hint of challenge from the two beings as both quietly snarl at one and other.

"Where's Winnie?" I ask frantically. Seeing her lying on the beach, I push away from Ryder and the siren and drag myself through the water towards her. I drop beside Toriq as he continues the chest compressions, stopping only to fill her lungs with air. Beneath her dark curls the sand is tinged in blood, and I belatedly realise she must have hit her head as well.

"Emery, I think...I think she's gone," Toriq whispers, continuing the life-saving manoeuvre.

No. She can't be gone. "You're not trying hard enough, you have to bring her back!" I scream. *Bring her back*...The witchlight.

Lifting the netted sack from around my shoulder, I remove the object, seeing it properly for the first time. A skull, perhaps no larger than that of a small child with swirls of golden alloys decorating the sides. I place it on Winnie's chest and Toriq knocks it away.

"What are you doing?" I cry. "This can save her!"

"Her *body*, maybe. But you don't know if it will bring back her soul," Toriq warns.

"I have to at least try," I growl and push him away as I place the skull back on her chest.

We wait...and wait. Ryder walks up the beach to stand beside me, his sword half unsheathed in case the Winnie we know is lost forever, just an empty shell walking around in her place.

"Why isn't it working?" I ask, turning to Ryder. He shakes his head and I look to Toriq who appears just as downcast and confused as I feel.

"Give it a moment, Emery," the siren calls from the shallows. "The child is searching."

"Searching?" Searching for Winnie's soul. I move to sit behind her head, lifting it into my lap to stroke the tight curls now brittle with the salt from the water. "Come back, Winnie," I whisper, hoping my voice reaches her soul before Death takes it for herself.

Winnie bolts up, the skull falling into her lap as she clutches her stomach and heaves up the water she had inhaled. I crawl along the sand to sit beside her, placing a hand on her shoulder to tell her everything is okay. She glances frantically from me, to Toriq and then Ryder, eyes wild and disbelieving. Looks down at the skull in her lap, she screams and knocks it away, scrambling back to get as far from the witchlight as possible.

"Winnie!" I call, holding my hands up as if to calm a wild animal. "It's us, you're safe, you're okay."

The *shing* of Ryder's sword cuts through the air as he pulls it from the scabbard, hesitating slightly when my eyes slide to him with a cold warning not to touch her.

Edging forward, I speak to Winnie in a calm and dulcet tone, repeating the same mantra over and over. She is safe. She is alive. We are here.

"Emery," she finally whispers, and I almost cry with relief. Surely this means her soul has returned to us? "Emery, I saw her, I saw both of them."

"Saw who?" I ask, edging closer.

"I saw the witchlight…and Death."

I crawl forward and close the gap between us just as Winnie sinks into my arms, her body shaking.

"Death gave me back, Emery," she whispers, clutching my forearm. "She wanted me to give you a message."

DEATH'S GIFT

FOURTH SEA ~ THE ISLAND

Winnie sags in my arms, and for a moment I'm afraid we've lost her again. My fingers fly to her neck when she refuses to rouse, but her pulse beats with life, her breathing slow and steady. Alive. I slump back and of all things, I burst out laughing.

"Emery, are you okay?" Ryder asks, sheathing his weapon and sitting beside me.

I nod my head, the moment of hysteria cooling as I look past him to the siren.

"You saved our lives…again," I call, the gratitude sincere despite my inherent disbelief. Lying Winnie on the sand, I rise and walk towards the water. "Why are you here?"

His golden hair catches the light as he tilts his head softly to one side. "I could taste your fear. I had to come," he says, his expression twisting to one of deep resolve. "You *must* leave, Emery. Now. Death has a claim here, and she does not take kindly to trespassers."

"I don't understand," I say, stepping into the water. Ryder takes my arm and holds me where I am, his eyes like jaded steel and full of warning.

"I know of your curse, Prince," the siren says with a sneer, his gaze flicking angrily to Ryder's hold on me. "My gift to you is this – a warning. Kiss Emery, and you will lose your heart forever. If the curse doesn't ensure that much, then I will."

A low rumble emanates from Ryder's chest, something primal answering the siren's challenge. "We'll see," is all he says.

The siren's teeth flash in a wicked smile, then he turns his gaze back to me, his eyes softening. "I'll be around, should you need me."

I call out, but he turns and swims away, once again leaving me with nothing but more questions.

"I can't believe I'm saying this," Toriq says from behind us, "but I agree with fish-boy. We need to get the hell out of here." He stands, lifting Winnie into his arms with little effort. "You get dressed, I'll get moving and you can catch up."

Picking up my breeches, I shimmy into those first, the residue of salt on my skin making it difficult and uncomfortable. As I pull the shirt over my head, I wince as the material brushes the scrapes along my skin.

"You're hurt," Ryder says, stopping me to assess the damage.

I tell him I'm fine, that one of the passages had been a little two tight for two people and I'd scraped my hands and arms along the rock.

He watches me carefully as I resume dressing, and I finally slide on my bright red boots. Turning away, I pick up the skull from the sand, wrap it in the netted sack, and then tuck it into my backpack before collecting Winnie's clothes and shoving them in alongside it.

We catch up quickly with Toriq, and Ryder takes over carrying Winnie, the two of them taking it in turns as we trek back through the jungle to the island's northern shore. The sun is close to setting by the time we make it back to the tender, and Winnie is laid on the sand so I can dress her.

Expecting the temperature to plummet the moment we leave the strange isle, I start to put on my coat when something by the treeline catches my attention. The lost boys are there, none moving to approach us, just watching, most staring at Winnie. Both Ryder and the siren had alluded to Lady Death's presence here. I think I understand what they meant now.

Collecting Winnie, we push the small boat into the water and climb aboard. As we pass through the fog, I turn to look back, to wave goodbye...but the lost boys are gone.

~

BACK ABOARD *THE ARCANA*, we're greeted by the worried faces of Ansel and Caleb who are eager to know how the trip went. First things first, I ask Ryder to take the sleeping Winnie to my quarters so I can keep an eye on her throughout the night. Second, we each need to get out of our wet clothes before we freeze to death. And third, I'm desperately hungry.

Ansel smiles when I make the last point and assures me a stew has been cooking all day and will be ready as soon we've settled Winnie and changed.

I thank him and promise to return soon with a tale they won't believe, then follow Ryder to my cabin. The prince sets Winnie on the bed and begins to remove her clothes, for which he gets a thump on the back of the head and instructions to leave and sort his own wardrobe out. He looks surprised by my reaction, failing to understand the issue when only earlier this day he had seen her in her undergarments. I shoo him out nonetheless and lock the door behind me.

Tending to Winnie first, I remove her boots, trousers and shirt, and not once does she move or bat an eyelash. I'd be concerned if not for the rhythmic rise and fall of her chest. When I'm finished, I make sure to cover her with several blankets before changing my own clothes into something dry and more comfortable.

With a last look towards her, I leave the cabin and return to the main deck where everyone is waiting with bottles of rum and our largest pot brimming with a salted beef stew. The men stand as I approach the table, their usual politeness and good manners never failing to catch me off guard, and I wave them to sit and dig in.

After two days of slugs, vegetables and fruit, I all but inhale the stew and fill my bowl a second time. Ansel seems pleased as he watches me, making sure my side plate is never without a slice of bread. Neither he nor Caleb talk as we eat, giving us the time to fill our bellies before loading us with questions.

"I don't understand," Caleb says when I finish recounting the events of the mysterious island.

"Which part?" I ask with a chuckle as I refill my glass.

Caleb holds up his hand and points to each finger as he lists off the many things that fail to make sense. "The tree man, the boys, the mountain, Winnie–"

"So nothing, then. You understood absolutely nothing," Toriq says dryly.

I laugh and sip at the rum, enjoying the warmth as it settles in my full stomach. "Well, do *you* understand any of it, Toriq?" I ask, raising an eyebrow. He opens his mouth to offer a smart reply, then realises he in fact doesn't, not really.

"I think I can explain," a tired voice calls from behind us.

We all turn to see Winnie walking unsteadily towards us.

Caleb rises from his chair and hurries to her side, taking an arm and leading her the rest of the way. She smiles gratefully up at him, in what probably amounts to the first pleasant interaction I've seen between the two.

"How are you feeling?" I ask, concerned and quite sure she should still be lying down. When I say as much, she insists she tried to go back to sleep, but the smell of the stew was too intoxicating.

Ansel clasps his hands together and his bottom lip practically wobbles with Winnie's words, the compliment considered high praise from such a wonderful chef. When she's settled in her chair, Ansel fills his bowl and passes it to her along with the remainder of the bread.

"You said you have a message for Emery. What is it?" Ryder asks, getting straight to business. I sigh and cut him a glare, telling the impatient prince to give her a moment to eat and relax.

"No, it's okay. This is important," Winnie says with a faint chuckle. Her smile fades and she sips at the stew. "When I died, Death was waiting. She knows what you have planned, Emery. And she knew you would use the witchlight to save me, so she spared my soul so that I might pass on a message."

Already my palms are damp. How could Death know my plan? I've never spoken it aloud to anyone, not even to myself. "I'm listening," I say quietly.

"She said you're a clever one, Emerelda Mirabel. And asks you to remember that Death does not offer second chances. Your plan will work, but it will cost you greatly." Winnie sighs and scoops up a few more mouthfuls of stew before regarding me again. "This is to do with the Guardian Pass, isn't it?"

"Yes," I say, taking another sip of rum. "It's the only plan I have that might concern her."

"You were expecting this? You planned for it," Toriq says, leaning back as the realisation dawns on him. *"That's* why you weren't worried about the book referring to you as *'the one who must die'*? I thought you were just..."

"Being ignorant, or foolhardy?" I ask, raising an eyebrow. He shrugs and smiles then raises his glass with an apology. But I don't accept it. "Now I'm not so sure the book *was* referring to just me." I look to each member of the table as I mentally run through the book's most recent verse.

...Rest and recover, girl with blue eyes,
the killer, the royal, and the one who must die...

I am the girl with the blue eyes, I am a killer, a newly appointed royal, and the one who must die in the events to come...but the other three members of the crew who stepped foot on the island *also* match that description.

I lift a hand and point to my chest. "Girl with blue eyes."

I point to Ryder. "The royal."

I drag my finger to Winnie. "The girl who must die."

And lastly, I look to Toriq...the killer.

Toriq stares back at me, showing no sign of being surprised by my deduction. He had clearly come to the same conclusion himself. "Firstly, I want you to know I would never harm any of you," he says looking at each of us in turn. "The life I took was not by my choice, she asked for it." Nobody speaks as he twirls the wedding band on his finger and stares into the knotted grain of the wooden table. "She was sick...I had no choice."

All of my suspicions dissipate when I realise who he's talking about. "A compassionate kill," I mumble. The hardest thing in this world, to end the life of someone you love and put them out of their misery.

He picks up his glass and downs the contents in one

quick swig. "My wife had suffered enough, so when she begged me to do it…I killed her. It was a marriage arranged by our parents when we were very young, but she was my best friend, and I loved her." He turns his gaze on me, desperation shining in his eyes. "The book called me a killer, and it was right. But I would never harm you, Emery. I care for you."

I reach out and put a hand on his shoulder, squeezing it gently. "I know, Toriq." And it's true. While our start had been rocky to say the least, he had shown nothing but concern for my well-being. Either he's being honest, or he's a very good liar.

"Well, with that settled," Caleb says turning from Toriq to Winnie, "I don't suppose Death gave you any hints as to what this cost might be for Emery's secret plan to trick her?"

Winnie shakes her head and looks to me. "What *is* your plan for the Guardian Pass exactly?"

I had wanted to keep it a secret, hoping Death might fail to discover my plans. But apparently that was a little too much to ask. "The guardians are known to ask the highest toll from any sailor who demands entry to the Fifth Sea."

"What's the toll?" Toriq asks.

I grimace. They're not going to like this. "I believe the price is life itself. With that in mind, when the time comes I'll need one of you to smother me," I finish quickly, downing the rest of my drink.

"So far I'm not liking the sound of this," Caleb says dryly. Beside him, Toriq crosses his arms and opens his mouth to protest.

"Ah, but this is where my *plan* comes in," I say before he can get a word in. "I will use the cloak to hide me from Death. Then, once we've travelled through the pass, one of you can revive me. It's quite simple really, but with the witchlight the plan is pretty damn solid."

"You can't, Emery," Winnie whispers. "We *must* destroy the light. We have to set the little girl free." She stands and walks to the side of the ship, leaning on the rail as she looks past the fog to the Lost Boys' Island. Bathed in moonlight, it looks peaceful, its beauty ephemeral, for in the morning it will look like any other island.

Ryder moves to say something, likely to object what with him being the witchlight's biggest advocate on my behalf. If this light can keep me alive, he will want to keep it.

"Why, Winnie?" I ask.

Her head dips slightly but she doesn't turn to look at us. "I understand what the island is now, it's Death herself. Those two little boys I tried to take with me when I fled all those years ago, I thought they had changed their minds, left the raft and swam to shore. But Death showed me they cannot leave. The island is a place for boys who have yet to reach adulthood, boys who died before their time. The island is her gift to them, to live amongst friends until they're ready to join her on the other side."

I had begun to suspect as much. It's why Ryder could smell death and the siren warned us this wasn't a place for our kind, for the living. They had both been right.

"I was able to leave the island because I didn't belong," Winnie continues. "Death could have taken me the moment those people left me on the beach, but she didn't. At the time she saw I needed the island just as much as those boys did, until I was ready to leave and...and to live."

"Winnie, I..." The words fail to form. I want to go to her, to embrace and take some of the pain from her shoulders.

She sighs and turns from the island to face us, her cheeks wet and glistening under the moonlight. "Emery, the witchlight is a trapped spirit. A young, female witch caught and killed for her power to channel the dead. There is another island like this one, an island for girls. But the witch can't go there because she's stuck in that...*thing*."

"I understand, Winnie," I say. It seems Death had divulged a great deal during their short time. And the book had been right in so many ways. By visiting the island, not only had Winnie been afforded the chance to free Peter from his torment and say goodbye, but now we can do the same for this young girl trapped in the witchlight.

I ask her to wait as I hurry to my cabin, hunting through my bag to retrieve the small skull and my dagger. I take both and return to Winnie, handing them to her. "I think if anyone deserves to set that girl free, it's you."

She smiles up at me as she takes the items and places the skull on the wooden deck at our feet. Kneeling before it, she raises the dagger and mutters a small prayer, then plunges it down into the centre of the skull. Bone cracks, and we each pull in a sharp breath as a chilly breeze blows across the ship. Then, the witchlight crumbles, turning to dust to be carried away on the wind.

The respectful moment of silence is broken when Toriq coughs and raises his hand. "That was great, and I'm happy for the spirit girl...but what the hell do we do about the Guardian Pass now?"

"My plan is still viable," I say, taking a seat and refilling my glass with rum. "We'll just have to be careful not to kill me *too* well."

A BOLD REQUEST

FOURTH SEA

After a long night of drinking and chatting, the crew sleeps in this morning and I enjoy the rare opportunity to be alone on the deck. Before starting this journey, I adored my solitary days on the open water. But slowly and without my realising, that seems to have changed. One could argue my travels would have been much smoother had I sailed the seas by myself, and that person would be right. But now I can't imagine *The King's Arcana* without our resident genie scribbling in the corner; or Caleb surreptitiously ogling either myself or Winnie; even Toriq would be sorely missed. Then there's Ryder. The ultimate puzzle.

"You should have woken me, I could have helped," the devil himself says as he heads up the stairs to the helm.

I watch as Ryder sits on the bench and looks out to the sea – his usual routine when I'm at the helm and there's nothing to do with the day.

"I didn't want to risk waking Winnie, and I'm capable of sailing *The Arcana* on my own," I say with a mock harrumph. I expect him to turn, to give me his usual, quizzical look. He doesn't, just continues to watch the ocean as we break through the waves. "What are you thinking?" What *does* a heartless man ponder?

"The siren wasn't lying when he said I would lose my heart forever if I kissed you," he says, finally turning to regard me. "He seems to know something we don't."

I had sensed the same. Though, what I struggled to determine was whether or not the threat was simply due to the siren's apparent jealousy, and our kiss *would* in fact break the curse, but the siren would kill Ryder for it.

"When do you read the next passage?" he asks when I continue to remain silent.

"Today. I'm waiting for the others to wake first." I turn to the table on my right, where a chart of the Fourth Sea lays open. While this is one of the coldest of the eight, it's also the smallest and one of the more treacherous. We have another two days of sailing before we reach the Guardian Pass, and the only way to get there is through Kraken channel.

Ryder steps up behind me just as I'm running my finger along the territory marked in red. "Are you concerned?" he asks, pressing his chest to my back and leaning forward to place his hand on top of mine."

"About what?" My voice is soft, as soft as the feel of his breath across my neck. He leans his body deeper into mine as he moves our interlocked fingers along the chart.

"About the krakens…the guardians…about me?"

"I'm not concerned about the first two. I'm confident we can avoid the krakens and–" my breath catches as he burrows his face in the crook of my neck, his hand abandoning the scroll to explore the different parts of my body. "You, however, are a tad concerning," I say quietly, making no move to stop him.

"When it comes to the Guardian Pass, I want to be the one to do it, Emery."

Ryder's touch suddenly turns cold as my stomach drops. I spin but get no further than his arms allow as he places both hands on the table to trap me. "You *want* to kill me?" I ask.

He moves and lifts one hand to brush his fingers along my jaw, his other arm possessing my waist. "No. But I want to be the one to bring you back. I won't allow anyone else to do it. Will you grant me that much, Emery? Will you let me give you the kiss of life?"

Just like that, the warmth seeps back in and my silly, fickle, *useless* heart dances to his words. I nod my head. I *will* give him that. If the siren is right then I can't break his curse, and Malka's warning doesn't count here, as a kiss of life is entirely different from one born of love.

"Eh-hem," Caleb coughs from the top step. "I hate to intrude, but Winnie insists you come and eat breakfast, Captain."

I try to move away from Ryder, but his grip only tightens as he tells Caleb we'll join them in a moment. Caleb shakes his head with a smile and turns to leave, only halting when I tell him to wait. The look in Ryder's eyes tells me he wants to keep exploring. And with everyone just below, I'm disinclined to open myself up to his temptations.

"I'm coming now," I say, wriggling free. Ryder finally relents and follows me downstairs, a sour, confounded look on his face as he watches me head towards the table where everyone is waiting.

"I brought the book!" Ansel says, waving it in the air. I smile as I take my seat, noting the genie seems chipper this morning, and oddly at ease. "I have a good feeling about all of this, my brother was scratching and scratching all night in the book. Surely that's a good sign?"

Ansel places it on the table and pushes it my way as the others sit. I take one of the steaming mugs of cocoa and flick the catch, opening the book to the fifth verse.

~ GO ON ~

By tomorrow night we should reach the Guardian Pass. I hope Ansel is right and whatever his brother has to say is only good news. I flip the page.

The boys are safe, all happy and well,
and the light of the witch is free of her spell.
But that was all easy, you must not unwind,
remember the story of a Pass so unkind?
Your choice comes to this, girl with blue eyes,
turn back and go home, go forward and die.
Your plan is quite good, I must say, I'm impressed,
trust in your prince, only fear what comes next.
Thanks go to Winnie, Death's warning is true,
die once, come back, but her chances are few.

Goodluck, My Queen.

.
.
.

~ TWO DAYS ~

Bloody, riddlesome book. This is a long one, meaning more to unwrap. All the other verses had hidden warnings and predictions. Words that mean one thing, and just as easily mean another. I read the verse again, unpacking it, trying to make sense, to glean as much from the text as I possibly can.

The first couplet is easy. The island of the lost boys was a success. Even Winnie's temporary death had been necessary, as now I know that Death really is watching, expecting my next move.

The second seems innocent enough as well. It's speaking

of the Guardian Pass, erected to span the length of the entire world, all to keep the krakens from the shores of the Fifth sea and beyond. That's the warning – beware of the krakens.

The Third...well, it isn't a choice. Not really. I'm going to see Mother Witch, and that's the end of it. Living a life not knowing, a life of wondering, isn't much of a life at all.

"What, exactly, are we trusting Ryder with?" Toriq asks, looking from the fourth couplet to me. I'm certain it has something to do with our earlier discussion, Ryder's request to kill and revive me.

...trust in your prince...

...the heartless man will kill you...

While the book's assurances do exactly that, reassure me...Malka's warning does the opposite. I lift my eyes to Ryder, to find him already staring back. He offers a single nod, so sure that this is the right decision, that *he* should be the one to do it. But what if he fails and Malka's warning comes true. I don't *think* I'm in love with Ryder. There are feelings, undeniable ones, but not love...not yet.

"I will be the one to kill and revive Emery," Ryder says when I bob my head in permission. "It must be me and nobody else." He looks to the crew, pausing on each face until his demands are met.

"What about the last lines, Cap?" Caleb asks, pointing to the page. "Sounds to me like Death is coming for you more than once."

"It says you have a choice as well, Emery," Winnie adds when I fail to respond to Caleb. "Maybe we *should* go home?"

From what I can tell, the danger lies mostly with me. By continuing forward, I'm the one taking the most risk. "I want to see Mother Witch. I want to go beyond and see what else is out there. I *need* to do this," I say, taking a sip of cocoa. "But I understand if any of you wish to turn back. I'll take you to the nearest port and wait until you have secured passage home."

The crew remains quiet at the table, none objecting to my wishes despite their clear concern.

"Of course we're going with you, Emery," Winnie says quietly and the others nod their agreement.

Taking the book, I snap it closed and slide it across the table to Ansel. He picks it up and secures the clasp before hugging it to his chest, a little sad that his hopes hadn't quite been met. I disagree. Death's warning is the only truly ambiguous part of the text, and considering what we face, his brother's passage could have been much worse.

We all disperse quietly after that; Caleb, Toriq and Ryder to resume their daily training and Ansel to his scribbles, while Winnie heads to the galley to prepare a stew to simmer throughout the day. I head to the helm to check our position and fill in the captain's log.

We're a day from Kraken Channel. Known to dwell in the deepest, underwater trenches of the Fifth Sea, these creatures are few but terrifying in every way. This time, we'll have to navigate carefully to *avoid* the deeper waters. I follow the line on the chart with my finger, picking out a path for us to carefully tread.

According to seafarers I've met, there should be buoys or markers erected over time to help sailors navigate the reef. I'm loath to rely on word of mouth alone, especially when one wrong turn of the wheel could set us on a path to deeper waters, where the krakens wait.

I guide my finger along the great wall to the Guardian Pass, the only means of crossing from the Fourth to the Fifth sea. As the story goes, when the first sea queen ruled the water, she grew tired of the humans taking her fish and killing her offspring, the sirens. Becoming desperate, she tricked Poseidon into her bed, and in a passionate kiss, stole a morsel of his blood. With this blood, the krakens were born and bred with a taste for human flesh. When Poseidon discovered her treachery, he banished the sea queen to a prison deep in one of the eight seas, and placed his own son on her throne instead. But the god could not kill the krakens, for they were made of his blood. Instead, he made a deal with the sky giants, requesting they build a great wall to span the world, cutting it in half. One half for his children *of* the sea, the monsters of the deep. The other half for his children who lived *from* the sea, the humans who once relied on his protection. The sky giants agreed on one condition, that their kind would be granted a means to travel down to our world and become human, should they wish it. And with that, The Great Tree on the Garden Isle grew and grew so that the giants might come down and become human.

Now, I must admit, I've never once seen a giant – or a human for that matter – descend our Great Tree. But I like the tale nonetheless, and I would always watch the Tree for a glimpse of a face in the clouds peering down, or movement higher in the branches.

"What are you doing?" Winnie asks as she joins me on the quarterdeck.

"I was thinking about the history of the wall," I say, turning from the charts to face her. "I don't suppose you know of the buoys that mark the safest route to the pass?"

She ambles up behind me, and regards the chart. "This isn't right, I'm almost certain the first marker is directly in line with the entrance to the pass. Right around here," she says pointing to a place about ten nautical miles from where the chart says the first is marked.

"Damn," I mutter under my breath. Her lack of certainty means we'll have to travel at reduced speed with everyone on the lookout. If we miss the first marker, we're in trouble.

Sailing blind through Kraken Channel is simply not an option.

It's almost noon, so I carefully plot our position, noting the sun is almost at its highest point. Then I check our speed and make a new bearing to where Winnie has indicated on the chart.

"If I'm right, we'll reach that marker by this evening," Winnie continues, looking from the chart out to sea. "We can't use the thrusters at all, Emery. If they hear it–"

"I know," I say, cutting her off. The thrusters will be too loud in the water, meaning we rely on the wind and my crew's ability to raise and lower the sails to control our speed.

"They can do it," Winnie assures me. Moving to the rail overlooking the lower deck, she watches the men train and I move from the table to join her. The corner of her mouth creeps up, her gaze transfixed on one person in particular.

"You and Caleb seem to be getting along much better than before." I give her a sideways glance and a sly smile. Being a widow, Winnie had made it clear she had no intentions of taking another lover, particularly of the male variety. However, I had seen the odd glance shared between the two, and how Caleb was always the first to offer assistance in the galley.

"We *are* getting along better," she says, her answering smile and candidness taking me by surprise. "Don't get me wrong, he's a lech, but he isn't all bad I suppose."

I lean my elbows on the rail and look down to Caleb now as he swaps places with Toriq to spar with Ryder. Both have removed their coats and stand on-guard, a thick sheen of sweat already coating Ryder's arms and face.

"What about you and our prince?" Winnie asks as she catches the direction of my stare. "For someone cursed with heartlessness, he sure seems to care a lot about you." She angles her body to face me, waggling her eyebrows for good measure. "He sure is handsome, too."

"He's being diligent in his duty as my guard," I say with a casual shrug..

Her face drops and she looks askance, clearly unsatisfied by my answer.

"Okay, fine. I have feelings for him and he's *'curious'* about me," I say, mimicking Ryder's deep voice and signature head tilt.

We both laugh and the sound must catch the men's attention as they all look up. My eyes lock onto Ryder's and he puts a hand to his chest, the corner of his mouth twitching, as if desperately wanting to curl up in the foreign act of a smile. It vanishes and he drops his hand as Caleb turns to duel him once again.

"What about Toriq?" Winnie asks quietly. When I stare at her questioningly, she jerks her head slightly to the side, indicating back to the men.

Down below, Toriq is staring up at me, a far off look in his eye, as if he isn't so much staring *at* me, but *through* me. I give him a small wave and he wakes from his reveries, offering a firm nod of acknowledgement, then turning back to concentrate on Caleb's lesson.

"What *about* Toriq?" I ask. "I suppose we're getting along better, too. He seems to trust me now."

Winnie shakes her head and sighs dramatically. "Emery, for someone so intelligent, you really can be quite dense."

I scoff, marking my mock offence as I push her lightly aside. "I know it's turning to more than just *getting along*, he's said it plainly enough...but–"

"But your suitors are growing in number and you're not quite sure what to do or think?" Winnie asks. She smiles and holds up a hand, pointing to each finger as she lists them off. "Let's see, there's the prince, Toriq, then there's that siren who keeps following us around and saving our asses. Oh yes, and I almost forgot about that husband of yours back in your little kingdom of Beggars' Cove." She laughs when I push her again.

"*Fake* husband! And please don't remind me," I groan, leaning forward to rest my head on my forearms.

She pats my back and in a sing song voice says, "Poor Emery. How terrible to have so many prospects."

I tilt my head to the side and give her a nettled stare, to which she smiles and rolls her eyes, insisting it could be much worse. When I question how that might be, she says I could be left with no lovers at all. But that doesn't sound so bad. I don't mind being alone so much…Though, perhaps that's the old me speaking. I think of doing this journey without the others, and a terrible loneliness descends on me like a blanket. In that moment I'm back in the wood by the sisters' house, with nobody and nothing. The thought is devastating, and I shake the feeling aside.

"What will you do when we get to Aurora Isle?" I ask, hoping my voice comes across as impassive, merely curious.

She steps back and looks down to her feet, rubbing her hands together nervously. "Ah, well…I was hoping, perhaps, if you don't mind that is," she sighs and steels herself, raising her head to look me in the eye. "I would like to travel with you for as long as you'll have me, Captain Emery Mirabel."

I burst out laughing, turning around to lean my back against the rail. "That's good, because I have no intention of letting you go, Second Mate Winnie Dawning."

We both link arms, our moods dramatically improved as we head to the lower deck for a second cup of Cocoa, my loneliness dispelled.

～

THE SINGLE LANTERN at my back sways as *The Arcana* silently glides over the choppy water. Only one lantern will be lit tonight. Not a word will be spoken and everyone will take care to quieten their footsteps across the deck. This is Kraken Channel, a place of silence. One foreign sound or beam of light is all it takes to garner the unwanted attention of the creatures below.

Posted at the bow, Ansel stands diligently watching the water for the large buoy, their night-time glow at times hard to spot against the churn of the dark sea.

Somewhere ahead of us, another lonely ship travels silently in the night, hoping to try their luck through the channel to the Guardian Pass. We had spotted them coming from the north only hours before, but lost sight of them with the setting sun. Their chosen route is approximately ten nautical miles north of our location, where the chart originally stated the first marker should be.

One of our ships will perish tonight. Only one path is safe through these waters. I hope Winnie is right, or the other ship will have a spectacular view of our almost certain demise. I'm once again thankful for our new, metallic hull. *The Arcana* is more graceful, no longer buffeting against the waves but slicing through them, a new level of stealth I never thought we would be afforded.

Ansel lowers his spyglass and waves from the bow. He's spotted the first buoy. I note the direction and watch the compass turn as we change heading directly to the southeast. I look to Winnie who has a knotted drop in our wake to monitor speed. She holds ups her hand to indicate five knots and I signal back for our speed to be reduced to three. The order is relayed to Caleb and Toriq who quietly, carefully, furl one of the sails to do as I've asked.

Glancing to port, my heart fills with pity. The other ship must know by now. Perhaps they'll turn about, maybe try again another day. Though, it's difficult to know exactly where you are in the water, especially at night. If they haven't realised, I hope they do before it's too late.

A full moon and a cloudless sky are considered a blessing to nautical folk. Tonight, it's unwelcome. With the moon lighting the water, the next buoy is difficult to spot, and it isn't until we're almost upon it when Ansel waves frantically and points to starboard. I open my spyglass and spot the marker's dull glow, spinning the wheel just in time to correct our position and line up *The Arcana* with the next predicted buoy.

Winnie approaches the helm, careful to avoid the squeakier steps. When she stops by my side I point to a quill and a piece of parchment, then hold a finger to my lips. She needs no further prompting and goes about writing her note to me.

If we maintain this speed it will be dawn before we reach the final buoy. Take the cocoa and have a break. I'll watch our bearing.

I look up and she hands me one of two steaming mugs with a smile, angling her head to indicate the lower deck where several blankets have been laid out by the table. I take it and silently mouth my thanks, then head down the stairs to take up a blanket. Waving to Ansel and the others, I invite them over to where Winnie has left a cocoa treat for each of them.

Just as Ansel reaches for his, a shockwave rips across the water and his mug falls and smashes against the deck. Nobody moves, we barely breathe as the sound carries. After a moment, I release my breath and the ship rocks as a second pulse shudders beneath us.

We stand from the table and move quietly to the port rail when the sound of distant cannon fire carries on the breeze.

The grind of wood cracking and harrowed screams comes next, and we each watch as giant tentacles reach from the water like fingers – blindly touching, feeling, tormenting their prey.

A fire breaks out on the deck of the lonely ship, the flames lighting the scene in a dramatic performance. Shadows dance across the deck, the crew running from a tentacle winding its way over the bow. But there is no escape. Two women scream as they jump overboard, just as the kraken raises its head from the water. The screams are cut short as they fall directly into the creature's open maw, a circular, spiralling chasm of teeth...and death.

Soon, all falls silent again, only the hiss of fire extinguishing, and the crack and groan of wood as it's dragged beneath the sea.

KISS OF LIFE

FOURTH SEA

RYDER'S POV

...

The last marker is almost upon us, and now as the sun crests the horizon, the Guardian Pass looms ahead in total clarity. Two stone giants stand patiently to guard a crack in the great wall, the rough waves of the Fourth Sea crashing against their knees. I watch from the bow as the final marker passes to port, and look up to the raucous cry of birds roused from their nests on the giants' shoulders. Stone cracks and groans along their necks as they each dip their heads to observe our approach.

Turning to the helm, we watch for Emery's silent command, ready and waiting to drop the sails. Great waves rock the boat as the stone giants move their spears to block our way. Emery grips the wheel and gives her command with a firm nod. We drop the sails as silently as we can, hurrying to secure them to each mast before turning towards the bow as we slowly approach the pass.

A shadow crawls along the ship as the sun vanishes from sight behind the stone wall, the shade apparently much cooler as Ansel shivers beside me. Though, it is said people shiver from more than just the cold. I gaze up at the giants, their stony faces expressing a warning to those who venture too close. Perhaps Ansel shivers in fear?

As expected, Emery has timed our approach perfectly, and the ship glides almost to a stop just before the hafts of the stone spears without any need for the thrusters. She motions to Toriq to drop anchor, not trusting *The Arcana* to remain stationary long enough to conclude our business with the giants.

Something in the hard lines of her expression seems to bother me, so I go to meet her at the base of the helm's stairs, turning and walking by her side as we head for the ship's bow. The boom of cracking rock pierces the air and Emery covers her ears as the giants bend at the waist to regard us. With their cold faces so close, you might expect a great breeze to blow as a result of their breath, but these beings don't appear to need the air as we do.

I put a hand out to steady Emery as she stumbles back, her body rigid and tense. Perhaps she's nervous? That would make sense. She's about to die. I'm about to kill her. I put a clenched fist to my chest as my heart thuds rapidly at that notion. I don't like this, I believe I'm uncomfortable, perhaps even... frightened. I've felt this only a handful of times before – when Emery was missing, when Emery was with the Beggar King, when Emery met the siren and the mermaid. It's always her.

As she steps forward to speak with the guardians, it takes all my strength not to pull her back and lock her away somewhere safe.

"We wish to sail to the Fifth Sea. May we pass?" she asks, her voice steady and strong.

A TOLL MUST BE PAID FOR THOSE WHO WISH TO PASS.

The giant's voice resounds across the silent sea, and yet he does not open his mouth.

"What is your price?" Emery asks, despite already knowing.

WE ASK ONLY WHAT WE GIVE. WE SACRIFICE OUR LIVES TO PROTECT THE SHORES OF THE FIFTH, ONE OF YOU MUST DO THE SAME.

"Then I offer my life for the crew's safe passage," Emery says without a moment's hesitation. The sound of rending stone rumbles across the ship as the giant nods his head.

Emery turns from the guardians, and I follow as she heads towards the table to Ansel. His cloak is already removed, and he helps her tie the strings and secure it tightly around her, whispering for her to think of Death and only Death.

Emery mutters she can hardly think of anything else, and climbs up to where blankets have been laid on the table. A sacrificial dais of sorts. My stomach turns as she lays down and looks to me expectantly. I walk around the table to stand by her head, her plaited, copper hair lying delicately across one shoulder. She nods and closes her eyes and I place my hands over her mouth and nose.

Toriq and Caleb look away as they hold her down on the table. Any moment now, natural instinct will kick in and she will fight it. That time takes longer than it might for most. Emery is accomplished when it comes to holding her breath after years of sailing and tending to *The Arcana* underwater. The time comes though, and her eyes fly open. She struggles against me, that instinct to survive fighting back.

I force my gaze to remain on hers, whispering words I'm

sure she wants to hear. *You're okay. Let go. I'll bring you back.* I mean the last with every morsel of my being. I will bring Emery back. I won't lose her. I *can't* lose her. Slowly her eyes flicker closed, and her body goes limp.

IT IS DONE.

The guardians return to their positions and Ansel cranks the lever to raise the anchor. Winnie, already at the helm, turns the thrusters as the guardians move their spears and clear the way through the pass. The ship rocks gently forward, then rocks again when a tremor vibrates through the ocean below.

The krakens.

"Full mast!" Winnie calls below, no longer cautious of being heard by the creatures. They know we're here, and they're coming.

Toriq and Caleb rush from the table to crank the masts, but it's too late. From the stern, a great mass of rubbery tentacle eases from the water. In a teasing, tormenting way, it caresses *The Arcana.*

"Ansel, the explosives!" Winnie all but screams the command to the genie.

We had prepared for this possibility, prepared the explosive charges for if the krakens caught our scent. Ansel races past as I jump on the table to straddle Emery, ready for the moment we clear the pass to begin her resuscitation. We have to hurry. I turn my head to Winnie and she looks desperately back after turning the thrusters to full forward.

The wood on the stern's rail groans and snaps as the kraken tightens its grip. We're no longer moving forward, but slowly shifting back, back towards its waiting jaws.

"Hurry, Ansel!" Winnie screams.

I look to where he's fumbling with the charges, only recently having been taught how to light them and how long he has before it detonates. The first is lit and he launches it with surprising accuracy out to sea.

One...two...BOOM!

The blast frees the ship and propels us forward, the shockwave so powerful, I hear the glass windows in Emery's cabin shatter as I'm blown from the table to the deck. I scramble up, stumbling to one side as the ship sways with the waves.

Emery is gone. I search either side of the table and see her sliding across the deck as the ship tilts. We're inside the pass now, in seconds we'll be on the other side of the wall. I stumble towards her and drop to her side just as the sun graces us once again and the Fifth sea opens up in greeting.

I begin the rhythmic compressions on Emery's chest, begging her to come back. Her face looks so serene, so peaceful, no sign of the hard countenance she had worn before the giants. "Come on, Emery," I call as I complete the last compression. Tilting her head back, I hold her nose and press my mouth to hers.

My heart seizes the moment our lips touch. Pain. I remember this feeling. I try to ignore it, breathing oxygen into her lungs before resuming the compressions. Still she refuses to rise. I touch my mouth to hers again and this time, when our skin meets, the pain in my chest is crippling.

I vaguely register Winnie's hands pulling me back and laying me on the deck. I scream at that, a blind rage overwhelming me. "Emery!" That's all I manage to say past the vice that seems to constrict my heart and lungs, like a snake has entered my body and now coils around my organs.

I try to sit up, try to reach for her, but Winnie holds me down, her palms rough and calloused, but...warm. This is warmth. With one hand holding my chest, I reach up and touch a finger to my cheek. It's wet with tears, but why?

"Toriq, revive Emery!" Winnie calls.

My anger resurfaces. I don't want him to touch her. But I'm forced to watch, unable to move and voice my protest as Toriq leans down and presses his lips to Emery's. My Emery. I can't breathe now, my lungs seem unable to function with the weight of this sadness, this possessiveness.

Emery coughs and rolls to one side gasping and drawing in air. She's alive. She's breathing. That's all that matters. My body relaxes and a darkness crowds my vision. I can rest now. Emery is okay. I can rest.

MOTHER WITCH AWAITS

FIFTH SEA

I take a lungful of air and close my eyes to the brightness of the sun. The *sun*. We must have made it through. Gripping Ryder's arm, I look up gratefully, only to find Toriq staring back. It makes no sense, Ryder had made it pretty damn clear he wished to be the one to revive me.

I glance to the side, to where Winnie is softly counting and carrying out chest compressions on Ryder. He's still, so still. I push from Toriq's hold and scramble across the deck as she finishes the last compression. She leans back when I put a hand out to stop her, instead taking her place and leaning down until my lips meet with Ryder's. They're soft and full and so much warmer than I expected. I release my breath, breathing my life into him and calling him back.

Ryder's eyes fly open and he bolts upright, his nose colliding with mine in the process. "Fuck!" he roars, holding the appendage and glaring at me.

"That was *your* bloody fault," I cry, holding my own nose and pointing an accusatory finger at him. My irritation evaporates as Ryder rubs the sore spot. Pain. Ryder feels pain. He shivers as a breeze blows across the deck and I slump back, awed, and amazed by such a simple gesture.

"How do you feel?" Toriq asks warily from beside us. The wide-eyed look he wears tells me he's noticed it too.

"Like I've been kicked in the chest by a horse," Ryder growls, holding one hand to his heart. Slowly his face opens up, and for the first time, the prince looks shocked. "I feel sore...and cold and angry and tired and...some other things I'm not quite sure of, but it's all there." He looks to me and my own heart breaks as he does what he so often begged me to do. He smiles.

"The curse is broken," I whisper. "The siren was wrong, it worked."

"It was all you, it was *always* you, Emery," Ryder says softly as he lifts a hand and brushes my cheek.

"Well, I don't know about that," Winnie says with a wide grin. "I mean, I helped a little while she was catching her breath." At her words we all laugh as what feels like weeks of tension falls away. Even Ryder cracks a smile, his hand dropping from my face as he winces and holds his chest.

I take Toriq's hand and rise to my feet, fumbling with the cloak's strings and handing it back to Ansel. The genie smiles and wraps it around his shoulders, then looks to the bow. Hopefully soon, he won't need it. In less than two days we should reach Aurora Isle. Though, if we continue at this pace, it will be closer to three.

Turning to Winnie I ask her and Ansel to make more cocoa and prepare for a celebration. Against the odds, we survived the Guardian Pass, we survived the krakens, and we're well on our way to what may be our final destination. Everyone whoops and hollers as Ansel and Toriq go to release the sails and I make my way to the quarterdeck.

"Seems someone is here to see you, Captain," Winnie calls.

I turn to see her pointing to the glow of the siren bell, and then to the water over the starboard side. Her lack of concern tells me exactly who to expect, and I hurry over.

The first thing I see is the golden hair, then the long, scaled tail of the siren, our rescuer, our shadow. As he swims closer, I call down and tell him to wait while I rush for the helm. Turning the thrusters, I call to Caleb and Ansel, telling them to drop the sails before returning to the starboard side.

"I felt your death, Emerelda," the siren calls up, his face creased with concern as he searches my body for any signs of hurt or injury.

"How did you get through the pass?" I ask, wondering if sirens are required to pay the same toll as a human.

"The sea is ours. We go where we wish," is all he says in return. His face twists in barely contained disgust when Ryder steps up beside me. "I see your curse is broken, Prince."

Ryder smiles down at the creature and steps closer to my side. "It is. Are you here to stop my heart as you threatened before?"

The siren sneers back, saying "All in good time." Looking from Ryder to me, his anger fades and he edges closer to the ship. "Emery, I'm glad you're unharmed. I'll be close, should you need me."

I call out as he turns to swim away. This time I'm determined to get his name. "What do I call you?"

At my question the siren smiles shyly back. "In our tongue my name means Hunter, perhaps you can call me that?"

"Hunter," I whisper, and he closes his eyes as if enjoying a soft song. "I have questions for you, Hunter."

His grin spreads from ear to pointed ear, and when he opens his eyes, there's mischief dancing behind them. "And I have answers, Emery. All in good time," he repeats, then flicks his eyes to Ryder as if to remind him.

Before I can begin my tirade of enquiries, Hunter slips beneath the waves, his smile never faltering as he swims away. I turn back to a quiet crew, everyone just as confused as I am by the siren's...by Hunter's actions. Thrice he's saved us, and now he comes to make sure I live. Why? How was he able to feel my death? Why does he follow us?

"So...anybody for a spot of cocoa?" Winnie asks, rubbing her hands together. We all smile back and she disappears below deck with Caleb to gather the supplies for a small feast. It's barely mid-morning, but after the weeks we've had, I think everyone deserves a day of rest.

I head for the helm as Toriq and Ansel go back to raising the sails. This territory is entirely new to me, and I haven't had a proper chance to study the Fifth Sea's chart. Under the table beside the ship's wheel, I take out the scroll marked with a yellow ribbon and lay it out to determine our position in relation to Aurora Isle. Our current bearing is significantly off, so I turn the wheel, taking us southeast.

Here in the Fifth Sea, there are plenty of smaller islands and waypoints to help guide us. We shouldn't need to stop; we have enough food and general supplies to last several weeks on the water. Still, it's good to know we won't be stuck should something happen...and knowing our luck, that's entirely likely.

"Emery?"

I turn to see Ryder standing by the stairs, a dark, almost unsure expression on his face. Even *that* is different, everything in the creases around his mouth and the emotion in his eyes. The heartless prince is no more. "What's wrong?" I ask, waving for him to join me as I go back to double checking the chart.

"Nothing is wrong. It's the opposite in fact."

I hear his steps grow closer and hold my breath when his hands snake around my waist. "Ryder," I whisper, "I really should copy our bearing to the chart." I close my eyes as his forehead dips to rest on my shoulder, his arms holding me in place.

"I killed you," he whispers.

My eyes open and I try to turn and face him. His arms only tighten, his warmth spreading along my back. "Someone had to do it. And you helped bring me back," I say, my tone soft and reassuring.

"The siren was right."

At that I wriggle in his grasp, making just enough room to turn. He raises his head slightly, but it remains bowed, his hair falling softly forward to brush the corners of his face. "What do you mean? I won't let Hunter harm you, Ryder. I promise."

He chuckles, the sound deep and guttural. It's the first time he's ever made such a sound in my presence, and I realise it suits him. I realise I want him to chuckle more often, and to smile and laugh – Gods what I wouldn't do to hear this man *laugh*.

"I'm not concerned about the siren. But he warned that if I kiss you, I'll lose my heart forever...and he was right."

"But the curse is broken, you can feel now," I say holding a hand to his cheek.

He leans into my palm and sighs as he lifts his eyes to look into mine. "My heart is returned, but it's no longer my own, Emery. It's yours. It's always been yours. Breaking the curse allowed me to understand that."

"Are you saying..."

"I don't know *what* that means, exactly. All I know is that when you were laying there, when you died and refused to come back, my heart was ready to stop. I didn't want to continue without you." His thumb brushes across my cheek, his eyes a caress along my lips. "I think that means *you* possess my heart, and not me."

Indeed, his heart has returned, but after twenty years of feeling next to nothing, he fails to understand these emotions. I rise onto my toes and touch my forehead to his, our noses brushing. "We'll figure it all out together, Ryder. I'm here, and I'm not going anywhere. Your heart is safe."

THE REST of the day and late into that evening is spent with the crew lazing about the deck eating fruit, cheese and biscuits, our hot cocoa fortified with copious amounts of rum. For hours we swap theories and tales of our biggest regrets, our worst mistakes and our greatest achievements. I find that with every question I'm asked, my answer comes back to a moment I've spent with these people...these friends. They are the ones I've faced some of my darkest hours with. I've cried with them, I've laughed with them, I've fought and survived by their side.

When the first rays of pre-dawn stretch across the horizon, Ansel returns to his cabin to retrieve the book. Those pages could speak of death and carnage to come and still we would be merry. I shiver at the fresh breeze and stifle a yawn, then turn to Ryder as he drapes a blanket over my shoulders.

"Seems you've found a soft touch along with that heart of yours, Ryder," Winnie says with a chuckle. She looks up wide eyed as Caleb mirrors Ryder and lays a blanket over her shoulders, then sits and shuffles closer to tuck her under his arm.

He grunts and laughs as she digs her elbow into his ribs, but neither moves away from the other. Instead, she lays her head on his chest with a sly wink to me, and I giggle as Caleb's cheeks flush and he coughs to stifle his surprise.

"So, shall we see what my brother warns us of this morning?" Ansel says, taking a seat on the blankets and handing me the book.

We all look to each other in turn. We've survived a lot. Surely it can't be *that* bad. I flick the catch and open to the sixth page. Seeing the familiar instruction to read on, I flip to the next and we all crowd in to read.

The giants have come, the giants have gone,
well done, blue-eyed girl, you play a good con.
Death has been tricked, but you cannot hide twice,
one day you'll see, but what is the price?
At Aurora Isle our queen will arrive,
her genesis revealed, her story contrived.
To the docks, blue-eyed girl, you cannot be late,
for there you will find, Mother Witch awaits.

~ ALL IN GOOD TIME ~

"I wish people would stop saying that," I mutter, looking twice at the last instruction. This is probably the best and the least ominous the book has been so far. Again, the same warning catches my eye, Death's price. I push the book forward, allowing the others a better look. Winnie and Toriq look up almost simultaneously, clearly having caught the same part that rubs me a little the wrong way too.

"Emery–"

"Nope," I say, cutting Winnie off before she begins listing her concerns. "We can worry about all of that when we reach Aurora Isle. For now, we're enjoying ourselves. That's an order." I smile and hand her the last dregs of the rum, stifling yet another yawn.

Caleb continues to read the passage, then stands to look out over the bow. "Well, we should be there soon enough. So, when should we start worrying?" he asks as he turns back to face us.

Confused, I hold the blanket around my shoulders and stand, wobbling slightly. Ryder slips an arm around my waist, smiling down as I'm forced to lean on him. Together, we all walk to the bow, where something rises in the distance.

I take the spyglass from its holder beneath the rail and hold it up to squint through the lens. "It's an island," I whisper. Only, where most islands meet the water, this one does not. Suspended just *above* the ocean waves, the entire isle sits amongst the low clouds of the early morn, the fog broken by great and fast flowing waterfalls falling from above, as if the Gods themselves had plucked the isle from the ocean on invisible strings. At the centre, towering above all else is yet another of the crystal towers we had on the Garden Isle, the same we had seen when we entered the Fourth Sea.

"How long until we get there do you think?" Winnie asks from behind me.

"Mid-morning," I say, continuing to scan the island. Beneath the rocks of the floating island's belly, a long spiral staircase descends to the water from the centre of the isle, to where a line of docks waits below, with many ships tied up and only a few making ready to sail with the birth of a new day. A solitary figure stands on the farthest dock. A woman, with long silver hair and…an impossibly familiar face.

"What is it?" Ryder asks as I slowly lower the spyglass.

"It seems we're late," I say softly.

"We're late?" He raises a brow and holds out his hand for the spyglass.

"What's wrong, Cap? Did you have a very important date you forgot to tell us about?" Caleb asks with a grin.

I offer a sardonic smile to Caleb and hand the cylindrical device to Ryder. "Not quite. I believe that's Mother Witch waiting on the docks, and it seems some of us have already met her."

As always, sorry for the cliffhanger!!

Thank you so much for reading UPON A WICKED TIDE!
Your support means the world, and goes a long way towards
making an indie author's career!

**If you have the time, dropping a few stars on Amazon
and Goodreads would be super duper awesome too!**

ACKNOWLEDGMENTS

My first thanks go to you, the person who picked up this book and invested your time in Emery's world. You're helping a small-time author's dream come true!

To my editor, Antony Walsh. Without you, my books would quite possibly sink. Thank you for all the time and effort you expended helping me polish these strange lands to the best of our combined abilities. I am incredibly lucky to have you.

Dad, your patience, kindness and encouragement has kept me forging ahead on a path riddled with hardship. Thank you for navigating these treacherous seas with me! And Mum, thank you for your unfaltering pride and unwavering belief!

The best partner a woman could ask for, my time is often divided between you and these worlds I create. Your love and understanding means everything to me. Without your blessing, this journey would be made that much harder.

To my BETA readers and promo assistant!! Abigail, Charlie, Gem and Sarah...you four dragged me from a pit of self-doubt and beat me with assurances until I once again felt confident about my work and this story. THANK YOU all so so much! I couldn't ask for a better group of wonderful ladies to help me. Love you all!

There are so many people who have continually helped or encouraged me along the way, too many to thank properly - Edna, Bridgette, Steve, Maria, Cat, Gus, Josh, Simmo and so many more! You all rock!

ARC-TEAM SHOUTOUT!

Check out these fantabulous booktok and bookstagrammers who helped me along the way!

@darklight_reads
@bookishcharli
@book_dragon_gems
@readit.with.red
@a_reads_alot
@noteriasu
@beastreader
@theratherslowreader
@book_reader_tiya
@ecBella76

ALSO BY KATE CRAFT

Wicked Tide:

Upon a Wicked Tide

The Chaos Covenant:

Chaos Forged a Fable

Chaos Deals in Death

ABOUT THE AUTHOR

Kate Craft is a British, fantasy author who debuted in March 2022 with her first book in The Chaos Covenant series. Stepping into the world of indie publishing, she continues to chase her dream of weaving new tales filled with love and mayhem.

Born and raised travelling the world, Craft finally settled in the United Kingdom to complete a BSc in Psychology and Criminology, before joining the British Army in 2016. She is always eager to hear from readers and writers, so feel free to reach out!

facebook.com/KATECRAFT.Author
instagram.com/book.cove